I0602085

THE CURSE OF THE CROW

THE WICKED KINGDOM

ABBEY FOX

Copyright © 2021 by Wild Rabbit Publishing
All rights reserved.

No part of this book may be reproduced in any form or by any
electronic or mechanical means, including information storage and
retrieval systems, without written permission from the author, except for
the use of brief quotations in a book review.

"To my mom.
Thank you for being my best book pal during this whole process."

THE
CURSE
OF THE
CROW

THE WICKED KINGDOM

CHAPTER ONE

They came like a summer storm, bringing bleakness and terror into her life. Two riders wearing darkness galloped down the long pathway to her home. Like beasts on top of their giant steeds, sending thunder roaring over the dull cobblestone road.

Nava regretted disobeying her mother's curfew. As the men dismounted, she stared around, trying to find a suitable place to run or hide in the garden. The stone rails of the terrace offered little cover. Both men took the stone steps two at a time, and when they reached the top, their gazes were heavy on her.

Time seemed to slow as they said nothing, clearly surprised to find her there. They wore ebony outfits with blue accents, the hoods of their cloaks large enough to hide most of their features.

"Excuse me, do you know if anyone is home?" A deep male voice like honey made her body go tense and soft all at once. His voice ignited flames that burned in the pit of her stomach.

What was going on with her? She swallowed, her hair standing on end. "N-no one's home."

He took one step forward to get a better peek at her. "Do you live here?"

Her body blazed when the weight of his eyes settled on her. Something was off with her body. "No, I'm just . . . the gardener." The moment the words left her lips, it was clear they wouldn't believe her. She was fifteen and the spitting image of her mother, with the olive tones of her skin, her unruly brown hair, and her full lips.

Nava tried to mask her nerves by pulling another dead plant from the ground, the painful pricks of the stem distracting her.

She lifted her gaze, something divine calling to her. Her heart fluttered as her gaze came upon him again. The sharp line of a jaw was barely visible outside of the shadows of the hood. The trail of a day-old stubble, and the start of thick lips that got lost outside of her view.

She couldn't see his eyes but knew deep within her that they were staring back at her.

"You have peculiar eyes." The second man's voice, cold like icy fingers, trailed down her skin, breaking the moment. He stayed back, however, his posture straight, observing while the other drifted closer to her.

"I get that a lot," she said, her hands growing colder. Her eyes had always been something people commented on since one was blue and the other one was brown.

"You look too young to be a gardener." The second man stepped closer. Nava felt like they were having a silent conversation as they looked at each other. She had to force herself to stay still. Focusing on their long legs, she was aware she wouldn't make it far if she decided to run.

"Do you know when Miss Celeste will be back?" the cold voice asked, startling her.

She shook her head, her long, wavy hair sticking against her sweaty skin. "She's out in the market with my mother because we are the closest neighbors she has." Nava tried to sound casual, but her voice shook. "I can tell them—I mean, tell her you came around."

She could see jet-black hair peeking out from the blue accents of the hood of the man with the cold voice. "Where did you say you lived?"

"I didn't." Nava placed her gardening tool inside the basket. "You aren't supposed to tell strangers where you live. I can tell Celeste you came by or you can try to catch her at the market." Her breaths faltered. Her mother always said Nava was a terrible liar. Would the men take her away? Like all the stories her mother had told her about children being seized.

The other man hovered for a moment that was like an eternity. They eyed each other in silence, in a daze. The first man shook his head, somewhat distracted, turning away from her. "Please tell her the Society of Crows came to see her."

She stood, focusing on his retreating shape as he followed his companion down the steps to their horses. He mounted a large gray horse, and as he settled into the saddle, so did the movements of the horse.

Nava. Something shook her, a tug of her shoulder, a voice far in the distance.

The prickling of her nerves settled in the pit of her stomach. She watched him go, trembling as heat coursed through her body and landed in her chest. An ache grew into a burning sensation.

Nava, wake up.

She slipped her fingers under the linen fabric of her shirt and moved it aside with a gasp of pain, revealing lines that marked her skin with the shape of three intertwining ovals that formed a flower.

Nava's body shook. It was like her parents' mark, though not the same symbol.

The mark of a soulmate.

Nava, please.

She wished she didn't have to wake up.

"Nava. Nava."

The pull of someone shook her as she tried to hold on to the dream for a little longer.

Nava's eyes opened. Her brother hovered over her face. A messy head of tight red curls, a small button nose covered in light freckles. A shadow of concern tinting his youthful expression.

She grumbled, moving her heavy arms outside of her worn cotton sheets. Her focus changed from the red curls of his hair to the gray tones of the wood beams of the ceiling.

"What a relief. You're finally awake." His hands dropped from her shoulders.

She smiled. "My eyes are open."

"You are a sleepwalker, though."

"I am not. Stop making things up." Her words were thick with sleep.

He laughed, getting up from her bed and straightening his pants. He was wearing his heavy wool school uniform. Indigo pants, a jacket, a stark white shirt with pearl buttons, and a striped vest. All were a bit tight on his body, getting too small for him after his summer growth.

She made a mental note to get an appointment with the local tailor. She'd have to dip into their savings once again to cover the expensive uniform. Not much she could do, as it was the only school on the island.

Nava refused not to send Cameron to get a proper

education, even though Laurie, their housekeeper, had insisted she could tutor him from home.

"I'm not making this up!" His eyes met hers again through copper eyelashes. "Were you dreaming about him again?"

She propped her body up with her elbows. Her muscles complained as she scanned the room. Judging by the light that filtered through the large double windows, she could tell it was early morning.

She shrugged, knowing he already knew the answer.

"Your dreams are getting worse, Nava. The bed was shaking this time." His hand grasped hers. "I don't want what happened to Dad to happen to you too."

She forced a smile. "It won't."

He studied her features, searching for a shake of her voice that would give away the lie behind her words. "You suck at lying. At least if you're going to lie, you should make it more convincing."

"It's not my fault I can't cater to your lying needs when I first wake up." She took a deep breath. "You don't have to worry about me, though. What happened to Father—it's different."

"Maybe you can tell Laurie about the dreams getting worse. I'm not great at keeping secrets."

Nava shook her head, knowing she was not about to go to the older lady with concerns she could do little about. "We don't need to add to her worries."

"I know you want to protect me. But I'm not a child anymore—I'm thirteen now. I can handle it." He pulled at the lapels of his jacket with uneasy hands.

"I know."

"He didn't wake up from the last dream about Mom. Lately, it seems like you don't want to wake up, either."

She tightened her lips, not wanting to worry him any

more. Because the truth lay somewhere between his words; at times, she didn't want to wake up.

Her body longed to know more about the man she was supposed to be destined with, anything that would feed the incomplete mental image she had of him. She wanted to see his face, to learn if the softness of his voice matched his features. Was his hair dark? Were his eyes mischievous or gentle?

"Why don't you help Laurie with breakfast? I'll be downstairs soon." Her voice was hoarse with sleep.

Cameron tapped the wooden frame of her door before leaving without another word.

Her mind wandered, caught in a fog left behind by memories. It had been ten years since she'd met him on that fateful afternoon when she challenged her mother's restriction of never being outside the house during daylight.

The songs of seagulls flying overhead brought her back. She pulled her legs out of the warmth of her covers, wincing when her feet touched the worn wood floors. Fall had arrived, making the rooms dry and cold. Her room lacked a wood-burning fireplace or a stove that would warm it up.

She would have to get the wool blankets out of her closet that evening if she planned not to catch death this winter.

The narrow stairs creaked under her feet, alerting the bottom floor of their home to her descent. The smell of smoked bacon enveloped her like a hug, and her stomach rumbled. Nava scanned the room as she padded to the kitchen, finding Cameron already seated at the table, happily eating his eggs.

Laurie puttered around the room, her age not slowing the quickness of her steps. She wore her favorite burnt-orange dress that had been pressed with care without a wrinkle in sight, the white apron a stark contrast against the bright color beneath. Her skin sagged with age. Her wise black eyes came to greet her as a smile graced her features. "Awake at last, Nava. If I didn't get Cameron to come get you, you would've missed breakfast again," she reprimanded, pointing a finger to a spot at the table.

It was like she was fifteen again, not the twenty-five-year-old woman who held the well-being of this family on her shoulders.

The table was rustic and well-loved, with ornate chairs painted in white and a vase filled with orange mums from her back garden.

"Thank you for breakfast."

The woman shook her head, her brow wrinkling as she stared deep into her. "You are skin and bones, girl. You've got to put on some weight if you want to carry children."

Her skin heated, her eyes flashing to Cameron, who had started to choke on his food. She was not skin and bones; nature had graced her with curves and an easiness to put on weight, but she didn't need to mention this. "I'm not having children anytime soon."

"You are twenty-five." Laurie's tone carried the burden of the societal pressure she'd been getting more lately, with all the pitiful stares people in town gave her.

Nava lifted her chin. "I won't wed anyone in this town. You know I haven't felt a true connection here. So no need to worry about my childbearing abilities." She had to worry about keeping food on the table for both Cameron and Laurie; she didn't have time to worry about missing breakfast.

Laurie's voice softened. "It'll be hard to make a connection."

Nava took a deep breath. There was no use getting into

this conversation again. A full plate appeared in front of her. Before she was able to muse her thanks, Laurie was already walking away, drying her hands on her apron.

"It's not like anyone is coming to see her lately, not after she booted Hale." Cameron shrugged, pushing another large bite into his mouth. Chewing loudly.

"Manners, Cameron," Laurie hissed to the boy as she walked around the kitchen, dropping dirty dishes into the basin. "She doesn't need to be courted by these fellows. She has a soulmate waiting for her."

A pit of dread started to build in her stomach at those words. Nava never asked about him, even though she wanted more. She didn't need any part of a false love where she had no real choice in the matter. She was sick and tired of magic and people making her life choices.

Because that was what a soulmate was, magic dictating who she was to love and be attracted to. Not that she was having much luck in the latter, as she hadn't been attracted to anyone.

"I told you before, I don't need my soulmate. I don't know him, and I don't want anything to do with him. I want to live in peace and be able to provide for the both of you the best I can."

"The gods brought you two together. It's not something you can outrun, Nava," Laurie said with a soft tone that hid a bite behind every word. "You should know this after what happened to your father."

Silence descended upon the table. Nava's eyes flashed to Cameron. She expected him to be saddened by the reminder; it had been a couple of years since they'd lost him. Cameron didn't appear sad. He was alert as he stuffed his mouth with a spoonful of eggs. "My soulmate is not here. I doubt I'll ever see him again."

Cameron coughed loudly then, his face red as he

shifted in his seat. He sprang up from the table, pushing his empty plate away from him. 'Well, this was great and all." He cleared his throat as his freckled hand brushed over his hair. "I guess it's time to go to school."

"Wait up. I'll walk with you," Nava said, pushing a couple of spoonfuls of eggs into her mouth and grabbing one slice of bread on the go, the loud complaint of the woman behind the only sound as she rushed up the steps to her room.

CHAPTER TWO

*T*heir home sat at the top of the town that was
built on the side of a cliff with long serpent
roads of warm-colored stones of all shapes that were worn
smooth by centuries of use. Their house was quaint, a two-
story home built of stucco that had cracked with age,
showing gray stone underneath. Sun-bleached large wood
beams held a roof of terracotta tiles, much like all of the
buildings in town.

She loved the little cottage and the small garden in the
front that bloomed in spring, with hydrangeas that lasted
all the way to late summer.

They walked down the street as Nava shrugged on her
long coat. She wore her simple grass-green skirt she'd tied
a brown belt over. A dagger was shielded within it, something she had carried around with her for the last decade,
always prepared to defend herself from an impending
attack.

"I wish I didn't have to go to school today. I could come
help you at the shop like old times," Cameron said. His
hair shone under the sun, freckles dancing on his cheeks. A

feature they both shared, freckled skin, though Cameron's was fair while Nava's was a few shades darker like her mother's had been.

"I would have done anything to go to school when I was your age, back when we lived in the Iron City and not on this island. To be able to make friends, to be *free* to leave the house," she said, lost in the moment.

"That's what you keep saying," he grumbled, shaking his head, half annoyed and half amused. "You can't keep moping about your stolen childhood. You are supposed to be the grown-up here."

Her mouth dropped, just before he started laughing. "Here I thought you had matured overnight." She pushed him by his shoulder with her own.

He was no longer that gangly, short, skinny boy. She hugged him close to her as they walked, the sound of their heels clicking over the hard stone to the rhythm of the birds flying around them.

He was tall, just a couple of inches shorter than her five-six, caught in that time where the proportions were too awkward. His voice was that of the boy she loved.

"My point was that you should enjoy your childhood with peers your age. It got lonely for me."

"You're still a hermit. What excuse do you have?" he challenged her.

Nava paused for a moment, taken aback by his observation. She guessed it had been naïve to think Cameron wouldn't have noticed how difficult it was for her to make connections. "I'm not a hermit—I see Simone often," she defended.

"One girlfriend. It's hardly a lot of friends. I'm saying I haven't seen you go out with anyone else. Hale courted you, then there was the excuse of me—which is a terrible excuse because I quite liked him." He shrugged.

"Cameron, the matchmaker," Nava joked. He narrowed his eyes. "Fine, he was boring, okay? There were zero sparks. Also, he kept implying I needed him."

Nava didn't need anyone, not even the man the gods had sent her.

Worry flashed through her brother's eyes, but in a blink, it was gone. He was much better at masking his feelings than she was. "Maybe . . . we need to leave this town, go back to the Iron City to try to find *him*. I know you hate for me to bring him up, but I'm afraid to lose you too, Nava."

"We aren't going to find him. There was a reason we ran away from the Iron City. I'm not about to put you in danger for my gain." After all, it was thanks to her they were in this mess. Had she not disobeyed her mother, the Society of Crows wouldn't have found her, and they wouldn't have had to run away from the city like the Devil himself had been chasing after them.

She was just thankful they'd never learned about Cameron's existence.

"Mom and Dad are gone. I want us to do more. It feels like we're here just because they said so." He crossed his arms, his brow dipped.

"Morning, witch boy." The voice startled Nava. She stared into the face of a fair boy who was smirking at them.

Cameron saluted the caller.

"Did he just call you witch boy?" Nava narrowed her eyes as she crossed her arms over her chest, puffing a breath out.

"Yes, he did."

She gazed at her brother before settling on his freckled face. Her anger wavered at his soft, relaxed grin. "It doesn't bother you?"

Cameron shook his head, shrugging. "Why should it?"

"Well, for starters, you aren't one," she stated. Those words had been used to mock her behind hushed tones, through tight lips and frowned faces—witch *girl*. The memories made her heart heavy.

Her whole time in this town, she had heard this. It was no secret her mother had been a spell wielder, and her father's gift with potion-making had shaped them into the outcasts of a town that had no magic.

Them calling her a witch was the worst insult, as witches were known for their cruel ways and working with dark magic. The reminder of side-eyes and mocking faces came to her, making her stomach heavy as if lead had filled it to the brim.

"Maybe not a witch. But maybe a warlock—or a powerful sorcerer." Cameron's excitement was a complete departure from the churning in her stomach as the words escaped his lips. "Stop shaking your head, Nava. You're going to rattle your brain." He smirked.

"You are most definitely *not* going to become one."

"You are free to be afraid of who we are or what we might be. I'm not. I want to figure it out myself."

A rush of energy ran through her body, and the sensation in her stomach grew more significant, making it hard to breathe. The chilly autumn wind moved her wild hair across her face. "Y—you never said you wanted to leave this town." Nava scanned around them, making sure eavesdroppers were nowhere to be found.

"I just did."

"Well, yes, I know. You were talking about my soulmate. Not about you and what you want." It was too early for her brain to fully take on Cameron's intent. At least she was glad no one was watching her panic. The town was still half asleep, the roads empty except for the odd student walking to school that morning.

"This town was picked by our parents, not by us." He shrugged.

"To protect us from the crown." Her voice came a bit louder than she intended.

"You don't have to come with me when I go, but I want to see what my nature is."

"Maybe we have no magic," she pressed, panic closing her throat.

"Then what are you so afraid for, right?" His smile grew lopsided as he gave her a side hug before walking away.

She raised her hand, waiting until he crossed the black iron gate that housed the school. A wooden sign with shiny brass letters spelled "The Walrod Academy." The school that taught no magic, a place that represented safety to her.

THE COOLING AIR OF an early fall morning. The old cobblestone roads were uneven under her steps, winding over a city built onto the steep side of a mountain.

Buildings of stucco, stone, and brick surrounded Nava. The doors of the shops and apartment buildings were bright, intense colors. The constructions weren't as tall as the ones she remembered from the Iron City the few times she'd been allowed to visit.

She stopped by her favorite bakery to buy a few loaves of bread and say hello to Simone, her best friend. The soft ringing of the doorbells welcomed her, along with a waft of delicious-smelling baked goods. Simone was behind the worn wood counter, her platinum hair pulled back into a tight bun that usually didn't let any flyaways escape their confinement. This morning, it was different, however, as wisps of hair were a halo around her head.

She was wearing a sky-blue dress and an apron that had been white earlier in the morning. Now it was stained by a baker's job. Her pink lips turned into a smile as soon as she noticed the new customer was Nava.

"Nava, honey." Her melodic voice broke the silence. She scurried to the baskets where she kept that morning's fresh bread. Her nimble fingers selected the ones Nava wanted before putting them inside a linen bag. "I was going to come to see you later today. I have completely run out of my migraine medicine and was hoping to bribe you with some of your favorite bread for a couple of bottles." She handed the bread over with a smile.

"Already?" Nava tilted her head. "I gave you some last week."

"Yes, you did—but Mother came by yesterday for dinner. We both ended up with horrible headaches after it. She took half of it, and I took the rest." Her flour-covered fingers came to the back of her neck.

"Is she still pushing you to marry Kyle?"

Simone winced. Nava turned, checking her surroundings. It wouldn't be the first time she'd spoken a bit too loud where strangers could hear a private conversation. Destiny had been kind to her this morning. The bakery was empty.

"Don't remind me." Her friend groaned. "I don't even know where she got that I would agree to this. Kyle and I are practically siblings."

Nava nodded. It would be amazing to have her mother here, pressuring her to find someone to marry and give her grandchildren, much like Laurie had this morning. It had been so long since her mother had been gone, she had already forgotten the sound of her voice, the softness of her embrace, or the spicy scent of magic when she'd come home from the garden when they lived away from here.

She remembered her father telling her he missed the tone of her voice as well, that he was afraid of forgetting it. Then the dreams had started. What once had been the healthy, round face of her father had chiseled down into a tired, gray complexion. He'd always wanted to sleep, had always wanted to be in whatever other world of dreams she'd awaited him.

"You went dark, didn't you?"

Her friend's voice took her out of her thoughts. "Yes, I totally did. I'm sorry. I'm feeling a bit—"

"Tired?" Simone worried her lip with her teeth. "Is it the dreams again?"

"Yes."

"Do you want to talk about it?"

Nava shook her head. "I will. I promise it's not something crazy. I know you get a bit anxious when I talk about M-A-G-I-C, even though I'm not one hundred percent sure this is in any way related to that . . ." Nava let her words fade because she didn't like lies. Magic was what was making her tired.

Even in this town that repressed magic, the soulmate bond was still there, beating inside her, haunting her night after night in dreams, reminding her that she had left something, *someone*, behind. The sorcerers and warlocks who'd set the wards in this town were all-powerful, though not more powerful than the gods.

Simone paled; she and her family were the only people in this town who accepted the Forrests openly, even though they were magical in a town that wanted no magic inside it. Simone's mother had been a good childhood friend of Nava's dad once upon a time.

"Honey, I don't want you to stop telling me things

because I might get nervous. You know, I have never seen magic before, but from the stories I hear, it's scary but also exciting?" Simone's voice wavered.

"Don't I know it."

"My point is, I want you to talk to me if something is happening to you, even if I don't understand it." Simone reached across the counter to Nava.

"Thanks, and I promise I will tell you more. Preferably over wine and chocolate," Nava murmured with a smile, trying to lift the sudden mood that had fallen over them. The impending doom of what she often referred to as her curse was present in her mind.

"I will come by tonight with both things, and you can spill whatever is bothering you then." Simone's voice carried around the room as Nava pushed the door of the shop open with her wide hips, turning to smile at her friend.

"Don't forget the chocolate or I won't let you in," she said before exiting the bakery, a bag of fresh bread in hand.

CHAPTER THREE

*T*he shop was slow that day. People had been buzzing around about a new ship that had docked earlier in the morning. Nava hadn't gotten around to checking it out, as it was always unnerving when a new boat landed in Willowbrook.

Nava had been a ball of nerves ever since she'd learned there were soldiers and a sorcerer onboard the ship. To most people, it was an exciting novelty. To Nava, it was her absolute worst nightmare.

Few ships landed on the island. Usually, kingdoms avoided sending crews here. The island wasn't wealthy, and magic got canceled inside the invisible shield guarding the town. Treaties made eons ago protected trades. City people rarely came to vacation or moved to the Grey Island.

Nava tapped her pen against the worn wood of her shop's counter, having abandoned the illusion of making any potions much earlier. She couldn't focus with a kingdom's army looming so close to Cameron. Much less if they had a sorcerer or warlock in tow.

Her gaze darted around people passing by her shop.

Everyone seemed to be in a cheerful mood, the novelty of the newcomers making the town buzz with excitement.

She took a deep breath and told herself for the tenth time that her paranoid nature got the best of her. The likelihood of one of two sorcerers who knew her face coming to this island was improbable.

The sun kissed the paving stones of the streets with orange and yellow hues at a quarter to five. The bell on her door rang. She lifted her head toward the newcomer, and her heart dropped.

The towering shape of a man, dressed in an ebony coat with indigo and cobalt-blue accents, came in, crowding her small potion store. Shapes embroidered intricate organic patterns across a broad chest. She had seen the exact outfit once before. Her heart pounded and everything went still for a breath as she considered her swift escape.

Once again, she cursed that the only exit of the building was through the narrow front door. Poor architectural planning had been a constant thought when the afternoons were slow. If she survived today, she would not be renewing her lease.

Her gaze reached his face. She expected to see *him*, her soulmate. She knew deep within that he wasn't it. He met her stare with eyes so dark they could have been pools of spilled ink.

Nava was at a loss for words. The knot in her throat grew with every step he took toward her. Like a wild cat hunting for prey. He reached the counter in a heartbeat, one pale, scarred hand resting on top of the glass, tapping a finger to a soft rhythm that sent her nerves into a frenzy.

His focus never left her as he smirked. Nava had never beheld anyone with such a fair complexion before. His skin was so pale he could have been a sheet of bleached parchment.

"Good afternoon," he purred. The scent of blackberries and mint wafted around him.

Nava blinked her daze away, swallowing loudly. The voice sounded familiar. Nava might have heard it that morning in a hazy dream brought by memories she could never forget. She had lost her voice. He lifted a brow, awaiting a response. Perspiration dampened the skin of her hands, and a prickle crawled down the back of her neck.

She managed to find her voice. "G-good afternoon. How can I help you?"

His hair was brushed back neatly, black as a moonless night. He leaned forward, resting the weight of his body on the old countertop. Nava pulled back and heard the clinking sound of glass bottles as she collided with the rack of potions she kept behind her.

He smiled crookedly. "We landed today, after many months locked away in a ship with hundreds of men."

A panther in front of a scared rabbit. Why did he try at small talk with her when he could be anywhere else in town?

Her nerves were driving her closer to a panic attack. She had not seen a Crow for ten years. A secret part of her, one she never gave a voice, had hoped the next time she encountered one, it would be *hers*.

Her Crow. Her soulmate.

"Is there something you want?" Words spilled out of her mouth before she could stop them, something that happened when her nerves took over. "Or are you looking for a potion?"

His eyes sparkled like polished onyx before his voice filtered out of his lips in an unnervingly calm tone. "Imagine my surprise when I see a potion store in a town that is supposed to suppress magic." He straightened to his full height. A whole head taller than her. By his intense scrutiny on her face, he had memorized every single one of her freckles.

"Oh, we don't use magic here—it's alchemy. The name potions is for novelty. No one is expecting a love potion or good luck in a bottle."

"How disappointing. I hoped someone had found a way around the spell that cancels magic inside this town," he said, peering across the shelves of potion-covered walls.

"Sorry to disappoint." She hoped with every bone in her body that he would take his leave.

"Forrest. I knew a potion maker with the same name back in the Iron City."

She stilled, considering jumping over the counter and bolting toward the door. If he was as skilled of a warrior as she assumed, he wouldn't have a problem catching her.

Still, she didn't spot a weapon on him, and he had no magic here.

"Forrest is a common last name."

"Is it?" A charged silence followed. He remembered her.

"Of course. There are a lot of Forrests in town," she lied through her teeth.

One of his brows lifted. He was toying with her, realizing her predicament.

She told herself he didn't have any magic here. No way to detect her aura or whatever other parlor tricks warlocks could do. He had a last name, along with a memory of a young girl picking plants from her garden. She wrapped her shaky arms across her stomach, grasping the hilt of her dagger.

Nava hoped it looked casual. Crows were skilled in weaponry, but so was she—sort of.

She had trained for many years to wield this weapon, to defend herself without the need for magic. No longer a defenseless teenager. Her mother had made sure of that.

"You have such peculiar eyes." He leaned in. His long fingers reached across the glass. The wood frame creaked with his weight.

"Everyone says so," she said. Her knuckles went white as her grip tightened around the leather handle of her weapon.

Perfect, straight white teeth flashed behind a truly mischievous grin. "I once met a girl with similar eyes. A gardener, a very young one."

Nava swallowed, not saying a word at first. "What can I say? I have a common face."

"No, I don't think you do." His gaze narrowed on her. "A friend and I were together that day. I haven't seen him since. He is dear to me, you see. I have been looking for him for quite some time."

Missing. Her soulmate was missing. Her mind reeled back to his words. Her body went cold and clammy. Why was he not in the Iron City? Was he searching for her? "I'm not sure what you are trying to find here, sir."

"Sir sounds old. Call me Devon or Mr. Black." He took a step back, focusing on the hand holding her dagger.

Her throat bobbed. Her stomach revolted with nerves. She might be sick at any moment.

"The crown became interested in my trip here. It's said Gray sorcerers tend to escape to this island—"

"I assure you, I was born and raised here." Another lie. "I have never seen you before—or your friend."

"Of course." He walked around the shop, his arms coming around his back as he studied the sage-colored walls, the dark worn wood shelves. "Perhaps you have seen sorcerers passing through town?"

She shook her head so hard a sharp pain extended down her neck.

"Another dead end, I suppose," he declared. The intensity behind his expression hid nothing.

"I'm sorry I'm not the girl you were looking for, Mr. Black. I don't mean to be rude, but we close at five, and check the time." She waved her hand, signaling the clock hanging on her wall. Steam poured out of the top, marking five fifteen with its brass arms. "I'm afraid I have to go. I have previous commitments."

He nodded, and the same side smile appeared on his face as he tilted his head, studying the clock on the wall. "Of course."

She walked to the front door of her shop, one shaking hand holding the linen bag with her bread and the other firmly placed on the hilt of her weapon.

"I was not aware this type of advancement had made it to this island," he said, pointing his chin to the clock. Her father had brought it over from the Iron City.

She stilled. "We don't. A tradesman brought it over five years ago. It's handy."

He dipped into a polite bow and sauntered to her. "Apologies for having kept you, Miss Forrest. I'm afraid I could not pick any of your potions to try for seasickness. I must come back at a later date."

"Please do." She clenched her teeth with the lie alongside false politeness.

He *knew* her. The safety of the town provided her a shield from his magic. He would be back and armed with soldiers later on.

She pushed the door open with too much strength. The old hinges screeched before it slammed against the exterior wall. She walked out of her shop, almost tripping over her steps.

He prowled to her, his hands behind him. Nava held her breath, trying not to catch his scent. The heat of his body almost burned her. She stepped back and hit the frame of the door, cursing she hadn't gotten out of the way fast enough.

His eyes fixed on hers, a promise of something wicked and bad shining behind them.

She pressed her lips together tightly, waiting with a forced smile as he turned to her. Devon lingered on her before he sauntered down the cobbled road. People all around ignored their exchange, talking lively about the day, unaware of the danger she was in.

She had never run faster than she did that evening toward her home.

CHAPTER FOUR

*N*ava had learned from her mother to be paranoid. The run home exhausted her, as she'd decided to take the long road at the last minute. Just in case someone followed her there.

If she lived through this mess, she would have to move out of town since she'd decided it would be a great idea to run through lady Mallory's yard as a shortcut. They would call her not only a witch but also a trespassing lunatic.

She heaved for air when she crossed the edge of her property, past the ornate black iron fence and the browning leaves of her hydrangea bushes in the front of her house.

Nava pushed the heavy wood door open, meeting the eyes of both Laurie and Cameron by the kitchen, the latter holding two plates while he padded to the table. Her blood boiling, she removed her coat, the fabric of her shirt stuck to her back.

She stared toward the street before she closed the door behind her and rushed to the side window, peeking through white curtains while gasping for air.

"Nava, is everything all right?" Laurie asked.

"He found us—me. He found *me*, Laurie." Her shaky hand came to her face, brushing away the hair sticking all over her sweaty skin.

"It can't be." Laurie shook her head as her skin turned a pale gray.

"Who? What's going on?" Cameron's voice wavered.

"The Crow. One of them is here. He came to the shop this afternoon. We aren't safe here. We have to go." Her words rushed out, and silence descended between the three of them.

"Your soulmate?" Cameron asked, his features appearing so much younger as he approached her.

Her hand came to his face. Tears prickled her eyes. It was her fault, after all, that they were in this mess. Had she not disobeyed her mother that afternoon, he would be safe. "No, it wasn't my soulmate," Nava whispered.

Laurie walked to them, and her heavy hand landed on Nava's shoulder. "If it wasn't your soulmate, you're in danger." She tugged her away from Cameron. "Do you think he would find us here in this house?"

It had been the one thing that had occupied her mind during her run home. Devon just needed to ask around town for Forrest, the potion maker residence, and someone would offer the information for the right price.

"We have to leave." Laurie's voice shook with emotion.

Nava nodded as her mind reeled back. "Why do you think I would've been safe if it had been *him*?"

"A soulmate would never hurt you. I never agreed with Celeste on keeping so much from you. You are her child. I respected her choice not to tell you anything until you asked." She moved her hand down Nava's arm, holding her with an underlying urgency. "You never asked."

"Laurie?"

"I did research on the subject of soulmates when you found yours . . . Celeste and I had extensive conversations about what was coming for you."

They walked past the kitchen and down a narrow corridor that led to Laurie's bedroom. It had the house's best view, with large windows facing the town's steep views and Nava's back garden.

Laurie let go of Nava's hand and stepped in, moving around her space, heading toward the heavy black-and-gold trunk by the end of her bed.

"I don't think we have time for this. Devon Black is here and might be coming to the house as we speak. We've got to leave."

"Yes, we do." Laurie pushed the heavy lid open and rummaged through the contents inside.

"I don't understand what's happening."

"Me, neither," Cameron piped up from Laurie's bedroom door.

"The Crows might think they have a claim over you—they might even know one of their own is your soulmate," Laurie said. She rummaged around her trunk, large hands pulling out an old leather-bound notebook. She got up from the floor, her face morphing into a pained expression.

Nava's brows dipped. "Yes, so?"

"We need to go to the Grey Forest."

Laurie's words hit her all at once. Dread crawled like an icy caress down her spine. A shot of adrenaline ran through her body. "The forest is full of magic. It's cursed. We wouldn't make it a day."

Silence descended over them, the weight of her words settling as the truth. Nava had trained with her mother in weaponry. She was barely able to defend herself, let alone Laurie at her old age and Cameron.

"They don't know Cameron exists. They aren't aware

you are here with us. It'll be safer for the both of you to stay in this town," Nava said, the air escaping her lungs in a whoosh. She rested her body weight against the cold wall.

It hit her at once, the relief that she hadn't put Cameron in danger. The dread of having to leave him behind . . .

"Not in this house," Laurie said with a stiff nod.

"No. Maybe the inn?"

Laurie nodded. Nava's fingers were thick and uncoordinated as she undid the leather string tying the notebook closed. Stumbling, she caught a piece of parchment that had dropped from it as soon as the bind had loosened.

She opened it and studied the ink lines that made a clear map of the Grey Island's forest. It was easy to see the town by the illustrations, the edge of Willowbrook where the spell ended and the magical lands began.

The forest took most of the island, with the shapes of trees, mountains, and lakes. Dotted lines marked directions she didn't understand. Nava blinked in confusion, her gaze zeroing in on the contrast of red ink circling one area in particular. The familiar scribbles of her mother's letters wrote a name.

"*Arkimedes*." The weight of two intense gazes fell upon her. She lifted her face to Laurie, a question about to spill out. Who was Arkimedes?

"Your mother didn't say much, just that he was someone we should go to if the crown ever found us." Laurie's face fell. "I wish I had asked more questions. I had so little time left with your mother before sickness took her."

"She wasn't one who liked to share truths." Nava's words burned her throat.

"No, I guess not." Cameron's voice shook with anger,

his fists clenched at his sides. "We should stay together. That's what family does."

Nava came to him, closing the map inside the notebook to inspect later. Her free hand reached to one of his, grasping it tightly. "Family also protects each other," she said. "You are the most important thing in my life, Cam. Believe I'll be fine and will come back."

His skin lost a bit of the color it had gained when his anger spiked. "I never doubted you would be fine. You're the strongest person I know, even when you are a butthead," he admitted.

A soft knock on the front door had them all jumping in their spot. Nava's skin crawled. Her finger pressed to her lips, signaling them to be quiet. Laurie rushed to the side table by her bed and blew out the candle that illuminated the room, bathing them in darkness.

"Stay here," Nava whispered, coming outside to the living area. The gentle light of candles illuminated the place, and the floorboards creaked under her quiet feet. She walked to the front door to see the shadow of someone peeking through the window

Nava took a calming breath and took the dagger out of the sheath as she approached the door. She might have the element of surprise. If she did enough damage, it might give her family enough time to run away from the back of the house.

She yanked the door open, raising her dagger. Simone yelped, stumbling back. It was a miracle the bottle of wine hadn't fallen to the ground.

"Nava, what the hell is going on?"

"Come in." Nava pulled her inside the house.

Simone focused on Nava as if she had at last lost it. Her attention followed a spot behind, where Cameron and Laurie were coming out from the back room, somber expressions on their features. "Nava, honey, what's wrong?"

"I don't have much time to explain anything, Simone. I'm in trouble," Nava said.

"Pack lightly, child. We must not appear to be running," the older woman said in an assured voice and pushed Cameron toward the stairs. Nava could tell by the crease of her brows that she didn't know what to do.

Simone paled. "The ship." Understanding shone in her blue eyes. "It's from the crown. They're chasing deserters. They don't know you are—"

"A warlock came on the ship, and he does."

Nava watched Simone's skin turn a sickly green. Her best friend took a couple of steps back, holding herself against the nearby chair. "Oh."

"They never knew of Cameron and Laurie. They'll be going to the inn. We don't know if the warlock and whatever army he has with him will come to look for me here."

Simone shook her head. "They'll go to the inn to search." Her gaze shone with conviction. "They can stay with me."

Nava swallowed, blinking to prevent from crying. "Are you sure?"

"Of course I'm sure, silly," Simone said, enveloping her into a bone-crushing hug. The steps of Cameron coming down the stairs distracted them.

"I'm ready," he whispered, tugging the canvas bag closer to his body.

Nava walked to her brother and wrapped him in a tight hug. The Society of Crows made children ruthless soldiers. She wouldn't let them take him. "You will be staying with Simone," she said in a shaky tone. "I'll be back before you miss me."

"We should go." Laurie came close to Nava. "You should leave tonight. Don't wait long."

"I won't."

"If you can't find Arkimedes, there is one village in the forest. You can go there, ask for help, and warn them they are coming."

Nava nodded, unsure if she'd make it to any village. At this point, she'd be glad if she survived one day in the forest.

"I will care for him, Nava. Don't worry. Go. Stay away. Don't let him take you, or I fear we might not see you again." Laurie enveloped her in a tight hug; the soft scent of cinnamon and cardamom reminded her of her childhood.

"I guess it's time," Nava whispered, dropping the fabric of the curtain. "Thank you, Simone."

"Of course, honey."

"We'll come back to our home when it's safe," Laurie said.

"Yes." Nava turned to Cameron. "See you soon, caterpillar."

"I want stories when you are back," he answered with a smile.

Nava held back as they said their goodbyes and the people she loved the most in her whole world left her behind. Once again running away from a Crow, from her own mistake. Her cheeks grew wet as she watched them walk down the pathway of their home and past the front iron gates.

CHAPTER FIVE

*N*ava frantically shoved supplies into a backpack that had once belonged to her father. It was old and tattered, made of thick canvas the color of green olives, with soft leather tabs and worn brass buckles that barely held it closed.

She could hear her neighbors chatting on their back patio, enjoying the cooling temperatures after a hot summer.

She swallowed, trying to rack her brain for tips her father had once given in their many camping trips. What medicine to pack if she were ever to cross the edge of town to venture into the forest. She shoved in the bread Simone had given her, a heavy breath escaping her lips.

Silhouettes came down the walkway to the front door of her home.

They had come for her after all. It had taken less than a couple of hours for Devon Black to find her. She picked up the heavy cloak that hung from the back of one of the dining chairs.

Avoiding making any noise, Nava moved to grab the

two daggers she'd lain on the table earlier. She took her backpack and headed to Laurie's room.

The window was heavy to open but large enough for her to sneak out. For once, she was grateful for the neighbor's overgrown, unkempt garden she often complained about. Relieved that none of the men checked the back of the house.

Nava tossed her heavy backpack out, snapping her mother's rose bushes in half as it fell down, and her heart ached at the sight.

She jumped out, and it wasn't a graceful fall. The hardness of the cold ground scraped her hands. Steam left her lips in a surge from the chilled air that burned her exposed skin.

Nava ran across the short, manicured grass. Their yard was a small rectangular space filled with dry plants. She jumped over the hedge that divided her home from the neighbor's, landing on a much more unkempt property.

Overgrown bushes hid her shape as she ran behind the home to the street. Her neighbors had decided to go in, chased by the cold air. She was grateful for the chilly night. The less they saw, the better.

Her feet pounded on the hard stone road. Her backpack buckles shrieked with the movements. The loud crash of a door getting kicked in echoed in the empty streets, followed by the breaking of glass.

Nava glanced and saw two of the guards around the front door, wearing black outfits with furs that adorned their necks.

"Hey, you!" one shouted.

Terrin, who owned the local flower shop, unloaded his empty buckets onto his home's front steps. His attention was behind her, his brow deepening.

Understanding lit his features as she ran past him.

Whatever he did next was unclear. Instead, the commotion of water splashing over stone came.

"I'm sorry. I did not see you coming." Terrin's loud voice gave her the fuel she needed to provide her steps with an extra boost of energy.

It was common knowledge to the townspeople that the crown chased deserters. She would forever be grateful for his help.

She cut through alleyways, making sharp turns that only residents knew. She went up the old, uneven steps, so many she lost count. Her lungs burned.

Nava kept going. She had at least two miles to run before she was out of the town, all uphill while carrying a heavy backpack and two steel daggers in her belt.

She struggled to catch her breath, her legs cramping. She didn't stop even as the buildings became sparser. Homes were smaller with larger front yards. Smoke billowed out of weathered, stained chimneys.

The Grey Forest stood tall, trees rising over a bed of mist. The fence dividing the non-magical grounds from the magical ones was near, made of the variance of stacked gray stones, bathed in the moon's blue light.

Nava stopped right before climbing. The shapes of the trees loomed in front of her. She wasn't sure what she was more fearful of, the people chasing her or whatever magical creatures awaited her inside the darkness of the forest.

Swallowing, she steadied her resolve and found the will to keep her freedom.

Sharp stones cut her palms and scraped her legs as she climbed over the wall, her green skirt making it harder. Nava couldn't stop until she was safe in the cover of the thick woods.

Safe—a word she would never take for granted again. At the top, she took another second to think of her family.

She jumped down the five feet of rock, across the invisible line that, for the past ten years, had separated her from magic.

NAVA WAS NOT SURE how long she wandered. Her eyelids were heavy, and she was drunk with exhaustion. She held the old brass compass that belonged to her father —and had given up checking on it.

The new morning sun peeked through the trees' tall branches, allowing her to better take in the magic around her. Trunks, thin and thick, extended high up, with limbs of moss-covered branches. The ground was softened with dried foliage.

She rested against a tree. Her breaths of air were loud. Dread pooled inside her stomach. She expected to see a three-headed something appear out of nowhere. The forest *was* full of life. Not in the frightening way she was expecting, normal somehow. The songs of birds singing with the morning sun calmed her. It smelled like cedar, pine, and morning dew.

To get to the red circle her mother had made on the map, she was supposed to head east. She searched for any shape that could represent danger but found nothing. The magnitude of her situation made her pause. Her house had been raided by Devon Black's goons. Her thoughts went to her neighbor Terrin. She hoped he was fine.

Nava dropped her backpack and lifted the top flap to remove the small notebook. Taking the map out, she studied the ink lines, hoping to find more information that would lead her *somewhere*.

She let her head fall back, the bark digging into her scalp. The truth was, she didn't know where she was or what to do. She dreaded trusting a stranger because her mother had left his name scribbled on a piece of paper.

He was likely an old haggard man who smelled funny and talked in riddles.

Her body heated as her hands tightened around the map, the crinkling paper somehow alien in her surroundings.

She startled at the feeling of a heartbeat that was not hers, a whisper of a tap-tap against the skin of her chest. Her fingertips touched her soulmate mark. It was warm under her touch, alive after ten years of slumber.

NAVA HAD BEEN WALKING for hours. She had occasionally stopped to eat and give rest to her tired feet. She needed to set camp soon. By following random notes her mother had scribbled on the map, it would be near impossible to get to Arkimedes's cabin in the woods until the next day.

The day had warmed up, and the forest was bright with golden colors seeping through the canopy's holes. A lingering scent of burning wood hung in the air. It had to be her imagination, as there was no fire or smoke in sight.

She jumped, startled by the sound of leaves rustling, her eyes fixing on the ground, watching them caress the forest floor. A bee struggled with an injury. It trembled on top of a dried leaf, its yellow body contrasting against the dried foliage.

Her heart pitter-pattered at the heartbreaking sight. Another one nearby, then hundreds of thousands peppered the forest floor surrounding her.

Following the path of the dying insects, she stopped, her mind screaming at her to get out of there, but her heart insisted she inspect further.

She always followed her heart.

The side of the tree moved, and long limbs took shape; spindly arms shifted, pointy shoulders decorated by protruding branches. Moss covered its torso and long legs, each the size of one of her. She swallowed, taking a step back. A scream held on her tongue.

He was a tall creature, his chest made of bark adorned by lichen. His long neck made him appear more fragile. His lips parted to reveal jagged teeth. He was staring at her, his movements frozen. What she'd previously read as a snarl was a pained cry. Her heart contorted at the horrible despair that filled the air.

The bees on the ground weren't dead. They flapped their wings in a futile attempt to fly.

The creature was afraid of her. She wasn't sure if whatever or whoever had hurt him was still lurking around.

She steeled her shaking body, forcing her eyes to find the reason for its pain. She gasped when she spotted another creature a few feet from the tree, the floor of the forest already hiding the decomposing body. Deep gashes ran through, and a thick, gooey substance that resembled honey spouted out of the wounds.

Her focus turned to the smaller shape crying by the tree, and a hand covered her lips on a shaky sob. It was the heart-wrenching pain of the creature in front of her. Whatever had attacked them had killed one of them.

There was a deep gash in the beehive that made the top part of the creature's head. At first glance, she considered it an enormous hat. It gushed honey down its face to its sharp mouth.

Nava was moving before she could think twice, running

to the spot behind the fallen tree, where she had left her backpack. She rummaged in the pouch where she had stashed her potions. She'd figured a healing potion would be handy at some point. It was unclear if the medicine would help the creature. However, she was determined to try.

She came to it, her arms out in a sign of peaceful approach. Its pitch-black eyes fixed on her, and it made no move to attack or retreat. Maybe it could read her intentions.

The bees on the ground flapped, their energy dwindling. Panic rose in her chest, but she didn't understand why. He was so high up in the trees she wouldn't be able to reach his head.

"If you can understand me, I have something that might help you. But I can't reach you," she said. Her fingertips couldn't even touch the bottom of the creature's feet.

He cried once again.

It had been many years since she'd climbed a tree, but the broken branches around this one made it a perfect option for her to try. She hoisted herself up the first branch, her leg coming up to secure her stance.

She steadied her hold, grasping the tree's trunk with shaky hands, and stepped onto the next branch, which cracked under her weight. She hiked up onto the next one, a thicker one this time, and continued one, two, three.

Nava was closer. The face of the creature made her pause. The pain in his expression stirred her to put aside any of her biases.

"I promise I won't hurt you," she said and reached into her pocket, fishing out one of the two vials of her healing potions. She brought it to her lips and bit off the cork that held the heavy liquid inside.

Nava reached, but the creature pulled away. She allowed it to come near, her heart hammering when its wooden nose touched her skin, sniffing. It would take a bite for her to lose her hand, her mind supplied, a spike of panic running through her. Her body slumped down as her adrenaline subsided.

"Please let me help you," she whispered. It dipped its head, allowing her to inspect the dripping gash.

Nava poured the potion down, digging in her pocket for the second vial, and repeated the process. She took a small gauze she'd also stuffed in her pocket and pressed it onto the wound with delicate fingers. Her hand became wet and sticky with warm honey, to her chagrin. She could never eat honey again.

She closed her eyes, the warmness in her hand extending through her body like a rush of energy. Nava hoped this could at least help this creature heal. Her skin glowed with power.

Panicked, she pulled her arm back, studying her skin as her heart fought to leap out of her throat. The wound in the creature's head closed a little—the goop had stopped oozing out of it.

Had she done magic? No, of course not.

She brought her hand back and stared—she could go fetch her last two potions to try again—but was interrupted by the creature. Its pained expression lifted somehow from the corners of its sharp mouth. The creature stilled, and his gaze moved to one side of the forest. And then it met her eyes again.

"*They are coming. Run,*" a buzzing voice thundered through her thoughts.

Nava's eyes went in the direction the creature stared. She didn't have to be told twice. Her legs trembled as she tried not to focus on what would happen to her if she were to drop.

The buzzing became louder, the bees waking up from near death. Nava jumped off the third branch, yelping in pain as she landed poorly.

She ran to the fallen tree and picked up her bag, hoisting it up on her shoulders, and she was off.

CHAPTER SIX

*N*ava couldn't keep running. She was afraid her body would collapse from exhaustion at any moment. Darkness was approaching, the days shorter as summer ended. She was tired, thirsty, and afraid.

The voices from her huntsmen came from afar. She tried to zigzag among the trees, to be hidden by their enormous trunks. She was running out of time. Despair moved her forward. Her hair caught the air with the quick movements.

They covered a vast amount of ground. She counted five, maybe six men in black coats. The buckles of her backpack screeched.

Nava didn't see the shape looming until it was too late. A firm grip locked on her arm as a gloved hand covered her mouth and pulled her behind a tree.

A warm body held her tightly. She writhed against his hold, pushing and pulling. She was against a wall of muscle. Her heartbeat drummed. They'd caught her. Nava bit hard, tasting salt and dirt on the leather glove. A deep gasp of pain was the only sound near her, and the hand pressed tighter against her.

"Stop that or they'll find us both," a throaty voice whispered against her ear. Warm air hit the side of her cheek, raising the ends of her hair. She stopped moving.

He turned her around, and her back hit the texture of the tree. His hand lifted off her for a second before covering them again. He stood over six feet. A brown hood hid his features, much like the one she was wearing. His hold on her loosened, a finger pressed against her lips in a signal to be quiet. She nodded curtly. His hand lowered from her face. He lifted his head and looked around.

"I swear I saw her run this way," one man grunted.

Nava moved closer to the tree, praying it sheltered her from view. She peered out of the hood of her cloak. The soldiers stared right where they were, with no recognition behind their features.

"He said she couldn't do magic," another one snarled. "Promised it would be easy, that she wouldn't expect us to come."

"Since when do Crows speak the truth?" another one asked as if bored, and the stranger next to her tensed at the words. "We are here for the money. All that matters is capturing as many deserters as we can. Twenty silver coins per head."

The other three grunted in agreement and walked on, their heads turning.

The stranger hid behind the tree, listening to the retreating steps. Her legs were cramped from the uncomfortable position she stood in. She moved, trying to bring circulation back to her extremities.

"Are they gone?" she whispered.

"Shh."

A spike of annoyance flooded through her. There was

no sound other than his breathing. The stranger's posture relaxed, so she took a deep breath.

He stepped away from her, crunching the leaves under his considerable weight. His hand came to lower his hood. The warm afternoon sun hit the sharp angle of a jaw. Fair skin came into view, gold under the sunlight. Bright green eyes stared back at her. Shades of chartreuse stormed inside his irises with otherworld magic. His umber hair matched his thick brows. His chiseled jaw showed the shadow of a beard.

Nava had never beheld such magical eyes before, the movements of colors. She studied his skin, his broad shoulders. He couldn't be older than thirty.

Her stomach twisted as she took in his features, a warm wave running through her body, spreading down her limbs, and pooling in her stomach. He was the most handsome creature she had beheld in her short twenty-five years alive.

"Why are those men hunting you down?"

She pushed down her hood.

His lips parted, softening his stern expression. He stepped back farther away from her.

Nava shifted the weight of her body as she searched the trees, trying to find her wannabe captors looming in the distance. "My name is Nava. I have been running from them all day. I'm looking for a man who lives near here. At least, I hope it's this part of the woods."

He paled. "You're Celeste's daughter."

Nava knew she had found him, and he was *not* what she'd expected.

She hadn't thought much about her mother's friend as she ran for her life. She had imagined him being old and wise, with a large potbelly and a long white beard. He was a fae of sorts, so maybe he was older than he appeared.

"Are you . . . Arkimedes? My— I was told you could help me. My mother knew you?"

He nodded. "We can't stay here. They will come back once they realize you aren't the way they headed." He focused on the direction where Devon's men had disappeared, and he took one long step back. "Come, my cabin is not far."

HOW HAD NAVA'S MOTHER met this man? Why had she trusted he'd help them if the crown were to appear on the island? It wasn't normal for someone as paranoid as her mother to send her off to a stranger.

She didn't know her mother at all.

Nava studied the sharp angles of his wide shoulders. His face turned from side to side, his steps lighter than hers even with his large stature. He was taller than average, and he gave away something that wasn't human. She realized she had never seen any of the magical species before, had read about them in books.

"Not so hard to be quiet, is it?" Arkimedes tilted his face back, his gaze flashing toward her.

"No one to keep up the conversation." Her stomach rumbled with hunger, loud enough it broke the silence. Her cheeks heated. "I haven't stopped to eat or rest in hours."

"We are close," he whispered. "We can't use any light to guide us after the sun is down. It will attract attention from things we don't want to follow us. Worse than the hunters."

She nodded, and her legs shook in protest. It didn't matter if a spirit of the forest or an ogre came out of nowhere to get them. Nava couldn't stand straight for much longer. If they kept going, Arkimedes would end up having to carry her the rest of the way or leave her behind.

She tightened her lips, the fear of being left behind to fend off the men on her own too strong to ignore.

The cabin became visible as they walked down a narrow pathway. Nava could hear a stream nearby, the rushing of water. They had traveled in silence for hours; he hadn't spoken much, other than the odd grunt, and she'd been too tired to do even that.

The cabin was quaint, with a thatched rooftop and stucco walls. Rough wood beams held it together in each corner, with moss growing from all horizontal faces. A stone fireplace jutted out from one side, covered by tree branches.

She had a decent warm place to rest tonight, after all. Unless he was expecting her to sleep outside in her tent, which she guessed wouldn't be so bad. Nava was tired enough she would pass out as soon as her head hit the— Wait, she had not packed any blankets.

She paused outside the home, studying her surroundings. It was cold in this forest, and she had her coat to keep her warm.

He was already halfway up the stone steps to the cabin when he turned around to her. His brows lowered.

"I followed you with no idea what I was to do once we got here." She crossed her arms over her chest.

"Other than being safe," he quipped in an amused tone.

She needed to get her plan together or she would mess this whole thing up. "It's presumptuous of me—" she started, and his lips twitched. Maybe it would have been the start of a smile, but he had schooled his features.

"Do you think I would leave you to be taken by the bounty hunters?" he asked in a soft voice, shaking his head. "You can stay here for a couple of days. It will give you enough time for them to lose your trail."

"I know it's moronic. I have no plan other than finding you."

"Most people who end up in this forest have no plan other than surviving." His voice was soft, almost lost in the noises of the forest.

The reality of his words hit her. She was fighting for her freedom. If the Crow took her to the city, she would be forced to a life of servitude for the crown. They would force her to marry, to make magical children who would be slaves all the same.

"I'll set my tent right over there." She pointed to an empty area at the front of his cabin. Dried foliage covered the ground, flat enough for her to set up camp.

He frowned. "What?"

She walked a couple of steps, lowering her backpack to the ground. The tabs screeched with the movement. "I brought one to sleep in."

With an amused expression, he shook his head. "There are wards around the house. The river nymphs tend to come out in the evening."

Nava nodded, opening the flap of her bag, searching for the heavy canvas of her tent. The heavy steps on stone called her attention to him.

He had come down a step. His brow was raised, a shadow of a smile on his face. "They have long, *sharp* teeth."

"Oh? *Oh.*" Her gaze traveled around the grounds. The tall grasses moved with the wind. She did not want to have to deal with those.

"Get in the house, Nava."

She nodded, fumbling to pick up her bag from the ground, and followed him up the stone steps, wondering about river nymphs and the fact that her stomach was doing somersaults.

The wooden door of the cabin was large, heavy, and rustic. She walked in and was greeted by a warmth that embraced her like a hug. It smelled like iris, sandalwood, and leather. Planked walls extended from floor to ceiling in brown tones.

It was cozy inside, the fire rolling in the small fireplace. There was a woodstove at the other end of the cabin, cabinets and a little rustic sink to one side. A small dining table with three mixed chairs.

There was no art, no bookcase in sight. Like he was ready to leave at any moment. Nothing personal in here, except for the weapons. Her gaze traveled to two large swords hung on the wall, their steel reflecting the fire nearby.

There were black lines etched on the blade, intricate designs she couldn't quite study from this far. Her attention shifted across the fireplace to the chair in the corner, covered in blankets and furs. Nava swallowed as she took in this one large room with *one* bed.

She was going to have to sleep in the tent, sans blankets and surrounded by river nymphs.

He moved around his home, taking off his coat and hanging it on a hook by the front door. She stood at the entrance, chasing his every move.

He was wearing a white button-down shirt that stretched over his muscular back, tapering down to his narrow hips. Brown trousers hugged his muscular legs. She bit her nails. He would take the whole bed.

Not that she was considering sharing it with him.

"Make yourself at home, and leave your bag at the door." He pointed at the place to her right, where he had hung his coat before.

He doesn't expect us to share the bed, right?

He huffed a laugh. To her horror, she had spoken the words out loud.

"You can have the bed," he said, his smile widening. Her heart stumbled at the beauty of it.

What was wrong with her? She hadn't meant to act so rudely to him when he was helping her out. "No, I can't take your bed. I can sleep in that." She pointed at a chair by the corner.

"It's fine, Nava. I won't sleep tonight. I'll do some rounds to make sure they didn't follow us."

She swallowed when his intense eyes met hers. She didn't like magic, but for his eyes, she could make an exception. "They will come here?"

How had her mother met this man? Had they been friends, acquaintances?

She could tell he was a sorcerer, not because he was skilled at veiling spells. The scent of magic in the air was a clear giveaway. The extension of his powers was unknown. She was confused why she was at ease with his company; she wasn't afraid of him—wary, perhaps.

"The house is warded by strong disorienting spells. The men who were chasing you wouldn't even know where to start. It will point them in a different direction if they get close." His veiling spell in the forest should have told her Arkimedes was remarkable.

Still, her mother had also been remarkable, and even she had not been confident to hide from a murder of Crows.

That was an exaggeration. There had been two Crows who knew Nava's face—three if she counted her mother.

"Aren't you afraid?" She voiced her fear. It occurred to her as she inspected the peaceful home.

He shrugged a shoulder, handing her a glass of water. She drank it all in one go, remembering how thirsty she was. "No. They are manageable and appear to be looking for deserters in general. They will be annoyed you disappeared. However, they will move to the villages next. My biggest worry is who hired them." He brought his hand to his chin, rubbing across the short stubble.

Nava's mind came to the word. Villages—as in plural. Laurie had mentioned something about one as well. He was in the kitchen, rummaging through the cabinets. She approached the table, unsure how comfortable she should be. Her rational brain told her it was strange she was at such ease. She pulled out a chair and let the weight of her body drop onto it. It screeched with her movement. He took the empty glass of water from the table.

"I know who hired those men."

Arkimedes straightened, his brow lowering.

"A man docked on the island yesterday morning. He made his way to my potion shop in the afternoon. I guess it was silly of my father to use our surname to name the shop. It led him straight to me." Her chest tightened. She wouldn't cry again today.

"Who?"

"Devon Black. I have a strong suspicion he will not stop until he finds me." Reading his stiff posture, she asked, "Do you know him?"

His expression shuttered; she had seen the same reaction on her mother before—always hiding information. The reality of it made her warm with anger.

He nodded, but he didn't elaborate as he walked farther into the kitchen and placed a kettle on the wood-stove. "This complicates things," he whispered, deep in thought. "He is powerful. If he's after you, Nava, we can't stay in this house for long."

"Us, as in *you* will come with me?"

"Is it true you don't use your magic?"

The warmness of her cheeks increased. "I don't care about magic." She paused. "And . . . even if I did, I never got the opportunity since I've lived all my adult life in Willowbrook. As you're aware, there is *no* magic there."

He let out a resigned breath. "I have to come with you. It's not safe for you in this forest by yourself. Not to mention you are being tracked by the bounty hunters."

"Your veiling wards could keep us hidden?" A slight tone of hope shone behind her words.

"My wards won't deter him. Devon is highly trained. He would perceive there's something off when he comes close."

The screeching of the kettle boiling broke the silence around them. His attention was outside the window. The sun was setting.

"Oh."

"Your mother was part of the Crows. Gaining you will give him high praise in the Society," Arkimedes proceeded.

"Where would we go? I'm—" Nava's brows lowered. "I'm not going to travel the forest to await capture. The ship was large. He told me there were *hundreds* of soldiers in there."

"Gray sorcerers, sent by the crown," he breathed out and poured boiling water into a mug. She focused on the liquid, the shining metal of a tea strainer. The water inside the cup turned a caramel color. The soft notes of chamomile reached her as the tea brewed.

"We need higher numbers. The both of us won't stand a chance against an army, but if we were to travel north to the larger village in the forest, we might."

She cleared her throat. "I know nothing about this village . . . ?"

"It's safer than here." He nodded. "We need to warn them since they won't be expecting this. They have families. Children." Something dark descended in his expression. He turned away from her scrutiny. "I have to go. Stay inside. You'll be safe here." His expression matched the grave tone of his voice. "There is a bath if you need it."

He left before the sun had fully set behind the tall tops of the trees.

She made her way to her bag and took out her bread to the cabinets by the woodstove. She drank her tea before heading to the washroom. A large wooden tub was in the middle of a decent-sized bathroom A metal pipe jutted from its side. A chimney twisted up to the ceiling. Her fingers grazed the wood.

Nava opened the faucet, and frigid water started spouting out. Upon further inspection, she found the coals in the small chimney were attached to it. Nava searched for matches all over the house and found none. Arkimedes never had to use them in his life. She left the bathroom to rummage inside her bag. Finding the small wooden sticks would mean a warm bath for her tonight.

Her muscles relaxed after the bath. Her skin smelled like sage and rosemary, some of the oils that were by the tub.

Nava padded barefoot across the room. The cabin was quiet except for the rolling fire burning from the fireplace. She searched for a sign of Arkimedes, but he was nowhere to be found.

The fluffy mattress was so appealing to her overtired body. Arkimedes truly meant for her to sleep in his bed. Otherwise, he wouldn't have offered. Right?

So much unknown was ahead of her. Now she was thrown into this world she had avoided for so long.

Nava crawled over the furs on top of the bed, the wool blanket woven in earth tones. She let her body fall. The surrounding scent lulled her to sleep.

CHAPTER SEVEN

*N*ava had been awake since before the sun came up. Her body buzzed with pent-up energy, even though she'd been exhausted both physically and mentally the day before.

Arkimedes was not back yet. Worry nagged at the edges of her mind. She figured he'd have returned in the middle of the night, and the thought of him being in the same quarters as her had woken at random moments throughout the night. Too self-conscious of sleeping mouth agape, kicking, or—worse—sleepwalking with a man like him around her.

When she was sure sleep wouldn't come back to her again, she rolled out of bed and made her way to the washroom. She tried to tame her wild waves to no avail.

Let it be, for now.

Nava washed her face and changed into fresh clothes. Today she put on her woolen trousers. They had belonged to her mother back when she'd served the Society of Crows. They were black, with a blue sheen, like bird feathers, in proper lighting.

She padded out of the washroom, appreciating the soft texture of the worn wood floor and the cabin's cozy atmosphere. Her gaze landed again on the swords she'd spotted the night before. She approached. There were ornate letters down the blades, spelling his name. *Arkimedes B. Valeron.*

She touched the cool metal, entranced as her pads explored the design's texture. A vague recognition hit her. She had seen this sword before, she thought. Or one like it. She was sure she had never met Arkimedes or his weapon. Nava looked at the second sword that hung above. Instead of his name, there was the etching of a dead tree.

Nava turned her head to the side, examining it in confusion. Curiosity got the best of her as she came closer to the sword, her nose almost touching it.

The door of the house swung open, startling her back. A scream escaped her lips. She leaped a couple of feet and hit the side of a table by the bed, pushing off all the contents as she fell right over it and tumbled down to the ground along with paper, glass, and more.

Arkimedes was by the door, looking tired from a night out. His eyes widened as she rushed to get up, her face warming with embarrassment.

"I'm *so* sorry," she blurted. "I was not snooping. I mean, I *was*. Only because it's such an interesting sword."

His attention traveled toward the sword, then to the ground peppered with his things.

Nava kneeled down and picked it all. She hoped he wouldn't kick her out of his house now that she'd made such a mess of his things.

She pulled her hand back when glass pierced her skin, examining it with a frown. A red drop was coming out of a slight cut. He was by her in a blink, his enormous hands bringing hers closer to inspect the cut.

Nava trembled under his touch A sensation ran through her skin and warmed her body. Her teeth captured her bottom lip.

Arkimedes's brows furrowed. His touch was leaving her speechless, which on its own was something to behold. She put her foot in her mouth when nervous, never one to lose speech.

"I left for just a few hours. You have already broken multiple of my things," he said.

Her skin grew warmer as she pulled her hand away. "You scared me."

Arkimedes huffed a laugh before starting to pick up the broken glass pieces. He walked to the kitchen while she finished settling the small table back into place. When she was getting up, he was by her, holding a wooden box. There were vials of potions and gauze inside.

"It's just a scratch. Also, what are those?" She studied his potions suspiciously.

His brow lifted. "I see. You destroy my property and snub my potions."

A bite of shame burdened her thoughts. "A good potion maker always questions other people's potions, *particularly* if they are magical."

Arkimedes laughed, shaking his head. He placed his first aid box on top of the table. "You've gotta clean it. Who knows what potion residual was in the glass that cut you?"

Her steps were quick to get to him, and she reached to pick the tiny glass vials from the box.

His hand stopped her before she got a chance to pick any. "I don't want you messing with them, potion maker."

He picked two out of the bunch and cut a small piece of gauze. He handed her the saturated cloth. She brought it down to her cut. From the smell and the sting of it, she could tell it was just a disinfecting potion.

Not unlike the ones she made daily in town.

"So. Nava Forrest. The potion maker of Willowbrook. Doesn't want anything to do magic but enjoys making potions," he said.

"Potions don't ruin people's lives. They improve it," she mumbled.

His playful expression faltered. "I see." He handed her a rag saturated with a different kind of potion, and he followed her movements.

She could tell by the soft lavender notes that it was a healing potion, much like the ones she had used on the creature the day before. She put it against her finger and met his eyes. "There, all clean. You don't have to worry about me losing my hand because you didn't clean your potion bottles."

A smile pulled the corners of her lip, and rolling laughter came out of him in disbelief—the sound making her insides swirl and heat pool in her stomach. "I saved you, let you sleep in my bed, and what I get in return is judgment."

"This will teach you next time you want to save a random person in the woods," she piped in, and his expression danced with mirth before he walked away toward the kitchen, shaking his head.

He reached for the bread Nava had placed on top of the counter last night, her favorite from Simone's bakery. "Yours?"

"Ours?"

"It has been a while since I've had sourdough bread." A wistful tone was behind his words.

"This one is the best one I have ever had." She made

her way to the small kitchen, intending to lend a hand with whatever breakfast they might come up with.

It was delicious, the warm bread with melted butter and eggs. Nava had to forgo the honey. After what happened yesterday, she was not about to consume the gooey liquid anytime soon.

"How do you get this food? Are all these things from Willowbrook?"

"I can't enter Willowbrook," he stated.

His swirling green eyes were a stark contrast to anyone's she'd ever seen before. Not even her one brown and one blue eye could compare. "Your eyes—I mean, your blood. You must be mixed, right? Magical beings can't enter, either?"

"Something like that. I go to the villages in the forest. They hold markets twice a week. There is also the occasional traveling marketer," he explained and took a sip of his herbal tea, looking already less tired than he had been when he arrived.

Her lips parted at the mention of villages and markets. She never expected this forest to be so alive with people. She remembered Laurie's words. Cameron would've been delighted to hear this. To just be in the presence of a sorcerer like Arkimedes would've been enough to send her brother into a frenzy. Her heart lurched.

"I guess I never knew this forest was so alive with people." Her voice was weak.

Arkimedes's gaze met hers, and she stirred under his scrutiny. "Yes, there are a lot of people in this forest."

"Are they all deserters from the cities?"

"All are escaping *something*." He nodded, taking a sharp breath. "We don't get bounty hunters often in this part of the world, much less the crown's army."

"And a Crow," she added.

Arkimedes nodded. 'It's not normal for Crows to work with other people. They work alone or with other members of the Society." He paused. "This is unusual."

Nava wanted to ask questions about how long he'd been here, what he had been running from. She guessed he knew about her situation, as he had known her mother.

The playful atmosphere had all but died. Nava popped a couple of tomatoes into her mouth. What would the next few days hold?

"When should we go?" she ventured, bringing the steaming cup of tea to her lips.

"Soon. Maybe tomorrow."

She studied his features. How could she be so attracted to this man she had never met before? Her soulmate bond should prevent it, as it had with all her suitors at home.

Nava paused. What if Arkimedes *was* her soulmate? It would explain why she was at such ease around him. A mixture of curiosity and dread spread through her at the prospect. She had to remind herself that even if he was, she didn't want her soulmate because the attraction would be a lie—something created by magic, not by her own choice.

Still, the attraction was strong. The play of Arkimedes's forearm muscles as he moved his arm across the table caught her attention.

No, he couldn't be him. Her mother would have *never* sent her this way, straight into her soulmate's hands, not after going through so much to keep her away in the first place.

Maybe, just maybe, this travel around magical lands would allow her to find a solution to her *curse*. Maybe these villages would be able to break the bond that attached her to a man she didn't want, therefore allowing her to make a real connection that wasn't forced upon her by divine intervention.

"I saw yesterday that you carry daggers with you." His voice shook her out of her musings. She nodded. "Do you know how to use them well?"

Her cheeks grew warm. "I trained for years before my mother passed away. It's been a while, and I have never used them in actual combat before." Her truthful words just made her that much more self-aware of the fact that she was unprepared for a Crow and an army.

"What about—"

"Don't say magic," she whispered, and his lips clamped shut. "I don't want magic, Arkimedes. I don't feel it is running within me. Maybe I didn't get the gene, after all."

"In that case, we should go outside, see how well your fighting skills are. I need to know what we're working with when out in the forest." Arkimedes pushed away from the table and made his way to the kitchen sink, where he dropped his dirty dishes.

She nodded, letting a mask of calm cover her features. Her hand shook as her insecurity with her fighting skills took over her brain; the rattle of the fork over the ceramic plate was the only sound in the cabin.

The sun was shining through the clearing of the forest. Soft warm light bathed her, a clear contrast to the cold temperature. Morning dew trailed down the black iron railing of the front steps. Now that it was bright out, she could focus on the details of the place.

The smell of grass hung around them, and the soft trickle of a stream nearby accompanied the sound of birds singing in the background. The land where the cabin sat had short grass, getting taller as it got closer to the woods' edge. The trees were different here. White trunks and moss-covered branches contrasted with the background of the dense forest.

Leaves covered the ground with red and yellow tones. She studied the property and met Arkimedes's expectant gaze. Her nerves came back alive, and her sweaty palms told her how ready she was to train with the man.

"We can go over there." He pointed to a spot far enough from the house.

She followed, taking both daggers out of the sheath and turning to him expectantly. He assumed a fighting stance.

"Where are your weapons?" She focused on his broad figure. His hands were empty, and he was wearing his regular clothes. Concern creased her brows.

"I don't need one."

"Wow, confident much?" She narrowed her eyes.

He circled around her like a giant cat sizing his next meal. She extended her arms, trying to keep the distance. Nava moved so she was facing him at all times. He was underestimating her, and it made her blood boil.

She attacked. For his large size, he dogged her with grace. He was well trained. Nava struck again. She was smaller and could get closer without him expecting it.

He grinned as he deflected her attack with ease. She didn't let him get too comfortable and moved quickly, changing directions as she attacked again and again. She was panting for air by the seventh attack.

It unnerved her more that he was quiet. Her mother had always talked to her when they'd been training, giving her pointers and praises when they were due. This silence was driving her insane.

She came at him more aggressively, letting her frustration take hold of her movements. He was close enough when she brought the blunt side of her dagger down. He blocked it with one arm. She brought the other one in, but before it could get anywhere near him, something grabbed her and swept her off her feet.

She screamed when she hit the ground ungracefully, staring at the mist that emanated from him, retreating from her body.

"That's not fair, Arkimedes!" she complained, rushing to get up.

"Why not?" His voice was a mask of clear danger. The dark tendrils rose again, shooting to her.

She gasped, dodging out of the way as she screamed in fright. "We aren't using magic!"

"You are not. I am." He was pleased with himself.

She stared him down in disbelief, right before she had to dodge another smoky tendril. She gasped in horror.

He appeared so calm, standing in the middle of the meadow, surrounded by shadows that could come out of anyone's worst nightmares. The spicy scent of magic enveloped her. She dove out of another one's grasp, swinging her dagger at it. The blade went across it like it was smoke.

She had a moment of confusion when something grabbed her other leg. She was falling again. This time, she didn't even get to scream, too angry to speak as she got up, threw her knives to the ground, and stormed at him.

The mist and shadow retreated from his body. The only thing left behind was his blackened hands.

"You cheating bastard!" she snarled, ramming into his body. Unable to move him an inch. This just angered her further. "Why did you use magic?"

"You chose your weapon, I chose mine. This forest is not for perfect techniques. We'll face magical creatures, warlocks, *an army*. There is no foul play when your life is at stake."

"I would've known this out there. Here, I thought you wanted to see my technique!"

"I wanted to see how you would defend yourself against someone—anyone out there," he countered, "but you are so afraid of magic, you lost track of who your opponent was. Magic is not your opponent. It's me."

She pressed her lips together, huffing in annoyance. Arkimedes arched a brow, and she choked out a cry when his power came out of his body. She stumbled back and rushed to get her daggers from the ground, heart hammering. A swooping sense of dread filled her.

Nava couldn't battle against magic. She could barely hold her own against a trained fighter with her weapons. Darkness surrounded him, swirling around his looming figure, and it paralyzed her. Her sweaty palms shook as she tried to keep a hold of her two long daggers.

She couldn't fight him. She wouldn't be able to win.

Maybe she didn't have to win. She had to fight just long enough to get away. She gripped the hilt of her daggers, walking with a determined pace toward Arkimedes. The surrounding shadows dispersed. Black tendrils pointed like the sun rays from his body, reaching out to her in thin, wispy fingers.

She found Arkimedes's gaze behind his dark cloud. Nava understood what he'd said. She had forgotten who her actual opponent was.

Nava couldn't hurt the shadows made of mist, power, and magic. She could attack their master. She leaped in the air, evading one shadow that dived for her, and landed with a wince. Her sore legs strained. She jumped again to one side, dodging another shadowy hand.

Arkimedes followed her every move. He was close enough for her to be on him soon; she wished her next jump would be higher.

She bounced, ready for an attack, when a shadow wrapped around her waist. The powerful movement jerked her around. The shadow dropped her, and she landed prepared. She had seconds. She jumped once again, but this time, the shadows came from everywhere and pinned her down.

She writhed on the floor, the heaviness of the spell constricting her. Or was it her panic? She blinked. Steps sounded near her. Arkimedes hovered over, studying her features. She stopped fighting the shadows, letting her body relax.

"That was better. Your focus was always on me," he commended, and the wisps of darkness retreated from her body. The ghost of magical fingers crawled over her skin.

She tightened her hand, and she rammed the pommel of her dagger against his foot with all her strength.

Arkimedes yelled and stepped back, and she bolted upright. Both blades ready, she attacked as he stumbled, not with the same grace he once had. The smugness disappeared from his handsome features.

He was slowed down by his hurt foot, distracted enough by the sudden attack that she had a moment of headway. She pushed forward and attacked, but both blades were stopped by the strength of the black shield.

For a being made of mist, it was hard like metal.

Arkimedes's expression shifted to something like appreciation, if not for her skills, then for her actions. "That was good, Nava."

She stepped back, panting. His shield was up when she dropped the blades to the ground, breaths coming out of her in a big whoosh.

She dropped to the ground with shaky legs and drew in a couple of deep breaths. "Don't mock me," she grumbled, aware of every ache in her body.

He settled next to her. His attention was fixed on his home. "I'm not. I mean it. You knew I would be confident. You could've taken the lead in the fight if this had not been a friendly match."

"It didn't feel so friendly, being hoisted around by your magic."

"I will keep that in mind for next time." His voice was tired. Magic was taking a toll on his energy or maybe it was the fact that he hadn't slept all night.

"Next time?"

"Yes. We'll need to train every day. Next time, if you catch anyone off-guard, wipe them off their feet." He moved to get up and offered his hand to her.

They were quiet, just listening to the song of the birds. Their calls were different to the seagulls back at home.

"Thank you," she said.

He turned to her. "For what?"

"Saving my life yesterday. I realized I hadn't thanked you for it." She met his gaze.

"You are welcome."

NAVA GREW AT EASE as soon as they crossed the threshold to his home, chills traveling down her arms when he hovered nearby. She found him staring past her toward the end of the room. Dark circles appeared under his eyes, making his bright, magical irises pop.

She followed the direction of his stare and found the bed, his bed. After being out all night, he needed to rest. "You are tired." She turned around to face him, miscalculating how close she would be. She met his gaze.

"I'm fine."

"Go. I promise I won't jam any daggers on your feet." She pointed at his bed.

He laughed. "If you promise to behave, I guess I could." They got lost in each other's eyes. His hand landed on her shoulder, just a touch that came and went too soon, setting her nerve endings aflame.

Nava sat on the table, spreading the contents of her backpack on top. She had packed in such a frenzy during the evening. She now had more time to go over her things. The cabin was quiet besides the soft crackling of the fire.

Her attention traveled to the sleeping form of the man she hadn't been able to stop thinking about for the past hour and a half.

Her hand stilled on top of her clothes, finding the leather-bound journal of her mother. She held it open. It was dated, narrating her findings in the forest. Her speculation of who lived here. Nava's heart grew heavy reading the words. She missed her mother, but her anger toward her grew larger the longer she read.

Nava's reckless nature brought us to this point. She was not ready for the world then, not for magic or the soulmate bond that came out of her disobedience.

She focused on the words, her vision blurred.

Nava closed the journal with a snap. She looked at Arkimedes sleeping on his back. Let destiny be cruel and tease her with this, a crush on a man she'd never expected, plus the sharp words of her mother hurting after all these years.

This soulmate bond was so much more like a curse this time. Even if he turned out to be the man, it would mean this was all a lie.

Nava sighed, focusing back on her potions. One of the things she had always been good at making. Her father had always praised her innate skills.

She packed them back with care. Nava hadn't brought much but the essentials and had used a couple of them already. She focused on Arkimedes again. Why was he helping her? Devon didn't know he was here. His hiding spell was so good, they would skip him in their quest of catching as many deserters as possible.

She guessed maybe he wanted to help, not only her but the rest of the villages as well. Perhaps he and her mother had been closer than she'd thought Nava pressed her lips together, making a mental note to ask him when she got a chance.

CHAPTER EIGHT

*D*eparting from the cabin in the woods had been difficult for her. Nava had started to feel comfortable there. She was also aware that whatever came next was going to be much more challenging.

Nava rested and was well-fed. Laurie would be proud. She studied the wooden walls with minor details that had felt like home for the past few days. The long swords on the wall, the gray-and-silver stones in the fireplace marked by soot. The small kitchen with the wood-burning stove, where iron pots and skillets hung on the wall. The box of potions hidden in a wooden box underneath the small ceramic sink.

Nava's heart squeezed at the realization that she'd never see this place again. What would Cameron think about it if he ever were to set foot here? He would try to pry the swords from the wall. Her gaze traveled to her companion, and she swelled with wonder and desire—the latter something she was too scared to look into.

He wasn't one for many words. Other than the light flirting she'd sensed from him the day she cut her finger, he had kept his distance for the most part. He was a mystery, one she was aching to solve.

"Arkimedes," she blurted, breaking the comfortable silence.

He stood by the front door, shrugging on his large coat, grasping a wool blanket he wrapped around his neck as a scarf. He smelled like pine and leather. He focused on her, his gaze swirling with an emotion she had a hard time deciphering.

She guessed he was not going to talk, but she had his attention, that was obvious. "I meant to say I was sorry to have dropped in on you and somehow dragged you into this mess."

"The crown sending troops to this island to gather people would have affected me whether you had come or not." He took in a breath.

"Oh, okay."

"I also escaped from the city—a long time ago. The likelihood of them knowing I'm here is small but possible. There are many innocent people in the village. Those who were born here have the right to stay. I can't just sit here knowing they will be hunted down and do nothing about it."

"I see." She understood a bit more. "So, it's not that you had a blood debt with my mother then?"

He laughed. "No, I did promise I would help her family if something like this would happen."

"Why . . . ?"

"Something like a blood debt, just not that bloody." He turned away, focusing on getting ready. He wouldn't say anything else on the subject judging by the tense lines of his jaw and shoulders.

Nava was used to not asking many questions. Her

mother had always admonished her and her curiosity in a much less subtle manner than Arkimedes had done.

"Are you ready?" His voice broke the silence.

"As ready as I'll ever be." She bent over to pick up her heavy bag. Her shoulders were sore from the day she had left Cameron behind.

Cameron's red hair and freckles made her heart ache. She was happy she had at least taken the danger away with her. Was he already at school? She hoped Laurie wasn't driving Simone crazy.

She took a deep breath, her heart heavy with sorrow. Cameron had wanted to see this world. He would've loved to see Arkimedes's magic, however scary it was.

"You wouldn't have to carry that backpack with you if you used your magic." He searched her face.

She tensed her jaw, lifting her gaze to him. Arkimedes put his hands up in a sign of surrender, a smirk pulling the side of his lips before he exited the door.

The cool air of the morning welcomed her outside, the sun kissing the roof of the cabin, highlighting moss and gold hay. The dewdrops shimmered like diamonds sprinkled over the blades of grass. Nava wrapped her woolen scarf closer to her neck, trying to find warmth in the cool morning. Arkimedes walked in front of her, tugging on his black leather gloves as mist billowed out of his mouth.

The forest seemed less daunting now that she wasn't alone. Arkimedes had her back somehow, allowing her to see her surroundings with fresh eyes. It was beautiful, imposing, large, and magical. Enormous trunks jutted out to the sky, branches covered in moss, greenery everywhere. Even though fall was in full swing, it didn't hit these giant coniferous trees.

"You mentioned there are different villages in this

forest." Her words came out winded. They had been walking for a while with no rest.

Arkimedes nodded, checking his surroundings before his face flashed to her.

It was no wonder he was in such good shape if he always walked around these woods at this speed with no rest in between. She was aware of her lack of endurance. Her cheeks heated when her mind went a bit south. Maybe he had endurance in other aspects as well. Simone always said that was an essential key with intimate partners.

Maybe if he wasn't her soulmate and they survived, she might get to see for herself. She fumbled in her steps, unused to this kind of curiosity before.

"What are the other villages like?" She pushed back her heated thoughts, giving way to another curiosity.

"There are a couple that are dangerous. Run by criminals." His voice was grave. "A mixture of cruelty and power. Those two are small and on the west side of the island. Most people don't head that route often."

Nava took a mental note of this. These villages were probably the ones the townspeople spoke of when they talked about the dangers of the forest.

"There is one in the north, which is the main village. It's not too different in size than the town you live in. A seasoned sorcerer who used to be a commander in the Copper Kingdom runs it. He transferred to the Iron Kingdom before he too ran away."

Nava struggled to catch on, her breaths coming out quickly. She brought her hand to her neck, using her icy touch to cool down her overheated skin. The terrain had become rocky, and they were trotting uphill. The path seemed to be well-traveled with a defined hiking pathway. "Those in the . . . north village . . . are . . . they good people?" she wheezed out. One would think all her gardening would help her some with endurance, but no.

"Like in any city." He shrugged. "There is one village to the east. Mixed races occupy it. Mostly fae. It's small, and the spells that protect it are powerful."

"Right, and you are sure Devon will be heading north first?" she asked in between breaths. Silence descended upon them.

"I'm hoping he goes there *last*. It will give us enough time to prepare, minimize any casualties," he admitted. He studied her flushed cheeks, his expression softening. "We are almost to the camp area."

"I don't believe you." She grabbed the straps of her backpack, trying to ease the weight on her sore shoulders.

"You have already said no multiple times . . . do you want me to carry your backpack?"

"I told you twenty times I don't want your magic's help." Her voice was sharp.

"I don't mean with magic. I mean *I* can carry it for you until you want it back."

Nava knew she should. The backpack was heavy. She swallowed, considering it. Arkimedes noticed she wasn't refusing him like she had done already multiple times and walked a couple of steps back to her. They were silent as they exchanged the heavy load.

She sighed, massaging her protesting muscles as they resumed their walk. They hadn't eaten since breakfast, and by the coolness in the air and darkness all around, she guessed it was nearing five o'clock.

Arkimedes, much like her, hadn't eaten after their breakfast, but unlike her, he knew the perils of the forest. Who was she to derail these plans?

They slowed down in an area where the trees were sparser. The sound of running water nearby was one of the first things she noticed, followed by how thirsty she was.

As if reading her mind, Arkimeces brought the canteen of water to her before dropping the bag to the ground. "I will gather some wood." His voice broke the tired silence.

Nava wanted to be useful, deciding she'd find the best spot to put the tent up. She cleared the ground from large debris.

Opening her bag, she reached for the thick canvas of her tent and pulled out rope and metal pegs. She had camped a lot while young. Her father used to make tents in the backyard to count the stars. She had continued doing so with Cameron, camping in the plains before the forest.

Her task took her full concentration, her fingers tying rope and finding the correct size branches to keep the tent up. She laid the floor down, a thick canvas coated with wax to prevent the humidity in the ground from seeping up. She didn't hear Arkimedes's approaching steps until he was next to her. He studied her hands as she worked the rope.

"What are you doing?" Arkimedes raised his brows, his deep voice a contrast to the quiet surroundings.

She yelped, jumping, and said, "I'm putting up my—our—sleeping tent," then frowned at his growing smirk. She unfolded the large, heavy canvas for the roof of her tent. "You don't have to do magic for everything. It's rewarding using your own hands to accomplish things. Plus, using magic will drain you, and you already look exhausted."

"You don't hold back, do you?" he said, amusement behind each word. The deep circles around his eyes made it apparent he hadn't slept enough again. He had been out all night and had come back home with sunrise.

Nava had been quiet this morning, trying to allow him rest. She had gone outside at some point while he'd slept and attempted to train. He had barely gotten four hours of sleep. The drawn appearance on his handsome face showed how tired he was.

He was busy making the fire while Nava finished putting the tent up and examined her excellent work. She brought her bag in, taking out the food she had packed earlier.

Dried meat, fruit, bread, and cheese. By the time she was out, the fire was rolling hot. Arkimedes was sitting by it. She extended him his food, and as he took it, their fingers grazed. The charged tension flowed in between them like waves of electricity.

"Thank you." His voice was quiet.

She plopped down next to him, focusing on the dancing flames of the fire, long tendrils of yellow and orange. "If there are all these magical villages, why live alone in your cabin?"

His eyes lifted, framed by his thick brows. "The people in these forests range from criminals to people searching for new beginnings. Because of who I am and who I *was*, I'm not welcomed into the ones I would feel comfortable being a part of."

Nava swallowed down questions that popped into her head. She shouldn't pry as much as she wanted. She had just met him and didn't want to be too nosy in his affairs. Still, they were to travel together, and a part of her craved to learn more, whatever he would give her. "I know about not fitting in. I guess that's not what you are saying—but what I'm saying is I understand about feeling alone, even when surrounded by people," she whispered. Memories of a lost childhood, awkward conversations, being an outsider.

Nava brought her hand to the spot on her chest where her mark lay, and her fingertips rubbed the area in a soothing motion. She often did this when she needed reassurance. Arkimedes zeroed in the movement, and she dropped her hand down.

"How did you and my mother meet?" There it was, the question that had been going around her mind ever since she'd met him.

"We met in the Iron City."

Silence.

"Just that—you aren't going to elaborate?" She frowned.

His cheeks turned red, and his features changed with embarrassment. "We met when I was very young. Celeste used to be a weaponry instructor for the Crows. She also oversaw the army camps' training. When we met here years later, the fact that one of the high-ranking commanders had ended up here was a red flag for her."

"Why would it raise a red flag if he was also running?"

"Because high-ranking officers of the army are not dismissed. They are a lot more likely to pursue him, to make an example out of his betrayal. Still, I guess it was safer for her to keep you and your brother here than in one of the cities." His voice was even, and it was clear he was studying her reaction.

She gasped. Her mother had spoken to him about Cameron. This tidbit of information shook her to her core. Her mother must have trusted Arkimedes much more than she'd thought. "You know about Cameron?" The words escaped her lips without permission, her heart stumbling over heartbeats.

"Not his name, but I knew of him," he answered.

"No offense, Arkimedes, but why would my mother think you would drop everything to help us if we needed it, if not because of a blood debt?" She gasped, filling the blanks. "A life debt?"

His lips parted to say something, but the crunching of leaves made their heads snap to the upcoming noise. A gray-hooded shape appeared between the trees, holding a giant wooden cane in one gloved hand.

The newcomer stopped at the edge of the woods, his face barely visible under the shadows of his cloak. Nava could tell by his build and frame that it was someone tall but likely human.

"Arkimedes Valeron, fancy seeing you in this part of the woods." The man's booming voice echoed around them. He was walking toward them with quick steps and without an invitation. His cloak swallowed his thin, tall frame. He pushed back the hood covering his face, revealing dark skin and a long face—sporting a crooked nose and a pearly white smile. Nava had never beheld teeth so large in a human before.

"Andreas, it's been a while." Arkimedes stood and walked to the newcomer, his eyes crinkling as his smile widened.

They embraced in a brotherly hug. "I was going to come to you after I went to Elise's," the man said, and when his attention came to meet Nava, the expression on his face faltered.

Arkimedes turned, following his gaze to her. By his expression, he hadn't forgotten the conversation they were having. It surprised her that she could tell it relieved him to have been interrupted. She crossed her arms over her chest as a wave of frustration built in her stomach.

"Nava, this is Andreas Mortimer, a friend," he said as if answering a question written all over her face.

She guessed it was evident by how comfortable they were. She stood, realizing she had been frozen in her spot, approached them with tentative steps, and offered her hand to the man. "It's a pleasure to meet you, Mr. Mortimer." Her voice was quieter than usual.

As his smile grew, the tension in her stomach lifted. "Please, call me Mort," he said, shaking her hand vigorously. "The only person who calls me Andreas is this bastard here. I'd rather not have anyone else use that name. My mother used to call me that. It makes me feel like I'm in trouble."

"Andreas is one of the traveling merchants I mentioned," Arkimedes explained, sitting down on a tree stump near the flames of the campfire.

"So what brings you two to this part of the woods?"

"We learned a Crow might be on the hunt on the island," Arkimedes said.

The man dropped onto the ground unceremoniously, his skin paling. "Are you certain?"

"I'm afraid so. Nava and I are looking to warn Roman's village. Also, staying in larger groups might be our safest bet. He has bounty hunters and an army."

"A Crow working with bounty hunters?" Mort repeated in disbelief, his brow bone lowering into a deep frown. "That is most strange."

"He can't be up to anything good," Arkimedes agreed.

"I'm on my way to Elise's village. I can tell her to up her wards for the time being."

Nava's eyes traveled to Arkimedes in question. His lips silently moved to form a word, "East," which answered her question.

The fae village.

"So you two are a thing . . . ?" Mort started.

Arkimedes lifted a hand, pointing at this friend. "Now, Andreas, I thought you knew better."

Mort laughed out loud, staring at Nava. "You can't

blame me for being curious. I have never seen you in the company of someone as lovely as her."

Nava's cheeks warmed at the praise.

"What is a beautiful lady like yourself roaming around this part of the woods with this scoundrel?" the man asked gallantly.

Arkimedes's brows lowered, his hand up. "Stop."

"Always in such a foul mood." Mort pulled a bottle out of his coat pocket. She stared wide-eyed at the large size of the bottle. "Rum, to celebrate the occasion."

Nava had one cup before she retired to her tent, a bit drunk and afraid her lips would be too loose to reveal something embarrassing.

Who had traveled with Arkimedes before? Her stomach sank. She had no reason at all to be jealous, so she blamed her curious brain for it.

She wrapped the wool blankets Arkimedes had brought in earlier around herself, grumbly admitting that even though magic had provided storage for them, she was grateful for them on that crisp fall night.

They smelled like the cabin, and the scent calmed her nerves. Soft voices of the men outside gave her a sense of safety. Would he come to her tent tonight? Her body prickled with excitement at the possibility.

It had been interesting to learn about how Arkimedes had met her mother. She had been an instructor of his, perhaps in the army. He could be a Crow. Nava had the distinct idea that if he had been, her mother wouldn't have trusted him to help her and Cameron in this situation.

She stared at the blank ceiling canvas on top of her. He could be her soulmate, even if it made no sense why her mother would send her on a gold platter back to him.

It was a possibility. She shouldn't let her heart get too

carried away. Whatever this was, it was doomed before it even started.

Magic would always win. Her soulmate would always be first. She guessed it was better Arkimedes had not shown interest in her thus far.

The sounds of the night enveloped her, and soon she was asleep.

CHAPTER NINE

*W*hen Nava came out of her tent the next morning, it felt like winter had arrived. The ground had frozen over, as it had dipped to below zero during the evening. The ice cracked under her boots as she made her way to the campfire. Rubbing her hands together, Nava tried to bring warmth back to her fingers. The sun was coming up, the rays sneaking in between branches and lighting the forest ground.

Mort sat by the fire, his hands clasped together in knitted gloves that didn't cover his fingertips. Brown eyes trailed the sound of her steps and settled on her approaching form.

"Mornin', sweetheart." His voice was throatier than it had been the night before.

A pot was boiling on the fire, and the fragrant scent of coffee came to her. She groaned as she took a seat. She hadn't had coffee for days. Arkimedes always made tea. A potent brew of herbs and spices that would wake up *anyone* but tasted like death.

"I take it you missed coffee." A big smile stretched across his thin face.

"Not sure what Arkimedes has against coffee. I have missed it dearly." She nodded.

Mortimer handed her a steaming cup. "Oh, he swears by that disgusting concoction he makes."

Nava's nose wrinkled at the memory of the mentioned drink, and she inhaled the aroma of the fresh-brewed coffee in her hands. The bitter, earthy scent of roasted beans came as a warm hug, and a smile tugged at her lips; she basked in the warmth the drink provided her cold hands.

She studied her surroundings, not finding Arkimedes anywhere. Mort's tent was still up. It was a monstrosity made of magic, two times larger than her modest setup. Her lips pursed as she stared at what appeared to be a house, thick gray-and-brown canvas, sewn together with gold stitches that matched the garish gold trim around the door. Tassels hung in places as decoration. It reminded her of a circus tent. She had never been to a circus before, but she had seen many illustrations.

"Where is Arkimedes, by the way?" she asked.

Mort took a loud sip of his drink, shrugging. "The man is a night owl, always gone when the sun goes down. Almost like a vampire—except reverse, I guess." His voice was amused.

Nava got the impression he found himself hilarious. He handed her a shiny apple. "Thanks." She took the fruit but didn't move to eat it. Her stomach swirled as she took in the reflective skin. Arkimedes trusted Mort, but to her, he was a stranger.

Her mother's warning voice telling her not to eat food from a stranger boomed inside her head.

She guessed Arkimedes was also a stranger she had met

four days ago. But getting to trust him had been as easy as breathing. She couldn't say the same for Andreas Mortimer.

"It's cold for being the start of fall." She spoke to break the silence.

"It's this part of the forest. It's charmed to be always cold, you see."

It must have been why Arkimedes had brought her so many wool blankets the night before. At first, she assumed it was one for him and one for her. He had never come to sleep, so in the end, she had hogged all the available blankets.

The soft ruffling of steps and leaves moving across the ground made both of their heads snap in that direction. Arkimedes ducked under a particularly low-hanging branch. He had to be at least six foot three. He strode as he approached them. He had not slept much at night. His short, wavy hair was awry, as if the wind had brushed it. His sharp gaze came to her first, a flash of relief passing across his features.

"Mornin', fae," Mort said and lifted a cup of steaming coffee up to Arkimedes.

He took a seat by his friend, a grumble of disapproval escaping his lips. "Good morning." He studied his newly acquired drink before his focus shifted to her. "Did you sleep well?"

"Wonderful, actually. Thought you would never ask." Mort's false excitement tickled Nava.

Arkimedes sent him an exasperated glance.

Nava huffed a short laugh. "I did sleep well. Thank you for the blankets. I didn't know it would get this cold so early in the season." She put the shiny, possibly poisoned apple in her lap and held her warm drink with both hands.

"You're welcome."

She missed being the two of them. She craved more of Arkimedes, her natural curiosity fueled by the fact that he always disappeared at night.

Mort extended him an apple, shiny and red like the one in her lap. Nava looked at it with the intensity of a hawk. Arkimedes lifted it to his lips, one of his brows raising as he read her expression before taking a large bite.

The movement made her body heat. Her focus zeroed in on the tip of his tongue as it caught some of the juice on the corner of his mouth. A grin tugged his expression, and his gaze flashed to her, a wicked realization in his features.

Nava cleared her throat, a wave of anxious excitement flowing through her.

"So what had you running away to this forest, Miss Nava?" Mortimer asked.

She brought the cup of her untouched coffee to her lips and took a tentative sip to prevent words from spilling out in a fit of nerves. She wasn't sure when she'd get to have coffee again and might as well enjoy it. "Why do I need to be running from something?" she asked, aloof.

Arkimedes sat still, to her surprise.

"My dear, everyone here is running from *something*." Mortimer bellowed a laugh.

Nava half shrugged. "I guess that must be true. I'm running from the Crow who came to town earlier this week —and the Iron Crown."

"Let me guess, a forced marriage? Maybe seventy percent of the people in this forest have run away from those. You would think the crowns would abandon their ridiculous law."

The law forbade magical people to marry regular humans and make families of their choosing. The one that had forced her family into hiding since her father had possessed no magic. Their whole relationship had been in defiance to the crown. They had been soulmates, which meant the gods had approved their relationship.

Once, Nava had read the soulmate bond ruled over any other law, but with the greed of more power, the Crows had chosen to turn a blind eye to this.

"I guess you could say that." Nava swallowed.

Arkimedes's back straightened as he looked at her intently. She had not told him about her soulmate and why they had run away from the kingdom. But she had to assume her mother had, given that she had been so forward to share the existence of Cameron with him.

"What had you running away, Mr. Mortimer?" she ventured to ask.

"Call me Mort," he said.

"He was running away from debt collectors," Arkimedes pitched in, and Mortimer opened his lips in false offense.

"Excuse you, *fae*, I was running from bounty hunters. Get it right."

Arkimedes's rolling laughter made her smile.

"How so?" Nava asked.

"Well, for starters, I could have easily taken care of the debt collectors. They have no magic and deal with measly Grays. I, Andreas Mortimer, am *way* more powerful than that." Confidence oozed from him. Arkimedes's laughter grew stronger.

"And you, Arkimedes, what made you run from the Iron City?" she asked, and his laughter stopped. She blinked. Both pairs of eyes came to her.

Had it been an arranged marriage or debt, like it'd been for Mort? A crime of passion? Defiance in the army?

"Miss Nava, you will learn this one shares very little about his past," Mort said.

Nava pouted, meeting Arkimedes's gaze, her own heart

hammering inside her chest.

"Self-preservation." His voice broke the silence. He took another bite of the fruit in his hand. "I had to leave to survive, or stay and die."

"It's extra scary *you* were running from someone, maybe *something*." Mort's voice was filled with wonder. Arkimedes didn't elaborate. He didn't smile any longer.

The heavy sinking settled in her chest. Arkimedes excused himself from their company and made his way to her tent, presumably to rest. She stayed by the fire, lost in thoughts. Movement in her peripheral called her attention.

Mortimer's tent was groaning and shrinking in front of her. She dove onto the ground, magic taking over her senses. There came the sounds of fabric ripping and folding. The spicy scent of magic overtook her, and just like that, the tent was out of sight.

"Woo, the look on your face, Miss Nava. It seems like you've never seen somethin' like it before." A smile tugged at Mortimer's lips. His hand was holding the cane he had the night before, the heavy fabric of his traveling coat swallowing his shape whole.

She found her voice. "I—I hadn't."

"Fancy that." The man's curious expression settled on her before he shook his head. "Well, here is where I say my goodbyes. It was a pleasure. I hope I get to see your lovely face again."

"But . . . Arkimedes, he is still sleeping."

"Oh, don't worry. We never say goodbye, him and I. I will see him when I see him," he said, lifting the hood of his cloak. With a small bow, he was off—a limp in his right leg.

She chased his retreating shape until the gray of his cloak camouflaged him, leaving her alone in the cold enchanted forest.

CHAPTER TEN

*N*ava was bored stiff. B-o-r-e-d. *Bored.* She was also tired. The crunching of forest debris under their feet broke the lack of sound around them.

Where were the birds? Weren't forests filled with them? Even when they'd been at the cold camp with Andreas Mortimer, she'd absently recalled listening to their songs.

It was hard to keep her mind from going to places it wasn't supposed to when the landscape was the same. All she wanted to do, other than wonder if Cameron was all right, was ponder how handsome Arkimedes was and over-read any attention he paid her.

She had become that pitiful.

"So. Arkimedes is a long name," she started. "Maybe I should come up with a nickname."

"Please don't." His voice was stern, but she couldn't care less. It wasn't like he kept up the conversation.

"How about Archie?" His whole muscular back became rigid. She chuckled. "Okay, fine—not Archie, though. I think it's cute."

"I don't need to be cute."

"Oh-kay, how about . . . Arch? No, too weird? Maybe Ark? I like Ark—"

"No."

"Val. That one is good."

He took a sharp breath. She was sure he tried not to show the full extent of his annoyance, or maybe the contrary. Maybe he acted this way to show her how annoyed he was. "Fine, I will bite. Why Val?"

"From your last name. I read it on your sword."

Silence. "I'd rather not have that one."

So he *was* considering a nickname after all! She would take the small wins where they came, happy she was wearing him down. A smile tugged at her lips, then faltered when something else came to her. Something a lot juicier than a nickname.

He didn't like his last name, Valeron. Why?

"Why do you ask so many questions?" he growled.

She had asked that last bit out loud. What in the actual hell was wrong with him? "Have you been cooped up in your cabin for so long, you forgot how to treat people?" she fired back.

His steps slowed down, and he faced her. "Perhaps most polite people are not this nosy."

Nava's mouth opened in shock. Why would her mother send her here with this hot, stubborn, insufferable man? "You are *so* nice." Her words dripped with sarcasm, her body heated. "I ask questions because I know little about you and we are traveling together. Seems normal to me."

Arkimedes was quiet for so long, she had given up on any hope of getting any answer at all. Her pride told her she didn't want him to give her any information. "The name Valeron means little to me. I barely knew that family. And I'm sorry," he added.

Some truth, but definitely, he kept most of it guarded.

She was happy he'd shared *something*. It gave her an insight into him not being close to his family. Nava also had the keen impression he didn't say sorry often.

"I'm curious by nature," she said.

"I'm finding that out." His face softened, and he resumed his walk.

"I will keep asking questions—*and* using nicknames." She would set a mental clock to know how long it took him to snap at her in annoyance again.

"You ran away from an arranged marriage?" he asked.

Her face went warm. "Oh, it wasn't that precisely. What did my mother tell you?"

"I— She told me enough." His face angled toward her, his bright green eyes turbulent. "But I want to hear it from you."

"Fine." Nava took a deep breath. If she wanted him to open up to her, she also had to do the same. "I found my soulmate back in the Iron City, ten years ago."

"How old were you?"

"It's rude to ask women their age," she pointed out with mock offense. His lips twitched. "I was fifteen."

"It's not quite an arranged marriage," he said, and she wished she could read his expression.

"I guess it's not." She shrugged. "But I don't want the soulmate bond either way, so in the end, it ends up the same."

He nodded, turning toward her. The light of the afternoon burned a highlight across his profile, marking his straight nose. "If you don't want the bond, I guess it would be even more suffocating since the gods, not humans, dictate it."

"Exactly." She paused. "Have you ever been curious if you would find your soulmate?"

"No," he said. "I don't want a soulmate, either.

Someone like me is not cut out for that kind of relationship."

Her whole body sank at his words.

I HAD TO LEAVE TO SURVIVE, or stay and die. Arkimedes's words had been going around her head throughout the night as Nava tossed and turned under the wool blankets he had given her days prior. She hadn't gotten much sleep with her busy mind.

The wind howled across the tall trees. The canvas moved like a sail in the wind. The thick wooden sticks she had found during the afternoon rattled along with her tent, and she half expected it to fall on her at any moment.

She had liked this campsite after they arrived, with ample flatter ground and massive trees.

When Arkimedes said he would do rounds around the campsite, Nava had offered to come with him, not wanting to stay alone to face her feelings, the way she missed Cameron and Laurie, or the comfort of her bed.

He had declined her offer, saying he'd be back and she should set her tent up, as a storm approached. Somehow Nava knew he wouldn't be back until the morning *again*.

Her heart shrank like a raisin, making it difficult to breathe. She wasn't sure if her mood was soured by exhaustion or the frustration of not understanding enough. Not about her nature, her soulmate, what to do, or how to do it. She didn't know about Arkimedes or his past, but she was hungry for more.

On the one side, if he was her soulmate, like it kept popping in her head, it meant he didn't want her. She was ridiculous for being disappointed, especially since she didn't want her soulmate, either.

He'd said he wasn't cut out for that kind of relationship. Whatever that meant. A profound, intense, dedicated love? It annoyed her further that he wasn't asking her questions. He gave her less of an excuse to pry into his life.

She blinked with heavy lids. The blue of the moon bathed one of the sides of the tent, showing the shadows of leaves moving.

Another blink. Why, even though she was tired, did her mind refuse to let her sleep? She focused on the heavy sound of steps, a deep voice in the distance.

Her vision was hazy, and it was bright, a clear contrast to the bite of the cold morning. Another slow blink. This time, her vision sharpened over the approaching shape of a large male body. Broad shoulders and a long, thick neck. Arkimedes.

"Nava! Are you okay? Are you hurt?" His voice carried a panicked undertone. His hand traveled down her arm, his touch warm over her icy skin. A current traveled through her body, awakening every nerve ending where he touched her.

"I—I'm fine." Her tent was a mess—tilted to one side, the weight held by a couple of her wooden posts. The other two had tipped over in the windy storm the night before.

Arkimedes's breath left him in a whoosh, his skin pale. He studied her face as if making sure she was *indeed* all right, then traveled down her body to continue his assessment before they settled on her chest. He didn't move, didn't blink as he stared, his pupils becoming wider. With a sharp intake of breath, he turned away.

"I will give you some privacy." His skin flushed, which was uncharacteristic.

She followed his shape as he awkwardly stood under

the half-fallen tent and exited. The heavy cloth of his coat billowed behind each of his steps.

Her gaze came down, and her skin heated when she realized she was wearing her nightgown—made of sheer cotton fabric that hid little of her breasts. Her nipples peeked behind the white fabric.

Her arms came across her chest, her hands grasping her cold shoulders as her stomach churned with embarrassment. A nervous laugh escaped her lips.

She was happy the worst of it was hurt pride over her fallen tent because even though it wasn't pretty, it had kept her safe and warm during the night. She shivered, her skin covered in goose bumps.

Okay, perhaps not warm, but it had kept her *safe*.

Nava got dressed in her traveling clothes and left her tent, finding Arkimedes by the fire. She was shy from the memory of what he had seen of her body but was determined to make nothing of it.

She had gotten a reaction from him—unknowingly, of course. Her stomach swirled upon remembering the heat of his gaze on her flesh. She found him not meeting her gaze.

No longer panicked and concerned, his expression not soft or worried as it had been a few minutes prior. His chiseled jaw was becoming more apparent by the rigid set of a strained expression.

"Is everything all right?" she asked as she approached.

Arkimedes stared at the pot resting on the fire. The strong scent of the godforsaken tea surrounded her. "No."

Nava's brows lifted up, nearly touching the edge of her hair. "Wha—?"

"You could have been hurt last night in the storm," he growled.

Nava's back straightened at once, heat prickling her

skin. Her stomach dropped, making her uneasiness grow. Long gone was his heated gaze on her. "And why is it making you angry with me?" she asked, unsure why his reaction was so harsh. She crossed her arms in front of her chest.

"This could have been prevented if you had reinforced your tent with *magic*."

The contrast of her warm skin against the iciness of the blood pumping through her veins was stark. Anger pooled in her stomach. "I don't need magic."

"But you do." He pointed to the spot where her lopsided tent stood. "Clearly."

"I have camped many times with my non-magical tent, using my own two hands, without a problem."

"Avoiding learning about your magic is not protecting you. It has given you a great disadvantage in this forest. In life."

Her chin lifted in the air. His imposing stature made her feel short, even though she wasn't. "How so? From where I stand, magic has been the one constant in my life that has brought me pain, has torn apart everything I held dear to me. It's magic that brought me to this forest in the first place."

"If you had used magic last night with your tent, you would have been protected from the elements and from the cold," he insisted.

"I'm *fine*. This has to do with more than my tent failing your standards. But the way I see it, I've been doing fine just the way I am."

"You had to leave your brother with someone else while you came out here to this dangerous *magical* place in searching of protection."

His words cut through her, the way he had intended them. The unpleasant churning in her gut wasn't anger any longer. She had a hard time putting her finger on what it was, but it was ugly and scary.

"You are running away from a world you don't understand."

"I know *something* about it."

"And what is that you know?" he challenged.

"People with magic have to serve, no questions asked, whether or not they believe in what they have to do. They're forced into arranged marriages, the sole purpose being procreation, even though you might not want children at all!" She took a deep breath. "Children are taken away to be forged into weapons. Do I know something or did I make all of it up in my naïve head?"

"It's true." His face softened. "That's the negative side of magic."

"It tore my mother apart to have to hide us from this. My brother and I were allowed to stay with our parents, to grow with their love, unlike most—if not all—magical children." Her throat thickened.

"But at what cost, though?" His gaze was hard on hers, unblinking. "Were you able to discover your true self? Are you happy with your mother about it?"

His words stung, reminding her of Cameron and the conversation they'd had before. Her brother wanted to find his true nature. If it weren't for a sorcerer and the crown, she would be with him.

"I don't need magic." She was supposed to be caring for her brother. It was her job to protect and care, but to do that, she needed love and strength. "So instead of judging so hard because of what I believe, maybe you can try to understand I'm not so ignorant."

"No, you aren't. But you are afraid—that often leads people to make decisions that hurt them in the end."

"Did I do that?" Her voice raised. "You must know all

about me. Tell me, Arkimedes, were you a believer of whatever they asked of you when you served their army? Or did you hate all of it like my mother did?" she asked, and his lips clamped shut in an instant.

"I— It wasn't so black and white." His throat bobbed. "We are not one extreme or the other, not usually either way." He paused. His large hand rubbed his face, out of frustration or plain exhaustion. The deep color underneath his eyes was more pronounced. "What I mean is if you push this other part of you away—"

"It's not another part of me," she interrupted him. "I have lived in the City of Iron. I have lived with magic. I'm happy with myself the way I *am*." She didn't believe her words, but Arkimedes didn't need to know that.

They stared at each other for a long, uncomfortable moment, neither of them saying anything else or making a move to leave. This first argument hung heavy between them.

Nava was the first to turn around, making haste toward her tent, not wanting to leave it up for a second longer than necessary. Her skin prickled with the weight of his stare following her. She touched one of the ropes before the poles fell with a loud thump.

Her annoyance with her tent spiked. She knelt, proceeded to untie her rope from the poles, and pulled the canvas away. The cold bit at her bare fingers, making her joints numb as the morning dew burned her skin.

Nava didn't put her gloves on. They were buried under the mess, and she was too self-conscious to try to find them under the thick canvas.

She turned around, and Arkimedes was still staring at her. He hadn't moved to get tea or even sit down. His jaw was tense, a clear warning to stay the fuck away. She proceeded with her task.

Eventually, he stopped following her. The intensity was driving her crazy, but it eased slowly. He had fallen asleep by the fire, his large body slumped against a tree. Her own heart leaped as she allowed herself to linger on him.

He was unlike any man she had met before, an otherworldly beauty that was more than human. The straight profile of his nose. The long, black lashes and the bow of his lips.

Her heart squeezed because he was so close but so distant. She had never experienced such an attraction to anyone before. Her hand touched the spot where her mark painted her skin.

You don't want a soulmate, Nava's mind repeated for the tenth time.

She wasn't available to fall for anyone and waste time in things like attraction. No, she had a task at hand, which was to stay alive and survive long enough to make it back to Cameron and Laurie. But it was more than that. Her quest for survival had grown when she learned other innocent people lived in this forest, and much like herself, they shared her fate.

Her anger subsided somewhat as she took in the way he slept. He couldn't be comfortable in the position he lay.

She had finished folding her tent and made a neat pile of the woolen blankets Arkimedes sent away with magic every morning. She took a deep breath and grabbed both of those. Her heart came alive in quick pitter-patters as the decision formed in her mind. She padded toward him, making sure her steps were quiet so as not to awaken him.

Nava unfolded one of the large blankets and laid it over his body. Maybe if he were warmer, he would get better sleep. She startled when his eyes opened and focused on her. Though no words left his lips, his brows furrowed. She continued, however, steeling her resolve, and put the second blanket on top of him, hoping he took the olive branch for what it was.

His lips twitched up into a whisper of a smile.

BY THE TIME ARKIMEDES WOKE, the sun shone in the middle of the sky, and Nava had packed her things away. She always admired how he was able to be fully alert as soon as he woke. He stretched like a cat, the movement making the muscles underneath his clothes more apparent. Her gaze followed from a distance.

He lifted the fallen blankets from the ground and eyed them before his curious gaze landed upon her. The blankets disappeared from his hand in a blink. Her heart sputtered at the vision.

"Are we leaving?" she asked, making scribbles over the mud by the fire with a stick.

"Yes." His voice was still deep with sleep. He cleared his throat. "Er, thank you for the blankets."

"I hope they helped. I like to sleep toasty," she said, avoiding his gaze.

"They did."

Her eyes lifted to meet his. They both stared at one another, and it wasn't uncomfortable but charged with something else entirely. She swallowed. "So . . . how far away from the village are we?"

They had been traveling for a week already. For an island she'd assumed only held her town and a vast amount of wasteland with magical creatures, it was huge and busting with human life.

"We're a few weeks from it. It will depend on the weather and what we might encounter in between here and there."

"What might we encounter?" she echoed.

He grabbed his kettle and poured himself some of his energizing tea. The smell alone made her nose crinkle. "The Neems, the spirits of the forest."

"The spirits?" Her voice was high-pitched. A pit of dread grew in the middle of her stomach. "What spirits? Like ghosts or like fluffy, leaf-covered forest spirits?"

"Fluffy? Where are you getting your information?" He eyed her with rakish amusement.

"Well . . . I have studied. Some forest spirits vary. I read some are protecting the forest and are not harmful to people who are passing by." She didn't mean for her voice to sound so defensive. She was trying to get along, after all.

He ignored her tone. "These spirits are angry. Those who were murdered here stayed behind. There is little known why these forests make it easy for them to stay. As we move north, we will cross some of their haunted grounds."

"Just great news all around."

He nodded, taking a long drink from his mug. "We could try to go around. If we do, we might get a bit too close to the West Village—which might be worse and would add an extra two weeks to our trip." He paused, frowning. "I'm not sure we have the time to do that. The village might be attacked before."

The reminder of her task was clear—innocent lives rested in their hands with the knowledge of the looming threat.

"Right." She nodded.

Following Arkimedes's cue as he killed the fire, she bent down and lifted her backpack and the remainder of their things.

CHAPTER ELEVEN

*H*aunted didn't begin to cover the feeling around this part of the woods. As Nava and Arkimedes progressed through steep climbs, their trips became shorter.

It had become of the utmost importance not to travel when the sun was setting. The trees had also changed, growing thinner and longer, the bark painted in silver tones. Nava had picked a couple of plants she hadn't encountered before, remembering from her studies that they were rare and full of heavy medicinal properties that would help with more potent healing potions.

The forest became muted, the chirping of birds and the croaking of toads ceasing altogether. Arkimedes seemed to be more on edge as the day progressed.

"Do not leave your tent in the night, at any cost." He studied the darkening sky, and he would be gone soon to do whatever he disappeared in the evenings for.

"I won't leave my tent at night. I got it," Nava said, taking a bite of her meal. The bland flavor of stale crackers and hard cheese wasn't exciting, even with her hunger. It was the third time he'd said the same thing with different words.

"Even if you hear cries."

She met his hard stare. "Cries?"

He nodded. "We are in the spirits' grounds now. It's *not* safe, much less at night."

"Are you leaving tonight as well?"

His face turned into a mixture of guilt and worry, his brows morphing as his skin lost all color. "I have to. The wards . . ." A whisper, then the words died on his lips.

She guessed he was done lying to her about this. "Are you a werewolf?" She had not meant for the words to leave her mouth, but this was her life, and her mouth had no filter.

"What?" His face snapped back his eyes wide in shock at her question.

"You disappear at night. I know there is supposed to be a full moon with werewolves—but maybe there's something I don't know," she continued.

Silence descended upon them before Arkimedes laughed, first a low sound that became rolling laughter.

She furrowed her brow. "Well, I'm glad *someone* finds me funny."

He shook his head. "No, I'm not a werewolf, Nava."

"A vampire, then?"

His lips twitched. "Not a vampire. Wouldn't you be concerned about being so close to me if I were one?"

She shrugged. "I guess that made no sense. I have seen you eat. Maybe that disgusting tea of yours curbs your appetite."

His smirk turned into a full-blown smile. Her stomach churned with the sight of those straight white teeth, such a blinding sight that she lamented she could count with one hand the times she had seen it. "It's not that bad," he said, half shrugging. "Maybe I shouldn't have let Andreas stay with us that night. Ever since, you haven't been drinking it. It's good for energy."

"Have you heard of coffee?"

"Not the same."

She scoffed. "Either way, don't think I didn't notice you changing the subject." She crossed her arms around her chest and leveled him with a stern gaze. "Why are you always gone at night?"

His face fell, his attention moving up. The blue tone of the sky peeked around sparse foliage, the smoke of the firepit billowing up. The expanse of his thick throat bobbed as he swallowed before he met her stare. "I'm cursed."

"I'm sorry. What do you mean?"

In a second, he was up from where he sat. He unbuckled the belt that held his sword and dropped it to the soft ground, taking a couple of steps around the area before facing her. "I was cursed many years ago. I can't speak about it much, but . . . the reason you haven't seen me at night is because when the sun goes down, I take the shape of a crow."

Nava's lips slacked. "Why?"

"I guess she thought it amusing," he said in between tight lips.

"How can you break it?"

He observed her, shaking his head. Was he unable to speak much about the curse or was he putting his walls back up?

"So, do you sleep in the trees?"

"Not usually. Sleeping is dangerous."

"Do you keep your consciousness?"

"Yes."

"What do they call you, the man with one-word answers?"

"I haven't spoken about it with anyone. I'm not used to divulging a lot of the information." His hands went over his head, the waves of silky hair falling over his face.

"No kidding."

The silence that surrounded them was long. What was going on inside his head? His shoulders were growing tense.

She took a few steps to him and reached for his shoulder. He stopped all movement when she touched him. A zap of energy ran through her hand, and she gasped, pulling her hand back. His gaze met hers. "Did you use magic on me . . . ?"

"Must have been static energy," he said, staring at the sky again and letting out a soft breath. "I have to go, please—"

"Stay inside my tent. *I know.*"

He nodded, and without another word, he turned around and disappeared behind the shapes of the twisty trees.

NOT WAITING FOR ARKIMEDES to come back didn't help with her nerves. Nava wasn't worried he would leave her, as she had been in the past, though it did morph into being concerned he would get eaten by a larger animal instead.

That night, however, she was worried about something else; much like Arkimedes had said, moans and cries happened through the night. Whispers sounded a lot like the howling wind, except she could listen to words mixed in between laments. Latin, the language of the fae, and others she didn't know. She couldn't tell them apart.

They whispered threats, cried for loved ones. They begged for mercy and asked for help.

The end of her hair stood up as the temperature dropped, so cold that mist billowed out of her mouth. Nava knew deep within her that she would not be able to sleep tonight, expecting a ghost to barge into her tent at any moment. The spirits, however, seemed to stay outside, as if her tent were warded.

She had the sneaky suspicion Arkimedes had worked up a spell while she had excused herself to take care of bodily businesses. She was so freaked out she wasn't mad about it. Of the two evils, the ghosts outside were the worst.

Something brown crawled over the roof of her tent, slow but steady, the size of a small coin. Nava blinked. It was a bee. The stripes of its furry body were gone in the darkness of the night. She fell back onto her bed.

Nava remembered the creature she had helped. It felt like a lifetime ago, but the memory was still fresh as if it had happened yesterday. She took another breath. The scent of mud and decay surrounded her, like flowers left in the same water for a while.

She buried her nose inside the fabric of the wool blanket, the soft scent of campfire holding on to the threads of the material. Nava could also pick up Arkimedes's scent, and she didn't want to dwell on the fact that her body relaxed a fraction.

When the sun lit up her surroundings, Nava rushed out of bed, making sure she was ready to run if she needed to. She folded the wool blankets and stuffed her bag. Her hair was wilder than usual, sticking out in all directions in soft curls. The last thing on her mind was to try to tame it. She put it up in a bun, eyeing the door of her tent warily.

Would it be safe for her to leave? To start the fire and wait for Arkimedes outside?

He said to stay in while it was nighttime, but the sun was already up, and he had to be on his way back to their camp.

The daggers would do nothing against a spirit, her mind supplied. She frowned as her stomach sank and the awareness of being ill-prepared hit her full force.

Steps over crunchy leaves made her head snap toward it.

"Nava."

She let out a sigh of relief before exiting the tent. He took her in from where he stood. A wave of intense need washed over her, startling her. "I'm okay. I stayed inside the tent."

"I know—I was nearby," he offered, his cheeks turning a bright shade.

Nava smiled. "Thanks." Even though he would've been unable to help her, he had stayed to make sure everything went okay.

"We shouldn't stay here for long." A crease formed in between his brows. "Did you get any sleep?"

Great, not only did she feel like dog shit, but she looked like it as well. "I guess my face gave it away."

"You look bea—" He stopped. "I *recognize* the appearance of being tired."

She was moving to pack the tent. She turned to Arkimedes in time to see a surge of mist and power form around his body. Black in color. His hand turned a blue shade, and gray smoke lifted from his fingertips. Soon after, a soft fire came to life in the logs.

His head tilted to meet her gaze. She always avoided

seeing him make the fire or do magic at all costs, but today, curiosity had won over her stubbornness.

THE TEA TASTED LIKE DIRT water and rotten fruit, but it did give Nava the energy she lacked that morning. Their meal had been light.

This dreary part of the forest made her blood cold. Maybe that was why this place was called the Grey Forest. The trees lacked the normal splendor. Mist covered the ground, and even though she couldn't see them, ghosts surrounded them in between infinite tree trunks that extended beyond what she could see.

Arkimedes walked a few meters in front of her, not resting. Their path was less traveled than all the previous places they had been before.

Nava caught something to her right, a gasp for air. She looked to the side. A shape of a woman stood in between the trees. Her head was down, with her long black hair covering her features. She choked. A rattle that reminded Nava of the last dying breaths her parents had taken.

Nava's steps slowed down for a second as her mind tried to catch up on what she was seeing. Her body already knew, though. The crawling in her scalp and the cold that extended through her body shook her.

The woman's gaunt white face lifted, and she stared at Nava, sockets where eyes once had been. Skin so thin it was translucent, the forest visible behind it. Teeth through a hole in her cheek, and her lips—or lack of them—open menacingly.

Coldness dropped through Nava's body as panic hit her hard. All she could hear was the drums, a hard beat taking over everything. It was her heartbeat.

"*Arkimedes.*" Her voice trembled.

"Don't look at her!" He sounded far away.

Nava's focus fixed on the dead woman's face. Her torn mouth opened again in a snarl. The pits of her eyes shone with light.

Arkimedes jerked her out of her frozen state, and before she knew it, they were running past large tree trunks. Her aching legs struggled to keep the pace, and her mind was behind her with that dead woman.

"Avoid their eyes at all costs!" he panted as they ran.

Nava could see white shapes pop around them, behind trees and closing in. "They're everywhere!"

"You've got to run faster."

It happened quickly; they hadn't been running long before a ghost figure appeared in front of them. Arkimedes changed directions, pulling Nava along with him. The ebony tendrils of his magic crawled over his body. A spell shot from him over one spirit, and the ghost evaporated in front of her.

A white shape reached out in between the trees. A gnarled arm with bone peeking through paper-thin skin. Fingers purple and blue from being rotten for days. They were spirits, but also corpses. Not entirely gone, but not here, either.

A scream escaped her lips as she jolted out of Arkimedes's grasp and the Neem's reach. Nava turned to it, and she stared right into a dead man's rotten face.

Fresher than the one before. Skin still clung to his swollen face. A scream left Nava's lips. Light shone behind his milky stare. A ray escaped out of his mouth, shooting straight at her.

Arkimedes came in front of her, and the ray hit him instead. He collapsed on the ground without a sound. Her gaze was on him as he lay by her feet. She had lost him.

Bile rose in her throat, nausea hitting her hard with the overwhelming sense of defeat. Her knees hit the floor as she dropped next to him. The backpack weighed on her shoulders.

Nava took off the heavy load and pushed it aside, her mind homing in on him. The spirits neared her, their laments coming closer.

A small bumblebee landed on top of Arkimedes's brown tunic. Its body was wide and fuzzy. Another one landed, and in the middle of her panicked state, she had the wherewithal to notice something was off. Her hands reached to the lapels of his coat and shook him. She called his name twice. Her voice was breaking with despair.

She tried to lift him, struggling with his weight. Nava was not weak. She often boasted that she was stronger than the average woman. Arkimedes was bigger than a regular man, however, pure muscle and utter dead weight.

Buzzing surrounded her, bees coming down from the tops of the trees. Wisps of Nava's hair escaped her bun and moved with the wind. She grasped Arkimedes's tunic harder.

"Arkimedes, please," she urged. She wouldn't run without him.

The bees surrounded her, forming a shield, and the gaunt faces of the spirits disappeared behind them. Confusion overtook her as she studied the wall of small insects. The buzzing became a clear whisper.

"*They are coming.*"

She had heard this before. The day she'd saved the bee creature when it warned her about the bounty hunters. Her back straightened, realization hitting her all at once.

Why did she know the bees weren't referring to the spirits, but to another more significant threat? Devon Black.

Without Arkimedes's magic, she was useless with her lack of powers. Tears pricked as anger ran through her. She hugged his warm body close.

She got up from her seating position, grabbed his arms, and pulled. The bees surrounded her.

"Tell me where to go," she gasped in between labored breaths. He was so heavy. She wished she were stronger. With the shield of bees, the spirits seemed to have less of a hold on Arkimedes. His tense posture was relaxing.

The bees opened a hole in their shield, and she could see the forest beyond her. She dragged Arkimedes over forest debris. The bees changed direction, and she followed, sweat breaking out on her skin and rolling down her face.

If she had mastered some spells, she could have been able to protect him better. She would have been able to help somehow.

Nava had been trying to get him away from the spirits and Devon's path for a while. Frustration with her mother and herself bloomed inside her. She spotted a large tree with a hole in the bottom. Large enough for them to hide.

The bees swarmed as she focused on Arkimedes's sleeping form. Ark had saved her, and it was her turn to do the same for him.

The tree was more prominent than she'd expected, smelling of mud. She gained strength once they were inside, hauling him until the walls of bark hid him.

"*He is coming.*" The buzz was distant.

Fear spiked through her blood. She rushed to cover Arkimedes's legs with leaves.

Nava pushed her back next to him, making them as small as possible. She studied her surroundings, and to her horror, she noticed her backpack was not there. She had dropped it when Arkimedes had been hit.

Dread trailed like a cold finger down her spine. Once, her mother had told her that magic was about visualizing what was needed. To home in on all the energy of her body and call for that to happen.

Magic always had a price, usually on your body's energy.

The bees settled in the hole and covered it. They weren't moving their wings. She guessed to an untrained eye it would soon appear to be tree bark from far away. Why were the bees here, helping her?

She pictured her backpack and wished for it to come to her. Cinnamon and cayenne, the spicy scent of magic, wafted to her. Warmth ignited in the pit of her stomach. Her hands tightened around Arkimedes's arm.

Exhaustion came. She pictured her backpack in that part of the forest. She imagined it disappearing, coming to her, and appearing inside the hole in the tree where she was.

Her body became numb, and even if she wanted to, she wouldn't have been able to open her eyes. Her head dropped and laid on something soft. A heartbeat lulled her down to sleep, then there was darkness.

NAVA'S SHOULDERS AND BACK ACHED, it was humid wherever she was, and she was lying on a hard, warm pillow that drifted. Her eyes opened, and she found Arkimedes staring back at her.

"Oh, good, you are awake," she whispered. She wrapped her arms around him in a tight hug.

"You saved me."

Her heart sped up when the weight of his hand landed

on her back. She shook her head and enjoyed the warmth of his body. "It wasn't me. The bees saved us."

He stared at the wall of insects. Their wings fluttered, but they didn't fly away. "I must know how you did this," he whispered, exhaustion marking every word that left his mouth.

Nava wished she could answer the question, but the reality was, she didn't get why the bees had helped them.

Her lips parted when she noticed the shape of her backpack a few feet away from her. She gasped with the realization of what she had done.

Magic.

He was sitting up, his large body crowding the space, like too much and not enough for her brain.

"They are still covering the entrance." She pointed to the bees. "I'm guessing it's not safe for us to leave."

He nodded. "The bees have an alliance with you. Can you control them?" His voice was low enough that she could hear him only because he was sitting next to her.

"No, I helped a . . . creature that afternoon, just before you found me. I put a potion on its head, and it warned me the bounty hunters were coming." She shrugged. "I don't know why they helped us today."

Understanding passed through his features. "A life debt binds you to your savior to repay in kind. You probably saved an essential creature. I have an idea of whom."

"Anyone would have done it," she said.

"No, Nava. Only a selfless act would form a life debt." A smile turned up the corners of his lips.

"How are you feeling?" She was glad there was no light in here or else he would see her blushing.

"I'm well."

Her mouth opened to respond when the buzzing interrupted her words. The bees were moving, flying away. Rays of gray light filtered through the hole. Nava brought her hand up to shield her eyes from the brightness.

"We need to go. It's almost nighttime, and it's not safe for us to camp here."

She followed him out of the tree, keeping her focus low to the ground. How long had she slept after her stunt with magic? Dread filled the pit of her stomach. She didn't want to dwell on what she had done as she grasped the straps of her backpack, a reminder that magic had saved them.

Arkimedes turned around and darted in one direction, and like she had done many times before, she followed him.

CHAPTER TWELVE

*M*agic had drained her. Nava struggled to catch up to Arkimedes, who, like her, seemed a bit off-kilter. She was too caught up in her fears to say anything. The silence was broken for brief moments when Arkimedes mentioned how much longer they would need to walk to make it out of danger.

The trembling started when the adrenaline dwindled. It went from Nava's fingertips, down her arms, and through her body. Her steps died down, and she grew numb as images of dead faces came flashing through her mind, but the worst was Arkimedes collapsing to the ground.

Again and again.

Ghosts were something she would see in a horrifying nightmare. Now it had become a reality.

A loud tapping distracted her, almost as if a woodpecker were nearby. She was shocked it was her chattering teeth. Her arms came around her to bring warmth back to her body. She couldn't find her voice to call for Arkimedes to stop.

Her vision was blurry as a panic attack closed in on her. Why had Arkimedes jumped in front of the hex? It made more sense for her to be hurt. He was stronger and able to carry her around or make it out of there alive. She was angry he had sacrificed himself—angry and touched.

The magic she had so vehemently denied just a day ago, the primary source of their fight, had been the thing that had saved her.

Arkimedes turned around, realizing Nava had stayed behind. His steps were quick to reach her, his face a gradient of emotions. "Nava?" Her name escaped his lips.

"Why did you jump in front of the Neem's attack?"

His brows furrowed, as if her question were the biggest puzzle. "Because."

"Just because? It could have killed you."

"I didn't think about it." His hand came to her shoulder.

"I—I thought they had killed you. Then I realized you were alive, but there was no way I could save you because I'm not strong enough. I have denied this part of me for so long. You were right, Arkimedes." Tears pricked her eyes.

His face softened. "We are fine, and you *are* strong. This is a new world for you. It would have shocked me if you weren't shaken by what just happened."

"They hurt you. I would have been able to do something if I hadn't allowed my prejudice with magic to take over."

"You *saved* me," he corrected.

"No, I didn't—the bees did."

"They were bound to you."

Shivers covered her body when his fingers traveled down her arm before dropping to his side. "That is true." She smiled, and Arkimedes mirrored the expression.

"Yesterday, I shouldn't have said all that I did." His

voice turned softer. "You were right. I don't know everything about you, but I want to know more."

His words took hold inside her because they meant something. He wanted to know her, and that was scary and exhilarating all in one. The fight had stirred something within her. She had been angry about him judging her decision to cut magic from her life. "You were right about something, though. I have never given Cameron a choice, much like Mother never gave it to me." Cameron had asked to see the magic books, to go to the forest and encounter creatures.

She had always feared this part of herself.

"However misguided your fear is, there is a difference between acting out of fear and acting out of spite."

"I have done a little of both," she said, lowering her gaze to the ground.

"Calling upon your magic can drain you. I meant to stop as soon as we were out of danger. It's still close to the edge of their haunted grounds. This could do for tonight if you need rest."

She nodded, her body screaming for her to lie down. However long she had passed out inside the tree had not been enough.

She inspected the area where they stood. Now that her nerves had calmed, she could take in her surroundings. Her boots weren't in two inches of mud any longer. The forest was humid, and moss hung from every surface sunlight touched, but it wasn't overwhelming anymore.

Nava laid her backpack on the ground, shaking from the remnants of her jittery nerves that lingered in her body. The tent was easier to set up this time; she let her hands go through the steps by memory, allowing her mind to wander.

THE WIND HISSED THROUGH the trees surrounding her. Nava opened her eyes with a gasp, the ghosts' images from the day before coming to her. She scrambled out of her bed. The furs, blankets, and jacket she'd hugged to her body fell to the ground.

It took a moment to adjust to the darkness. The off-white of the canvas flapped around with the wind, and there was no sign of Arkimedes.

He is a bird now, her mind supplied.

She needed to stop listening to the howling of the wind that sounded an awful lot like the cries of the ghosts and try not to remember the haunted grounds she'd slept on the night before.

She tried to focus her mind on pleasant things, like the smell of Laurie's blueberry pies or the Iron City's summer days. When that didn't work, she tried to focus on the reason she was here. Cameron came to her.

Her mind supplied the image of Arkimedes and Cameron, training outside his cabin, and her heart almost couldn't bear it. Why would it keep bringing this image back? He hadn't shown any interest, and she wasn't convinced this wasn't some magical trick of destiny.

Nava didn't know when sleep took her, but the wind was gone, and the soft light of the morning's first rays of sunshine brightened the canvas ceiling of her tent.

The ruffling of leaves had her jolting up, rushing to the flap that served as the door. Arkimedes was sitting by the fire. His coat lay next to him. The white sleeves of his shirt were rolled a couple of times, showing the play of his muscular forearms. His handsome face was focused on the rabbit he was cleaning.

His gaze came to meet her face and raked down her body. It was a subtle movement she would have missed if she hadn't been staring so intently. As it was, she *had* noticed. A sense of smug pride washed over her. Nava walked toward Arkimedes, putting a bit of extra pep to the movement of her hips. Simone had told her to do this plenty of times before.

"I would like to train and learn magic," she said with a voice she hoped sounded strong, unlike how she felt. Arkimedes's eyes widened at her words. "Don't look so surprised."

"Okay." He nodded. "We can start later today after we make it to the new camp."

"After you get some sleep, of course. I don't want to hurt you with the undeniable power I have running through my veins." She reached for an apple from the dwindling bag of food they had gotten from Mortimer days prior and bit a big chunk of it. She enjoyed the sweet, tart flavor that took over her palate.

He huffed a laugh, amused. "Who knew you would hide such an ego under that big hair of yours?"

She choked, coughing loudly. "I don't have big hair!" Her hand came to her messy waves, puffier than usual from the lack of her everyday hair products from back home. Her cheeks heated.

So much for the wave of her hips. He didn't see her that way.

"It's beautiful," he breathed, and for a moment, she thought she'd imagined his words. Her gaze met his, and she could tell by the color in his cheeks that he was surprised he had said this out loud.

"Thank you." She grinned at him.

The silence that followed was charged with under-standing. She buzzed with emotion at the idea that maybe her growing feelings weren't so one-sided. Then it came to her again. "Are you my soulmate?"

Oh, no, had she said that out loud?

"What?" He straightened, his skin turning pale. Now she had shocked him well. His brown, bushy brows dipped. His previously relaxed pose was long gone.

It was her gift to society to ruin something with her big unfiltered mouth. "Well, I just—I . . ." Her face was so warm she could have fried an egg on top of her cheeks. Her stomach twisted, and she swallowed, trying to get down the heavy constriction in her throat.

"What gave you that impression?" His voice was cold.

He had called her hair beautiful. Oh, god, she was so stupid. A compliment didn't equal being a soulmate! "I— Nothing. I just wondered because I never felt . . . attracted to anyone before . . ." Her voice became almost a whisper by the end.

She couldn't dig herself out of this one. Not only had she asked Arkimedes if he was the most important person in her life, but she'd also admitted she was attracted to him. She swallowed and understood her mistake.

There was no warmth of recognition. He *had* told her he wasn't ready for a relationship, then she'd gone ahead and asked him—just because she had a crush? Ordinary people had crushes all the time. She wasn't normal, though, but her pride prevented her from telling him so.

It wasn't like she wanted to dwell on the fact, not after he appeared so put off by her question.

"Just because someone gets along with you doesn't mean they are your soulmate." The almost imperceptible shake of his head made her stomach drop lower.

Fine, he wasn't her soulmate.

"I get it." Nava stepped back. Maybe she would get

some of the rabbit later. "I'm going to go and see if I can find a place to . . . die of embarrassment."

"Nava." His voice was a bit softer, but she didn't stick around to see pity. Oh, no, she was out of there.

A good walk would clear her mind, and maybe by the time she was back, he would already be resting inside the tent.

CHAPTER THIRTEEN

$\mathcal{T}$he new camp was bright. The trees had changed once again to white bark, and bronze leaves peppered the ground. Unlike the day before, this area felt calmer. Birds chirped. Squirrels ran around the trees.

Or maybe they weren't squirrels. Upon further inspection, they had long fluffy tails, but their ears were large and fox-like, and they had lizard-like hands.

"The Northern Village, can they help you with your curse?" Nava asked, hitting the pegs into the ground that would be her tent. Neither of them had brought her floundering words back up. She pushed back her hurt pride and acted as if nothing had happened.

Arkimedes got up from his spot by the fire, dusting his pants from forest debris. "Unfortunately, they can't break the curse. Only I can unravel it," he said, meeting her eyes.

"What do you have to do?"

His face hardened. "I can't say. The curse prevents me to."

"How long have you been cursed?" she proceeded, walking toward him.

"Nine years."

"Was that what brought you here? I know you said you had to leave the city to survive."

"I was cursed here, not far away from where we are," he said in a reflective tone, his eyes lost somewhere on the horizon.

Nava opened her mouth to ask more. She remembered he had said it had been a she—had it been a companion he often traveled with? Mort had made it appear as if Arkimedes did travel with others.

She would ignore her turning insides and the unpleasant heat that settled in her stomach.

"So, how about we start with your training?" His focus shifted.

A wave of excitement ran through her. "Here?"

He pointed to a clearing a few feet away from where the tent stood. Their steps were a mixture of crunching leaves and rocks. His body turned to face her. She was unsure what was coming next.

Conjuring magic from thin air sounded ridiculous to her. If anyone had told her a few weeks ago that she would try to do this, she would've laughed in their faces.

"Magic comes from within. To call to it, your mind must be free of noise."

"Noise?"

"Distractions—you must quiet your thoughts and focus on calling the energy within you," he explained.

"Fine, no distractions," she repeated, but just thinking about doing magic sent her mind reeling.

She tried, however, not to think about Cameron or Simone, who had offered to help her and had asked nothing in return. About Laurie, who had been by her side since she could remember.

She stared at a blurred spot in the autumnal colors of

the trees, and she tried again. Her mother popped into her mind. Anger took over her, suffocating her. Why had she never spoken about magic, taught them to fight back? Why had she never mentioned Arkimedes before?

Why had her father stopped caring about living and left his children behind? Chose to die bedridden like a skeleton over being with them. *Alive.*

"I can see you are spiraling." His voice brought her back.

"Sorry, it's hard not to get attacked by thoughts when there's so much happening here." She waved a hand over and around her head.

"Close your eyes and focus on the noises around you. It's like meditating."

"Do you meditate?" she teased, trying to lift her mood after the sour memories.

"Every time I do magic. Now, focus. Magic comes from the energy within our body, our surroundings. Those of us who have the gift can harness the energy and transform it into what we all perceive as power."

She took a steadying breath and did as he asked. The breeze of the cooling afternoon air hit her face. Her skin prickled in goose bumps.

"It's different for everyone. It differs in intensity and in what it can or can't do." His voice was low.

She didn't have a hard time pinpointing where he was as he circled her. The rustling of dried leaves on the ground, crunching under his feet. She took another slow breath and focused on his steps.

"We know you can heal and enhance your potions. This is true."

Not true. She wanted to protest this. The words were on the tip of her tongue.

"Focus."

The leaves were soft as paper, swaying in the wind. Could she lift them in the air? She remembered how the bees had circled the two of them a couple of days before, protecting them from the spirits that haunted the forest and forming a barrier of winged insects. Nava hoped she could create such a thing to protect Cameron, herself, and Arkimedes.

The silence was suffocating. The nothingness that happened made her skin prickle.

She opened one eye to find Arkimedes looming a few steps away from her. He lifted a brow in a challenge, and she closed them again.

"This isn't working," she said, splaying her hands out before letting them drop to her sides.

"You're overthinking it."

She met his gaze, full of disbelief. "Maybe it was a fluke—the backpack coming to me."

"Did you also accidentally alter your potion with magic to cure the Beekeeper?" he challenged.

Her lips parted in shock. "That wasn't— I didn't."

"You most definitely did. An alchemist potion wouldn't have cured a wound that would have bound the Beekeeper to you," he said with conviction. "Your potion likely had magic, and it runs deeper than just a small dose of power."

"Fine." She remembered how her hand had heated when she touched the creature's wound. "I still don't know how to harness it. When the attack happened, I needed to protect us. I was between a corner and a hard place."

"That is not how the saying goes." He smirked.

"Whatever. You get what I mean."

"Maybe I should make it harder on you."

Her eyes widened. "Like how?"

Arkimedes shrugged, walking around her. She smelled it, the scent of pepper in the air as the dark tendrils of his magic appeared around his body. Nava steadied herself for whatever attack he had prepared for her.

She trailed the long tendrils that surrounded her. But unlike that day training outside his house or the days after, this time she was at peace somehow. The magic didn't scare her as much anymore. It had her in awe.

It rushed to her and wrapped her in a hug of cool mist and spice. She gasped before it pressed her to the hard, warm body of Arkimedes.

"Get out of my hold," he commanded. His voice came out in gasps. He was as affected by the nearness to her body. He focused on her lips.

The warmth of his body molded against her. The rising and falling of his chest was slow as his breaths hit her cheeks. Warmth pooled in her stomach, extending lower, reaching a pinnacle between her legs.

This would not work out. Nava couldn't ever tell him she didn't want to be out of his grasp. She wanted to be even closer, and judging by her body's awareness, Nava wanted much more than his hands touching her.

"I don't want to," she blurted. "What I'm trying to say is *I don't know if I can.*"

Arkimedes held his breath, and she struggled in the magic's grasp. She wanted to disappear. Why, oh why, did her mouth keep running away from her? She had to get these nervous outbursts under control. She didn't want to appear a fumbling mess in front of him, not after what had happened earlier.

Her face was hot with embarrassment. She wished the earth would swallow her whole.

The ground beneath her feet shook. She reached for him, trying to gain balance. The surrounding shadows of his power had dimmed somewhat. Arkimedes's shocked expression told her it had not been him.

A wave of energy pulsed through her body, and shock ran through her. She searched Ark's face, and he nodded before a smile took over his features.

"Unexpected could be very effective," he said.

Nava was aware of how close they were. In her panic, she had jumped to him. Nava needed to put distance in between them. He'd told her he was not available, but neither was she. She dragged her feet while taking a couple of steps back.

A wave of exhaustion hit her almost immediately. Similar to the first time, when her body had drained and she'd fallen asleep. "Is it normal—for this to feel so exhausting?"

"At first. Eventually, you will learn to take energy from your surroundings as well, not only your body." His voice was distant.

Two muscular arms lifted her from where she was standing with a swift movement. One arm under both her legs and one holding her back. She laid her head against his chest and enjoyed the soft drumming of his heart.

"Maybe try not to conjure an earthquake to start with," he teased, and an edge of pride lingered behind each word.

Nava grinned against the soft material of his linen shirt. He laid her over the furs of her bed, which smelled like him.

She was out before his steps left the tent.

CHAPTER FOURTEEN

aw, caw, caw.

The constant loud sound woke Nava from her dreamless slumber. It shook her awake as if an invisible hand had landed on her shoulder. The bird's cries carried a haunted sound, along with the crunching leaves from footsteps around her.

"Get the bird!" A loud, deep voice.

She stumbled out of her bed, sleep clouding her senses. Her heart was hammering as the shadows came closer to the fabric of the tent, silhouetted by the dim light of the moon.

She reached for her coat, the bone-chilling cold air surrounding her as she abandoned the warmth of her furs. The ominous shadows approached, shooting spells from their hands as they pointed to the sky, trying to get to Arkimedes, as he was stuck in his animal curse. Bile rose in her throat as a wave of panic navigated through her.

She picked her blades from the ground, the cold of the metal seeping into her skin and chilling her bones. She was in trouble. Arkimedes's caws still echoed around the emptiness of the night, along with a few screams of pain.

"What the hell is wrong with this bird?" another voice called. They weren't even trying to be quiet. That was how fucked she was.

Nava took a deep breath, steeling her resolve. She guessed she'd rather go down fighting than cowering inside the tent when there was nowhere else to go. Her knuckles turned white as they tightened around the tan worn leather of her weapon's handle.

She lifted to her feet and bolted out of the tent, ducking through the heavy fabric. She held in a scream when she met three large men in black leathers. Time froze as panic overtook her.

Her fight-or-flight mode kicked in, and then she was dodging out of the thick arms of one and running around the tent. There was no use trying to fight them when she was so outnumbered.

Feet pounded against the wet dirt, and icy wind burned her throat and lungs. The screeches of the bird were distant. For a second, she thought she could do it. She would escape.

A black-gloved hand appeared out of the shadows of the night, holding a shiny blade. It hit the side of her head with its cold hilt. Blinding pain shot through her body, making her lose her footing seconds before it all went dark.

IT WAS BONE-CHILLING COLD.

"Miss—are you all right? She's waking up," a low, raspy voice said to someone, his tone concerned and a million miles away from her.

Nava winced when her head rattled in pain. Her eyesight was blurry, and her body ached all over. Her consciousness became sharper as memories of the night came to her in quick flashes. She squirmed under tight ropes. They'd bound her arms and legs. Nava's shoulders hurt almost as much as her head. There was a large cut oozing cold, sticky liquid on the side of her right cheek.

"Miss," the voice repeated.

Nava blinked up in confusion, trying to find the owner of the spoken words. There were two shapes near the trees by her. The drumming in her ears muffled his voice.

It was still nighttime. The morning peeked soft yellows through the canopy's sparser leaves. She traced back to the last thing she remembered as her blurry vision focused on the shapes. She didn't recognize the voice.

"Arkimedes!" She let her head fall back on the bark behind her.

"Shh, you're gonna call them back in here," another voice said in a higher pitch.

A man and a woman were three meters away from her, both bound to a cedar tree that, judging by its sheer size, had to be hundreds of years old.

Was it the night before? How long had she been out? Was Arkimedes all right?

"Who are you?" Nava asked, keeping her voice low. "Where are we?"

"Move little. You hit your head pretty hard—or I guess maybe they did that," said the guy.

"She asks so many questions. This situation could not get any worse, Gavin." The woman rolled her eyes.

Nava stared at her surroundings in silence, trying to find Arkimedes somewhere. Her body tensed, and anxiety built in her chest, making it harder for her to breathe.

She didn't recognize where she was. Nava's attention came to the woman who had spoken. She had smooth bronze skin, a face that would have been pretty—gorgeous, even—had she not been scowling so profoundly. Her hair was a nest of tight curls that spiraled out of her head at a hand's length.

"What are you looking at?" The woman sneered.

Gavin, who was working the binds around his wrists, lifted his head toward the other woman. "Why do you have to be so hostile?" he said in between his teeth. "Don't mind her. We've been tied to these trees for way too long and are tired and hungry."

Nava didn't answer, her mouth dry like sandpaper. Her headache was too intense for her to focus on anything for too long. How long had they been here before her?

She would never see her family again. Never see Cameron grow older, graduate, and become a man she would be proud of.

There was the noise of chattering around them, the soft crunch of twigs. Nava guessed the camp of their abductors wasn't too far from them. Tears dampened her cheeks. Her throat grew swollen as she swallowed her cries.

"Where are we, and who are you?" she asked again, adjusting to the darkness around them.

"My name is Gavin Luna, and this is Violet Ash. As you can see, we have been taken." He focused on her face before he resumed his task of moving his arms, letting out a groan. "I can't even seem to loosen them up a smidge." His head dropped back, hitting the tree with a thump. His Adam's apple bobbed.

"I told you, it's futile," Violet said.

"I'm not trying to escape them—they're too tight, and it's cutting the circulation from my fingers." His black hair was wet with sweat. He had a nasty gash on the side of his head. He moved his arms again with more fervor, grunting as his face turned red with exertion.

"You aren't going to be able to," Violet said, shaking her head in disapproval. "We won't gain anything by having you out for good from exhaustion as the damn ropes drain you."

"It will be worse if we let them take us back to the Iron City." Gavin sneered.

Nava's stomach dropped. They would take them back to the ship and away from this island.

"Bounty hunters—who would have thought? Probably trying to gather as many deserters as they can before heading back." He stopped what he was doing, studying her. "You don't look familiar. Are you new to this part of the island?"

Nava was aware of both of their gazes studying her. "I was on my way to the magical village of the north."

Violet grunted. "Oh, great. What we needed—a Willowbrook girl wanting to see a magic trick."

"I do not want to see any magic tricks." Her voice matched the woman's tone. "I'm trying to warn them about—well, the bounty hunters." She didn't feel like sharing all the details with these strangers. The bonding of their mutual kidnapping only went so far.

"And this Arkimedes you were asking about . . . did they kill him?"

Nava's stomach dropped, her skin growing cold at the words.

"Violet!" Gavin chastised her.

"What? They probably killed him if they didn't bring his ass back here." She shrugged.

"You are such a bitch." Nava's voice shook with anger as she stared at Violet's passive face.

The woman acted like she didn't care that her words had hurt anyone. Gavin shook his head before pushing it back against the tree trunk.

The sky was turning ominously gray. When had the sky turned so dreary? Nava could have sworn the tones of the morning had been present in the sky minutes ago.

"What is all this fuss about?" That voice was silk and cold.

Dread pooled in her stomach as she met the upcoming shape of Devon Black. He radiated elegance even in these humid woods. He wore a black cloak that was iron-pressed with no wrinkle in sight and a purple silk button-down shirt, which made a stark contrast against his milky pale skin. He fixed the cuffs of the shirt.

"They told me they found you last night, Nava Forrest. I had to come to see for myself." He knelt next to her, his ebony eyes shining with contained excitement. His leather-clad hand touched the side of her forehead.

She winced as pain came thundering in her head. "Don't touch me," she said, moving her head out of the way.

"Feisty little kitten." He laughed. His hand dropped from Nava's face. The scent of blackberries and mint lingered on her skin.

"Let me out of these at once, Devon," she demanded, struggling against the ropes that bound her. The movement weakened all the energy from her body.

"Tsk, tsk. It's no use for you to struggle, kitten. The rope will cancel your power. The more you fight them, the more it takes your energy." He pushed up to his full length. Imposing. Not in the same way that Arkimedes was. Devon looked out of place in these woods with his fine silk clothing and the stiff set of his shoulders. The man was slim, with a sinewy, muscular body.

"I see you have met your people." Devon's voice was elegant, as if they were talking over tea. His hand signaled the other prisoners.

"Why do you have us tied to this tree like we are animals? I've done nothing wrong," Nava said again, her pounding headache making her vision blurry. She didn't miss a smug smile spreading across his features.

"Kitten, your rights are nonexistent, worse than any animal. All of you are a shame to our kingdoms and a disgrace to magic," he said, fixing the collar of his new outfit.

She was aware of the stark contrast between them.

Clear societal differences between Devon's expensive, tailored outfit and their clothes. The Society of Crows was the elite force, detached from the crowns' interests. They were meant to protect the citizens, to guard the balance between magic and non-magical people, but they had been seduced by power and money.

It had been one of the reasons Nava's mother had left the Society years before they had to run away. Nava remembered their manor's size back in the city, a palace if she compared it to her home in town.

She focused on Gavin and Violet, who observed their interaction with murderous intent painted on their features. They were both stained with dirt and blood. Their skin was shiny with sweat, their lips dry from not getting enough water to drink while being tied up.

"You can go to hell, prick. No Crow ever needed a bunch of goons to carry his duties. You, however, might be weaker than most if you have to get help from a lot of them," Nava spat, her attention flashing to the noise in the campground.

Devon's face turned from false agreeableness to one of pure fury. Surprised to be called out and insulted. She guessed no one ever challenged him. He laughed and knelt over her, his gloved hand holding on to her chin. She hissed when a spark burned her skin as he came closer. The peppermint smell of his breath hit her face. Nauseated by his closeness, she turned her head away.

"I'm going to enjoy breaking you," he said, and it was the first time the true fire of anger burned behind his expression.

He got up and dusted his hands before throwing a glance at the other two, as if Violet and Gavin were cockroaches in his way, not worth more than a dismissive gesture.

"Enjoy the rain," he mused.

Thunder roared in the sky, followed by the pitter-patter of freezing rain. Their place among the trees had fewer branches and leaves to shield them from the weather.

Coldness seeped into her body. She followed the retreating form of the Crow. His coat flowed in the air. Gavin cursed in another language, staring at Nava, a spark of curiosity and annoyance tinting his features.

"I didn't know one of the Crows was working with the bounty hunters." Gavin's voice was more concerned than before, his skin pale. Mist came out of his lips, caused by the drop in temperature.

"We are even more screwed than I thought." Violet's gaze fixed on Nava. "You taunt him recklessly, not thinking of what your actions would cause. Not to you but for us by approximation."

"Let me remind you. It's not because of me they tied you to this tree. So focus your anger on the person who did it and not someone who's also sharing the fate," Nava said.

Violet bared her teeth. "No, but it's because of you we will get hypothermia by the end of the morning."

Nava pressed her lips together, forcing down the bitter

words that tasted like bile in her throat. There was no point in arguing with someone like Violet. She needed to focus on warmth and how to get out of this mess.

Devon Black had not come to this island in search of the Forrests, but for deserters. She had been found by accident because Devon knew what she looked like. Bad luck, yes, but at least she was happy her brother was not in danger. Not unless he ever decided to find her.

Her stomach sank because, without a shadow of a doubt, her spirited, brave little brother would do that as soon as he came of age.

She studied the cloudy sky as it poured icy rain over them. Sunrise had come; it was only a matter of time before Arkimedes would come. Nava wished he would leave, save himself, and warn the village people like they'd intended.

There was no victory against a Crow. They were the most skilled soldiers—the most powerful sorcerers and warlocks in the kingdoms. Even though Nava had taunted Devon, his strength terrified her.

If she were to judge by her companions' faces, her fears were based on reality. She tried to tune out their voices as they talked about escapes. Her attention traveled up the trees. She blinked at the heavy drops of rain that hung in her eyelashes, her body numb from the cold.

At least the headache was duller, driven down by the temperature and the exhaustion of her body.

A tree moved, and Nava blinked in confusion, her focus sharpening as she followed its movements. Bark sticking off places, a waxy chest, and a deep hollow gaze trailed her. Gnarly teeth shaped from tree bark turned into an expression of despair. This creature intended to come to aid her.

Nava was unsure why she could tell his intentions as if

she were staring at her own. She tried to find the sign of bees. The frozen rain would prevent them from coming.

She shook her head at the creature, hoping whatever connection they shared, it would read her mind. Nava didn't want it to get hurt. The risk wasn't worth it.

Stand back.

CHAPTER FIFTEEN

*T*he magical rainstorm didn't waver, not after the temperature had risen with the apparent passing of time.

The agonizing screech of a man by the campground jolted her awake. Arkimedes had arrived.

Clear commotion boomed around them. The three of them stared through the forest where the tents stood, where men in heavy cloaks and furs were running, carrying heavy weaponry. They couldn't see well what was happening behind the screams.

Thunder boomed.

A tree fell with a ferocious bang. Arkimedes rose in the distance, as if suspended in the air. Nava blinked at the sight of sable wings that jutted out of his white shirt. With long feathers that spread out, he perched onto a tree branch. Tendrils of magic radiated from his body like hands, arms—like he was carrying people's souls within his power. His face contorted in rage.

Nava's heart skipped a beat when she took him in, and the palms of her hands tingled as her nerves flared. Her worry shot up for him. He could be harmed, captured, or, worse, killed. She struggled against the binds around her body, ignoring how exhausting it was.

The sight of Arkimedes and the fight against a whole group of bounty hunters rendered her companions speechless. Nava followed Devon Black, who was crouched down on the floor, an arm to his side with the power of ice swirling around his hand. His face was not so polished and cocky anymore.

Thunder roared in the sky again, and a bolt of lightning struck down. Her hair stood on end with static, her ears ringing as one tree went up in flames. Arkimedes dodged the weather attack, jumping out of the tree branch with barely enough time. Shadow figures made a shield and chased after him.

The tree went up in flames. Devon screamed something in a clear commanding voice. Arkimedes didn't answer. His wings expanded, like the most magnificent vision she ever saw. Gavin stilled at the sight of him.

He was muscle and strength. A plume of smoky ink followed his movements as he leaped down on Devon. Ice and snow exploded around them. Smoke billowed out, hiding them from view.

A man's cry of pain echoed in the camp once again, and her blood chilled with the thought that it could be Arkimedes. She resumed her fight against her binds, having stopped to stare wide-eyed and open-jawed at the man she had been traveling with. Her friend. Nava's body ached, her extremities numb.

Nava could see little from her vantage point but could hear the hits of pounding flesh. The smoke cleared, and Arkimedes came into view. His hand raised as an upcoming bounty hunter ran to him, weapon lifted. A wave of shadows left his hand, and the man collapsed to the ground.

He didn't hover, but he met her gaze from across the clearing. His usual stormy green eyes were shaded by anger as he took her in. Nava's stomach dropped. The realization of his power hit her hard, then he was gone.

Her lips parted in shock when the swirls of charcoal smoke were left in the spot he'd been mere moments ago. The screams and the clanking of metal echoed around them.

Gavin became frantic, studying his surroundings.

"It's one of them," Violet hissed. "Gavin, I don't want to go back."

One of whom?

"Don't worry, Vi. It seems he is fighting against the ones who took us," Gavin said, his voice winded.

Nava turned to Violet, who also was trying to get off her binds, and the realization hit her: they were afraid of *Arkimedes*, more so than Devon.

Something heavy landing on the ground next to her had her gasping. Gavin and Violet let out a scream. Her attention was on the shape of the Beekeeper in front of her. The stature of it was imposing. Its long, wooden fingers came to the rope and winced on contact.

Its sorrow-filled face came to her, and she realized it couldn't help her even though it wanted to. The magic in the ropes would cancel the Beekeeper's magic.

"Go. I will be fine," she said with a conviction she didn't have before, but it was rooted deep within her stomach.

The creature nodded, its movement jerky, and with a speed hard to register, he vanished up the trees.

Nava met the shocked gazes of her captured companions. She didn't like saying or explaining anything to these strangers. Especially since her own brain was trying to figure it out. When silence descended upon the campground, the eeriness of it became real.

Nothing besides the cold remained. Thunder came, and rain fell heavier upon them, making it hard to see anything.

The silence lasted longer than she cared for. Her sanity hung by a thread as she waited on a string of hope for something that told her Arkimedes was all right. A tall shape appeared from the darkness of the trees.

She recognized the way of walking—no, running as the person came closer to them. He was wearing his coat, also drenched by the rain. Wings no longer grew out of his back.

"Are you okay?" Arkimedes's voice was soft as puffs of breath left his body.

His blade cut through the rope that bound her. Nava shook free of it, and as soon as the textile dropped, the exhaustion lifted from her body. The tentative, soft caress of his fingertips against the side of her cheek ignited the nerve endings of her skin.

"They hurt you." His jaw tensed as he trailed his fingers down, gently touching near where her open wound was. He was examining it with a frown.

"I'm fine. It's just a scratch," she assured him. Her hand came to rest on top of his, giving it a tentative squeeze.

She *was* fine, now that he was here and could scoop her off the ground, where she had turned into a gigantic pile of mush.

"It's more than a scratch." Gavin's voice shook them out of their exchange, making both of their stares travel to him. "You might have a minor concussion. You were a little dazed, and the bright light seemed to bother your eyes."

"Are you a healer?" Arkimedes stood and meandered toward Gavin, who nodded.

Nava got to her feet and took a tentative step, her surroundings spinning as she winced and reached toward the nearest tree, trying to steady the dizziness that engulfed her.

"Easy," Arkimedes urged her and was next to her in an instant. He studied her features with worry etched on his handsome face.

"Might be best if you sit for a moment," Gavin said from his spot on the ground.

"Nava. My name is Nava."

"Nava. If your friend here can let me out of these, I would love to look at your wound," he said, staring at Arkimedes, whose jaw tensed.

"He won't let us out," Violet mumbled, speaking for the first time in a while. Nava had forgotten she was there. For someone who had chastised Nava about baiting a powerful warlock, she didn't seem to take her own advice.

"Of course we will." Nava met Arkimedes's gaze. However, he did little to move from his spot. Nava took a step toward Gavin, intending to get him out of the binds. Her steps faltered, and nausea hit her hard again. The ground spun. Her cold, wet clothes made her movements stiff.

"Don't move. The healer said you might have a concussion."

"Please help him out of those," she said in between her teeth.

"Of course," he said.

Her headache was too intense so she sat down, struggling with her garments that were stiff and half-frozen, taking a calming breath. The rain was ceasing, becoming a drizzle. She wasn't sure if the numbness around her body was due to disorientation or the fact that the cold wind made it more apparent she'd been rained on for a long time.

It was clear by the tense lines in Arkimedes's shoulders that he trusted the strangers as much as they trusted him. They eyed him when he took a knife out of his belt and knelt in front of Gavin. A silent exchange happened before the sharp blade cut through the binds.

Gavin's chestnut eyes focused on Nava. The softness behind them spoke volumes of how thankful he was. He was up on his feet before Arkimedes was done cutting through Violet's binds and walking toward Nava with assured steps.

"Let me see this." Gavin possessed a calming smile. His touch was cooler than Arkimedes's had been, his fingers damp and stiff from the cold or lack of circulation. He studied the unbroken expanse of skin on the side of her face. "Are you feeling dizzy?"

She nodded at his question and winced as the pain in her head intensified.

"We don't have time to play healer, Gavin. We need to warn Roman." Violet's sharp tone drove all eyes to her. She was rubbing her wrists as she stared down at Arkimedes.

"Nava might have a minor head injury. Her speech pattern appears normal. She lost consciousness for a bit when she was brought over and looked dazed. She needs to rest—we're to set camp somewhere safe. The village is three days away. She won't be able to make the trip there so quickly," Gavin said, choosing to ignore his companion.

Arkimedes's face turned to one of more concern. "Devon escaped. I don't think anywhere in this forest is safe." Something heavy was in his expression.

"You cannot seriously be considering sticking around them." Violet's body shook with tension.

"I am, dearest." Even though Gavin used a loving name with her, his voice was anything but.

"We would just be sitting targets for more of the Crow's goons to come and get us." Her purple eyes went to Arkimedes. "Or worse. She's useless and is going to slow us down!"

The tick in Arkimedes's jaw told Nava his patience was running thin. If she were honest with herself, so was hers.

"I would like to remind you this useless person just saved your sorry ass's life," Nava snapped. And it hadn't technically been her who'd saved them, but those were semantics.

The air of Gavin's laughter hit her face as he shook his head, amused. "You don't have to stay with me, dear. For one, I'm grateful to them for saving us and would like to help Nava."

"You gotta be kidding me," she huffed, not moving a muscle to leave.

"Am I wrong to assume our kidnappers won't be waking up soon?" Gavin's attention came to Arkimedes.

"Not in this lifetime," he said with a shrug. His brow dipped into a deep frown. Her stomach knotted. He'd killed them.

But, her mind supplied, if he hadn't, they would have hurt or killed all of them.

He had killed all but one, Devon Black. How was he feeling about this? Had he killed before? It was a silly question. If he had been a part of any of the crown's armies, he'd *had to*.

"We can't stay here. They aren't the only ones in their group. The others will come searching for them. From what I gathered from their conversation, they're expected to be back at their main camp within the fourth night,"

Gavin said. "That was before the Crow showed up, of course."

Arkimedes nodded. She wished they could talk more freely, as they usually did. Even though she liked Gavin, she wasn't sure she trusted either of them yet.

"I can carry Nava so we can move faster," Arkimedes said.

"With the magic you just used, you'll be drained of energy for a while. We can take turns."

"I'm here, and I'm sure I have a say on whether I get carried around like a fra-fragile doll or not." Nava's words came a bit harsher.

"Kitten does have a bite." Violet's voice was amused.

Nava shot her a glare. "D-don't call me that." The reminder of Devon's nickname rattled around in her brain. By Violet's smile, the intent had been to get a rise out of her.

"I'm sorry, Nava," Arkimedes said, kneeling in front of her. "We have to move quicker than you can manage since you're injured. We need to gain distance from this camp," he said as a matter of explanation.

"B-but is it necessary for you to ca-carry me . . . ? I might be too heavy." Her voice became a whisper at the end.

His expression softened. "You'll be just fine." His smile eradicated whatever resolve she'd had before to be less codependent of him after he'd saved her. *Again.*

"Okay. Fine." She wasn't unreasonable. "Is-is the village that's three days away the-the Northern Village?" she asked Arkimedes, who nodded.

"Roman, who Violet mentioned, is their leader—you might remember him from our conversation with Andreas." Arkimedes's voice lowered enough that she wasn't sure the others could hear him. So close to her ear, the air of his breath hit her skin, raising goose bumps everywhere.

So they had a common goal, the Northern Village, the path they'd been traveling for weeks to warm them about their common enemy. To stay in more significant numbers and avoid being taken back to a life of servitude.

"You should be better within a day. We can reassess then," Gavin conceded with a nod.

Nava met Arkimedes's gaze as his hand went under her knees and behind her back and he lifted her from the ground as if she weighed nothing.

CHAPTER SIXTEEN

*I*t turned out they were right. Nava couldn't walk even if she wanted to. The forest was disorienting on its own. With her injury, she had a hard time focusing on where they were going. As soon as Nava pressed her feet to the ground, everything spun around. They walked and walked.

The camp they found was terrific in the darkening light of the day. Arkimedes sat her on the ground, while Gavin stood in a wide stance and conjured two large tents out of thin air. Those were perfection in a tent. She squinted when she found Arkimedes's amused expression fixed on her.

His lips pressed down into a thin smile as he averted his gaze to the handiwork of the healer. Violet had left to check on the perimeter of their camp and make sure Devon hadn't followed them.

"Ark—medes," she whispered, nausea hitting her hard.

He was kneeling by her in a blink of an eye. The sun was setting, and Gavin focused on them. Curiosity tinted his features.

What did he think when he looked at Arkimedes and her? Was he wondering why Devon Black seemed to pay more attention to her? Or how Arkimedes and her knew each other?

"M . . . not."

"Shh, bee, the tent it's ready. I'm sure it's not to your standards." The playful smirk was back on his face.

Nava narrowed her gaze as a soft laugh escaped him. At least his mood had brightened somewhat.

She didn't want to go in alone; she dreaded going to sleep to find people lurking over her tent once again and taking her against her will. She shook her head, finding words weren't coming to her.

His hand came to her shoulder, squeezing it softly. "I understand you probably don't want to be alone, and you won't be. I'll stay with you tonight. The only way I can, but I will still be there," he promised.

A knot formed in her throat. She lunged at him, hugging him. He held her just as firmly. Perhaps he had been as afraid of losing her as she'd been of losing him. Her energy was dwindling once again, and she was out before she had much more to worry about.

THE SOFT MELODY OF BIRDS chirping around her woke Nava from slumber. The warmth of the morning filtered through the fabric of the tent. This was the most comfortable she had slept since her nights in Arkimedes's cabin. She groaned at the throbbing pain in her head, like her skull was splitting open.

"Are you presentable?" Gavin said.

Warily, she studied her state with horror. She was still

wearing her dirty clothes from the day before, caked in mud and blood. Covered in a familiar woolen blanket.

She pulled the fabric up more and brought her hand to her head, patting down her matted curls. "As presentable as I would be in my current situation," she answered.

His head peered in through the flaps of the tent. "How are you feeling this morning?"

"Like my head is being hammered by river-dwelling sprites."

He walked in with a tray of potions and gauze in his hands. He knelt by her and, with nimble hands, checked the previous bandage. One she didn't remember having on.

She sniffed, trying to catch the scents of the potions to get a sense of what he was using to aid her healing. But she couldn't pick a scent. Her injury must be the most annoying thing she'd ever had.

He answered her questioning gaze. "It's looking better already, but you need to lay low and rest for at least another day—maybe two."

"Isn't it dangerous? With Devon Black at our heels, I'm concerned that staying here and waiting for me to feel better will make us be sitting ducks for him to come and snatch. "

Gavin nodded, but his gaze didn't shift from hers, his fingers patting a potion against her wound. Gentle enough not to be too painful, but a simple reminder that she was unwell. The room spun, and she leveled him with a glare.

"We worked some spells last night and a few more this morning. They aren't the strongest, but they should hold for a couple of days." He smiled. "I'm not sure how much you know—but your boy, he is one of the most powerful sorcerers I have ever met, and I've met my fair share. He seems intent on protecting you. I wouldn't worry about it. Concern yourself with recovering."

Nava understood his words. Arkimedes's power was something that had left them all speechless the day before. Still, Nava preferred him to be far away from the Crow. Also, Gavin wasn't aware that Arkimedes wouldn't be able to help them if they were to be attacked in the middle of the night, like it had happened to her.

It wasn't her secret to tell, so she guarded it and nodded.

"We aren't too shabby, either," he said, reading her concern. "Violet and I—and you, if I were to judge a sorceress by the fact that a *Beekeeper* tried to save you."

Her bee creature. Wait, why did she call him *hers*? The thought was so natural, it came to her as easy as breathing. She blinked in confusion.

"I meant to ask you how something so rare and pure came to be bound to you."

Nava shrugged, wanting to protect it at all costs. She didn't want to divulge that she had found it dying, mourning the loss of someone he loved. Another Beekeeper had been murdered. She guessed the culprits were the bounty hunters, though at this point, she wasn't so sure. "I don't know, either," she said; it wasn't a lie, but she kept it simple. Even though she liked Gavin so far, Nava was not so naïve to trust blindly. It didn't mean that because they had a mutual enemy, they would become automatic friends.

Her brain supplied Arkimedes's image almost immediately. Deep down, she knew that whatever was happening with *him* was anything but ordinary. She had to be cautious about letting her feelings drive her actions.

She had never been attracted to another person this way before, both physical and emotional, and at such a fast rate. She was mated to a stranger she had never seen before, and it made her cautious of any man. He had so much power, it could mean he had been a Crow in his past.

But he wasn't her mate. He had told her so.

"There, you are ready. I was going to bring you some food, but I think a bit of sunshine and fresh air might be nice for you." He got up to his feet and left her alone.

Nava got up. Her equilibrium was off but not like the day before. The backpack sat against the wall of the tent. She walked to it, taking slow breaths to calm her sudden dizziness.

She picked her last set of clean clothes and found her canteen of water. She dampened her towel and cleaned her skin the best she could with what she had available. It took time, but by the end of it, she was a lot cleaner. The grime and memories of the day before were fading into another nightmare.

Nava battled with her tangled hair for an eternity before she tied it into a quick braid. She remembered how her mother had braided her hair before going on missions as a Crow.

Her mother always told her that their wavy hair was a blessing and a curse, but it was still better to keep it out of the line of vision when in battle. Nava liked to have hers wild and long, flowing against the salty ocean wind in town. Free, unlike her.

She picked a pocket mirror from one of her backpack pockets. When she shoved it there, she'd thought it was silly. She stared at the reflection of her face, the freckles that speckled her nose, her wide lips that were paler than usual. One blue eye and one brown eye, framed by thick brows.

Her fingers combed her eyebrows. Coming down to her cheeks, where she pinched some color back.

She had lost weight since she'd last seen her reflection back at Arkimedes's house. She guessed it was expected with all the exercise, the energy spent using magic, and the lack of substantial meals. She pushed the mirror back into the pocket and took a steadying breath.

Nava pulled the flap open. Black things hovered on the ground by her backpack, calling her attention. She stared at the fluff floating in the air. Black down feathers, the color of the night.

She picked one up between her fingers. The tiny strands shimmered indigo when the light hit them—the same color as the enormous wings that had grown out of Arkimedes's back the day before.

He had kept his word and stayed with her last night the way he could—in his cursed body.

CHAPTER SEVENTEEN

*H*er healing came quicker in the forest than a wound this bad would have healed in Willow-brook. Magic had a big part in it. At first, the tingle of worry was present every time Gavin applied the salves and potions to the gap on her head. By the second day in this camp, Nava was less worried and more curious.

Arkimedes slept most of the day and spent the night as a prisoner inside an animal body, perched on top of her backpack while she spoke about Cameron. He was obser-vant, and she didn't know if he understood a word she said but was comforted by the swirling magic in his irises, so much like his human form.

By the third day, the nausea and dizziness had all but gone away. Gavin's wounds were just a small scratch. His face had been swollen, presumably by someone hitting it repeatedly. With the bulges gone, he had to be around the same age as Arkimedes, maybe in his late twenties or early thirties. He was handsome in a rugged way.

She sat by the fire, watching Violet and Gavin spar a few feet away from her, following their movements when fists connected and grunts were voiced. Violet cursed when he connected a mean-looking punch to the side of her arm.

"You dirty slob of a bastard." She jumped back into a crouch, like a feline ready to pounce.

"Tsk, tsk. You've gotta protect your weak spots, dearest wife," he said but didn't sound apologetic. His face twisted into a wicked smile.

"Don't call me that." Her voice went up an octave. Nava's lips parted when her brain caught up to his words. *Wife?*

Violet leaped toward Gavin, who was ready to meet her attack. They weren't holding back. Nava winced at the pounding flesh, watching their every move.

"Intense." A voice behind her made her jump, and a scream escaped her lips. She met the looming shape of Arkimedes. He was holding a steaming cup of his tea in one hand, an eyebrow raised at her reaction.

"You scared me to death, Ark!" She brought her hand to her chest.

"I wasn't quiet." He smirked, sitting down next to her as his attention followed the pair's sparring.

"They aren't holding back at all—aren't they afraid of hurting each other?" she asked, meeting his gaze.

Arkimedes shrugged, taking a long gulp of his disgusting drink. His complexion was golden, rested. "By the looks of it, they want to." He pointed.

Violet screamed, round-kicking Gavin, who stumbled back with a gasp of pain.

"I can't watch this," she said, her focus trailing them with intent. "I can't . . . look away, either."

Arkimedes laughed, and a comfortable silence came over them. It had become second nature to enjoy the other one's company.

"How are you feeling this morning?" His deep honey-like voice broke the insults from the other sorcerers.

She nodded. "Much better today. No dizziness, headache seems more manageable. Gavin said the wound is almost all healed."

"Perfect." He studied the sky. Blue peeked through the tall forests, and it was warm for a fall afternoon. "The wards are fading. It should be our last night here."

She followed his gaze, squinting at the sky, trying to see whatever he saw, but all she could discern was nature. Wind stirred the leaves on the trees, the slow movement of white billowy clouds that painted the sky. Branches shifted when squirrels ran by them. "I can't see anything," she grumbled, staring at her half-eaten bread, annoyed at her lack of impressive magic.

Surrounded by Gavin and Violet, who could fight, or Arkimedes, who had displayed magic unlike she'd ever beheld before. She was not knowledgeable on the subject of magic, but she *knew* she was unimpressive.

"We should resume your training now that you are feeling better," he said.

Her cheeks burned. Memories of their last training session came to her in flashes, how close they had been, how much she had wanted him to kiss her. She never knew she could be this romantic before. Never again would she poke fun at Simone and her romantic tendencies.

"Like now?" she asked. A rush of excitement went through her body, surprising her. She turned to Gavin and Violet. They were both resting against separate trees.

Violet fixed her shoe, quiet while observing Gavin, who massaged his shoulder and returned her gaze. Their expressions confused Nava, a mixture of longing and anger.

Arkimedes dropped another log onto the fire. "No. Tomorrow if you are fully recovered."

She bit the bread, enjoying the softness of the texture, its delicious buttery flavor melting against her palate. She had woken up to a fresh loaf of bread earlier this morning. When asked how it had appeared, Arkimedes had been intentionally cryptic.

His expression danced with delight. He'd been teasing her previously strong dislike for magic and her change of heart. Still, magical bread tasted better than no bread at all. Even though her skin still prickled with fright when the spicy scent of magic wafted through the air, she was finding comfort in it.

Love was such a big word, one she'd only used with her family. She never imagined she would feel this way for another human, having decided at an early age she wouldn't pursue searching for her soulmate.

Could she grow to love him? It was so easy to care for him. To get lost in this attraction that burned in her veins and extended through her body.

"Yesterday, you said Cameron wanted to travel the world, to get to know his nature." His comment made her head snap back to him.

She had a brief mention as she'd stared at the ceiling of the tent. There had been a black bird perched on top of her backpack. "Yes, I was so afraid that day. Then Devon walked into my shop, and my life changed forever."

"Do you think he would like magic?"

"Oh, yes. Unlike myself, he is so brave and smart." Nava beamed with pride. "If it had been him, he would've mastered a spell by now."

Arkimedes's brows deepened. "You are brave and smart."

Her face warmed at his words. A smile pulled at her lips. "Thank you for noticing."

"Of course." His gaze moved to the other pair.

"Do you have siblings? Family?' Her voice was tentative. "I know the crown takes children away from their families once the magic comes. I always wondered if you had one to go back to."

Arkimedes was quiet for a long time, his gaze back to her. Her breath caught in her throat at the raw pain behind his irises. His expression wasn't guarded, however. "I never knew my family." He added, "I was dropped at the doorstep of an orphanage when I was one. Or so I was told."

She tried to mask anything he could see as pity, even though her soul ached for him.

"I presented magic at a young age. I was five when they came for me. The orphanage had written them, claiming they had a half-fae in their care." Arkimedes breathed and took a long pensive sip of his drink.

"Couldn't they tell before, by your eyes, that you were mixed?"

"The eyes came when I was five. It was the first sign a different kind of magic ran through me."

She had known Arkimedes for weeks, and this was the first time he'd shared something like this. The truth behind his words horrified her. He had been part of the army of the crown since he was five years old? Raised by soldiers. "It's horrible that they gave you away so young."

"The crown pays a pretty penny for a magical child. I'm guessing my bounty alone covered their expenses for a year." He shrugged. "I was treated well, better than the orphanage. It's more than I could have hoped for."

Arkimedes's guarded nature became so clear to her. Abandoned at such a young age, moved around, and raised to be a weapon. "Do you know anything about your family?"

Silence.

"No." He was quiet. They both followed the other pair sparring once again. This time, magic was part of their training.

"I guess they don't deserve you," she said, and the intensity of his gaze burned her. Nava's hand came to his, the warmness of his skin a welcome change to her chilled fingers.

"Your hands are freezing," he said.

Her chest tightened. "That's because there is nothing I can use to warm my hands. I'm talking about a hot cup of something to hold while we talk. All of you heathens like that disgusting tea."

Arkimedes's soft roll of a chuckle made her smile. He had changed the subject, and she was not eager to bring that pain back to his face. She was glad he had shared a part of himself with her.

"I guess I have to start drinking it if I want to be part of the sorcerer team," she said.

"It's a drink they give us in the army," he said with a shrug. "After a while, you grow used to the taste and the energy it gives you."

"Coffee is great with cream or milk. Two cubes of sugar." She sighed. "Oh, how I miss it."

"I'll make sure next time I see Andreas to get you some."

She beamed. "Is that where you got the bread?"

"You would never know." His lips tilted into a rakish smile.

Nava had been staring at him while she chewed her bread in silence. She forced her focus on the other sorcerers.

Gavin walked in their direction, more at ease than they had been before. "Good morning," he greeted.

Arkimedes nodded, taking another sip of his drink. Gavin sat on the other end of the fire. The impacts had reddened his skin, already bruising in places. Nava gaped wide-eyed at the angry hits on his glistening skin.

"They don't hurt anymore," Gavin explained.

"Why train so hard when it's just the two of you?"

"Because our adversaries won't hold back. It's of no use to hold back on punches and not do our best. We don't want to get hurt, so when we are training, we must get out of the way."

Nava focused on Violet, who walked the camp's perimeter, checking the wards that undoubtedly they all saw but Nava.

"Violet holds back," Arkimedes said.

"I know." Gavin shook his head. "I taunt her to see if anger gets her to give it her all, but she is strong-willed."

"Arkimedes can train with her," Nava offered, and the relaxed ambiance darkened around them.

"No." Both of their words came at the same time, with the same intensity.

"O-kay," Nava said.

Men.

They ate in silence, and by the time Violet joined them by the fire, the tension had lifted somewhat.

"The wards are weaker. We have to move." Her voice was sharp and unwavering. Her smooth skin was tainted red, her knuckles bloodied.

"We can't. Nava needs at least another night." Arkimedes's flat tone matched hers.

"I wasn't asking you." Venom dripped off every word, and distaste painted her features.

Arkimedes's face was unmoving as he shrugged. Nava's turned from one to the other; she stirred in her spot.

"You are more than welcome to leave," Arkimedes said and pointed away from the camp. "No one is holding you back."

"Maybe I will because if the Crow doesn't get us, the Neems will. Tomorrow is a full moon. They will be here come midday." Her words and expression lacked the sharpness of distrust, unlike the day they'd met.

"Violet, please, Arkimedes and Nava saved us. You know better."

"I don't want us to be here and get kidnapped again," she said.

Gavin lifted a piece of bread to her. "Eat something. You're angry because of the lack of sugar."

Nava's lips twitched.

Violet snatched the bread out of his hand and stormed off to her tent without another word.

CHAPTER EIGHTEEN

*T*he next morning, they left their camp when the sun was rising. Nava opened her eyes to a mild headache and Arkimedes's head poking through the door of her magic tent. He'd recently trimmed the beard he had been growing the past few days down to a stubble. He looked absolutely delicious.

When had she become like this?

"We should get going in the next fifteen minutes," he said, and before she could say anything, he was gone.

She jumped out of bed and stuffed her clothes into her backpack, making a mental note to wash them in the next day or so. She braided her hair and resumed the washing routine she had done for the entire trip. As her second foot met the cold dirt ground outside, the heavy scent of magic came around, and wind enveloped her. She blinked and turned to find an empty spot where her tent had been.

She stepped back from the spot, magic still lingering in the air. Violet's hand came down in front of the campfire, and the flames suffocated. Gavin was finishing with his tent, his steps bringing him over to her. His hands reached for her bandage.

"Hey—" she complained.

He peeled the bandage back and leveled her with a glance. "We don't have time for you to complain and proceed to tell me how you have rights, blah blah. The spirits will descend upon us any moment now, from whatever dimension they come from, and we *don't* want to deal with them."

Nava shut up. She didn't need to be reminded of the horrifying truth of the ghosts that haunted these forests, angry spirits taken by magic and brutality, never able to rest, always coming back for vengeance.

"Where is Arkimedes?" she asked after Gavin had finished setting her straight. She helped pick up a couple of leftover bowls, which soon disappeared out of her hand.

Violet gave her a pointed look. "The kitten is always worried about the fae." Violet's mocking ground on Nava's nerves.

"He went to do a perimeter check before we leave." Gavin ignored Violet. "I didn't paint you for someone who cared about whether people were fae or not, my dearest."

"I don't, for regular people *I like*, which is not him," she said with a shrug.

"Do you even like anyone?" Nava's chin lifted in the air.

Violet smiled like a cat. "Not usually, no." Her eyes flashed to Gavin.

Nava was curious once again, then she found she shouldn't care. Violet was rude and mean, and she had better things to do than worry about their love life, even though it *was* interesting.

Arkimedes came back down from a tree. The daylight was dim enough that it gave the illusion of him floating, his wings like shadows. They disappeared behind his back in a blink. Her heart sped up at the jarring image, the beauty, and the strangeness of it all.

In the middle of her recovery from her head injury, she had forgotten to ask him about it. Why did he have wings? Was it something he had inherited from his fae genes? Or was he bending his curse to his will somehow?

She walked to him, curiosity blooming in her chest, and grabbed the straps of her backpack, trying to alleviate the heaviness of the load she carried. The weight of it dug into her shoulders.

"Morning." His gaze avoided hers, swirling with raw emotion, guarded.

"Good morning." She brought her hand to his arm. Maybe her questions about the wings could wait longer.

"How are you feeling today?" His voice dipped lower in concern.

"Just a *very* mild headache left. It's the heaviness of the backpack. It's killing my shoulders."

Nava regretted it when it left her lips. She had forgotten who was around her. All three of them lacked a backpack but were always wearing fresh clothes. It had her face burning.

She pulled at the sleeve of her tunic, trying to hide the stain that peeked from her long-sleeve shirt.

"You can—"

"No."

"Hear me out," he said, and she pressed her lips into a thin line. "It can be part of your training, so you don't drain your body when you do magic."

"Fine, so what is it I'm supposed to do with this training of yours?"

"You can make your backpack weigh nothing," he said

with a shrug. "That way, you can stubbornly carry the thing but won't throw your back in the process."

"Ha-ha, it's not that I'm stubborn." She crossed her arms over her chest at his pointed expression. "It's not. I don't know how to do what you do, and I don't want you or anyone else fixing everything for me. The situation is frustrating enough as it is."

"Fine. In this case, it wouldn't be the Grays taking care of your problem for you or me. It will be you alone."

She focused her mind on her backpack, reeling back to what Arkimedes had said. "The Grays?"

He pressed his lips together, lowering his head to the ground. "It's a way to refer to deserters."

Her face was slacked. "Arkimedes!"

"Okay, fine, I'm sorry."

"What are you sorry about? Does that mean I'm a Gray too? Is it a negative word? It sounds like it," she sputtered.

His face lost color with every single one of her words. Regret shaded his expression. "Yes—no." He took a breath. "It makes us *all* Grays. In the eyes of the kingdom, Grays are sorcerers, warlocks, and sorcerers who have mid-level magic and run away from oppression to forests where magical creatures live." He brought his hand over his face. "These lands, where we all ran to—the ones that are habitats for fae, spirits—are usually called the Greyland. The unwanted places."

"Like Willowbrook?" Which was located on the *Grey Island*. It made sense.

"Yes."

"So is it used as a bad word?" she asked again.

"Yes."

"What are we? Why aren't you considering yourself a Gray?" Her voice carried some heat.

Panic took over his features. His lips parted to speak when a bee landed on Nava's hand.

The soft fluttering of wings hit her skin, sending shivers down her body. The bee's fur tickled her. The contrast of its colored body against Nava's olive skin was jarring. Nava focused on the insect with curiosity when another one landed next to it, then another one.

What concerned her wasn't the bees. It was the sense of dread growing in her stomach. Nava faced Arkimedes, whose eyes were wide, staring at them with equal shock.

"Wha—?"

"*Run.*" The voice came into her mind, jolting her. She didn't have to wait to figure it out. She had to be out of there immediately. She grabbed Arkimedes's hand.

"*Run!*" She sprinted. The bees flew, and she followed them without a doubt crossing her mind.

It nudged the back of her mind, telling her it was strange that she trusted these insects, that she sensed their intent and where to go when she followed them. Her human brain thought this wasn't normal, but her magical side *knew* it was right.

Arkimedes ran next to her, checking his surroundings where ghosts materialized. She didn't stare at the dead faces this time. The bees surrounded her, leading her way. Gavin's voice boomed in the clearing, yelling at Violet to run, and their steps tailed not far behind.

She wanted to run faster, make her body weightless. Her backpack hurt her shoulders, so she called it to be light as a feather. The bees pivoted, and so did she, jumping over a fallen tree.

She let go of Arkimedes's hand, using her motion to propel her forward. She needed to be faster. White bodies appeared in the hole between the thick trees in front of her. Her mind supplied the gnarled image of a pale man, dead, having been taken long ago if the state of decomposition was anything to go by.

"Dammit, they are everywhere," Gavin gasped, his voice sounding far.

Arkimedes's presence next to her provided a sense of relief in the chaos. He had no issue keeping up with her, with his fit body and long legs, following her direction even though she wasn't voicing them out loud. This other connection was strange to her.

Five more bees appeared, their round bodies making it clear where she needed to go.

A face appeared in front of her, and her heart jolted in fright.

"*No!*" Nava gasped, memories flowing through her mind of the first time she had seen the Neems.

The ghost, which wasn't so much a ghost but a lifeless body made of pale rotten flesh, opened its mouth, a ray of magic inside the pit of death. She wished for a thousand bees to shield them from their attack.

Thousands of bodies came flying down, some real and some made of light, shielding Arkimedes and her from the upcoming attack. Arkimedes grabbed her hand and pulled her in another direction, running faster.

Nava turned around to make sure Gavin and Violet were following. They weren't far behind, their magic emanating from their bodies in shades of gray. The bees resumed their spot around them, buzzing. The spirits disappeared behind their small bodies.

They ran. Nava's ragged breath burned her lungs, her body hot from exertion, even though the chilled air burned her cheeks. When they left the area where the spirits of this Greyland were haunting, her body relaxed. The forest was alive with nature.

Birds chirped. The air was less muggy. The smell of rot lifted from the air.

She slowed down as the bees disappeared from view, flying off to somewhere else in the trees and around the forest. The ones that remained were made of yellow light, landing on her and Arkimedes protectively.

The bees' brightness contrasted with the gloom of power that emanated from his body.

Arkimedes's green eyes focused on them in awe. The heavy steps of both Gavin and Violet came around them. The four of them were gasping for air, their faces shiny with sweat.

The bees faded away, and the heaviness of exhaustion swathed her before everything went dark.

CHAPTER NINETEEN

*W*hen Nava opened her eyes, she was staring at the same ceiling she had woken up to the past few days. Not her beloved handmade tent that had belonged to her father, the one she put up with sticks and flimsy materials. This one was built with magic, making its construction stronger.

She groaned as pain extended down her arms and legs, sore muscles complaining about being overused. Her head spun, but not from her head injury. It was pure unadulterated exhaustion. She racked her mind, trying to come up with memories. All of them came rushing back. Ghosts, them running, and bees—real bees and ones made of *her* magic.

Nava's brain conjured the image of the Beekeeper. It kept helping her. It came for her even though she wasn't calling it. She was not afraid of it, like she had been the day she met him. Her need to protect him was intense. Something had happened that afternoon. An invisible connection had formed in between them, helping her hear it, feel his pain.

She studied her hands. Freckles peppered her skin, but nothing appeared different. She was the same woman who had left Willowbrook, except magic had awoken inside her body. This time, it was she who had saved them.

The idea made her heart soar. Warmth traveled through her body, and she smiled. Her breaths came out easier. She was where she was supposed to be, however scary. Now she needed to survive long enough to bring Cameron to it.

Her spirits deflated. Why would she bring him to danger? To ghosts, murderers, and kidnappers? She bit her bottom lip. She had time to figure things out.

Nava walked out of the tent, bringing her hand to shield her face against the brightness of the fire and the morning light. She met Violet, who was sitting by the fire, picking food out of a brown linen bag on the ground.

Nava hesitated, sitting in front of the woman who studied her movements with interest.

"Kitten." A greeting.

Nava narrowed her gaze at her. "Please stop with the name."

"Why? The guy is a complete dick, but the nickname fits," Violet said lazily.

Nava shook her head and decided ignoring her would be best. She picked up the kettle by the fire and filled a cup with steaming, disgusting army tea. Nava dreamed of the days she could drink something other than this.

"Yesterday's stunt, I must admit . . . it was pretty impressive, kitten." The irony in her voice had toned down a bit.

Nava stared at her over her mug. "Thanks?"

"So, what's up with the bees? Are you and the Beekeeper connected somehow?"

Nava didn't want to talk about this with her. "Are you and Gavin married?"

Violet paled, not having expected this change of subject. Her face changed to a guarded expression. "That is none of your business."

"Oh, well, I guess my issues aren't any of yours, either," she snapped.

Violet's lips curved up into a small smile. "Cute."

"What?"

"You getting flustered. It's cute. I guess I understand what he sees in you," she said and stretched her legs in front of her.

"Who sees what in me?" Nava asked but was side-tracked by the sound of steps.

Arkimedes was coming out of Gavin's tent, scrubbing his face with his hand. He stopped when his eyes met Nava's questioning gaze.

Something was wrong.

She stood and walked to him with long strides. "What happened?"

"Good morning to you too, Nava."

"Are you hurt?"

His brows lifted. "How did you . . . ?"

"It's easy to figure it out. The sun just came out, and you went to find Gavin *the healer* first thing after you transformed back into yourself." She listed the points with her fingers and stared.

He let out an amused laugh and nodded. "I might have gotten hit last night with an arrow."

Nava gasped. She studied his body, trying to find any sign that pointed to a wound.

"It is not visible," he said.

"Where? Are you okay?"

"I'll be fine. It was a clean shot. It happened close to

sunrise. I could transform and walk instead of flying back to our camp."

"Did it hit one of your wings?" She shifted her body weight around, her hand dragging down his arms before reaching for his hand.

He nodded, his hand squeezing hers. He was reassuring her when he was the one who had gotten hurt. "Gavin said I should be fully healed within a week. You don't have to worry."

She got lost in him, enjoying the closeness, her worries dissipating. "Who did it? Do you think it was Devon?"

"I know it was him. It wasn't close to our camp. I flew in a different direction—I couldn't tell how many people he had with him."

"Do we need to leave today?" Her body tensed with dread.

"Yes, we need to get closer to the Northern Village. They'll need time to prepare for an attack."

"You should get some rest before we head out."

"I will," he promised. "I'll go around the perimeter to check that our wards are still strong. Gavin and I set them wider this time to hold back any spirits *and* Devon."

Arkimedes walked past Violet with a polite nod she barely responded to before disappearing in between the trees. Would his wound be visible if he were shirtless? She would work on her healing potion while he rested.

She picked her now-cold cup of tea and brought it back to her lips. It tasted worse when chilled by the weather. Maybe this watered-down, mud-tasting drink had started as a way of torture.

"That's never gonna happen." Violet's voice jarred her attention back to reality, to the campfire and purple irises staring right through her.

"What will never happen?" Nava asked, blinking in confusion.

Violet threw another piece of wood onto the campfire and settled back in her spot. "You and him." She stuffed a large piece of potato bread into her mouth and chewed loudly while her finger traveled through the air, pointing to where Arkimedes had disappeared earlier. The exact place she had been staring at.

"I don't know what you are talking about," Nava blurted. Mortified that anyone else, meaning Arkimedes, might hear Violet's words. The woman wasn't quiet.

"Oh, please. You do a terrible job at hiding it." She scoffed. "With all the heart eyes and nausea-inducing smiles."

"I *don't* do that."

Violet stared at her with no words as she moved to cut a slice of apple with her knife. "Look, I get it. Most people would fall for the chemistry, his body, and the pretty-boy looks," she said. "A ray of sunshine will come out of my ass before he breaks his precious rules and does anything with you."

"What rules?" Nava furrowed her brows. "Have I missed something here? Now you and Arkimedes are good friends and he's shared all his secrets with you?"

"Pfft, we would never be friends," Violet said. "He is one of those who followed the crown's rules. He would never get serious with you unless the crown dictated he had to marry you."

"How do you know?" Nava squinted. "In case you haven't realized, we aren't in the city anymore. No one is forcing anyone into marriage here."

Violet half shrugged, as if Nava's comebacks meant nothing. "I guess I owe you an apology from my outsider's point of view. After all, I must have missed all the ways he's been courting you."

Nava tried not to let the disappointment show on her features. She tried but was unsuccessful, clearly, by Violet's softening expression.

"Please don't cry or something."

"I will not because there is nothing to cry about." The knot forming in her throat told her quite the opposite.

Arkimedes had told her he was not available, that someone like him wasn't ready for a relationship—not in those words, but she got the gist of it. She couldn't be with anyone. Either way, she was mated to someone who wasn't him.

Violet's voice broke the silence "I mean, it wouldn't hurt you to bathe. Perhaps a fresh smell could do wonders."

She brought her nose down to her shoulder and sniffed. "I don't stink!"

"Kitten, you reek." Violet shrugged. "Men in the village wouldn't mind, but pretty fae there . . . he does."

Nava's mouth fell slack. "You don't hold back, do you?"

"Look, I can see a virgin from a mile away. I'm just trying to help you."

"Oh, god, please stop!" Nava rushed to get up, done with the conversation. She took five steps toward her tent before turning back to face the dark-skinned woman sitting by the fire, whose lazy stare came up to meet Nava's fiery one. "I'm *not* a virgin," she declared.

Violet's lips pulled up into a smile.

Nava tried to get along with the other woman. She did. Violet was the only other female in the group, and it would be nice to connect with someone who didn't have massive amounts of testosterone running through them. She tried to fill the void from missing Simone, but she was done.

Nava turned to find Gavin a few steps away. She winced when she noticed his amused expression. His mouth was opening to say something, but she stopped him by lifting her hand and shaking her head.

"Not a word, Gavin," she said through clenched teeth and rushed past him.

NAVA HURRIED TO HER TENT, going for her backpack. She picked fresh undergarments, her thin worn-in towel, and a set of clean clothes she had washed by the stream five days ago. She also rummaged around, picking the handmade soap she had packed once upon a time. It smelled of roses and cardamon, a present from Cameron for her birthday.

He had worked in Simone's bakery during a busy summer day to save enough money to buy it for her. She pursed her lips and told herself she would use it a little today.

Nava hid the clothes under her tunic, pausing, considering taking the whole backpack with her. She shook her head, groaning at the thought of having to carry the heavy thing with her when her neck and shoulders were healing. She could try to make the backpack lighter, but the idea of draining her energy was less appealing than being dirty.

The lake wasn't far away. With the sun out, she hoped the water wouldn't be so cold.

Out of all their camp spots, this one was her favorite. The ground was less muddy and covered in fallen leaves of various red, orange, and brown shades. The colors reminded her of the tones in Cameron's hair.

Nava had always liked camping, her love of nature still a part of her. She'd always had a connection to plants, to the trees around her. Her mother had been good at gardening and had encouraged Nava's love for it.

That was, until Nava disobeyed her, went out of their manor, and got caught by the two Crows. One had happened to be Devon, and the other her soulmate. How a simple rebellious decision and a hobby could change your life forever.

Her mother had hated camping; she used to say she loathed sleeping in uncomfortable beds or dealing with bugs and mediocre food. Nava's ties to nature grew when she was out and away from the town—looking at the stars in the sky.

That was something she'd shared with her dad.

She missed him, missed the way he'd been when he was healthy and robust with so much energy and a jolly mood. Cameron always reminded her of him.

The trees were changing as she got closer to the water. The view was magnificent. The jewel-blue tones of the water reflected the blue sky above her.

Her chest squeezed at memories. She swallowed the thick knot in her throat, urging her mind to move elsewhere. *Anywhere* but her dad. It wasn't hard. Violet's words came back to her brain as she made her way to the shore. She was thinking of Arkimedes, her undeniable attraction to him, and what Violet called his pretty-boy looks.

The vision of his stormy green gaze flashed to her, and she let out a sigh. At first, her feelings had been a gradual thing, the pitter-patter of her heart when he glanced her way with a particularly intense stare. When he saved her from the spirits, somehow it had changed something else, something more significant.

She wished he'd opened up more, share his past like he had done a few days ago. It made sense that he was reserved. After what he had gone through as a child, she understood and wanted better for him.

Her gaze was lost on a spot at the end of the lake, where mist hid the connection between the water and the land, her boots hitting the smooth rocks in the shore with a crunching sound.

A virgin.

Nava might not be experienced in the lovemaking department, but she was not ignorant. She grew aware of the growing needs in her body. After that disappointing first time with Hale when she was twenty, drinking had never been the same since. She stayed away from hard spirits.

She made it to the lake, distracted as she admired the splendor of her surroundings. She stopped at the sight of the naked chest of Arkimedes. A large expanse of golden skin and overbuilt muscle. Thick strong core marked with cut abs that looked a whole lot like the chocolate bar Simone used to bring to her.

Her mouth watered, not from the memory of the sweet chocolate, but something else. Her eyes followed a drop of water that glistened as it dripped down toward the taper of his navel to the beginning of hair and more. Her eyes zeroed down on the promise of something great.

She flailed her arms, dropping all her clothes. Undergarments and soap flew down to the rocky ground.

Arkimedes gazed up. "Shit!" He submerged himself back in the water.

Her throat was dry as she stood frozen, fingernails digging into the palms of her hands. Of course, she'd never expected him to be bathing.

Stop staring! But her eyes refused to move, too afraid to lose a second to marvel at his toned physique. Heat traveled down her body and pooled in her core, throbbing with want.

Nava had imagined him, fantasized about what it would be like to touch him. To kiss him all over. She had fantasized more heated exchanges; the reminder of those made her blush intensify.

Her imagination had not done him justice.

"Nava," he called. His cheeks were also a deep shade of crimson that was crawling down his neck.

"I'm *so* sorry!" she exclaimed, urging her body to move, to turn around and give him the privacy he deserved.

Her legs refused. Her gaze was fixed on the way his skin wrapped around the muscle—he was the prime example of health, and Nava ached to touch and savor it. Her breaths were coming out in puffs. She wanted the earth to open up and swallow her whole immediately.

She stopped, remembering the near earthquake she'd almost caused before. Maybe she didn't need the earth to swallow her up.

Turn around! her mind bellowed.

Arkimedes's embarrassment eased when he noticed her immobile. He raised a brow and rose from the water. Steam was coming out of his body. He was so goddamn *hot*, the water evaporated from him.

"I'm so sorry. I didn't know you were going to come here when you said you were going to check on the wards!" she babbled, and finally, her body moved. She crouched to pick up her items, her hands shaking.

Moving water had her turning in another direction. She exercised extreme self-control not to turn around to get another look at his . . . manhood.

"I promise I saw nothing. I mean, I did see *something*. A lot of muscle and . . . things." Her voice lost its power in the last word, and she cursed her awkwardness.

She picked at the last remnants of her things. Nava lifted her head at the sound of approaching steps, and Arkimedes walked toward her. He was wrapping a towel around his waist, his eyes shining with much more than amusement.

Nava bolted up, her back straight, her legs shaking. She tried to ignore the tingling sensation between her thighs and swallowed the thickness in her throat.

"I'm done here if you need to . . ." His voice was deeper than usual. Arkimedes's arm moved across his chest, holding onto his shoulder. She guessed he was trying to hide his wound from her.

But the wound was the least of her worries.

He was going to kill her. She shook her head, and long locks of waves hit her cheeks. "No, no, it's okay. I will come back later." She was dying for a bath, if just to cool down her heated skin.

"Are you sure?" he asked. Why had he decided to walk to her? There was no way he wouldn't be able to notice the red in her cheeks now.

"Yes, *very*. Sorry again, Ark." She took a step back, her attention drawn back down, raking the planes of his chest, so close she could lift her hand and touch.

Bad idea. Nava couldn't remember why she had to keep her extreme lust for him under control. It had something to do with an army coming for them and the fact that she had a soulmate.

When she reached the top of his towel, his skin shook from the cold. She snapped her focus back up. His pupils were blown wide, and he was not bothered by her admiration. Her mortification grew as she kept ogling him.

"I'll see you in the camp." She had never walked so fast before, running past the trees she had been admiring the splendor of a few minutes ago. The soft gray color of the smoke of their campfire billowed in the air. It reminded her of the way magic swirled around Arkimedes when he was in battle.

Both Gavin and Violet turned to meet her approaching body. Her unmentionables were held against her chest. She hoped her undergarments weren't visible but couldn't care less to check. Things could not get any more mortifying.

"How was the water?" Violet asked in a sing-song way.

Nava halted, focusing on the other woman. Her full lips pulled up into a smile.

Nava gasped in horror. "You knew? You conniving, evil—"

"Mastermind," Violet supplied.

"You would like to think so." Nava scoffed, shaking her head.

"I feel I'm missing a critical piece of information right now." Gavin's voice was soft and entertained.

"I figured you needed a bit of a push. Trying to help another girl out." Her smile grew, her eyes dancing with laughter. It was all a fun game for her, embarrassing Nava further.

It wasn't like Nava needed to be fueled into it. She did and spoke her fair share of embarrassing things already; she didn't need for her self-awareness to grow.

Gavin turned to Violet, a brow raised.

"Don't"—Nava pointed her hand to the other sorcerer; she might have been holding the soap in said hand—"help me again."

With those words, she left the campfire, intending to stay in her tent for the rest of the day before they had to go.

CHAPTER TWENTY

*T*he sun had set over the horizon. The sky was painted with oranges, reds, and purples. The soft scent of the fire Gavin had been working on for the past ten minutes surrounded them. He was at last successful.

It was a bet he and Nava had struck earlier in the day. She'd challenged him to make a fire without the use of magic. His laugh of victory echoed around their campsite, and even though Nava had lost, a grin tugged at her lips.

The air was crisp as fall carried on, getting colder by the day and dropping lower in temperature at night. The color of the changing leaves of fir and maple trees was a welcome change to the constant pine and cedar they had been in for weeks. It had been almost a month since she'd left home. Much had changed in her since, like the nature that surrounded her.

Nava tugged at the tent Gavin had put up for her. She was deciding how she could improve her regular human tent when someone came behind her.

She turned and yelped, her hand coming to rest on top

of her chest as she met Arkimedes's looming form. Gavin laughed, staring at the pair with increased curiosity.

"Archie, you are going to kill me sneaking up on me like that!" Nava said, and she had no moral ground to be complaining about him sneaking up on her. Not when images of his naked body flashed through her mind as she stared at him. She turned away to hide the blush that crept onto her face.

He chuckled. "I guess you're not the only one sneaking up on people when they least expect it."

Her lips parted with complete shock and mortification.

His grin widened. "Also, we said no to the whole 'Archie' thing?"

"*You* said. I happen to be still deciding which nickname I like best." She would tease him with all her ideas except for Val.

"If I may suggest not to use Archie because it sounds like a child's name, and I don't look like a child, do I?" His gaze shone with a rakish light.

Her face boiled with heat. They both knew the answer to that question. She looked at him before dropping her gaze down, her stomach churning. "I'm *so* sorry for earlier. I didn't mean to see anything. I saw *nothing*," she babbled. "Not a thing, just a large . . . tattoo?"

His lips twitched. At least he didn't appear to be furious with her. Though blurted in a panic, her words made her rewind back to what had happened earlier. The expanse of his skin. She *had* seen a large tattoo. Black ink wrapped around his shoulders and arms like feathers.

"It's fine."

"I swear, I didn't intend to . . . intrude. In my defense, I thought you were checking on the wards, and it never occurred to me that you would be there bathing."

"Nava, it's okay," he repeated.

"Violet knew. I don't understand how." Arkimedes lifted a brow. "She told me I needed a bath—so." Nava's lips clamped shut.

Arkimedes's eyes lit in recognition. "When you were asleep, I mentioned to them that I would do a recognizance of the area and strengthen the wards. Gavin offered to come with me, but I said I intended to take a dip in the lake by myself."

"Ha! That conniving . . ." *Genius.* "Still, I'm sorry."

"I meant it when I said it was fine," he said. "So—training tomorrow morning?"

"Yes, training. I want to hone my skills and do more." An awkward silence followed her words.

His hand rose to her shoulder in a soft touch that ignited the nerve endings of her skin. He read her like an open book, every single one of her insecurities spelled out in a language he understood well. She turned away, not wanting to be so bare with all her shortcomings to him.

"Hey, there is nothing wrong with the way you are. I keep telling you this." His voice was low and intended for her ears only. "It's not ideal in such a volatile situation that you haven't gotten proper training with your magic. Being kidnapped by trained fighters, or attacked by the Neems, isn't something even a trained sorceress can handle with ease."

"You're saying that to make me feel better."

"Gavin and Violet, they have both endured more than we know. Battles and hardships have shaped them. They were trained since they were children, and they also got kidnapped."

"Yeah, and what about you?"

"I was a Crow. They didn't even know they should have paid attention to me when I was stuck in my animal shape. Maybe the one good thing that has come out of this whole curse situation." Arkimedes's slow grin spread across his features.

She tugged the magical canvas of the tent, not moving it but an inch. How could it be this strong?

"You seem extra annoyed at your tent. Put up a complaint with Gavin. His tent-making skills must be abysmal if they do not measure up to your standards." Arkimedes could barely hold back the smirk.

Nava turned around, hitting the side of his arm. "Stop it, you tent snob. My tent is normal and would pass any test. It failed me in the wind storm."

"Be careful with your use of strength. I'm injured."

Nava brought her hand back, searching his face, expecting him to be in pain, and instead found a knowing smirk. "You are incorrigible." She shook her head, focusing on his shoulder that was covered by his thick tunic. Would the arrow wound be on his back, or perhaps his arm? She didn't remember it from earlier when he'd been with no shirt on.

Though, to be honest with herself, and she often tried to be, she was looking elsewhere.

"Getting easily distracted today, Lee."

Nava smiled at the use of such a fitting nickname. She shook away her memories of naked bodies and the desire pooling within her. "It's hard not to get distracted with all that I did manage to see." She was surprised she admitted this and didn't fret about it.

Arkimedes's expression intensified over hers. What had been a light ambiance became charged with much more.

They stared at each other. His gaze dropped to Nava's lips. He was so close that if she lifted on her toes and kissed him, he might not pull away.

She had to be careful about her fast-developing feelings when it came to him.

"You have a tattoo?" she asked instead.

He lost some of the heated darkness that had taken over. "Yes."

"Your wings?" He was so close, the scent of leather and cedarwood still surrounded her.

"They represent my wings, yes," he whispered.

She understood this was information meant for her alone. "I meant to ask you, are those wings part of your curse? Have you found a way to make it work for you?" She hoped he had. It would be a great way of giving the middle finger to the woman who had cursed him.

"No, it's not the curse. I have been able to call upon my wings since I was five." Arkimedes's eyes evaded her, as if he were battling a harrowing memory.

Nava's lips opened, and her heart squeezed at the sorrow that shaped his handsome features. She didn't want him to be in pain, not by a memory from her questions. Her hand came to his chest. He met her gaze. "Was that how the orphanage found you possessed magic?"

He nodded. At first, the giveaway had to be his eyes, so beautiful with raw power. "It wasn't the only thing that I developed at that age," he said. "They are pretty large, and I was unable to call them off. So they were always there, a constant reminder that I was different."

"Are you a shapeshifter?"

"Yes and no." He turned to the steps of someone near them. Violet was walking toward Gavin by the fire, not paying any attention to them, not even acknowledging that they were standing so close. "I can change my shape as I call upon my wings and withdraw them at will, but I don't shift into an animal." He paused, his brows furrowing. "Except now, because of this curse."

"Is it because of your fae origins?" Nava hesitated, her

THE CURSE OF THE CROW

hand still on top of his chest. She was aware of the touch. However, she didn't drop her hand. She liked it there.

If Nava were to judge his emotional state by the thundering in his chest, she would venture to guess he was nervous.

"Yes, or at least that is what I believe. They didn't leave a note that explained what to expect from my powers when they abandoned me." His expression darkened.

"Food is ready," Gavin called them from the fire, and both of their gazes traveled to the other pair. Nava dropped her hand, the cold air prickling her skin at losing his warmth.

She was happy he had decided to open up to her. It helped her understand, to fill in one of her many questions. Nava opened her mouth to say something, but her stomach decided to speak instead, making them both aware the scent of bread and meat by the fire was of the utmost importance.

Her cheeks grew warm. "I'm sorry." She should stop being sorry for everything.

"I guess we'd better get you some food then." He smiled, the heaviness of the last subject lifting from his features. He pointed to the fire where Violet was sitting, filling her plate with food.

She and Gavin were immersed in a lively chat that mentioned sweet liquor and wine. For the first time, they all ate in a companionable conversation, not with a lack of ironic remarks from Violet or grunts from Arkimedes to her.

Nava enjoyed the casual conversation right until Arkimedes had to leave, before the sun dropped behind the treetops.

WHEN SHE WOKE UP the next morning bright and early, Nava went to the lake before having her first drop of what she called war tea. By the time she was clean and back to their camp, she was crankier than usual. The water had been freezing. She couldn't understand how Arkimedes was at peace, like a statue carved by a skilled artist.

She had managed to make her body warmer. Magic had flown to her easier than the last few times. Her walk back to the camp had been slow and tiring. At least this time, she'd managed not to deplete her body's energy to zero. She plopped down on the ground, taking the mug Gavin extended her and wrinkling her nose at the bitter dirt taste. At least the warmth was pleasant.

Positive thoughts.

"Good morning." Gavin's voice took her out of her sulking.

Nava grunted. It had been good and bad. Bathing in a lake that held magical beings made the freezing dip in the turquoise waters more unpleasant. The coolness of the bath had cleared her groggy brain, however, so even though her exhausted body needed food and rest, her brain was sharp.

She imagined Cameron screaming at the cold water but braving it either way.

"Arkimedes . . . is cursed, right?" Gavin's words took her out of whatever trance her mind had gone to.

"Uh . . ." She blinked as her brain caught up to his words.

"It's easy for us to know. He is *always* gone at night and sleeps during the day. I'm guessing he gets trapped inside something. I'm thinking an animal. By his injury and his clear experience with wings, I'll guess a bird?"

Nava shifted, uncomfortable by the line of questioning.

"I don't think it's my place to say anything," she decided, and the man in front of her nodded. Nava didn't like lying, but she wasn't doing that now—she was deflecting.

"It's fine. It was more a comment than a question. He came back and has gone in your tent to rest."

"Is his injury better?" She glanced at her tent.

Gavin agreed with a hum, taking a substantial bite of the half-eaten apple he was holding "I thought you would have seen it by now, with all the questions about the healing potion I applied."

Arkimedes's naked skin still played in her mind. She deviated her attention somewhere else because she had no shame and was apparently a pervert

"He was lucky. Wherever the arrow hit, it was a clean shot. It didn't harm any tendons or ligaments."

"That's very good." She took a plate and filled it with food.

By the time Arkimedes joined them by the fire, the sun was nearing the sky's highest point. He was wearing all dark clothes, a navy shirt, and black pants. His brown jacket had been replaced by a thicker gray one.

He quietly took a seat by Gavin and poured a cup of warm tea, accepting Nava's offer of a food plate.

"We aren't too far from the village. I'm concerned we are leading Devon straight to it," Violet said.

"It's not like we have any other choice. Devon will get there. We can keep running around, but it's best to warn Roman. There needs to be enough time for us to gather the children and elderly. To take them to safety." Gavin's hand tightened on top of his knee, his knuckles whitening.

They had been talking about this for a while. Nava was listening. She didn't know about the village other than by mention, but she wanted to help and prevent families from being torn apart, everyone rounded up and taken to the city to be slaves.

It had stopped being about saving Cameron and herself alone. It had ceased being about running away from magic and all that entailed.

"Maybe the bird here can bring the warning to the Commander on his own. He can fly, after all."

Arkimedes's groggy gaze sharpened. "I won't be leaving Nava. Also, I don't believe Roman would listen to me on my own, even if I were to do so."

"You got the point—why would he trust one of your kind?" Violet's words dragged, and for the first time in a few days, her eyes narrowed into slits.

"Hey!" Nava complained. They were past this. Anger flourished in her chest as Gavin rested his hand on Violet's leg, giving her a warning.

Nava didn't understand why Violet held such a strong dislike for Arkimedes's kind. She remembered the other woman mentioning he was a hybrid and Gavin reminding her she didn't have those biases. Somehow, whatever Arkimedes was, it made a difference.

She wanted to save the innocent people of the Northern Village, and she would not stand back and let Violet bully Arkimedes because of his breeding, even though he seemed to be unaffected by the woman's opinions.

"Please, let's eat—we will leave this campsite tomorrow morning as planned."

The rest of the meal was quiet and uncomfortable, and by the time they were done eating, Arkimedes was up as if sprung by something else. "It's time."

Why did he often speak in such short sentences? She turned around in confusion. "For training?"

He nodded, walking away without another word.

"Well, *someone* is in a foul mood this morning—multiple someones." Nava side-eyed Violet.

"Not all of us need to be a ray of sunshine at all times, kitten."

Nava shook her head and stormed off, shadowing Arkimedes. The area he picked was in between significant trees. He stared at her as she prepared for training, dropped her coat to the ground, and searched around for a couple of sticks she could use instead of a weapon.

His face darkened as his black aura of magic enveloped his body, tendrils coming out. The sight was no longer scary. It filled her with awe and wonder, nonetheless. Why was his aura black when Gavin's and Violet's were gray?

She widened her stance. Nava gripped the stick she had just foraged, the same size as her actual blades. She was no longer in the mood to train against him with something so sharp. No matter how great of a warrior he was.

She took a measured step, and a bee landed on her hand, the buzzing of its wings sending a shock of power through her skin. However, it didn't jolt her. She followed Arkimedes's body. He walked around like he had done that day in the clearing of his house.

Nava had changed ever since. She was like a different person. She was no longer scared of everything that surrounded her. No longer would she be able to see the shadows in the forest and not remember the gnarled faces of dead people with vicious intent to kill.

No longer would she be able to eat honey.

Magic was not only evil but also beneficial. She was not a regular human; she had never fit in because she wasn't around her people. She focused on Arkimedes, knowing without a doubt she was where she belonged. Cameron had been right.

That alone was scarier than the magic had been the afternoon they'd trained for the first time.

Nava exhaled, her breath billowing up to the sky. She attacked him, her movements as fluid as her mother had taught her. Black tendrils pushed her stick away and wrapped around her body, lifting her off the ground as if she weighed no more than a leaf. She winced as air escaped her lips. Her weapon sliced through mist and fog. They were not harming it.

Bees kept landing on her skin, more than she could count. This time, though, the pinch of impending doom was not there.

They weren't here for a warning; they were coming because she had been calling on them. Nava was not aware she had been doing so.

When had bees begun to signify her power? At some point in the past three weeks, she had accepted them as if they were part of her. It was still confusing, yet here they were, responding.

Nava imagined what would happen if they wrapped around Arkimedes, blocking his view of her, enveloping him in a small bubble. As if she had whispered the command out loud, the bees flew at incredible speed toward him. Arkimedes gasped, and the magic that held her wavered. Her body weight fell a fraction before his magic held her up again.

Her own body was warming up, and the mist evaporated from where it touched her. She dropped to the ground and landed on her feet, wavering but recuperating her balance before toppling over.

The bees enveloped him, and she took the advantage to run toward him at the maximum speed her legs could carry her. The bees opened up a hole when she was close enough to him, and she hit Arkimedes on his side with her stick before jumping back when an arm of black mist came out for her. The bees covered the hole, and a gasp of pain came.

Were they stinging him?

She could do this, though her strength wavered as magic sucked the energy out of her body. Nava's arm shook as she gripped the stick harder.

She ran to the other side, her steps slower, and the bees opened a new hole. Arkimedes's surprised face was now covered in crawling insects before she swung the stick once again and hit him on the side of his arm. He winced, and before the bees could close in, his giant wings expanded, sending bees flying everywhere. Darkness enveloped him, and she gaped, wide-eyed and in complete awe of the magnificent sight of him.

His wings were at least seven feet long, with black feathers that shone an iridescent blue and gray. She took a few steps back when his magic's spicy scent burned her nose. He attacked her this time, and she winced at the unexpected move.

His body was surrounded by shadows popping out and around him. The precise shapes made her skin crawl.

It was like something made out of nightmares. Nava had time to cover, crossing her arms in front of her chest, both sticks up, but the wood broke with his power. Black tendrils sent her back, gasping and flailing. He grabbed her arms, bringing her toward his body before she stumbled to the ground.

The force of Arkimedes's pull brought her floundering into his chest, and she grasped the soft fabric of his shirt. Their eyes met with intense heat, their gasps for air mixing, and she let her body relax in his embrace.

He followed her closely, the thick veins in his neck visible from her vantage point. He was frustrated that she'd gotten a couple of hits before he'd had enough. His pupils were blown wide, and it was much more primal than she had noticed before. It wasn't anger.

It was arousal.

She relished the heat emanating from his body and the way he held her near him. His large hands were going down her arms in a soft caress that lifted the ends of her hair and made her lips open with a gasp.

Her legs shook under her, and heat rushed through her body, pooling between her legs. Arkimedes came closer, his forehead touching hers. His breathing hit her face. She swallowed, finding she had to come up a fraction and she would discover what his lips tasted like.

The sound of clapping had them breaking apart from whatever spell they had been under. He stepped back as if she had burned him. Nava let out a breath. Gavin and Violet were standing nearby, their faces shaped with different emotions.

"That was something else!" Gavin's excitement seeped through his skin. He was clearly unaware of the tension in the air.

How *not* to be annoyed at their presence? Nava shot a frigid glare to Violet, who dropped her hand and grabbed Gavin by the arm, hauling him away. He complained but let himself be dragged back to their campground.

Nava met Arkimedes's gaze, her body cooler than it had been seconds before. She was shaking with want. Would it be too off-putting if she kissed him? He pulled back another step, adding to the distance, and shook his head as if trying to get rid of fog.

"That was impressive." He cleared his throat.

"T-thanks." Her teeth caught her bottom lip as she tried to distract herself from her desire.

His eyes zeroed in on the movement. "The bees—they

are still coming to aid you." His voice was quiet. She didn't get protective when *he* spoke about them, like it had happened when Gavin or Violet inquired.

She nodded. "I don't know why they seem to keep coming. I think about it all the time." It made the worries clearer. "I—I want to protect it. The Beekeeper, I mean. It's almost like we are linked."

His face grew concerned, but he kept his distance.

"Maybe the creature has taken the place of my actual soulmate," she joked, and a soft laugh escaped his lips.

"It seems that when you healed it, the connection went both ways. It came to you in Devon's campground. If it had been a life debt, it would've been repaid when it saved you from the Neems the first time."

"Yes."

"The bees are with you, not only real ones but ones you create with magic." Arkimedes's brows met in the middle. "When the Beekeeper is around, does it speak to you?"

"It does—and doesn't. I sort of sense his intent, his and the bees."

Arkimedes nodded, shoving his hands in his pockets.

"It's not a bad connection." She walked to him. His whole body tensed at her proximity. She realized belatedly that he was trying to put space between them. Her stomach churned, and her warm body turned cold.

He was regretting almost kissing her. She dropped her gaze. Her pride took over. If he wanted not to talk about it, she would oblige. "It's natural, like breathing. Like it feels being with you," Nava whispered. To hell with her pride.

"Nava," he pleaded.

She lifted her gaze to him, searching for something that told her he might feel the same way. His expression was guarded, his body rigid while his fingers rubbed together in a nervous tick.

She took a step back, her heart contracting. "I'd better go. I'm just making this more awkward than it needs to be, like usual."

"It's not that."

"I felt . . . We had a moment, right? That wasn't me making it all up in my head." The words were spilling out. Magic had weakened not only her body but also her sense of self-preservation.

"We did. It was something," Arkimedes said, keeping his feet grounded in his spot. The pit inside her stomach grew. "It's not the right time, Nava."

She nodded. Violet's words came back to her mind. She had warned her Arkimedes would not be with her, even with their undeniable chemistry. She hadn't paid attention at the time, focusing more on the flirting and the intensity of what they'd shared after their training session.

Anger was coming at a fast pace. Why would he flirt with her if he wasn't ready for anything else? Why lead her on—almost kiss her—then push her away?

Nava didn't want to risk falling for anyone, but she was willing to do so with him.

She opened her mouth to say that before snapping her lips closed. There was her pride coming to her again, maybe a bit too late. She turned on her heels and walked away before she could pass out from her drained energy and embarrass herself any further.

CHAPTER TWENTY-ONE

*N*ava's surroundings had not changed for hours. Tall trees covered in green moss extended high in the sky, making their walk dark and cold. The air was more humid the more north they went, and she was happy this was their last day traveling.

Everyone walked in relative silence, alert for possible attacks. Arkimedes was in front of her. The tension was palpable in between them, and it almost suffocated her.

As desperation hit her, she considered telling him to forget their almost-kiss ever happened. She didn't know if it would make things even worse. Nava didn't understand what he wanted but wished they could go back to being normal.

She studied the surrounding trees. If she were to be here on her own, she wouldn't be able to find her way. Not to this village but back to Cameron and the town she avoided thinking of much.

Nava's heart contracted with dread as she imagined being immersed in Willowbrook's boring simplicity once more.

"I haven't been forthcoming with you." Arkimedes's whisper had her head snapping up toward him. His face was beautiful and lethal, with the sharp angles of his high cheekbones.

"What do you mean?" Her steps were longer and quicker to keep up with him.

He was quiet for a moment that extended too long. Nava didn't reach to grab him, however. She had been trying to keep her distance since the day before. "When Devon's army shot me, I did notice he might have come with a larger army like you mentioned when we met."

Her lips parted in shock. "How large are we talking about?"

"Hundreds."

"Why didn't you tell me before?"

He pressed his lips into a thin line, evading her pointed gaze. "I wanted to give you a few days of normalcy and allow you to focus on training. I'm sorry." Honesty tinted his last word.

The heat of annoyance still swirled inside her stomach. "Are we going to stay at the village or leave and keep on the move?"

"Our best option is staying with bigger numbers still. He didn't come looking for you or me. I believe he had been tracking Roman since he used to be a high Commander in the army of the Iron City, but after finding you and, in return, me, he is after us more so than them at this point."

Nava opened her mouth to say how little sense it made that Devon Black had his attention set on them when he had a whole village of sorcerers to raid and capture. Still, her mind supplied memories of the day in the clearing when his magic had rained down on her. Devon had made it a point to come and talk to her. He had ignored Gavin and Violet.

She swallowed. Devon knew her from before. Her mother had been a Crow once upon a time. Arkimedes had defeated a small camp full of bounty hunters. That alone would drive the warlock insane. She was sure of it.

She said flatly, "No more secrets, this includes withholding information."

His eyes held hers for a long time. "No more secrets."

"Are you two lovebirds coming?" Gavin's words shook her. Heat traveled to her face.

Arkimedes turned and walked toward the other pair without another word.

THE VILLAGE APPEARED as they crossed the wards that protected it. Nava took in the magical ambiance. Homes and buildings made of stucco, wood, and stone were built against tall trees with massive tree trunks as large as her house back in town.

Lanterns shone with magical flames, lighting up the dark streets shaded by the giant trees that hosted it.

Three-meter-wide roads were paved with smooth stone aged by lichen and moss. Life burst through the seams of this little section of the world. Carts were being pulled by large stallions or donkeys, but upon further inspection . . . said donkeys bore large horns in the middle of their heads.

Her head moved to the sides as she studied the people who walked by. They wore earth-colored tunics similar to Violet's and Gavin's. Children played in the streets, chasing each other. Their laughter echoed around, mixing with birds chirping and the casual conversations around them.

Kids ran around her. They couldn't be older than five,

maybe six. Two women wearing dresses and heavy coats chatted among themselves as their offspring played. Not a worry in sight, ignorant a monster was coming to take them away.

Nava had come to this village first for protection. Now she wanted to help them. Devon Black arriving here without warning would lead to failure for these people. Seeing this place, the life here made her aware of how similar her situation had been when she was a child and her mother had protected her from slavery.

Her anger toward her mother, the one always burning beneath her skin, subdued a bit.

The air smelled of a mixture of spices—saffron, cayenne, cumin. Incense burned in the air, and beneath all these scents was the particular smell of magic. It was different from what she remembered from the Iron City. This was breathtaking and booming with life.

Dread bloomed in the pit of her stomach as she took on all these people who could lose if Devon Black got to them.

She followed her group of people as Gavin and Violet greeted a few who were walking by. Arkimedes walked next to her, his own gaze fixed on a point ahead. A tall man wearing a black tunic with a dark fur collar stood by, talking with someone, unaware of them approaching. Both men in front appeared militant, even though their hair was long and wild. Their statures were imposing, much like Arkimedes.

"Roman." The man's gaze searched for Violet's voice, relief and surprise flashing across his worn features.

He had to be in his mid-forties. His expression was of a much older man, worn by battle and hardship. His face was a mixture of strength and wariness, high cheekbones, and a straight nose. A large scar marked the right side of his face, sparing his dark eye. His hair was peppered and tied into a low ponytail.

"Violet, Gavin." His face twisted into a smile that morphed his face. "I'm so happy to see you. We have been hearing rumors of a crown ship landing in Willowbrook and expected the worse."

"I'm afraid the rumors were correct." Gavin shook the man's hand, turning toward both Arkimedes and Nava, who waited behind. "We met these two in our captive time."

Roman's focus shifted to them. He scanned her before moving on to Arkimedes. He paused. "Arkimedes."

"Roman."

"I hope you had nothing to do with this." His voice held an aggressive undertone, and Nava's skin prickled.

Violet's face showed no signs of embarrassment by the words of the Commander.

"He did not, Roman. He was the one who released us." Gavin's hands came up.

"Or that's what he wants you to think," Roman said.

Arkimedes's jaw tensed. "Why would I do that?"

"Who's to tell with you?" Roman's eyes narrowed.

Nava pushed forward, much more petite than Arkimedes, but still, she walked in front, wanting the man's attention to be elsewhere.

Curiosity caressed her mind at this, settling on Arkimedes and his tense jaw. It was ridiculous that this man would blame him for this. Yes, Arkimedes had been part of the army, but so had this Roman guy. Arkimedes had also run away and was living in exile in this forest.

Nava's breaths came out quicker as heat traveled through her body. It was clear Arkimedes was an outsider, much like she had been in Willowbrook. He had not shared many things about his past and was an enigma, but she also knew he had wanted to help them.

"He did not plan this." She took a sharp breath and squared off her shoulders. "The bounty hunters who took them also took me—and Arkimedes was there to get me out."

When she finished, a weight lifted off her shoulders. She wanted to speak up for him. Even if they had met not that long ago, he was her friend.

"And you would be . . . ?"

"Nava. I met the Crow in Willowbrook. We have been running away from him for a few weeks."

Roman shifted his focus to Arkimedes, ignoring her words.

"Roman, he took care of the bounty hunters. *I* saw him fight the Crow—please, there is no need for this," Gavin said, his brow furrowing.

Violet let go of a sharp breath, her face soured. Nava guessed she had been enjoying the way Roman was making Arkimedes a villain, right until the point Gavin decided to side with her and Arkimedes.

"What brings you here?"

Arkimedes stiffened, but other than that, his expression remained neutral. "We were on our way to warn you of Devon being on the island and targeting *you*. He comes with a large army."

"Targeting me?" Roman snarled. "What makes you think he is here for me and not *you*?"

Nava turned to Arkimedes, her heart pounding.

"He didn't know I was here until I attacked his camp to get Nava out."

"Rather convenient no Crow or crown has an idea where you are."

Arkimedes shrugged. "I have been on this island longer

than you. They had stopped looking for me. However, you left with a big splash, didn't you? The crown probably put a pretty penny over your head."

"Crows don't work for money," Roman said.

"No, but bounty hunters do, and he comes with those as well." Arkimedes seethed.

Silence descended upon the group. Nava swallowed.

"He is also after us. We figured if we stayed in larger numbers, everyone would fare better luck," Arkimedes said.

"I see."

Conversation followed, and Violet explained what had happened and how they had been ambushed in the middle of the night the day before they had taken Nava.

Nava glanced at the trees around her, curiosity taking a firm grip on her thoughts. This was the first time she had been inside a magical village, and it was unlike anything she had ever seen. Something moved, long limbs made of tree bark. She blinked, and the vision was gone.

She walked away from the group, searching for her Beekeeper up in the foliage. Nava pursed her lips and considered the possibility that she was going crazy. A small fuzzy body flew down in a zigzag and hovered close to her face.

She turned her hand and offered it her palm. As it landed, Nava waited, holding her breath for words to echo in her head. The bee walked and turned up its little head as if waiting for a command.

Nava's eyes changed focus, from the insect standing on her hand to the shape of someone in front of her.

She met irises the color of vibrant cobalt blue. The woman's skin was blue and leathery, its shine reminding her of the pearls sold in the town's market by the ports.

Her dark blue hair was in an elaborate bun on top of her head, and she had long, pointy ears. A fae.

The closest she had ever been to a magical creature like this before was Arkimedes, who talked little of his past but had shared a small fraction of what he knew. Her lips parted as both of them stared at one another with increasing curiosity.

"I haven't seen you in town before," she sing-songed, walking around Nava, studying every inch of her body. The movement made her want to cover herself somehow.

"We got here with Gavin and Violet," Nava said, pointing behind her, where the four of them still stood.

"Your name, girl?" the woman whispered.

Nava blinked, a daze forming around her mind. "Nava."

"Nava," the fae repeated, long white teeth revealed in a smile sharper than she cared to dwell on. "I'm Thea. The Commander called, so I came," she said as if this would answer the question going through Nava's head.

Steps came behind her, but she couldn't move much. She was entranced by the cobalt eyes and an increasing prickly sensation inside her head.

"Is everything all right?" Arkimedes's voice shook her out of her trance. "Roman said there is a cabin for guests. You can have it." He fixed his gaze on the fae, who stared from Nava to Arkimedes, buzzing with excitement.

"What about you?" Nava lowered her voice.

"I don't need it. You know why."

"That's not true—"

"Oh, how exciting! Anima-mate. I haven't seen the likes of you for so long, I almost forgot what it looks like." Thea smiled, buzzing with delight.

Nava focused her attention on the fairy before lifting a brow. Arkimedes's expression differed from what she was expecting. His face was suddenly pale. He shook his head, his lips pursed together.

"The likes of who?" Nava said.

The fae's leathery hands landed on each side of her cheeks. Thea chuckled with excitement, turning Nava's head as she examined all of her exposed skin. *So, I guess me?*

"Um," she said.

Arkimedes's hand landed on her hip, pulling her back a few steps and away from the eager fae. "I'm sure we should get going," he whispered into Nava's ear.

From the air of his breath hitting her neck, goose bumps awakened and traveled down her body, making her aware of how close he was.

He held her against his warm body, but his attention was fixed on the woman in front, wariness tinting his features. It hit her with the realization that whatever the fairy had said had him in a frenzy.

"She doesn't know. How is it possible, girl?" Thea asked, her brows dipping down into a frown.

Confusion was creeping in as she took a sharp breath. She was tired of always being the one out of the secret. Never understanding what was happening around her. Was the fairy referring to her connection with the Beekeeper?

"*What?* About . . . the curse?" She turned to Arkimedes in a warning she hoped he heard. She was not buying his need to get her away from the fairy.

"You must have missed the sign or something is blocking you from finding it."

"Get out of our heads, Almathea," Arkimedes warned.

The fae took a step back and crooked her head, studying him. "The Commander demands if you are to be trusted," she said, her sing-song words dying down.

Nava understood the prickliness inside her head and the fogginess that had occupied her mind. Thea was a seer.

"I don't care what he says," Arkimedes hissed.

Nava crossed her arms in front of her chest. The woman had been inside her head, and she had found something that was different in there—had alluded to something Nava ought to know. Her mind reeled as she took Arkimedes's features. Something he didn't want her to.

"Roman, what is the meaning of this?" Arkimedes's voice boomed.

The Commander, who had been talking with Gavin and Violet, came hurrying. His expression shuttered, his hand resting all too casually on top of the hilt of his sword. "What is the problem?"

Arkimedes turned and pulled her along with him, still holding her hips. It wasn't as if they didn't touch. As a matter of fact, the longer they spent together, the more touch became part of their routine. A shoulder graze here, a caress to one's arm. He had never held her like he was doing now, however, and she couldn't help what blossomed in her chest.

"You had the fae get inside our heads," Arkimedes snarled.

Roman's lips twitched. "We do it with *all* newcomers. It's a way to ensure we have no moles."

"Let me remind you. You need us as much as we need you—you do not get to get inside our heads without us agreeing to it." Arkimedes's expression didn't waver.

Roman's tense shoulders relaxed a bit. "I apologize." His eyes flashed behind them, where Nava assumed Thea still stood. "It seems it's all okay. With that, we will escort you to the guest cabin. You can rest tonight, and tomorrow we will prepare for whatever might come our way."

Silence passed with a beat as Roman walked away, followed by Violet.

Gavin walked to them, both hands inside his pockets, his face apologetic. "I'm sorry for his behavior—but I hope you have grown to trust me. You will be safe in here. We need you to help us fight against the Crow." Gavin's face morphed to one of concern, his attention fixed on the children playing in the street, the laughter, the normalcy. His pronounced Adam's apple bobbed. "I will take you to your cabin. There will be a small celebration this afternoon. I hope you two will join us for drinks and dancing."

Nava smiled, eager. It had been a while since she had been able to do something she loved. She and Arkimedes fell behind Gavin's steps, walking down the wavy stone roads of the village. The smell of burning wood, dirt, and moss was a pleasant combination.

Gavin stopped in front of an old tree. A small cabin jutted out with ceramic tiles on top of the roof and small windows. The door was much too small for someone the size of Arkimedes.

"Your home." Gavin's hand moved in a grand gesture, making Nava smile. It was pleasing that someone's mood was not being shifted after arriving at this village.

The door was heavy, and as she walked inside her home for the night, she studied the warm, rustic wood tones and the wool rugs over terracotta-tiled floors. A small living room surrounded a stone fireplace and worn leather chairs with thick colorful blankets layered on top.

To the side, under a small window covered in forest-green curtains, there was a small shelf filled with curiosities: a half-burned candle, three hastily stacked books, and a glass vase filled with dried flowers.

Someone had once lived here. Nava turned to ask Gavin whose cabin this was but stopped when her attention landed on both Arkimedes and him. They were whispering outside. She took slow steps toward them, trying to make out anything of what they were saying.

Curiosity was her worst trait, her mother had said. She happened to think it was one of her best.

"He understands we also need you, but you need us too," Gavin said.

"I won't leave Nava, if that's what you are thinking. I'm not going anywhere while she's still here."

"Good, I will see you later."

"I'm not one for parties."

"Don't do it for you but her. It's clear Nava has never been to war." Gavin added quickly, "A large army, you said, coming this way to take every deserter—but we both know what they do to the elderly, the disabled, or fae. You and I have fought on the other side."

Nava walked closer to the door and peeked through the small opening, focusing on the hard planes of Arkimedes's back. The afternoon light graced the sharp angles of his features.

"Yes." His face turned dark.

"The ones who are worthless to them will get killed. We'll put up a fight, and this will become a bloodbath. War is coming, and you are aware of what that entails. Drink some wine, make love to your woman, and prepare yourself for hell."

"Gavin—"

Nava stepped back. The war was coming, whether or not she was ready for it.

CHAPTER TWENTY-TWO

*A*rkimedes entered the house shortly after, bending under the worn doorframe. He straightened while he studied the small space, and then his eyes settled on Nava.

His cheeks blushed, and she knew he was remembering Gavin's last words. To make love to her and prepare for battle. The tension increased as her own blood boiled in her veins.

"Do you think we need to get dressed up for the celebration? Because I have nothing other than trousers and shirts—in various states of filth." Her voice was less convincing by the end.

Her mind supplied the image of her green skirt. She had worn it little on the trip because the excess fabric made it hard for her to walk in the forest, but maybe she could use it for today's festivities.

"I won't get dressed up, either," he offered with a shrug.

She studied his dark clothes and wind-brushed hair, which had gotten longer in the past few weeks. It swooped over his forehead. He was the most handsome man she had ever seen with his stubble.

She grimaced. "Of course, it's not like you need to, with the way you look." Realizing all the words had left her lips, she winced but decided it was too late to salvage it. "It's something silly to be concerned about, not with what's coming." She walked around the home, her cheeks flaming. "This reminds me of your house." She took in the play of his muscles as he removed his coat and dropped it over the back of one of the kitchen chairs. "I like yours better." She met his gaze as he turned back to her.

Curiosity piqued his attention. "You do?"

She nodded, walking around while her fingers brushed over the stucco walls. "Yours felt like home."

His lips twitched into a smile she might have missed had she not been staring so intently at his face. He took a step forward, and she held her breath, unsure what he would do. They had been dancing this strange game of giving in, then pulling back.

"Have you thought about what you want to do when all this is over?"

Silence. "Are you going to return to your town?" The muscles of his jaw tensed.

Nava's throat went dry, her palms sweating with uneasiness. "I have to go back to Cameron and Laurie," she admitted. "I don't want to be in that town, far away from . . ." *You*. This time she held back, afraid to say too much and have him pull away again.

Music drifted through the air, reaching them. They both turned their heads at the sounds of the cheerful tunes.

"I'm going to freshen up before we head out." She carried her backpack with her. For once, she wished all her clothes weren't inside a town where no magic reached or else she might attempt to bring something new for the celebrations using her magic.

That alone made her pause as she dropped the heavy backpack on the floor. Her lips parted as she stood still and enjoyed the quiet to reflect on the changes that happened within.

The washroom was narrow, illuminated by a tall stained glass window with intricate designs, arranged in a mosaic that formed trees and leaves. There was a wooden tub with a coal-burning stove attached to it, similar to what Nava had seen in Arkimedes's home.

There was a small vanity with a copper bowl and a pump faucet to the side. This whole village would have been connected to a septic system, unless it all worked with magic—which, based on where she was, she guessed was plausible.

Nava splashed cold water on her face, taking a deep breath to calm her nerves. She was not only nervous about her lack of proper attire for the celebration.

Water filled the tub with steam. The air was thick as she took another breath, closing her eyes as her mind rushed through memories of what she knew before and knew now.

This village proved she had been misguided her whole life to fear, hating what she was, a magical person with power running through her veins. She was not a damsel in distress. She should have been able to protect Cameron and herself.

Her mother had been an instructor, a powerful sorceress, and part of the Society of Crows. A respected weapons master. She had been Arkimedes's teacher, for god's sake, yet she had chosen to leave Nava in the dark. To let her believe the best option was to be wary and afraid of magic.

Nava guessed she could understand why she had been

so sheltered. Her mother had gone through a lot to protect them. She wished she had thought of their future more.

Arkimedes's question came to her mind—would she return home to Willowbrook? The answer was an easy *no*. Nava craved knowledge, wanted to work on her confidence and self-worth. For the first time in her life, she was not feeling inadequate, but powerful instead.

Cameron had wanted to learn this side of their nature, and she would work on that. They could move to this village, or she'd search for somewhere they could go, because it was clear the crown would not stop seeking deserters even in this remote place.

She got in the tub and let herself soak in the warm water as it soothed her sore muscles, and for the first time in weeks, she was truly clean.

She settled on her green skirt and a shirt she had washed in the lake. She braided her hair in one of the styles Laurie had taught her. By the time she was out, Arkimedes had settled into one armchair and was paging through a book.

His gaze raked over her body before settling on her face. "You look beautiful, bee," he breathed.

Her stomach woke up in a flutter. "Thank you." She didn't need to dwell on his appearance. "I like the nickname, by the way."

"Yes?"

"It suits me, I think.

He smiled, and the expression reached his eyes. "I like it too. Ready to go?"

THE VILLAGE WAS ALIVE with people on the streets, loud voices, and laughter. The smell of tobacco, beer, and rum filled the air, along with something spicy. Magic was everywhere.

Nava and Arkimedes followed the crowd to the village's center, a small plaza shaped like a circle with smooth stones that matched the roads and walkways. Large planters housed four weeping willows that clashed among all the other trees. A band played music on a wooden stage, all wearing matching outfits of moss-green tunics and brown hats. People of all ages were dancing.

Lightning bugs flew around in the air. It wasn't night yet, because Arkimedes was still here. Under the trees' dense canopy, it was dark and magical.

She followed the men, women, and children wearing dressier attires, unlike herself. Women wore long dresses in saturated colors that popped against the trees' brown bark and the yellowish tones of the stucco buildings in the background. Her insides sank with self-awareness.

Even though she wore her best attire, her skirt was torn after climbing that wall when leaving town. Still, green suited her.

Nava's gaze followed the direction Arkimedes was staring and found Roman and Gavin, both men wearing dressy attires. Gavin's face was shaven neatly, making him look so much younger. His nose had a shadow of a scar from their captive days.

They made their way to them, around the dance floor and between a sea of people. She spotted Violet by one of the willow trees, wearing indigo pants and a clean black tunic. One of the few women she had seen *not* wearing a dress. The weight of self-doubt lifted from her shoulders.

"You made it." Gavin's voice was cheerful as he patted Arkimedes's arm twice, then took a drink out of a pint of beer. "Nava, may I get you a drink?" Gavin searched

Arkimedes's face, as if checking he was not overstepping on some alpha male thing.

She squirmed in her spot at the heaviness in her chest. What had she been expecting? That Arkimedes would offer to get her a drink instead? It was precisely what she'd wanted, him jumping at the chance of courting her. Instead, he was keen on keeping the distance he had set since their *almost*-kiss.

"I don't want to trouble you. Where may I find one?" She was also not ready to deal with a possible hostile Violet if the woman was a jealous type. She spotted a lady with a tray filled with cups of overflowing drinks. "Never mind. I think I found her. I will be right back."

Nava made her way across the crowd in search of something to calm her nerves. The three men fell into a hushed conversation, reviewing what had happened in the last few days while they'd traveled.

She didn't need to stay behind to hear what she already knew, reliving moments where she had been paralyzed with fright or swiped away by another array of feelings she cared not to dwell on. The woman holding the tray couldn't be older than forty. Her ash-blond hair was pulled back into a bun with ringlets framing her thin angular face.

She was beautiful in an otherworldly way. Nava knew she wasn't just human. She paused and stared for longer than necessary before those magical orbs came onto her, a thin brow lifting in question.

"Is there something wrong?" Her voice held a bit of a bite.

"Oh, nothing wrong. May I have one?"

The fae hybrid sized her up from the bottom of her worn, dirty boots to the top of her head and shrugged. "You look old enough." She extended Nava a pint of beer.

The foam spilled over her fingers as she tried to steady it so it wouldn't make a mess. "T-thanks."

The fae with the drinks was already walking off. Nava shook her head and brought the glass to her lips. The fermented taste of homemade beer came to her palate. She had never been a particular fan of the drink, preferring wine any day, but this celebration called for it.

Nava walked closer to the dance floor as if hypnotized by the dancing. She stared at the shapes, sipping on her beer. Her legs ached for her to let go, to loosen up a bit and forget the things that haunted her dreams or her concerns about whether she wanted to return home or stay in this new world.

Or the fact that she was falling for an unavailable guy when she should be uninterested.

A female voice called her attention. "Have you seen the new guy?"

She was near enough that Nava could tell she was young and eager. Nava studied the crowd as curiosity piqued her interest.

"The one next to Gavin? How could anyone *not*?" another voice replied.

Nava blinked as she found two girls huddled together, a couple of meters away from where she stood, their eyes fixed on a spot in the crowd.

"He is scrumptious," said the blonde, whose hair fell down her back, contrasting with her shiny silky blue dress. The shade reminded her of one Simone wore often, and her heart contracted with the memory of her friend.

"He *is*, Mina. Mother told me he was dangerous," the other said. This girl had warm copper skin and jet-black hair. Her dress, much like her friend's, was a silky gown but light green.

Nava took another sip and followed their gazes,

peeping across the crowd. Her gaze landed straight on Arkimedes, and her cheeks flamed at the vision of him. His arms were crossed over his chest, the pose displaying the bulge of his muscles. His attention traveled across the sea of people as he studied his surroundings with a bored stance. Gavin was near him, still chatting with a man of medium stature, muscular build, and long, wavy caramel hair. She didn't recognize him, which wasn't surprising as she was new here.

Nava breathed her disappointment. She had hoped he would come and look for her, but instead, he was biding his time before he had to depart, forced by his impending curse.

"I'll let him do whatever he wants to me. You know how I like a bad boy," said the girl with the pale hair.

Nava's chest burned with flames that flowed through her body as she huffed at the girl's words. She couldn't be older than twenty, and her rosy round cheeks and clean face made Nava ruffle like a wet hen.

Arkimedes was indeed too old for her. She grumbled, tilted the pint to her lips, and finished her drink. When the last drop was gone, she stared in awe as the ceramic cup disappeared from her grasp. Her lips parted in shock, but she held it together long enough not to make a scene.

As Nava followed the dancing bodies, a man, not much older than the girls she had been obsessing over, came to her. He was tall and slim with blond hair and bright blue eyes. He reached a hand out with a broad smile, and she tried to find who he was inviting to the dance floor, only to realize he had come for her.

People moved in circles in a lively rhythm, a dance pattern she knew from back in town.

"Could I interest you in a dance?" His voice carried a heavy accent, and his cheeks were flushed.

Giggles came from nearby, and the girls, Mina and black hair, were staring at them. His smile faltered at her hesitation. She took a sharp breath to steel her nerves and took his hand, letting herself get carried away to the dance floor.

Her smile grew as they jumped around and forgot about everything. He smelled like pine, and his hands were much softer than the large hands she longed to hold. She stared over her partner's shoulder to the spot where Arkimedes stood, and she was shocked when her gaze met his across the dance floor.

His shoulders were tight with tension, his expression filled with emotion. Nava swallowed and looked away, back to the present.

She clapped to the sound of the music, following everyone else. Their complexions were shiny with sweat, all happy and *free*.

Devon Black was still out there, getting closer to them with every second that passed by. These people, like her family, had run from the crown and made their lives away from servitude.

She sobered a bit, and her attention stopped on her dance partner as she took in his features. Much like what had happened to her in town, there was no connection or attraction, though her brain supplied he was handsome. His face was sharp and smooth.

The song was ending. She jumped around the dance floor along with the guy with blue eyes. The last notes of the song were hanging in the air, and everyone stopped dancing and clapped at the band.

"Thank you for the dance." Nava managed to curtsy. Laurie would be proud she had not forgotten her manners.

The man who had invited her smiled and bowed to her. "It's my pleasure." He paled as he looked behind her shoulder and then he disappeared from her view before she could say anything else.

She turned around and found Arkimedes looming. His jaw was tense, his stance wide. He stared at the retreating form of her dance partner. A part of her wanted to be annoyed at whatever this display was. Another, more significant side wanted to rejoice.

"You have scared away my dance partner with all the crankiness happening on your face." She eyed him sharply.

He extended her a hand. "Then I'd better rectify it. Would you join me for the next dance?" he asked in a refined, high-society tone she hadn't heard before. It was like he had grown up going to such events, maybe even much fancier than this one.

Nava took his hand, and butterflies flew inside her stomach. She hoped he didn't notice the tremble as he brought his body closer to her and his other hand came to rest on her lower back. They moved to the slow rhythm of the ballad playing.

She broke the silence. "So what was that about?"

His dark lashes lowered. "What was what about?"

"The display with . . . my dance partner."

His lips lifted into a side smile. "So you didn't even get a name? Ruthless, bee."

Her cheeks went warm. "It's not like we had a lot of time to speak. We were dancing." She smiled. "Maybe I was too lost in the moment to speak."

"Or too busy looking elsewhere," he countered.

"Do tell. Since you were paying attention."

"*I was* paying attention." His hand squeezed hers, his eyes dipping down to her lips.

A breath caught in her throat, but she didn't want to fall into the abysm of her desire. Not this time. They had gone down this route before, and it had burned her. "So, what was I looking at, Arkimedes?" she pressed.

He spun her, making her stomach swirl. He pulled her back and held her close. The warmth of his body seeped through the layers of clothes, burning her. His breath caressed the side of her neck, his lips against her ear. "You were looking at me," he whispered.

"I was reading the room." She could tell by his amused expression she was not fooling anyone. "You can't keep doing this to me, Arkimedes, playing with my feelings."

"I'm not playing. I told you it wasn't the right time a couple of days ago—and maybe not now, either."

"It makes no sense." She huffed. "Why not? Last time I checked, neither you nor I are with anyone. We are free to be with who we want, and I want . . . you." Were they moving to the sound of the music or standing still?

Silence.

"Is it because of my soulmate thing?" she asked.

His brows met in the middle. The song ended, and he pulled away from her as if she had burned him. Her mind went haywire. Was he retreating because he thought she was trying to pin him about being the one again?

She was *not*—right? A prickle crawled across her scalp.

"I'm going to head back. I only have minutes before nightfall, and I don't want to transform in front of all these people." He took a couple of steps back, facing her, before spinning around and stepping past the crowd.

For such a large man, he was a quick one. She followed behind, steps faltering as people came in front of her, covering his retreating form.

"Excuse me." She pushed between bodies but was unable to make any headway. Instead of moving away, they came closer together. She pushed and pulled and soon was out of a wall made of people.

Everyone was laughing behind her. She studied the darkened streets. Nava's stomach sank. The tall trees crowded her in the noisy background. A spark of recognition. Somehow she knew where to go, which made little sense to her human non-magical brain but worked with her awakened senses.

The whisper of magic caressed her mind, giving her flashes of images that told her where to go, showing her a way back to him. She would not stop their conversation there.

She would take any minute he still had this evening. Nava wanted to use it to clear the air. Questions swirled in her mind, Amalthea's words coming to the forefront.

Nava hated secrets having grown up in a family that said too little and left her living adrift.

Arkimedes was swift on his feet. Even though she was practically jogging behind him, she could not catch up.

By the time she made it to the cabin, the light of the fireplace illuminated the windows, and as soon as she opened the door, the largest raven flew out of the house, cawing as it disappeared between the shadows of the night.

CHAPTER TWENTY-THREE

*N*ava woke up in the morning to a cold cabin. The fire had gone off in the middle of the night, and with the dropping late-fall temperatures, the stone floors were frigid when her feet touched it.

She made her way to the fireplace, searching for kindling to light it up again. When she found none, she moved to her backpack, but her matches had gotten soggy.

Nava dropped back onto the floor. The smooth stones' coldness seeped into her body, and she wallowed for a couple of minutes—before she would pull herself together again.

She had never relied on anyone so heavily that despair took over her, not being able to do something so simple as making a fire. Lighting a fireplace was something she'd done over and over with non-magical human tools.

Life had forced her to grow up when her father had fallen into the daze that had taken him. He had chosen to die with his soulmate instead of living with his children. Her body warmed as anger flowed through her veins at that.

If anything, these weeks had made her aware of her resentment toward her parents. Sure, her father had taught her to make a fire using matches. He could have demanded her mother teach her how to make such things with magic, instead.

Her world closed in, suffocating her. It was not because of her soggy matches or because she was cold, hungry, and alone. It was because of the constant feeling of being the weak one—something she was unused to.

She was used to being the aloof person who didn't need help. Taking care of her home, her brother, and the family business when she'd been twenty.

She didn't need a man. Nava had dismissed her suitors when they'd implied she *needed* their support. Like hell she did. Sure, her funds were dwindling because people in town were unwilling to give a woman of her age a shot, even though her potions were just as good as her father's. She didn't need a man or her soulmate.

Being rejected for something she had no control over made her blood boil.

Her lips shook as she swallowed down a heavy knot in her throat. *You don't want a soulmate. And if it's not your soulmate, then it shouldn't be anyone.* Her brain repeated the words Nava had been telling herself since she was fifteen.

While she had been attracted to Arkimedes from the get-go, it had developed slowly, from attraction to friendship to more. Or maybe it had come all at once, and she was better at lying to herself than she thought.

Nava stared at the fireplace. The ashen wood stared back at her defiantly. She had magic. It was about time she used hers for things other than a panicked attempt to save herself.

Focusing on the energy that coursed through her body, on what she wanted to do, she buried away all negativity.

Her mind narrowed to the cold that surrounded her and called on fire.

A tingling traveled down her spine, over her skin, through her veins, and to her fingertips. She smelled spice, smoke, and burning wood. Nava gasped when orange-and-yellow flames danced in front of her. She fist-pumped the air, right before a wave of tiredness ran through her body.

She got up and headed back to bed, plopping down while her eyelids drooped. A smile tugged at her lips, and exhilaration mixed with exhaustion.

The knocking brought her back to the present time. She must've dozed off at some point, and she blinked at the haze inside the cabin before she moved to the door.

The door was heavy, and when it cracked, a wave of frigid air hit her like a hurricane. She squinted against the bright light outside, coming to the familiar shape of a woman. Flawless copper skin, wearing a burgundy coat and dark pants, hair pulled back in careful braids that made her already fierce expression even more intimidating.

"You are alive," Violet said, walking into the cabin and examining the area.

"Good morning to you too," Nava said, closing the door behind the other woman.

"You mean good afternoon."

Nava swallowed. "Afternoon," she corrected, emphasizing her annoyed tone. "Can I help you with anything?"

"We're preparing for an attack. Roman thinks it's prudent to have you train with me since the Crow seems especially keen on you."

"Oh?"

"Gavin and I noticed how even though he didn't bother to come to us after we were captured, he made it a point to see *you*." Violet studied her nails, but by the vein throbbing on her forehead, Nava deduced this didn't please her, her pride not too happy with the revelation that Nava was somehow more prized in the Crow's eyes.

"Why you?" Nava challenged. She would prefer to train with Roman himself rather than with the woman in front of her, remembering how she had hit Gavin in their training sessions.

"Why not? Are you afraid of me?"

Nava frowned. "Maybe I am," she admitted. "Look, I'm not here to measure our pride. I'm not an experienced warrior. I never used magic before a month ago."

Violet scoffed. "You expect me to believe this, that you have discovered power. Yet you have a significant amount of it. You control the bees. The Beekeeper comes for you. One of the scariest men I have ever seen protects you, and the Crow hunts you."

Nava lifted her hands in a sign of peace, and Violet's frown deepened. Why did people keep saying Arkimedes was scary? Powerful, yes. But scary . . . ? Her mind supplied the image of him raising his hand and one of the bounty hunters collapsing to the ground. The man had been alive one second, and next, he was dead.

Yep, she guessed he was scary.

"The Beekeeper is something I'm trying to figure out myself, but I don't control him. Arkimedes is not that scary, and my mother pissed off the Society of Crows when she married a non-magical man, lied to them, then escaped with me in tow." *And* Cameron, but Violet didn't need to know that.

"I'm not sure if you are just naïve or stupid. Maybe both."

"You are so nice. I wonder why I even try with you."

Violet's lips pursed as she walked around the house, abandoning Nava. "Let's give you the benefit of the doubt, kitten. You are new to this life, that much is clear. Why would I risk everything I love to protect you?"

"What—?"

"Arkimedes bringing you here put us all in danger. Devon will come for you *and* him. To him, we are insects. You two are his prize. Why should I not take you there myself?"

"Oh, you think Devon is here for us alone?" Nava challenged. "He came searching for *deserters*. He didn't even know I was on this island until he found my shop. Taking me to him won't stop him. Once he has us, he will keep coming for more. His ship is large. It will fit this whole village in it, and the ones who don't fit will likely get executed."

Violet's nostrils flared, her face and throat flushed.

"You are counting on Arkimedes to help." Nava's voice was unwavering. Violet had come of her own will to train her so she was ready for what was coming. She was not a burden but an asset in the eyes of this trained warrior. Her soul soared. "You need me."

"We don't need you." Violet's gaze narrowed. She walked toward her bag, trying to find a set of clean clothes.

"No, you do." Nava's throat became a knot, the knowledge making her dizzy.

Violet's lips pressed down, and she didn't argue any further. "We have been sending sentinels to see if they can find the army, if they are coming north or heading east. Arkimedes and Gavin went with them earlier today. They haven't returned."

He had left without saying goodbye, even though he'd said he would never leave her behind. Her heart squeezed at this, and she sobered her features. This situation was more significant than whatever was going on between her and Arkimedes. This meant freedom for everyone on this island, including Cameron and Laurie.

"They left before I woke this morning. He should have come to get me as he promised." Violet shifted, her face tinted with concern, and Nava understood. While her concern had been for Arkimedes, Violet's was for Gavin.

"I want to train," Nava said.

"I won't go easy on you, kitten. Not like he does."

Nava opened her mouth to counter that Arkimedes didn't go easy on her, but Violet's knowing expression made her shut her mouth. "Fine, but please don't kill me."

"I'll try my best since, according to you, we need you." Violet's voice held mockery.

"I'll get dressed and will be right out." Nava headed to the small bathroom in the back of the house.

"Hurry up. We need to get you fed before you pass out on me, as you like doing."

NAVA HIT THE GROUND WITH A GROAN, her hands scraping over rock and dirt, her muscles sore by their training intensity. Violet was standing over her, still in a fighting stance. This time they were training sans magic, per Nava's request after she had hit the ground more times than she cared to admit.

Violet had street fighting skills, and she moved with precision over grace. Her hits were hard, and by the third punch, she had left Nava winded right before the woman had swept her off her feet.

Nava had, however, gotten several hits, and Violet's pointers were helpful.

"C'mon, kitten, I'm not getting any younger," Violet

said, her voice never abandoning that bored tone that ground on Nava's nerves.

She pushed up, her arms trembling from exhaustion. They had trained with magic before, and that duel had gone better for her. Now, her body was too tired even to get up.

"Draining your body of energy while using magic might as well be a death sentence," Violet said.

Heat flooded Nava's cheeks. "Everyone has failed to teach me how to avoid it." The heaviness of her limbs refused to move, dragging over muddy soil.

"It's not something we can teach you. It's something you learn by practicing every day. Things like energy from your surroundings become more apparent." Violet lazily poked at her side with her foot.

The movement made Nava's blood boil.

No.

Heat rushed over her body, and her muscles trembled as power ran through her, her limbs not so sore anymore. No, she would not get kicked while defeated on the floor. She had fought her entire life to keep afloat, head over water, preventing her from drowning, and her body would not give in yet.

She swept her legs under Violet's and pushed her body from the ground with unnatural power. No, it wasn't artificial. It was *her* power. Her skin buzzed with energy, shining white and yellow.

Violet gasped as she fell to the ground and stared back at Nava's glowing skin. "You are cheating."

"There is no cheating in war, especially against someone who kicks the person who's down." Nava's power was shining brighter.

Violet was up from the ground in a blink. Both

attacked, hitting a target as they grunted, and pain extended through her extremities.

Nava knew she had little energy left. She had to get the other woman down one more time. She shifted her attention from the energy that ran through her body to the earth beneath her feet. Her power hummed with recognition of the natural magic around her, pulling energy from her surroundings instead, as Arkimedes had once told her.

Nava stepped back away from Violet. The brisk air burned her lungs. Her eyes snapped to the large tree roots by Violet's feet, thicker than her legs, and she imagined them moving, grabbing the woman, and holding her down.

The trees moved, and Violet gasped as thick roots lifted from the ground and shook the two women on their feet, making them lose their balance. Faster than she could imagine something so significant moving, the roots grabbed the slim figure of the warrior and pinned her down.

Everything went quiet except for the intense buzzing inside Nava's head. She stumbled forward to check if Violet was all right. Her face slacked in shock, facing the open sky that peeked over the tall branches of trees. Nava held her weight against the wood of a nearby tree. The noise around them became louder. Voices exclaimed, and the loud steps of people approached.

"A-are y-you all right?" Nava's words were slurred.

A genuine smile appeared on Violet's face. "Not so much a kitten," she groaned.

Nava leaned against the tree, closing her eyes

"I'm impressed, tiger."

Nava's lips twitched before her legs gave in. She was falling before it all went dark.

CHAPTER TWENTY-FOUR

Nava . . . Nava . . .

Her eyes fluttered open, burning from the brightness around her. She closed them again before letting them adjust as strong hands held her head, and her blurry vision focused on a familiar shape of a man.

"Welcome back," a soft voice said.

She focused on Gavin's face as it became clearer in front of her, his crooked smile more apparent.

"Thanks." Her voice was hoarse. "Water?"

Quick feet behind her and a canteen of water appeared. She drank as if water hadn't touched her lips in years. And she didn't stop until there wasn't a drop left.

"That was quite something you did, pinning Violet down with a tree—I had never seen that before," Gavin said.

"Is that judgment I hear?"

Gavin laughed, shaking his head. "On the contrary." His gaze came up, and she followed it toward Violet, who was standing nearby with her arms crossed, eyeing him with anger.

"Well, she's up now, so I'm going to make myself useful. Not all of us have the luxury of sleeping in the middle of the day," Violet snapped.

Nava didn't get to ask her if she was okay. The other woman had already stormed off.

"She is fine," Gavin reassured her. "The anger isn't directed at you."

Nava blinked. Understanding rang inside her head. Gavin and Arkimedes had left them to go on a mission and hadn't bothered to let them know. Her brow furrowed at the memory. "Arkimedes?" The word left her lips before she could stop it.

She turned her head, trying to find him among the people nearby. Gavin's hands left the back of her neck, and she pushed herself up with her elbows, muscles screaming in protest. She spotted him talking with Roman in the distance, not here checking on her.

"He is fine," Gavin said.

"I get it." Her bitter tone said more than her words.

"It makes me happy I'm not the only one in trouble." Gavin's voice was amused.

Nava eyed him, shaking her head. "It's not funny, Gavin."

"It's a little funny," he disagreed, and his hand came to her head again. She winced when his fingers grazed a susceptible spot. "You've got to stop injuring your head. It's not smart to pass out and fall straight on it. Every. Single. Time."

"I'll remember it the next time I lose consciousness—to make sure I don't hurt my head in the process."

"Your healer appreciates it."

Nava sat down. "Why did you leave without saying a word?"

Gavin put a vial of potion back into a leather pouch that hung from his side. "Not all of us have to go all the time," he said with a shrug. "I have my reasons not to tell Violet. The last time I asked her to come with me, we were kidnapped, held, and tortured for days. I'm sure Arkimedes has his reasons."

Nava frowned, and her mouth parted to refute, but she caught Arkimedes's approaching form. His tentative steps brought him over. Her eyes narrowed.

His hands dug inside his coat pockets. "How are you feeling?"

Had he come to check her when they arrived or had he been too busy to care before? How much of the whole thing had he seen?

"Never been better," she said, moving to get up. Ready to go back to her cabin and take a long warm bath to soothe her muscles. Maybe if he was so eager to distance himself from her, she should do the same. She was never one to pine and beg for attention. It was annoying her heart had decided to start now.

"Take it easy for the rest of the day. No more training." Gavin's voice broke the uncomfortable silence that had fallen in between them before he lifted to his feet. The man's hand landed on Arkimedes's shoulder, and they both shared a look of mutual understanding before the healer walked off, leaving her alone with him.

She winced, her muscles and sides protesting from the hits her body had taken during her sparring with Violet. Her head throbbed, still weakened by her display of magic from before.

"Do you need me to—"

"Don't say it," she snapped. "I can't believe you left this morning to find Devon's army with these people who hate you and conveniently forgot about me."

He shut up. More hurt than she cared, she pushed the knot that had formed in her throat down.

Her legs moved, anger driving her forward. She wanted to be out of there and away from Arkimedes. His steps followed. The temperature was colder today. The sun was hidden behind heavy rain clouds.

"It was early, and I thought it would be best for you to rest."

She turned around, and he almost ran her over. Nava poked the hard planes of his chest, raising her face to meet him with a challenge. "No, you felt I couldn't handle it."

His brows lowered into a deep furrow. "*Not* true. I wanted to protect you."

"Please. I'm not a child." She turned around. Nava spotted the cabin as raindrops started to fall, rustling the trees' leaves with the wind, first a slow pitter-patter and then thick, heavier drops.

She pushed the door and went inside but didn't bother to close it, aware he wasn't far away. She turned after the door locked. Arkimedes stood ruffled, his hair pointing in different directions.

It was clear they had left before he'd gotten much rest, if his tired face was anything to go by.

"It's dangerous. You have never been in something like what awaits us," Arkimedes rushed to say, taking wide strides straight to her.

"And you—"

"Yes, I have."

"Well, since you like to keep secrets from me, I barely know anything about you. What did you do before coming to this island? Why are you alone? Why do these people dislike you?"

Hurt flashed through his features, and he crossed his arms over his chest. "What do you want from me?"

"For you to tell me things!" she snapped. Groaning, she stepped around the living area.

"It's not a good story to tell. It's not nice to remember my family abandoned me and that I have spent my entire life being feared for something I don't understand! I don't know much of where I come from. The little I know, I don't like."

"I also did things I'm not proud of when I was trying to fit in. It's hard to find a moment to explain all of this when we are trying to survive."

Her ire softened a fraction, the fire burning in her veins dimming somehow. Arkimedes had told her he had been abandoned before, and when his magic presented, the orphanage had been eager to get rid of him. "I guess I understand," she said, but something kept nagging at her, scratching in the fog of her memories. "Why does everyone here say you are dangerous?"

Silence descended upon them. She shifted her weight around. He would not say anything of the matter. Disappointment took over.

"The magic that runs through me is dark and old. It comes from an elven bloodline in the Copper Kingdom." He shrugged. Judging by the tense set of his jaw, this was anything but trivial to him. "I stopped trying to find my origins a long time ago. I accept people will not trust me and that I'll never understand why."

Silence took over. The only noise around them was the heavy rain falling.

"How can they sense you are different?" She didn't understand.

Arkimedes's expression softened on her. "It's my aura. Unlike most people with magic, mine is always present."

Nava blinked, confused as she studied his body. Flesh

and blood. "I don't understand. I don't see anything but you."

"Have you ever seen my aura before?"

She nodded. "Your magic aura is black. It's present when we are training. It's like mist."

His lips flattened, and his hand came over his head, brushing his hair out of his face. "Most people here can see it, even if I'm not using any magic. It's a curse on its own. It stirs fright in people, mistrust." He paced around for a while and stopped, his back straighter. "My magic works in sinister ways. It takes energy from people. Suppose I hurt someone. I kill, even if it's in self-defense. I absorb part of their power."

Nava gasped, and her mind supplied a memory of the day he'd rescued her from Devon's army. The mist that had followed him around showed shadow arms and hands. Her skin went cold.

"You have seen it." He deflated.

"I—I think I have, the day the bounty hunters took me from our camp."

"Well, that's what they see of me all the time."

No wonder everyone feared him. "Ark, I just see you," she admitted, swallowing.

"I have been alone in this world since I was born, bee. You are one of the only people I have let get this close." And by his morphing expression, she couldn't tell if this pleased him or made him even more hesitant.

The sizzling of affection and trust surrounded them. They had been through so much already and had fought to protect each other. Had confided in one another—more so her than him, but still.

He walked past her toward the fireplace and leaned against the cold stone while he got lost in the dim embers, the fire coming to life.

The scent of magic surrounded her, and it didn't make her panic as it once had. Much had changed in such a short time, a life of prejudices shaken so. After so many weeks together, him using magic was as normal as breathing.

She remained quiet, allowing him time to come up with another slice of truth he would share with her. He would shut down if she pushed him too hard. He was afraid, but she didn't understand why.

His nature reminded her a little of her mother, and it made her pause. Her mother had always had a problem opening up. She'd liked to keep secrets, not saying anything when it could help.

Why did life keep making her care for people who were afraid to let others love them?

"Do they have reasons to fear you?" she asked, trying to focus on the present, to take advantage of the fact that even though she could sense he was close to closing himself off, he was still sharing.

Maybe leaving her behind today had made him feel guiltier than expected.

"Yes," he said. "Whatever is in my nature, it's not light. My thoughts sometimes are harsher than normal. I have an easier time making hard choices, but it doesn't mean I lack empathy, though."

Nava came one more step closer to him, giving in to the pull between them. She was close enough that her body touched his. Arkimedes's head dropped, his forehead pressing into hers. She had never been so close to him. The scent of cedar, leather, and the intoxicating smoke from a campfire enveloped her. She enjoyed the intimacy of it all as the air of his breath hit her face.

She forgot her insecurities.

You should pull away, her mind supplied, worrying

Arkimedes would pull back once again, as he had done before.

Maybe this was magic-induced love, after all. No, not love—care.

"You don't have to be so afraid of letting people in, of letting *me* in. You won't lose me," she said and met his gaze. Her hand came to his face, and a spark of electricity ran from her fingertips.

Her body shook with anticipation, and she was drunk with desire, needing to explore his body with more than her mind.

Her fingers trailed his face across his soft skin that was golden after traveling for so many weeks. He went still under her touch. She wasn't sure when she'd become this bold. Maybe she had always been.

Nava took a calming breath, waiting for him to pull back again. He stayed, his black lashes fluttering. His eyes opened, and without preamble, he kissed her.

It was unlike anything she'd ever experienced before, and it took her by surprise. Her body buzzed with aware-ness. Her skin raised in goose bumps when his lips demanded more of her.

A wave of desire crashed into her, pooling in the pit of her stomach and extending to her core. She wrapped her arms behind his neck as his skilled tongue caressed the bottom of her lip and his arms dropped to her hips, lower, resting on the curve of her ass.

She opened her mouth, meeting his tongue in a deli-cate dance as her hands held strands of his hair. He grunted in response and dove deeper into the kiss as he pulled her closer. She was burning up. Nava's fingers teased his hair, and she gasped when his hands grasped both her legs and lifted her off the ground.

Nava wrapped them around his hips. He was so close

to where she wanted him. She let out a soft moan when the hard shape of his cock pressed against her. She straddled him as he walked blindly. Wherever was he taking her, she hoped it was somewhere horizontal and soft.

She rocked her hips, and they broke apart for a few seconds after he hit the side of a table. He was great at this. While Nava was not experienced, she had been kissed a few times before. None had caused her toes to curl and her desire to spike.

She gasped when her back touched the hard cold wall, and her stomach tightened. He pushed against her center. There were too many layers of clothes in between them. She traced her lips down the thick expanse of his throat, rejoicing in his taste and the soft sounds he made. His hands weren't idle as he pushed her coat off, and this time she was the one pushing against him, trying to calm her burning desire.

Her head thumped against the wall. Arkimedes took that as an invitation, and his teeth nipped her neck, sending shivers through her body. The way he pressed against her told her how he would move when he was inside her, and her blood burned hotter.

It wasn't lost on her that he could hold her body weight up while moving and not have to put her down. His strength made her hunger for him grow, and she moaned.

She pulled his shirt out of his trousers, an edge of desperation in her movements. The fabric was off his body, and her hands lost no time exploring his newly exposed skin.

Mine.

It made her pause. Arkimedes's lips trailed down her chest, his fingers unbuttoning her shirt.

She blinked. Desire pushed aside the random possessive thought that had crossed her mind. Her shirt pulled open, revealing the freckled skin of her chest, her breasts covered by a sheer layer of lace and thin cotton.

His lips traced feather-like kisses down her clavicle, down and down. She writhed against his hips, trying to no avail to bring him closer.

He stopped.

Nava stared down to find him paralyzed, his face a few inches away from where her soulmate mark was. Three circles that could have been confused for a birthmark to an untrained eye.

"Ark?" Her voice was small. She traced a few strands of hair out of his face, and he tensed.

He pulled away, and his hands came to her waist, making it easier for her to unwrap her legs' firm grip from around his hips.

She stood, shaking under her weight, and he was off her body as if she were on fire and it had burned him. "What's happening?" His reaction was making her self-conscious about her state of undress. She pulled her shirt closed, her brows furrowing.

"I can't." He shook his head.

She pressed her lips together. Her soulmate mark was visible, and suddenly, he wanted nothing to do with her. She guessed knowing it and seeing it made a difference.

She couldn't believe she had allowed herself to get pushed away *again*. She swallowed her anger, as it had formed a thick knot in her throat. *I guess you don't want me, after all.*

"It's not that."

Of course, her brain filter had failed to do its job once again, and she had spoken all those insecurities out loud because the situation wasn't mortifying enough as it was.

She didn't want his pity, and the way he was staring at her grated on her nerves. She clumsily closed the buttons of her shirt, aware of how much easier it had been for him to work them open than for her to close them. "Well, it feels that way." Hurt seeped into every word. "I would like to be alone." She stepped away from the wall with shaky legs, her vagina demanding something to happen. She had clearly not gotten the memo.

Not tonight, and not ever again.

"Bee," he pleaded as she walked past him toward the bathroom.

She appreciated that he didn't follow her or try to hold her back for a heart-to-heart. His self-preservation was not *that* lacking.

She slammed the door behind her and leaned against it. The kisses, hard and passionate, flashed through her mind, and she let herself slide to the floor. Her heart felt tight, as if it had been shrunken down after being so full.

Tears spilled down her cheeks. She hugged her legs and let herself think. Nava shouldn't be this upset. She had made it possible for him to hurt her this way. Arkimedes had told her from the beginning that he wasn't ready for this. She understood he had the right to change his mind. Maybe he didn't love her the way she did him.

Love—did she love him? She had never been in love before. It was the first time it had come so clearly that she allowed herself to admit her feelings.

He might be the one, her soulmate, hidden in plain sight. He had told her that he wasn't, and yet, she had still fallen.

Something in between a laugh and a cry escaped her lips. Leave it to her mother to play with her truth this way.

She didn't hear him leave.

So Nava allowed herself to cry over her broken heart on the cold stone floor of the washroom. The light of the fading afternoon seeped through the stained glass window in colorful speckles that slowly fell away as her heavy lids closed, giving way to the darkness of sleep.

Powerful arms carried her, and she nuzzled her nose against a chest that smelled like home. Nava was caught between reality and a dream, but she was being moved, the coolness of the surrounding room a clear contrast to the warmth of the body against her.

"Arkimedes?"

"Shh. Sleep." His voice was whisper-quiet enough that if she hadn't been so close to him, she would have missed it.

A soft feather-like kiss to her forehead and the heaviness of sleep pulled her under. She hadn't dreamed of him for so long. She'd almost forgotten what it felt like to be in his arms.

The arms of her soulmate.

CHAPTER TWENTY-FIVE

*K*nock. *Knock.*

Soft knocking woke her up. Nava blinked her sleep away, focusing on the pale gold-and-beige tones of the dry bamboo ceiling. Its imposing rustic wood beams held it up.

She had cried all her tears away the night before. The heaviness of her breathing reminded her that her heart had been shattered. Nava didn't understand why it had happened. Her raw and well-kissed lips, and the memory of how his body had responded to her, told her he had felt the connection like she did.

Knock. Knock.

She pulled the soft wool cover higher, trying to wrap herself in the comfort of the bed, so different from the cold hard floor in a sleeping bag. She sighed and enjoyed the feather mattress beneath her.

His scent lingered on her skin.

Nava sat up. How was she in bed? She racked her brain for memories and an explanation of how she had gotten here. The last thing she remembered was being on the washroom floor.

Had she sleepwalked? She guessed it wouldn't be the first time, according to Cameron. She had been known to walk to the kitchen in search of evening snacks.

Knock. Knock. Knock. Whoever was outside was getting impatient.

"Nava." Gavin's voice took her out of her sleepy musings, and she pushed the covers aside, swinging her legs out of the soft comforts of the bed to the floor.

She winced as the cold traveled through her body, and she rushed to the door on her tiptoes, combing a hand through her wild hair, surveying the state of her undress. She was wearing her indigo trousers and a lopsided shirt, none of the holes matching.

"Coming!" Nava brought her hands to the buttons and fixed them. She took a calming breath and put on her best forced smile.

The chill of the morning enveloped her, but the warmth that radiated from Gavin's smile was as contagious as ever. She found her smile grew when she met his gaze.

"You are hard to wake up." He inspected her ruffled state.

Her hand patted down her hair again. "Don't you have someone else to torment? Violet perhaps?" she said in a false snarky tone.

He shook his head, laughing. "Oh, no, I value my life too much to mess with Violet this early in the morning. Plus, she is pissed at me."

Maybe Nava was too soft. Had she been more rigid and taken longer to forgive Arkimedes for leaving her behind, she would have avoided the big mistake that was last night. "What brings you here?" she asked and opened the door to allow him to enter as she made her way to the washroom.

"Roman wants to speak with you," Gavin said, walking in with both hands shoved in his pockets. He was wearing a forest-green shirt and gray trousers, his face bright and rested.

"Please, make yourself comfortable. I need to freshen up." She pointed awkwardly to the door at the end of the narrow hall.

Gavin nodded, walking to the fireplace, a spot where Arkimedes had kissed her senseless the night before. She wished she didn't have to be reminded of it.

Nava found Gavin sitting in one of the leather armchairs, his legs crossed casually as he flipped through the same book Arkimedes had the day they arrived here.

"Ready?" He closed the book with a snap.

"He doesn't waste any time. Roman, I mean."

"We don't get town dwellers here, much less a magical one who brings us news of impending doom. One who comes accompanied not only by a powerful sorcerer, but one that seems to have a history with the Commander."

To her, Arkimedes being powerful was no secret. They had all seen him fight that morning when Devon held them captive. It made sense now that she was aware of his history, of what the others saw. "I would never lie about Devon coming. Arkimedes is powerful, but he wouldn't hurt you or the people in this village," Nava said, even though there was a piece of the puzzle she didn't have.

"I'm aware of that . . . now." He paused, sauntering out of the house.

The splendor of this village took her breath away once more. Buzzing with life in earth tones, the setting was beautiful. People of all shapes and sizes walked by her in colorful robes and tunics. Pointy ears. People with horns.

Small children who seemed to have shadows following them around. The view would have been creepy, but the child was laughing.

Here in this village in the middle of the forest, magic didn't look like a curse, but something that brought life and joy. Her heart squeezed.

Why had her mother decided to live in a non-magical town when this was a possibility?

Well, had it not been for the name of her shop and her peculiar eyes, Devon Black wouldn't have found her. She begrudgingly gave her mom a point.

If it had not happened, she wouldn't have made it here to warn them about the threat. She wouldn't have learned about magic and her Beekeeper and . . . love.

"Roman doesn't trust your boy yet," Gavin said.

He was unaware of Nava's train of thoughts or the way she cringed at him calling Arkimedes hers. His words were a bucket of cold water to her senses. "He is not *my* anything, I told you."

"Does he know that?"

"Gavin, he's the one making it so." Nava shook her head. "His hot and cold is giving me— He doesn't want me."

Her brain supplied plenty of memories of Arkimedes pushing against her the night before, his groans and kisses. Nava pressed her lips into a thin line. Maybe he wanted her body, but there was something else preventing him from letting go, and the other side was stronger than whatever attraction he had for her.

Gavin stared at Nava with a raised brow. "I don't get it, and I'm a pretty good judge with these things."

They walked through roads of dirt, rocks, and pine needles. There were homes against and up trees as if suspended in the air. A street market, where people gathered and chatted vibrantly, bustled with activity. The smell of saffron, rosemary, and other spices wafted into the air. Wooden crates were filled with fruit and vegetables.

Dried meat and cheeses hung from tent roofs. The place was popping with life, and if Nava didn't focus on the different creatures surrounding them and the magic scent sparkling in the air, she could almost forget she was in a magic forest away from home.

She focused on a small creature inside a cage. It was scaled and small, painted in bright colors. Pink, teals, and blues. A Dragon?

"Yes, a young one," Gavin answered with a laugh. "I assume you have never been in a magical market before?"

She shook her head, pressing her lips together. Her mother had gone alone to the magical markets when they lived in the city, always leaving her behind with Laurie, and when Cameron had been born, he had also stayed. "My mother said it was dangerous for me to come, back when we were in the City of Iron."

Gavin nodded. "She was right."

"I have feared magic for so long, for it to cause despair and death. It shocks me to see it so alive."

"Magic can be both death and life. It's up to us to find the balance and to defend our freedom, to have the choice to do so."

Nava understood Gavin's words more than he knew.

"I was taken by the army, never to see my family again, until I was old enough to get a break. I was one of the luckier ones who got to stay with them longer. Most, like Violet, are taken when they are twelve years old, and then the training starts." His words matched his sad expression.

Nava stared horrified at Gavin. The Society of Crows took their members as children, but she had never heard of the army recruiting theirs so young.

"I found another family here amongst all these people after I escaped the kingdom with Violet."

"Did they make you do things you didn't want to?" she asked.

Gavin's face turned more severe, and his Adam's apple bobbed. "We were prisoners. We had to follow or face the consequences."

"Did they try to force you to wed? Violet and you, I mean," Nava asked.

"Aye, they did. The crown doesn't care about who you love, whether you are already with someone or have a soulmate. They will match you with another equal sorcerer or sorceress, and you have to procreate. They want to keep their army going."

A crawling sensation traveled down her spine. "You had a soulmate?"

Gavin raised a brow. "No, no. Soulmates are hard to come by, Nava—one in a million, they say. I was young, and I was lucky I had not found anyone at the time."

He kept talking, unaware of how she had stumbled on her feet, her throat going dry all at once. She was grateful she could avoid this prison and ungrateful because she didn't want her soulmate. Right?

"What happens if you are barren and can't have children?" she asked.

"Oh—they will cancel your marriage and arrange another union."

"Wow."

"Either way, it was better to join Violet on her crazy escapade than be murdered on our wedding night," he joked, and a breath of a laugh escaped his lips.

Nava shook her head, smiling. From both of their interactions, they had grown to care about, if not love, one another, so at least, even though they were forced, the crown had not ruined them. "I guess I felt like I was in prison as well," she admitted, remembering the long days inside their manor when she was fifteen, wanting to feel the sun, to make friends. "Except mine wasn't imposed by the king and queen's greed, but by my mother." It was the first time she had voiced it, and it shook her how bitter she sounded.

"Sometimes we do stupid shit for the people we love most," he said.

Both of them fell silent as they walked past the market to a quieter part of the village.

There was a large campfire and a long table with mixed food laid over it—cheese, crackers, dried meats, fruit, and bread. People walked around with bowls and plates, filling them with food and heading on their way to unknown places.

She spotted three large men speaking on the side of the campfire, their expressions solemn. Roman, Arkimedes, and the same guy Gavin had been speaking with the day of the celebration.

Her heart dropped when her gaze settled on Arkimedes. He was wearing new clothes, a black shirt, gray pants, and brown leather belts that held his enormous sword.

Nava's steps slowed when his eyes met hers across the way. She swallowed as the images from the night before came crashing down, and she cursed her vibrant memory and hurried to catch up to Gavin, who didn't seem to notice her falling behind.

Her heart hammered in her chest as they made their way to the three men. Arkimedes's arms dropped when she was but three meters from him.

"Good morning, Nava," Roman said, taking her out of her inner turmoil. His voice was a lot less tense than the day she'd arrived. Nava wished the passing days had brought her the same peace.

The night before, she had imagined sleeping deeply after a few hours of intense lovemaking, but that had been replaced by intense crying instead.

She slept well, and today at least, she was rested. It was more than she could say for Arkimedes. His expression was shuttered and tired. He had come here right after changing back to his human form.

"Morning," she responded to the Commander because the good part was debatable.

"Nava." Arkimedes's voice was a plea.

She wished he wasn't so ruggedly handsome with his fresh clothes and trimmed stubble. Her attention deviated to Roman.

"You called for me bright and early, so here I am." A forced smile tugged at her lips.

"Let's talk about Devon and his ship," Roman said.

Her cheeks warmed. She was afraid the information she had was lacking. "Uh, okay."

"We are trying to figure out the number of Devon's army. It's hard to tell what to prepare for by something so ambiguous," Roman started.

"I'm not sure I will be much help. I didn't see his ship —had intended to go and take a peek at a later date, but he came to my store, and I had to run." She shrugged. "He told me there were hundreds—but I didn't see it myself, so I'm not sure."

"You are right, that's not helpful at all," Roman said.

"Better than what you had a week ago." Arkimedes's voice was low and cold. "We could go and investigate again today, make it closer to their camp."

"We are not in the kingdom anymore. You do not call

the shots." Roman's body had gone rigid with tension, his golden skin turning red.

These beasts of men couldn't wait to jump at each other's throats, and by the looks of it, they would get there before Devon even made it here.

Her money was on Arkimedes, if she were a gambler.

Her mind reeled back to Roman's words. Arkimedes had called the shots over the Commander, a high-ranking soldier in the army?

"Let's calm down. We aren't enemies here," the third man said, and Nava turned to him. His expression was gentle, his face was all sharp angles, and his caramel-colored hair was wavy and long. He was in his late thirties. Unlike the other men, this third guy didn't appear to be a trained fighter.

"I agree," Gavin said next to her.

Roman's gaze fell on the third man, and his own expression relaxed. He cleared his throat. "You are right, Mars."

Mars approached the Commander, and his hand came to his back, rubbing calming circles up and down, a smile on both their faces. She understood by their body language they weren't friends but lovers.

"If you want to do another round, I will send some men with you," Roman agreed, and Arkimedes nodded.

"Breakfast?" Gavin's voice startled her.

She nodded and was happy to be pulled away from that uncomfortable conversation. "Are the Commander and Mars together?" she asked when they were far enough from ears to reach.

Gavin chuckled. "Curious, aren t we? But yes, they are. The reason why Roman left the kingdom was because of their relationship, if I'm not mistaken. You could ask Mars. He is an open book."

"He doesn't look like you all. He looks . . . normal."

"Ouch, normal? Who wants to be normal?"

"I used to," she mumbled. "What I mean is he doesn't give me the soldier vibes."

"He is not. He was an actor in the city—a quite popular one at that. The girls used to flaunt themselves at him, or so he says." Gavin chuckled. "The kingdom forces us to marry but never listens to what you desire. Who you love. A man and a woman are forced to marry because they are after our children. We were all screwed."

When would this crazy world rebel against them and claim their freedom back? Nava hoped it was in their life-time. Maybe Cameron would be free to visit the kingdoms and chose who to marry outside of the Greylands.

CHAPTER TWENTY-SIX

$\mathcal{N}$ava filled her plate. Her stomach rumbled at the sight of the food. Bread, butter, and cheese. She gazed at Gavin as he put a healthy serving of honey on top of his bread. She took a deep breath to calm her uneasy stomach and filled her plate with it all, except for the honey.

"Comfort food today, eh?" Gavin commented, glancing at her plate.

"Oh, shush." She appreciated him. He wanted to cheer her up, and it was working. Distraction over food made her not be consumed by rejections or heart-melting kisses. Her eyes traveled to Arkimedes, who was sitting by the fire with Roman and Mars.

Violet had joined them, and the four of them seemed to be caught in a vibrant conversation. Judging by Arkimedes's frown, whatever the subject, it wasn't a pleasant one. A warm wave of protectiveness washed over her.

It didn't matter what had happened in between them.

She didn't want him outnumbered by people who clearly mistrusted him. "We should go back there."

Gavin stared at the heated conversation with a curious expression.

They weren't sitting too far from the table of food. She walked around the fire and plunked down across from Arkimedes. She wanted to be there for him but not too close. She took an absent bite of her bread, and the salty flavor of butter dominated her palate.

It took her a minute to note the conversation had paused. She studied the group. Gavin was sipping on his steaming drink with a wondering expression. Roman was giving Violet a warning.

She focused on Arkimedes. He was sitting tenser than usual, his face troubled.

"So what? We're supposed to stop talking because Nava is here?" Violet snapped, and it was Nava's turn to straighten up. It was a miracle she had not choked on her food.

"Violet!" Roman's voice was a warning.

Arkimedes didn't flinch, his stormy green gaze coming up to meet Violet's with a cold, unmovable expression.

"What's happening?" Nava's gaze moved across the fire to Violet, who was scowling at Roman. It had been a while since she had seen that severe expression on her face.

"You two are here talking about how she doesn't know yet. She deserves to!"

"About what?" For once, she agreed with Violet, albeit blindly. She had the inclination it had to do with the secrets between her, Arkimedes, and whatever hostility these rebel sorcerers harvested toward him.

"It's not ours to tell. We don't have all the history," Roman warned.

"I want to know," Nava whispered.

Arkimedes's face turned into one of pure panic. Long gone was the calm, collected expression. His mouth opened as if to speak, and the knot in her throat became thicker.

Violet's voice interrupted the thick silence surrounding them. "He was sent to hunt us, over and over. Keep us under their shackles. Am I supposed to forget this?" she challenged Roman.

"Before two weeks ago, I had never met you in my life." Arkimedes answered this time, his voice matching the coolness of Violet's voice. "Last I checked, I saved your life from the ones who were keeping you prisoner."

Violet's lips pursed. If her stormy gaze could kill, Arkimedes would be dead. "You are all alike." Venom dripped from her words. "Breaking families apart, not caring that besides our magic, we are people."

"We are not servants of the crown," Arkimedes snapped. "The Society is meant to keep balance. We take on the task and teach magic. We defend innocent people. The crown and civilians are all subject to the law of life."

"Is that so? You are more focused on maintaining their armies, following their nonethical coupling rules—taking children away from their families," Violet hissed.

Arkimedes took a sharp breath, eyeing Nava, concern back on his features. Nava's brain was fighting to catch on. Society . . . ?

"We—they don't take children away. The Society only takes the ones who offered to join because it's an honor to serve our gods. But not everyone's intentions are good," Arkimedes agreed. "There is good, bad . . . and in-between. There are people in our—the Society who are fighting for people's rights."

"Yet here you are, cursed by a sorceress you chased down, and the Society of Crows is not tailing your whereabouts," Violet said. "This is because you are one of them. You leaving doesn't bring the same repercussions as *us* leaving does. We are hunted down like animals."

Nava tensed, her mouth as dry as sandpaper as she met his eyes across the fire. Nothing and no one was around them. The silence that descended was absolute. Her breathing was loud to her own ears.

She'd known it from the beginning. A fog lifted from her mind, taking her own stubborn denial. She focused on his lie, clear as day. At first, she had been doubtful her mother would ever send her straight to him, but Nava hadn't wanted to accept it as the days turned into weeks.

He was part of the Society of Crows, and in a flash, she could see him, behind the blueish tunics, his voice asking her if her mother was at home in a distant memory.

The earth shook beneath her, and she bunched the fabric of her coat in a fierce grip. She shook as adrenaline ran through her veins. Trying to discern the truth behind his tumultuous expression, to find something that would ground her, to tell her what she was conjuring in her mind was not true.

Even if he was a Crow, that didn't mean he had lied to her about being her soulmate, right?

No, she was doing it again, making excuses and trying to find other truths when reality was staring her straight in the face. It had ever since the beginning.

Regret, worry, and pain were etched on his face as his lips parted, his expression changing to one of pure panic as he realized she had put all the pieces together at last.

"Nava." He rushed to his feet, and absolute silence descended upon the group.

She stopped him with a raised hand, going over memories, things her mother had told her when they'd been escaping the kingdom. How afraid she had been because *he* had been chasing after them.

Him . . . the one Crow with the most power her mother had known. From that fateful afternoon, he'd turned her life upside down. Her mother had been afraid of him, of the darkness in his power. Arkimedes had revealed as much the night before, how people feared him for what he represented.

The magic of her *soulmate*. It made sense why she was not afraid of him. Why, even though everyone could focus on his aura, she could only see him.

"You are *him*," she murmured. Adrenaline pumped through her veins as she stumbled off the log she had been sitting on.

He was up in a blink of an eye, so fast she stumbled backward, trying to gain distance in between them. He was around the fire and over the log she had been sitting on. As he took slow steps toward her, his voice turned pleading. "No. *Yes*. Nava, please let me explain."

She could barely register the shapes of the rest of the group in the background. When had Roman stood up? Her mind was spinning, her hands shaking more as tears ran down her cheeks. "You *lied* to me."

"No. I . . . diverted," he said, and there was a ruffling sound around them.

She turned to Roman, who clung to the grip of his sword. The weapon meant nothing. All Arkimedes had to do was raise his hand and point it at the leader of this town for him to crumple down.

However, Arkimedes wouldn't hurt the man.

"Arkimedes." Roman's voice was filled with a warning.

"Stay out of this, Roman," Arkimedes seethed.

"You are my soulmate—all this time." Her voice shook

with pent-up emotion. He was quiet, and his silence was all the confirmation she needed.

She had asked him before, and he had denied it. The answer had been there all along. In her mind, he was always the one, but each time she'd come close to admitting it, she had pushed that away, overlooking something so obvious. Like his voice, how easily she'd fallen in love with him when her entire life she'd had no connection or attraction to anyone.

Why would her mother send her straight to him? Her mother, the most aggravating person she'd ever known.

There was a gasp from around them, and both Nava and Arkimedes turned to face the others. The audience made her already clammy skin prickly with their stares. They were too close. Her clothes were too tight, suffocating her.

Roman dropped his sword back to its sheath and, with a quick nod, walked off without another word. His large hand grabbed Mars and pulled him along. Gavin followed behind, a bowl of food in his hand as he pushed a spoonful of eggs into his mouth, chewing like nothing else was awry.

Violet stood frozen, her features twisted in so much confusion.

"Violet!" Roman's stern voice shook her, and without another look back, she walked off.

Nava wrapped her arms across her stomach as a wave of dizziness ran through her body.

"Can we speak in private?"

She shook her head. Walking might not be an option for her with her trembling legs. "We are alone now."

"We are never alone in this forest." He came one step closer, and she took a step back, desperately putting distance in between them. "Please."

Her mind rushed through memories. All the rightness

of his kiss. Was that even real? Was it all a magic trick? She wasn't sure anymore.

She turned on her heels and forced her body to move, numb as she walked the stone road toward the cabin that had been theirs for the past few days. He opened the door for her. She stepped into the home, flustered, unsure, and confused.

"Let me see it," she said in a biting tone, turning to face him.

"Bee . . ."

"Arkimedes, let me see it," she begged, her voice shaking with emotion.

He stared. "I don't think—"

"You owe it to me," she snapped, a wave of pure rage rushing through her.

He didn't move, his breathing hard, matching hers.

"Show me your mark, Arkimedes. "

His hand came to his chest, dabbing the center between his two pecs. She knew where it was located, a place she had so eagerly touched and kissed the night before. "Why? Would that change anything in between us?" he challenged, his expression shuttering.

"What is that? I don't know anything."

"How does this change anything of what you feel— what I feel?"

"And what is that?" she snapped. "You haven't said anything. I have been throwing myself at you since we met, unable to control this crazy attraction, while you knew all along why and you—"

"What? I didn't take advantage of you. At first, I didn't want this either, Nava. You might remember our conversation."

How could she forget? He had all but told her he didn't

want her. Granted, at the time, she had said the same thing
. . .

"Much like you, it was also a surprise to find a teenager who was meant to be mine. Before I even figured out what I felt, your mother was already taking you away."

"She was protecting us." Cameron and her.

"From whom?" Arkimedes lifted both hands in frustration. "From her selfish decisions? You are aware we cannot outrun fate. The mate bond will claim us whether we accept it or not. She doomed us both."

"You chased us down across towns, villages, and a whole freaking ocean!" she exclaimed.

"What would you have done? Little is known about soulmates and how it works, other than we are rare and that if we are apart from one another, the dreams will become our reality. If I were not at least close to you by approximation, I wouldn't have survived—neither would you."

"Well, maybe she was scared of you!"

"We already established everyone is scared of me, whether they have to be or not," he said. "She was not letting you decide anything. You were a prisoner in that house."

Nava wanted to refute this, but it was true. She had grown inside the four walls of her home without meeting anyone or anything else. Tears spilled down her cheeks. "I was just a kid. Not ready for a forever match," Nava whispered.

His face morphed into a pained expression. The words hurt him, she could tell. "I was twenty when I found you. Wouldn't say I was experienced and mature. Or ready for a forever match, either."

"She was afraid for me—of you, like all these people, Arkimedes."

"I was young and craving acceptance when she left the Society. She was not perfect, either. She was just as quick at hunting down people who broke the law." Arkimedes shook his head. "They told us lies, and I realize it now, after being away for this long, after meeting all the people who run from who I was."

"Why did she curse you?" She pressed her lips together after the words left her mouth.

"The spell the town has, it doesn't allow magical beasts to enter. As part fae, I was already pushing the limit. She threw in the curse to make sure I could not make it to you."

The conniving, brilliant mind of her mother would never cease to amaze and paralyze her with anger. "Did she tell you how to break your curse?" She knew by his conflicted expression that she would not like the answer.

"Yes."

"Arkimedes, out with it."

He hesitated. "Nava—"

"How do you break your curse?" she pressed.

"I'm supposed to do a selfless act for you," he said.

Silence descended upon them. Pieces came together in her head. Her mother had been mindful that she couldn't stay away from Arkimedes forever. It would eventually kill her.

"You accepting to help me, it was always to break the curse, not to save all these people?" Disappointment flooded her system. She stormed to him and pushed against his chest.

"No, I wanted to help these people. It's not all about us."

"It was always a lie! You never wanted to be with me, to help me. You have been lying to me all this time."

His face was tight and flushed. "At first, I didn't know

you. I had been cursed for ten years. I wanted to be free of it. Don't mistake that for being the sole reason. I also wanted to keep you safe. Protecting you was always my primary goal."

"Somehow, I doubt it." The ground beneath her shook, and she wasn't aware if her emotions had been kicking magic around and she was causing another earthquake. "Why did you lie to me when I asked you if you were him?"

"I—I wasn't ready. I wanted to tell you. I was afraid you would pull away."

"If you are here in this village to be *selfless* and break your curse, congratulations, you brought me here. You can go."

"You don't have to do this."

"I don't want you here, and they don't want you here, either," she said, hoping the words would hurt him at least half as much as she hurt.

The memories of the first time she'd met him, *truly*, inundated her brain.

He winced and frowned. "I can't leave you. Devon is almost here. I can't go."

"Whatever. You can stay if you choose, but don't expect me to speak with you—and when this is all over, I will be going back to my town."

He paled. "It will be a death sentence to us both."

"What do you want from me? You lied. You have done all in your power to reject me when you could have been truthful. Yesterday you left me here, and you didn't consider telling me anything."

"It's not true. I held back yesterday because I did not want our first time to be like that. With a secret so large." He paused.

She had wanted him. Ever since she met him, her

dreams had always been of him. She'd held on to his voice, imagined how he would be. She'd never expected Arkimedes. He was too powerful, too handsome, and apparently too wicked, at least in his past.

She took a breath. Tears spilled down as her throat thickened with emotion. "You should have told me," she repeated.

"To have you run away when I had just found you?" he pleaded.

"Please go."

He hesitated, but Nava stayed where she was, her face unmoving as she pointed in the direction of the door. She was done with the conversation and with the lies. Her heart sank when he turned around and walked away from her.

CHAPTER TWENTY-SEVEN

*A*rkimedes did leave, but not permanently. When Nava went out during the evening for food, she learned from Gavin that he had gone with other sorcerers from the village to investigate how far away Devon's army was and gauge its size.

She took her food and excused herself home, or the home she had for the time being. She didn't eat much, hunger escaping her. The light in the room changed, and she didn't know how long she had been sitting in the leather chair, staring at the red embers of the rolling fire inside the fireplace, lost on the spot in between the gray tones of soot and the dancing flames in front of her.

It could have been an hour, maybe a day—perhaps two. Time was going slower than normal. By the ever-changing shadows across the room, its passage registered in her mind.

She woke up to dreams on and off, of dark gray trees and bloody feathers. Her chest burned with an intensity that made her eyes tear. She guessed the dreams were back, though these were different from what she was used to, full of despair and pain.

Nava wished she were not worried for him as the anger settled in her chest, but she would be lying, and she was going to try to be truthful with herself from now on. After all, nothing came from denying truths to oneself.

She had lost him before she'd ever had him, and who was to blame? Him, her mother, herself, their destiny? Even though her logical mind had let her do it, her heart rebelled against this development.

Nava never got a good glimpse of him in the dreams, and that was even worse. Seeing him again, though briefly during sleeping hours, allured her.

She had been so distracted by her developing love that she had never reflected on why she had stopped dreaming of her soulmate. She had somehow enchanted her mind not to acknowledge him for what he was. It was so much clearer, her memories there for her to study.

Getting to know him, fighting alongside him, fighting *for* him. A sob escaped her lips. The sound of the fire was too loud in her ears, the weight of her body too heavy. Her chest contracted.

"Well, this is even more depressing than I believed it would be, and believe me when I say I could conjure a pretty depressing image when it comes to you." Violet's voice made her jump in her spot. She was standing right beside her, her purple gaze studying her, and even though her words were snarky, her expression was soft.

Nava didn't care. Violet was the last person in the world she wanted. She narrowed her eyes. "Is there a reason you are here? If you're looking to feel better about your sorry existence, congratulations, mission accomplished. Now, leave me alone."

There was a pause, and Violent put down the tray filled with bread and soup that she had been holding onto the table next to Nava, but she didn't move to leave. "You are doing this to yourself, self-punishing. It's weird, coming from you."

"What does that even mean?" Nava's tone had a bite to it.

"It means he is your *soulmate*. What did you expect by rejecting him? That you were going to be fine after sending him away? You have given the both of you a death sentence."

"Why are you here?" Nava exclaimed, getting up from her seat, not wanting to hear this. Concern took over her. "And what do you mean, I rejected him?"

"Did you deny the bond?" she asked. "You have been pining after him for weeks. I don't understand what the big deal is about. So you have this gift, that it's real, and you send him on a mission when his head isn't right, to get captured or worse. Do you think what you're feeling is happening to you alone?"

"No." *Yes.* Her mouth went dry.

"Refusing your mate when you are already half bonded would mean certain death for the both of you," Violet said matter-of-factly.

"Half bonded . . . what are you even talking about? We haven't half bonded anything."

"Do you love him? Did you say it to him?"

Nava closed her lips before the next words came out of her mouth. Violet seemed to know something more, and she was at least sharing the information.

"From what I have studied, admitting the connection already sets the process in motion."

"I didn't say that I loved him, not out loud. He doesn't love me. He never said it."

Violet's brows furrowed. 'Oh, god, you are even more stupid than I thought."

What the hell? "If you are trying to help me, which I'm not even sure that's your goal here, can you please stop insulting me?"

"Look, kitten, it's not a secret I don't like him. I have been running away from the Crows my entire life. I found out he was one recently. I obviously knew he was a Dark One. But having a soulmate, it's a gift from our gods."

"A gift?" Nava's voice echoed with anger or with sadness—she didn't know. "You have been claiming you want freedom, you want to choose your destiny, no? How is this different? I have no choice *but* to love him. I have no say in the matter."

"You have a say. How is it working for you?" Violet asked. "You were all about him before you knew who he was, so did a title change it for you? You have stopped caring for him?"

"No, of course not."

"So what then? You found out who your destined love is. God split one soul into two bodies for them to find each other. Someone most of us never get to have—is that so bad?"

Silence. Did knowing it was him change her mind? She loved him desperately. She always told herself she wouldn't trust this affection being true once she'd found him, but did it make a difference for her?

Her heart ached the same. Her desire for him was still there, untouched. She was angry, sure, but she had been angry with him before.

"When a child is born, a mother loves the baby. Most do, anyway. Nature dictates that for the preservation of *any* species. No one questions it because it's meant to be. Do you question a mother's undying love?"

"No." And for all the wrongs her mother had done, Nava had never questioned the woman's love for her and Cameron. Not ever.

All her decisions were making more sense to her.

"So, nature—the gods, it gave *you* that out of everyone."

"It's not the same. It's magic. Magic gave me this."

"And what is magic, if not our own nature? You have denied it to yourself for whatever stupid reason your brain has come up with. Don't get it wrong, Nava, you are blinded by ignorance."

Even though the words hurt and she wanted to ask Violet to leave once again, deep inside her brain, she got it. She had angrily sent him away, had abandoned him like she had promised she would never do.

Just like his family and the orphanage had done.

Her heart hammered as she lifted her gaze to the other woman.

"And there it is. She gets it."

"You seem to know a lot about soulmates," Nava commented.

Violet nodded and came to sit next to her by the fire. "When I was young, I was one of those who secretly hoped I would find mine." Her delicate brows came down. "Of course, that was silly. One in a million people might find theirs, and many times, they aren't matched."

"What do you mean?"

"I mean, even if they find each other, if one happens to be the wrong gender, non-magical, or the wrong species, the crown would void a soulmate bond over having a sorcerer for their army."

Like her parents, Nava thought, and the pain on Violet's face made her keenly aware of what her mother and father could have gone through had they chosen to follow orders.

"That world is not one for love, kitten," Violet said.

"Unless you end up falling for your assigned partner," Nava piped up.

Violet's attention fixed on her, a smile pulling at her thick lips. "Unless you fall for your assigned partner, eventually," she echoed, nodding, and they both shared a look of understanding. They didn't need to say more. Nava knew that, while it hadn't started as a love match, Violet loved Gavin.

VIOLET STAYED, AND THEY both ate in companionable silence. It was a first for the both of them to converse and not bicker.

When the sun came down, a blinding pain bloomed in Nava's chest. Her mark. She hissed, and her hand came to it. Her skin was hot to the touch.

"What's happening?" Violet's brow rose in questioning.

"I don't know." Nava rubbed the sensitive spot, and her heart stumbled. Something was wrong with Arkimedes. She got to her feet, a cold wave spreading through her. Nausea hit her hard.

"You are pale." Violet rose to her feet.

"Arkimedes is in trouble.' Her gaze turned to the other woman. Her voice sounded panicked even to her own ears.

Violet's face sobered. "We can ask Roman where they went. I will go with you."

Nava probably said thank you or something of the sort, but she didn't remember anything as they exited her provisional home and walked the streets. Cold dread crawled inside her, clogging her throat.

Roman was giving orders to a couple of men by the plaza where she had danced what felt like ages ago. When his eyes locked on them, he dropped his hands and came to them.

"Where is Arkimedes?" Nava's words escaped her lips without preamble. Violet grabbed her elbow, and she wasn't aware she needed the support until it was there. Why was she so panicked? Her throat closed in. Her mind provided images of gray trees and bloody feathers.

Something was very wrong. She could sense it.

"He hasn't returned." Roman focused on Violet. "None of my men have. What's going on?"

"Something is wrong, Roman. I can sense it. My—" She hesitated but pushed forward. "My mark aches, and I have had dreams. Something happened." No one in their right mind would believe her.

Roman's jaw clenched. "They were going southeast, retaking the path we traveled before."

So she was wrong. They did believe her. They believed and cherished soulmates, she realized, remembering how all four of them had walked off when she'd revealed Arkimedes was hers. She guessed they'd understood why he was here trying to protect everyone. He had something larger to lose.

As panicked as she was about something hurting him, she had time to figure out how furious she was with him once he was safe and sound. Her mind was supplying another set of questions of how she could get to him when a bee landed her on her hand.

Her stomach dropped, and she got the message: it was a warning sent not by the insect but by a powerful old creature that was somehow linked to her.

Something bad was going to happen here.

Nava turned to Violet, grasping the thin shoulders of

the woman. "He is here, " Nava said, and Violet followed another couple of bees.

"What's going on?" Roman demanded.

"I have to go to Arkimedes," Nava said with urgency. She had not walked even two steps when thunder boomed in the air, and heavy rain fell out of nowhere.

Her heart contracted, and panic came upon her. It wasn't the rain scaring her, but the fact that seven bees landed on her arms. She remembered how Devon had called in a storm when they'd been his prisoners. She studied her surroundings, paralyzed, with her feet glued to the wet, muddy soil.

"He *is* here," Violet said in an icy voice. She also remembered.

"What? Who?" Roman looked around the place, on high alert.

"Devon Black. He can control the rain." Violet's words were louder, and Roman took a step back. Urgency took over his battle-worn features before he took off running. "Go now," Violet said, pushing her by her shoulder. Gray tendrils of magic emanated from her body, and a couple of bees landed on Nava's chest. Violet's face was void of any color. "I can't come with you. You have to find him—we *need* him."

"But . . ." She needed Violet. How was she to travel in the forest on her own?

"Find your soulmate and come back! He is stronger than any of us and knows how to fight Devon. The small army Devon has with him might be held back for a bit. We are families here. Not many warriors."

Nava nodded, and her hand came to the top of her mark. The dread in the pit of her stomach grew.

With the third boom of thunder, the start of screams filled the humid air, along with the loud hissing sound of magic and fire. Both Violet and Nava ran as sorcerers and fae rushed in for cover, pulling children along with them. Nava chased after Violet.

A couple of soldiers loomed in the distance, wearing black and gray tunics. Smoke raised over a house next to a tree. Their hands were covered in blue flames that rolled near their skin, their faces covered by their hoods.

These were not the Society of Crows. These were the army of the Kingdom of Iron, formed mostly by sorcerers. Violet was right. They needed Arkimedes to help whatever chance they had of defeating them.

"Go!" Violet said to her before she ran in another direction.

Nava pulled out one of her blades and ran as fast as she could, her steps faltering as soldiers appeared behind a cloud of mist in front of her. Their attention fixed on her, and her blade wouldn't be enough.

She was no longer shocked by the prickling of her magic awakening. After training day after day, the sensation was familiar.

The energy of her nature. She focused on the large trees that surrounded this town. The long, knotty branches twirled, thick with age and memories, the earth beneath their feet, and the energy coursed through her body as anger pushed her forward. The trees groaned, and the branches lifted from the earth, pulling chunks of dirt with them.

Nava didn't overthink that she was able to sense nature this way. It was not the first time she had moved the earth or commanded the trees. If she thought about it, she had always had a connection with plants. Her hands always focused in the garden.

The soldiers ran toward her, unaware of the movement beneath their feet. Still, blue flames raised from their hands. The men lost their balance as the ground shook. Her energy soared as she took some from her environment.

She had to persevere to get to Arkimedes. They yelled as branches shot to them, pinning them to the ground with a heavy thump.

Nava didn't stick around to see how hurt they were. She jumped over the large branches and the hidden boots beneath them, the buzzing of bees around her becoming stronger, and her soulmate mark seared her skin.

Was it true she was somehow connected to him already and the mark was telling her this?

Panic flooded her veins, and another fire of motivation lit within her as she pushed forward. Her boots made a wet sound in the mud. The whizzing sound of magic and the screams grew stronger.

People's cries pierced her ears, and she almost stopped. The heavy knot in her stomach intensified. The rain was falling harder, but it didn't stop the blue fire from burning the Northern Village's treehouses.

She dogged a blinding light coming for her, her own heart hammering with adrenaline. Her lungs burned with the heavy intake of cold air.

The secondary white light hit her straight on the back, sending her tumbling down onto a pile of mushy leaves. Blistering pain extended through her back where she had been hit. Her vision blurred as a cry escaped her lips.

She dug her hands into the soft mud, and bees landed all around her as she rolled on the ground, putting out the fire that scorched her tunic. She did not let the panic or the intense burning pain slow her down as she tried to get up, but she slipped on the wet ground. Steps came close as she struggled to gain speed before falling again.

Heavy hands pulled her hair up as she yelped in pain and met the gaze of a man in dark gray clothes.

"This is the one, the one with the blue and brown eyes." He pulled her up to her feet by her hair. Her scalp burned.

Her hands grasped his arms and she thrashed, trying to kick. One of his fists met the side of her face, making her vision blur. She tasted the tangy flavor of blood on her tongue and knew her teeth had cut her mouth by the intense blow.

"This one?" The other man came closer, his eyes raking down her body. "I can see the appeal. Maybe the Crow wants to have some fun before the trials."

Nava tried to push against them, panic rising in her body. The grip on her hair tightened before another hand wrapped around her throat.

"We can have our fun before he gets her." The man leered, and bile rose in Nava's throat.

Her body went limp as she waited for the moment he believed she was losing her grit and loosened his grip on her, so she could make her move.

It came sooner than she expected. His hand loosened just a touch, and she smacked her head back with all her strength and heard the loud crack of his nose breaking. Warm liquid fell over the skin of her neck.

"You bitch!" he screamed.

Pain radiated through her scalp and neck. A breath escaped her lips.

"Maybe he doesn't want her alive. I would enjoy killing her."

She was going to die today. Panic rushed through her body. The surrounding screams matched the ones inside her. Tears ran down her cheeks, and the freckled face of Cameron came to mind.

"No, Tiberius, we have our orders. He would have our

heads on a pike if we killed her. He is keen on bringing her, along with the one we captured yesterday."

Her blood chilled, her movements freezing. There was one person Devon Black would obsess over who wasn't her —Arkimedes.

She stared at the one talking. His dark skin peeked through his gray hood.

His rotten breath made her want to retch the contents of her stomach. He stepped closer. A mocking smile appeared on his features. "Have you met a fae with brown hair and darkness that follows him? The Crow insisted we set a trap for him."

"She knows the bastard," Tiberius hissed, and he squeezed Nava's throat tighter. "Did he make you feel good, sweetheart?"

They had Arkimedes. They had hurt him. The bloody feathers, the gray trees. Her fear was pushed down by anger.

She focused on the man in front of her, and she imagined him being swarmed by bees. The sky darkened as bees made of light appeared everywhere, furiously swarming the thinner man with the gray hood and rotten breath.

His screams were loud and pained, and the hand holding her neck lost a bit of its grip as Tiberius shrieked his friend's name. She didn't care to listen to it. The screams died down in front of them as he fell onto the ground, a pile of swollen meat.

She used the distraction to move and grabbed the hilt of her dagger. She pushed with all her strength out of Tiberius's grasp, took her blade out swiftly, and stabbed him.

Her eyes bore into his until the light behind them vacated and his heavy body fell to the ground.

Warm blood had splattered her shaky hands. One second, she was standing surrounded by swarming bees, and the next, she was emptying the contents of her stomach onto the ground next to the bodies of the men she had *killed*.

CHAPTER TWENTY-EIGHT

*N*ava moved through the forest at a quick pace. The sound of the attack fell behind, her ears drumming in the quietness that surrounded her.

Her breaths came out of her lips in pants. She didn't slow down, however. She was exhausted but not as she usually was after a display of magic like she had just performed. She was learning to take some energy from her surroundings—the skill was yet to be mastered in so little time.

When they'd traveled this forest, she never imagined her way home would be racing to her soulmate. She guessed it made sense.

Arkimedes had become one of the most important people in her life when he stepped in her manor that fateful summer day. Her mark throbbed, and Nava knew somehow deep within her stomach that she was going the right way.

The bees still swarmed around her, following or leading, she didn't know. It was unclear when they had become one entity with her.

It had been wet and humid in the Northern Village when the storm had hit them. Her steps were loud with the crunching of dry leaves and sticks. Between trees, the poking shapes of tents appeared in the background. Smoke billowed out of a campfire, and her steps slowed down until she was walking. She made sure the trees covered her.

The bees followed suit, landing on top of the bark and crawling over her hands and face, on top of her coat. Branches moved over her, and her gaze lifted to find the shape of the Beekeeper.

It was staring at the campsite, ten feet up in the air, its twig fingers gripping the tree. The Beekeeper had been with her the entire time.

Nava swallowed. Her shaking hands pulled the hood of her tunic up, covering her wild, wavy hair. She took a couple of deep breaths to calm her breathing and heart rate.

Crouching down closer to the ground, she strolled behind the trees. No one had spotted her yet. The campground wasn't empty, as a few soldiers seemed to have stayed behind. A couple by the fire, talking calmly, not expecting anyone to come here.

Nava peered over the brush she was hiding behind and counted two by the fire. She stared at a couple who walked and talked in low voices. She focused on a particular tent. One guard stood by the door, arms crossed over his chest.

It had to be where Arkimedes was. She hid behind the bush, and her attention came back up to the Beekeeper. His brows morphed into a concerned expression, but it didn't move or tell her to stop this suicidal quest.

"I don't have a choice." She swallowed the thick knot that had formed inside her throat.

Her body was yelling at her to get in there and save

Arkimedes, stat. Every cell in her blood was angry that she had sent him away to come here on his own.

Tears pricked as guilt invaded her.

She was not strong enough to battle five men on her own, especially ones who were sorcerers—better trained in both magic and combat. Devon had left them all behind to guard one powerful prisoner.

She studied her surroundings, making sure they did not see her. She had the element of surprise. She was not alone, and she was angry.

Nava let it wash over her and tasted her magic as it coursed through her veins. She studied the areas where she could hide.

If Nava were to get to the tent without being noticed, she had to make sure the walking soldiers were on the other end of the camp. Then she could take care of the one guarding Arkimedes's tent.

Her mind supplied that she would die today, but she would do so trying to save her soulmate, and that was a good way to go.

Nava willed her steps to be light as a feather. Power rushed through her body, and her feet were weightless on the ground.

Her palms were clammy as she came closer. She unsheathed one of her daggers and took a calming breath. The two soldiers on foot were almost out of sight as she walked between tents, making her body as small as she could. She moved quickly behind the next one.

Nava's power hummed through her veins. Her hand gripped her weapon tighter. She had to catch the guard by surprise. She focused on his back.

It smelled like mud, body odor, and tobacco in here. The soldier was unaware of her proximity. She was about to pounce on him when bees landed on the yellow-stained canvas of the tent by her, making her pause.

A muffled voice came from inside the tent. The tent flaps moved and revealed a man she knew. He was thin and tall, his cloak swallowing his body. Andreas Mortimer, Arkimedes's friend.

His face still sported the same smile she had seen that morning when they shared stories. Once, she had thought that smile to be friendly, curious, but in this new light, it was a wicked pull of loose skin.

He was massaging his red-stained fist as he came close to the guard. Her stomach rolled. "The prisoner is incapacitated. As promised, he won't be giving you grief at the moment. Can I go?" His voice was easygoing, like it had been that night she'd first met him.

Nava's eyes narrowed, heat rushing through her body as her hands went clammy.

The soldier nodded, grunting something Nava couldn't understand.

"The gold?" Mort inquired.

"Martin has it."

Her mind built a puzzle that told her with blaring awareness that Mortimer had betrayed Arkimedes.

"I will go to him then and be on my merry way." Mort dug his hands inside his pockets before walking with his limp and a cheerful whistle.

"Did you say goodbye to your friend?" The guard's voice dripped with sarcasm.

Mortimer smiled as he turned to face the guard. Wicked large teeth appeared behind thin lips. In the light of the day, tiredness drew his face, and he was not as lively or healthy as he had been. "I try not to befriend faes, much less a Dark One, my man. They are evil creatures, you see.

They will snuff your magic away from you." Mort snapped his fingers. "Like that."

The guard shook his head, muttering something under his breath, and the absurdity of the situation hit her. The sense of betrayal was bitter on her tongue. Arkimedes deserved better.

She took advantage of the guard who followed the retreating form of Mortimer as she ran to him, her steps no heavier than the wind, and she brought her blade up, hitting him in the back of the skull with all of her strength.

The crack of bones shattering rumbled, and her hand shook with the impact of the hit. Blood stained the bottom of her dagger's pommel, and the man crumpled to the ground as a heavy, unconscious mass.

Blood splattered the skin of her fingers, still warm against the cold air of the afternoon. Acid churned in her empty stomach again. Nausea hit her fast, and her body grew cold and shaky.

She cleaned her hand against the cloth of her tunic before reaching the door of the tent. It was made of rough canvas, dirty with age and wear. Inside was dark and musty, but she could see the shape of a man tied to a pole in the center.

Arkimedes's head lifted, and when his eyes met hers, they widened in shock.

CHAPTER TWENTY-NINE

*T*hey had tied a dirty rag in between Arkimedes's lips. Gashes and blood marked his face. One of his eyebrows was swollen and discolored, and a heavy cut on his brow was still dripping blood from a recent hit.

Nava grabbed the guard by the shoulders and dragged him inside, making sure he was fully covered, and ran to Arkimedes, kneeling in front of him. She dropped her dagger as her trembling hand pulled down the cloth in his mouth.

"I'm going to get you out of here," she whispered, guilt tinting her every word. Her fingertips lingered close to his eye. The blood underneath was sticky and cold. His skin no longer held the healthy glow she was used to.

Nava didn't linger. She got up and walked behind him, pulling out her second dagger and slicing through the ropes wrapped around his arms. His body slumped forward, a pained sound escaping his lips. She caught him before he toppled over. His skin burned like hot coals, and he was too heavy.

Her arms shook from the strain, but she willed her body to be strong, holding him with one arm as she pushed the ropes away from his body. Touching them made her energy drain. She had felt these before, the same ropes they had used on her.

"Go." His voice was a weak, muffled sound.

"What?"

"You—have got to go," he pleaded, his parched lips pressing into a thin line.

"No." *Never.*

"Nava, I can't . . ."

She paused as something wet seeped through the fabric of his shirt. She gasped in horror as she stared at her blood-stained hand. Their gazes met, and her resolution grew. Long gone was her weak stomach. No longer was she afraid.

"Who did this?"

His face lowered. "Andreas."

Of course, it had been that sleazy snake. Nava wished she had brought her potions with her, but she had left them all inside her backpack. Her world closed in on her, but the desperation extending through her body came to a halt.

Nava didn't need to have her backpack here. She could call on the potions with her magic like she had done before. She closed her eyes and pictured the exact spot in the cabin she had left it. She could almost smell the fire around the village.

She focused her attention on the olive-colored canvas of her bag and the pocket where she kept her potions, the same ones she had used to cure the Beekeeper. She pictured them and willed them to come to her. Her skin heated as energy coursed through her veins again.

"Please," she murmured, and the cold glass vials

appeared in her open palms. A wave of exhaustion reached into her, but she refused to let it take her.

She opened both bottles, holding them as she lifted the fabric of Arkimedes's shirt. A deep gash was right below his rib cage. Deep crimson blood dripped down from it. "Can you lean over?" Her voice shook at the end, and she pressed her hand to his shoulder.

He did as she asked, his arm braced against the ground. His body shook as she poured the liquid over the wound and placed her hand firmly over it.

How did she do it with the Beekeeper? She needed Arkimedes to be healthy. She needed this wound to heal faster. Her fingertips tingled as her skin warmed, and white light shone in between their skins.

His gaze met hers before tilting down to examine what she was doing, his features illuminated by the brightness of her magic.

"Bee——" His voice held a tone of reverence.

She pushed the second vial to his chest. "Drink this, please."

Arkimedes eyed the potion before emptying it in his mouth. His brows knitted together. "Let the record show I drank one of your potions." His lips pulled up into a grin that disappeared as steps came closer. Both of their eyes snapped to the entrance of the tent.

"Igor, where did you go?" said a male voice with a heavy accent, the shadow of his shape coming closer to the tent.

Nava stood, holding her dagger with white knuckles. Before the person finished pushing the flap open, Nava pounced. Anger fueled her movements. She sliced through the chest of the soldier, who screamed and fell backward. She stumbled out of the tent, her face snapping up to the sound of men running to her.

She grabbed her second dagger from the floor and straightened. No, she wasn't as trained as these men, but she was much angrier.

Arkimedes's wounds flashed through her mind, and she jumped, the memory giving her an edge of strength. The earth shook, and the men lost their footing, gasping as the tree roots lifted from the ground with a clamor, and some of the large lower branches swung.

They dove out of the way, screaming, and Nava got closer, unafraid of the branches, as they were avoiding her.

The tree branch hit one of them hard and caught him by the stomach, and the man's eyes went blank before losing consciousness. The tree swung him through the air and across the field.

The other soldier lowered his long sword on her, and she met his with one of her blades. Her muscles shook with the power of the strike. His blade was blazing, making her wince as her weapon lit up.

She pulled back. Her skin sizzled while she focused on the soldier. His own power rose around him as a light gray aura. She brought her other blade across and sliced his arm. He gasped, and she barely dodged his long sword.

Nava's shoulders slumped, her body aching in places they hadn't since the beginning of her journey. Her energy was nearly depleted. The rest of the guards were coming closer and closer.

"There is no way you can win, bitch," the man snarled.

Her lips curled, and waves of energy came to her, out of every pine needle, leaf, and bark. The strength in her body soared. She wished the forest would help her again, and the trees cracked. The man's attention darted around, trying to find the direction of the attack. She took advantage of this, ignoring the upcoming steps, and attacked him.

She jumped high and brought down both of her daggers in succession across his chest. Blood stained his cloak, and his hand dropped his weapon, coming to hold his chest before he too fell.

Nava turned to the upcoming men. She had used too much power in too little time and with no rest. Her vision blurred, but she willed herself to keep going.

A spell hit her and sent her flying back. The pain scalded her skin, and her bones shook inside of her, aching through her body. She cried, her palms sore from the burn and the rough landing.

The sorcerer's steps were slow as he approached. A sneer painted his weathered face, and his hands lit up as energy swirled around his fingers, then a tree fell on him with a bone-crushing crack.

Nava gasped, pushing away from the fallen tree and the dead man under it. Branches and leaves stuck every-where. Her heart stuttered at the vision. The second guard screamed as the Beekeeper landed on the ground. It was tall and slim, its sharp teeth twisting in a ferocious snarl.

A swarm of bees came around him and straight to the retreating body of the last sorcerer. His screams of pain echoed in the clearing as the bees caught up to him.

Nava lifted to her feet and ran to the creature, studying his face, making sure he was all right. His gaze fixed behind her shoulder.

Arkimedes was coming out of the tent. His body slumped, his skin green and pale, almost getting lost against the fabric behind him. His hand pressed to his side, and he was turning around, trying to find her in the chaos. She was walking to him before her head caught up to the fact that she had not died.

She wrapped her arms around him, careful not to do it too tightly. Arkimedes's chin rested on top of her head. His hand landed on her lower back, bringing her closer. The heat of his touch seeped through the cloth of her coat. His hands and body were feverish.

"Are you hurt?" he asked.

She shook her head, ignoring the pain around her body. "Mortimer is still out there." She glanced from side to side, trying to find the dark cloak between the sea of yellowed stained tents.

Arkimedes left out a forceful breath. "He doesn't stick around."

Her hand trailed up his arm soothingly. "Devon attacked the village. Violet said you might be their only chance—"

"They put too much faith in my power." Arkimedes groaned, clenching his jaw. "We have to go and help them."

"Shouldn't you rest? You are hurt."

He straightened, his brows meeting in the middle. "I will rest when we are there. We can't stay here, not knowing if sentinels will come back. I don't want you alone when I turn into a bird at night."

It was irrational to expect that he could rest when heading into war. Nava guessed at least this way it was somehow on their terms. "I'm sorry this happened to you, Ark. I shouldn't have told you to leave. It was selfish and . . . Had I not pushed you away—which I had every reason to do, by the way—you might have been less distracted, and maybe Mortimer wouldn't have double-crossed you—"

His lips came crashing onto hers in a short, hard kiss. "I am the one who has to apologize," he said, his face hovering near hers. "I shouldn't have kept that from you. I hope you can forgive me."

Nava's fingers came to his cheek. "We can take it one step at a time once this whole mess is over. "

"Thank you."

"You are still in trouble," she said, but the heat had escaped her body when she realized Devon had taken him. She was happy he was alive and free.

"I know." His expression softened. His lips came down on hers again in a slower kiss that made her skin tingle.

The sound of steps broke the moment. They focused on the Beekeeper. He poked one of the dead men on the ground with his long fingers.

"We have to go."

"Are you fine to head back into battle? You don't look too good."

"I have been better," he admitted with a grimace, his eyes flashing to her, and a smirk brightened his features. "Your potion is surprisingly effective. Who knew?"

"He did," Nava quipped, pointing to the Beekeeper, who had straightened and was staring at them with curious intent. "What about Mortimer?"

"Andreas is halfway to your town by now." Arkimedes studied the surroundings, but the only sound around them was that of the crackling campfire.

"What happened to him?"

Arkimedes shrugged. "Andreas came to us yesterday when we were setting camp. He said he was coming to meet us in the village. He was happy to find me alone and was curious as to what had happened to you." He shook his head, pinching his lips. "I didn't think of anything because he had met you. It seemed natural for him to be curious. I mentioned you had stayed back at the village."

Nava ached for him. "There is nothing wrong with trusting someone you thought was a friend."

"It doesn't feel like that, Nava," he said, and his voice shook. "It's like I led Devon straight to you."

"How would you have anticipated Mortimer working with Devon? How did that even happen?"

"Andreas told me Devon had made him an offer he could not refuse. Right as he stabbed me."

"What a piece of ogre shit."

Arkimedes's chest rumbled, and his lips parted with a laugh.

Her lips pulled up into a half-smile. "Should we be worried about him?"

"He is not a fighter. The reason he got to me was I trusted him enough to drink some of the wine he offered."

Nava had not been incorrect not to want to eat Mortimer's apple that one morning.

"He killed Roman's guys. They were good people, out here trying to protect their families." Arkimedes lowered his gaze as he walked up the hill stiffly. "Devon counted on me trusting Andreas enough and was waiting for me. He always knew I had a weakness for my friends."

Nava's chest ached as anger took over her. "Well, Devon's weakness was being a cocky bastard. He misjudged that I would come and save you."

"Thank you."

"Not too shabby of a soulmate you got yourself. Who knew?" She smiled as he turned his head and studied her features.

"I did."

Her cheeks warmed as Nava and Arkimedes edged over a well-traveled path toward the village. She slowed when Arkimedes paused, his face morphing with pain as he took a deep breath and leaned on the side of a tree. They needed to rest, for Arkimedes to find time to regain some energy and allow her potion to heal him.

"I have meant to ask you about your past. Now that I know who you are, you might share more?"

"There is one way to find out."

She nodded and took a deep breath, steadying herself. "If the orphanage sold you to the Crows when you were five, where does the name Valeron come from? Do they have anything to do with you?"

Arkimedes dropped his gaze, his jaw tightening. "The Valerons crave power. They want to be feared. Brody, my adopted father, wanted to be able to brag about my skills being in his family."

"So . . . they weren't a family to you?"

"I was no more than a showpiece. They expected me to attend celebrations, dress to impress, and speak little."

"Well, you being quiet wouldn't have been difficult for you. It's hard to get you talking."

He huffed a shadow of a laugh. "Do you want to know or not? You curious creature."

"I do."

"They made it clear behind closed doors that I was no more than an abandoned hybrid. They mean *nothing* to me."

"I'm sorry, Ark." She stepped closer to him, wishing she could somehow make up for that sense of abandonment that loomed over him.

His fingers caressed the side of her cheek. "You have nothing to be sorry for. It brought me here to you."

She smiled. "I guess that's true. What about the B?"

"The B?"

"Yes, on the sword, it said Arkimedes B. Valeron."

"Oh. It stands for Black."

Nava gasped. "Black, as in Devon *Black*?"

Arkimedes's cheeks flushed. "We were like brothers. In the Society, they assign you a partner. He was mine since we were twelve."

That would explain why both of them had shown up at her house that afternoon.

"So you decided to make a last name and share it?"

"I couldn't tell you before that we had been close. We had no surnames in the Society. At some point, we decided we would be each other's family." Arkimedes shrugged. "When the Valerons forced their way into my life, I kept Black as a defiance."

"It makes sense why Devon said you were very dear to him." Nava leveled Arkimedes with a glare. "You have got to stop with these secrets. Your *brother* had you stabbed."

"Sometimes it is hard to open up," he admitted. "Especially when everyone I trust—"

"Stabs you in the back?" she offered.

"Yes." He took a deep breath and held her hand. "I get that's not you, but give me time, Nava. I promise I will give you everything."

"Okay. Like I said, we can go slow. I think we both need it."

His eyes lowered to her neck and his brow dipped. "What's this?" he growled, and the touch of his rough fingertips lingered on the sore spot of her neck, where Tiberius had choked her.

"Oh, on my way here, two soldiers got a hold of me." Her hand came up to his. Her stomach dropped as she remembered their dead bodies on the muddy ground of the village.

She was not going to be sick again today.

"Did you kill them?" He knew the answer already by studying whatever was painted on her face. "War is not easy. The first person you take will haunt you for a while, but the fact that you did this in self-defense will help you keep up with the guilt," he said in a gentle tone, and his finger caressed her bruised skin.

It did make it better somehow. Her hands were still soiled by blood, and she had changed so drastically today she might never be the same.

"I'm here if you need to talk."

"Thank you," she said back, and they stayed there resting for a while before they continued up the hill and toward the village.

CHAPTER THIRTY

$\mathcal{B}$y the time Nava and Arkimedes made it to the village, the whole place was a mess of smoke and fire. The laments of people were a whisper in the air, not loud enough to discern if it was the howling of the wind or the cries of war.

Nava and Arkimedes held back behind the trees, trying to get a hold on what was happening. Her eyes burned from the smoky fog that lifted from the earth. The sun was fading behind the trees. Her attention deviated to Arkimedes, and they had little time left before he turned back into a crow.

"They don't know I'm cursed," he said. "I might be able to use this to our advantage and get closer to their camp that way."

"They shot you when you were one."

His brow deepened. "Yes, I guess that's true. I'll still get close."

She nodded and swallowed. "How were you able to avoid it last night while you were a prisoner?"

"The ropes. It cancels magic—even the curse." He

shrugged. "The first time I haven't been a bird at night in nine years."

"Not the most rewarding way," she murmured.

"I could think of better ways," he agreed.

Even though it was clear he didn't mean anything sexual, Nava's mind went there. The wave of warmth that ran through her took over her senses.

She also could think of a couple of things she would rather do with him during the night. Nava should be too angry with him for that to be a possibility. She was embarrassed about her evident lack of control with her hormones.

As he read her expression, Arkimedes's pupils took over his irises, and she could tell that his hunger for her was present.

"I can't tell what to do," Nava admitted after clearing her throat. She hoped Gavin and Violet were safe. The village wasn't as small as she had once thought. Housing hundreds of sorcerers and fae. She guessed even with Violet's urging, they would have held them back for a day.

They waited as the sun dipped down lower, and the time for them to be apart grew near. She had never witnessed him turn before.

Arkimedes's voice filled the quiet space. "I'm going to fly over to get a sense of what's happening."

She nodded, for once not finding words—the idea of separating not appeasing the nerves that had surged through her. "You are injured. I'm extra concerned about how that will affect your transformation."

He swallowed, and his head tipped back. He studied the night sky behind smoky clouds. Time extended, and they both waited and waited, and nothing happened.

Nothing happened.

She blinked and studied him as the darkness enveloped them. He was here, in his human form.

Arkimedes's expression lit with understanding. He lifted both of his arms, inspecting his body with a frown. "What is happening?"

Her hand came eagerly and grasped his coat. Walking around his body, she focused on the large planes of his muscular shoulders and his handsome face.

"Is the curse broken?" she questioned in a voice that was almost too small.

He swallowed and dropped his arms, grabbing each side of his coat, opening it and inspecting his stomach and legs. "I don't understand." A smile pulled his lips. "I don't know."

"But why? How?" Nava's mind went back to what had happened, trying to find an answer that would explain what had lifted the curse. Had it been because Arkimedes had urged her to leave him behind and save herself? Or maybe it was another layer her sneaky mother had set to the curse, her forgiving him?

She doubted her mom had thought that through, but maybe it had something to do with them being in mortal danger and choosing each other?

They stayed in silence for a while longer, waiting for the curse to settle, but it never happened.

Arkimedes let go of a breath. "I still have to go. Devon won't expect me—since they think I'm a prisoner. The smoke and the night will be a good cover." He studied the trees and the quiet buildings by their hiding spot.

Nava pressed her lips together, holding back her comment. She had no better ideas, and walking into the village without knowing what to expect was reckless. Arkimedes's expression softened when he noticed the worry that etched her features.

He brought his hand to her face and caressed the side of her cheek, smoothing the crinkle that appeared over her nose. She jumped at the touch.

"You don't have to worry."

"Promise me you will be back."

His expression faltered, and she understood it was not something he could guarantee. He came closer, and his lips landed on her forehead. She enjoyed the softness of his touch, her breathing shaking.

"*This* is something I have done before," he said instead as he pulled away, his face changing to one of stern determination.

The wind that came from the reappearance of his wings whipped her hair around, and she took in the magnificent shapes of them.

She would never get used to them because they were fantastic and something she had only seen in books. She reached to them, caressing the edge of one particular feather and the soft hairs that formed its shape, smooth like velvet under her touch.

She swallowed when his darkened eyes met hers. He had cleaned the blood from his forehead earlier in the afternoon, but his right eye was swollen and bruised.

"Don't move from here."

She studied the wings as they flapped with ease, sending leaves and stones back. His face morphed as his brows knitted. Before Nava could say a word, he flew away, a flurry of dark mist following closely behind.

Nava heard a whimper and turned around to find the face of the Beekeeper. He was holding on to a tree, his gaze following the retreating shape of Arkimedes. She could sense his distress toward her soulmate, and her hand came to the spot on her chest where her mark lay.

Come back to me.

The soft pant of the creature was the only response in the quiet evening. He landed next to her with a thump.

"I'm worried too," she mumbled.

The creature didn't say a word but stayed right next to her. Bees buzzed around both of them as if it were the most natural thing in the world.

Once upon a time, the vision of a swarm of bees would have petrified her. Even one little winged bug would have made her cautious of its sting. But her feelings had morphed to one of strange care and admiration.

Nava took a moment to stare at the bee creature. "I'm confused about us, about our link," she said, and his eyes bore into her. "Are we somehow connected?"

Even though it could talk inside her head, the creature said no words. It seemed to reserve speech for life-and-death situations. She was disappointed about being in the dark once again. The creature nodded.

"Because I saved you?"

He looked at her, and Nava knew deep within her that wasn't it.

"Was it my magic that bound us?'

He shook his head.

Nava's lips parted in shock. "No?"

"Destiny binds us." His voice came inside her mind, and the bees around them stopped flying. Some landed on trees nearby. Some went into the beehive on top of the Beekeeper's head.

Nava's fingers came to her lips as she held a breath. "What do you mean, destiny?"

"My name is Aristaeus, but you might call me Ari, dear one. Alongside you, I am the keeper of the bees. We keep the forests alive." His voice was louder in her mind. Their eyes connected.

What could this mean?

"There are always two Beekeepers in the forests. Never has a

human been one of us. But the gods decided we needed you to defeat our enemies."

Their enemies? Which enemies? Devon?

Ari shook his head, reading her mind.

"The ones who killed the other Beekeeper?"

Ari nodded, and his brows, or what could be his brows, dropped. *"We are bound together to protect the world from the Zorren, demons that come to our dimension, seeking destruction."*

Her lips parted as his words caught up in her brain. The gods wouldn't tie her to two people.

Aristaeus tilted his head as if it had read her thoughts, and it amused him. She could *almost* sense his laughter. She didn't find the situation funny at all.

"I already have a soulmate, Ari!" she said sternly, shaking her head.

"We are not soulmates, dear one. We are companions. Arkimedes, your soulmate, is our protector."

"What?" she breathed.

Ari's branch-like fingers came to her and touched the mark on her chest. Her eyes dropped down to it. Her skin sizzled under his touch—magic awakening.

"Three circles. Three of us."

CHAPTER THIRTY-ONE

*H*er eyes came to Aristaeus's chest, and Nava gasped when noticing that in the texture of his torso, three circles made a flower.

Her soulmate mark.

Out of all the strange shit that had happened to her since she'd left home that fateful morning, this had to be the strangest one. "I don't understand."

"*The day we met was set in motion, not by chance. It put me in your path, and it called Arkimedes to us.*"

Her lips parted, and her mind filled in the gaps. Yes, of course. Arkimedes had been near her and Ari, something calling to him. Their marks. She hadn't known how to travel the forest, but she had found her way to them.

Something landed next to them, and both of their heads snapped to the newcomer. The wind tossed her hair back as she focused on the shape of her soulmate.

Arkimedes lifted his handsome face to meet her gaze, his full height imposing. His wings disappeared behind his back. His turbulent green gaze traveled from Nava to Ari next to her.

If he thought it was weird that the Beekeeper was around, he didn't say a word about it. Maybe he could feel the connection between the three of them.

"Is everything all right?" he asked. He was reading her tense pose.

She nodded, curious how he would react when she told him their insane destiny. It would have to be a conversation for another time, however, so she kept the secret burned in her mind.

"What did you find?"

Arkimedes's head snapped around the place, as if he expected something awry. His brow dipped. "You are acting odd."

No shit. Nava shook her head and forced a smile. "I'll tell you later. The war situation is more pressing."

Arkimedes's gaze cut to Ari. "Devon and his army have taken prisoners. Some of the fae didn't make it. It seems the Iron Crown isn't interested in them."

Almathea and the fae who had served her the beer at the party flashed in her mind as well, and a heavy knot settled in her chest.

"The rest have barricaded themselves in the west side. Their wards are strong. I did see some of Devon's sorcerers attacking them. They might have until nightfall tomorrow."

Nava's brows creased. "Gavin and Violet?"

"I was too far," he admitted. "We can go around and reach Roman's people from behind. None of Devon's soldiers had made it there, and we will be safer inside their warded shield than here."

She nodded. Exhaustion peeked around the corner of her brain. Her stomach grumbled with hunger, and she was aware she was pushing her body too hard. Nava wasn't sure how she had managed to endure all she had with an empty stomach, then Aristaeus's presence scratched the back of her mind, and she had borrowed someone's energy, after all.

They were the same. Keepers of the bees and the forests helped each other, as their safety was imperative.

She would protect Ari and the bees the best she could and would learn whatever knowledge he needed to teach her to do so.

"How is your injury?" Nava said, reaching to her soulmate. She pulled the side of his coat open and studied his shirt, searching for any possible traces of blood from his wound. It was clear.

"Sore," he admitted. "I need to rest. I won't be able to get too far like this."

"Would it be safe to stay in one of these vacant houses?" she asked.

"Safe is not the word I would use." He focused across the trees and on the homes in front. "It might be better than walking around the dark forest without energy and with the spirits on the hunt."

Right, the spirits and the constant haunting.

Ari made a rough sound that came from the back of his throat. It seemed he was not happy with either option. It wasn't like Nava or Arkimedes could climb a tree and blend in, though.

"We will have to stay in one of these homes tonight. Get some rest and depart west before sunrise. Devon and his people don't know what happened in his other campsite, and from the looks of it, this side of town was hit earlier and is empty," he said, walking to her and reaching for her hand.

Nava wanted to protest about invading someone's home, but her body was too tired to be able to do much else today. She found herself nodding, and they both walked across a ghost town.

What once had been roads filled with laughter and children were empty, with rubble and debris polluting the streets. Most buildings were charred and smelled like soot and death.

Scorch marks went up half of the length of the trees. Nava walked behind Arkimedes, scanning the place and avoiding anything that appeared like it had once been a human.

This peaceful village in the middle of the forest had been destroyed by greed. Why wouldn't they let these people go? Why kill faes? Why kidnap children and take their parents for trials that surely would end in executions?

Her heart slowed down to a painful beat that cried for this destruction, the dark side of human greed. Her mother had warned her about the horrible sight. She had been so angry with her mother before. For once, she understood why she'd gone to such depths to keep them safe.

"Wait here." Arkimedes went inside a particular home, one that was less affected by the destruction of Devon's army.

Ari was walking next to Nava, his eyes shaped in horror as he also took in the forest's destruction. The cold, dreary air chilled her to her bones.

Arkimedes scanned the area and, with a silent signal, told her this was where they would stay for the night.

The home was dark and messy. Someone had left in a hurry, leaving everything behind in their wake. The dining table, a small rustic-looking thing, was still set for breakfast. The food had long gone cold. Even with her previous hunger, her stomach revolted at the sight.

"We will be safe here," he told her in a soft voice. "I will walk the perimeter to make sure there are no soldiers around and will set wards so we can rest."

"Arkimedes, I fear you forget you were stabbed and are *injured*. Maybe it's smart for you to take it easy," she said. "Maybe I can do something?"

"Do you know how to set wards?" he asked, raising a brow.

"No need to be a smart-ass about it," she grumbled, crossing her arms over her chest.

He took a deep breath and walked a couple of steps to her. "I *need* to do this. It will guarantee your safety."

"Maybe I want your safety, as well."

He mimicked her stance as a frown darkened his features. "I won't go far, but it needs to happen. I'm aware this is hard for you, bee. But I am feeling better."

She understood Arkimedes's reasoning, even though it crushed her spirit not to be able to help. Her attention went around the room, and she noticed their Beekeeper wasn't around.

"Where did Ari go?" she whispered.

Arkimedes lifted one brow. "Ari?"

"Yes, Aristaeus. The Beekeeper," she explained.

His face changed from a brief amusement to confusion. "You know his name? Did it talk to you?"

She nodded, gripping her hands together to keep them from fidgeting. She avoided his curious gaze. "He did—" She took a deep breath and knew the truth was about to spill from her lips. "He also told me we three are bound together."

Arkimedes held his breath, his eyes widening. "What?"

"Maybe you should sit down."

"Out with it, Nava."

"How to say this . . ." And not ramble? "Ari has our mark."

Arkimedes's back straightened, and his whole body stilled.

She swallowed. "He said I'm one of the Beekeepers and that you are our protector."

He shook his head. "No."

"Ari also said his—*our* enemies, the Zorren, whatever they are, have been coming to our dimension more and more."

His complexion paled. "The demons of destruction?" Well, at least he knew what they were. He reached for her. "Nava, little is known of the Zorren or the Beekeepers. I don't like this."

"Same with soulmates, yet here we are."

His lips pinched. "He has our mark?"

She nodded. "Ari said the three circles represented the three of us."

"Why don't I have the connection, then? Why can't I call the bees like you? It makes no sense. Does this mean we aren't soulmates?" His voice came a bit louder, his skin turning red.

"Oh, no, we are soulmates all right. He said we aren't his soulmate. However, our destinies bound us. Me being a Beekeeper, you being our protector."

He growled. "No."

"I don't understand, either. The day I left town, he said we called one another. I met him—he was in my path, and so were you. Did something call you that day?"

His brows lifted. "Yes."

Her lips pursed together. "Maybe we'll focus on this when this whole Devon war blows over?"

Arkimedes's jaw was tense. His breath shook. "I will be right back." He stepped out into ash-covered streets. Nava could listen to the laments of people around in the distance.

294

She forced her eyes away from the door. Tears pricked as the intensity of the horror hit her. It shook her to her core, and her hands muffled a cry. She hoped no children had been captured with all her might, however unlikely.

Mother was right. Right for protecting her at all costs to save her from this destiny—but instead of being a victim, maybe she would've been the one inflicting the punishment.

CHAPTER THIRTY-TWO

There was a large brown sofa surrounded by a stone fireplace and a wooden table with books neatly piled together on top. Nava's gaze traveled up to a loft area above. A mattress lay on the floor with piled linen sheets and wool covers. She dragged her feet, trying not to disturb the things that made this someone's home.

Her focus came to the kitchen, and hunger became too strong to ignore any longer, so she begrudgingly walked there and opened the cabinets in search of something they could eat.

She was finding bread, dry meat, and cheese. She made a platter with these and chopped an apple into quarters. Every creak and whisper of the wind made her heart jump.

Her muscles shook with tired spasms that screamed exhaustion. Her eyelids were heavy. These past few weeks, she had pushed her body to the limit again and again. Nava had grown stronger. Her previous soft curves had trimmed and now showed the apparent shadow of muscle under her skin.

She was used to being hungry by now. However, she hadn't eaten anything since this morning with Violet, and she had thrown up most, if not all, of her food right after.

Magic, constant running. and panic had led her to complete and utter exhaustion. Her back was still sore from the times the spells had hit her and burned her skin. She didn't even want to check that.

Moans filled the air, carrying haunted undertones that could have been the Neems in the forest but weren't. Her vision blurred as tears accumulated, and she took another shaky breath.

Arkimedes came in the door, a large shape of muscle and strength. His gaze raised from the floor to meet hers, and the normal healthy glow in his skin was gone. His complexion was pale, and his frame slumped unlike how he usually held himself. He closed the door shut behind him, and Nava kept busy as she watched his familiar body move around the home, closing blinds and curtains.

His breath billowed out in front of his lips. It was cold inside the home. He approached her, his attention going straight to the food as she removed her daggers from her belt and placed them on top of the table.

She studied her fingers that were marked with dirt and dried blood, and her stomach churned.

Nava went into the bathroom, and the whole day's events caught up to her. She held her body against the bathroom sink, trying to keep the food she had just consumed inside.

She met her reflection in the mirror in front of her. Brown dried blood and dirt marked her skin, and her hair was a mess of tangled brown waves. She turned on the faucet and splashed icy water on her face, scrubbing it clean. Her breath shook as the images of the men she'd killed flashed through her memories. A sob escaped her lips, and a deep cry overtook her body.

Nava hadn't locked the door and didn't see Arkimedes come in until his hand touched her back. She straightened and met his eyes before crashing her face into his chest and breathing him in. Never again would she take a moment like this for granted.

He wrapped his arms around her body and buried his face in the crook of her neck. Neither of them said a word.

"I killed them, all of them," she mumbled.

"Shh, Nava. If you hadn't, they would have done worse." He held her back, grasped her chin, and lifted her head. "War is not easy. I wished you hadn't had to experience it."

"I thought I had lost you."

"I'm here now." A side smile appeared. "We should get some rest. Tomorrow will be a long day."

He pulled her out of the bathroom in silence. Both of them were aware they had to be extra quiet not to call any unwanted attention if someone was walking outside. Nava focused on the loft and the only bed available. Her cheeks burned hot, and she swallowed, avoiding his eyes.

It was silly to be getting nervous about sharing a bed with her soulmate after it had been a fantasy of hers ever since she'd met him. Especially considering how exhausted she was. Yet her mind was not tired enough not to go there. She studied his profile in the darkness.

His jaw was tense as he also took in the bed. "I can sleep on the couch."

She shook her head. "Aren't we past that?"

His lips tilted up in a whisper of a smile. "Are we?"

Memories of their kiss in the last cabin flooded her mind, and her blood lit within. "Yes, we are," she said, resolution settling in her stomach. Nava climbed the steps that took her up to the loft, managing to calm her breathing and shaking hands.

If they were to be taken as prisoners or die tomorrow, she was at least going to enjoy this last night of peace with him.

It took Arkimedes some time to come upstairs. She couldn't see much in the blackness of the room, but she noticed he was fidgeting. Arkimedes was not the nervous type who held back. He was the one who stormed in. For as long as they had been traveling together, this was the first night they had to share with one another.

She kicked her shoes off, removed her dirty coat, and got in between the sheets. She followed his movements as he imitated her and then his gaze raked down her body. The mattress dipped as he got settled next to her, his large frame occupying most of the bed.

He stayed over the covers, and she found herself annoyed at his gentlemanly behavior and endeared by it at the same time. She cuddled the pillow, closing her eyes, and her body sank into the soft mattress beneath as sleep reached in.

"Good night, bee," he said.

"G'night." And she was out.

CHAPTER THIRTY-THREE

"*N*ava, wake up. It's a nightmare." A heavy hand shook her shoulder as Nava teetered on the edge in between consciousness and the nightmare that held her.

Her eyes opened quickly, blinking away the daze, barely needing any time to adjust to the darkness of the room.

"You are fine." The voice appeased her nerves, allowing the weight of her body to sink back into the soft mattress beneath.

Arkimedes was leaning over her, the hard planes of his chest touching her shoulder. The warm air of his breath caressed her face. Her breathing calmed, her mind becoming more lucid. The clutches of the nightmare had lost their hold.

Her gaze traveled to her soulmate's, meeting eyes that shone with green shades and illuminated the room, like something magical she had never seen before. The beauty of them was hypnotizing.

Nava's hand came to his face, the pads of her fingers

going over the rough texture of his scruff. His beard had grown in these past few days. She allowed herself to enjoy the feeling of him near her, of being alive and free. The distance between them was too large.

Her teeth caught her lip, and a wave of warmth ran through her body, her hands tingling.

Arkimedes's fingers pulled her lip from the rough ministrations of her teeth. "Nava . . ."

The room didn't feel as cold anymore, his heated gaze warming her. "What?" Her hands traveled down, caressing the skin of his neck and down his chest, stopping where his mark lay.

His expression shuttered. "We need rest. This is making it harder for me to keep my hands off you."

"I don't want to sleep. I want *you.*" She was shocked she'd said those words out loud.

A breath caught in her throat before his lips crashed down onto hers with barely contained desire. Energy crackled in the kiss, and an awareness ran through them with the knowledge that this was more than either of them had experienced before.

Nava understood that coming together would forever change them, even if the extent of how much was uncharted territory. Arkimedes's tongue swiped across her lips, and she pushed off the blankets that covered her body in an attempt to be rid of an extra layer that separated them.

He deepened the kiss as her hands fumbled over his shirt's buttons. She groaned in frustration, her fingers stiff and uncoordinated.

Arkimedes's hand skimmed over her clothes tentatively. His fingers were reaching down to where her shirt gapped. His soft caress of the sensitive skin on her chest made her warm and wet.

His lips abandoned hers, traveling across her face, down her jaw, and to her neck. Her wanting hands pulled his shirt out of his pants and settled against the exposed skin of his lower back.

They rolled in bed, and he was over her. She sank into the mattress as he finished opening her shirt, and his lips followed a trail to the newly exposed skin. Her body quivered as soon as his kisses met the raised skin of her soulmate mark.

The intensity of what ran through her took the air out of her lungs . . . Heat traveled through her body in waves and settled in her core. She spread her legs open to allow him to come closer, finding him hard and wanting.

His fingers came around to her back, working the strings of silk ribbon that tied her bustier to her chest. Her breasts came out as the loosened piece of clothing sagged. His fiery gaze raked over her body, making her squirm.

He was kissing her again, making her forget the wave of insecurity that had taken over her thoughts. It wasn't enough. The feel of his hand over her breasts, his fingers raking over her hardened nipples . . . She needed *more*. To find relief somehow for the ache that lit her with desire.

He groaned and rolled against her, relieving some of the pressure in their aching bodies. His tongue stroked a path over her chest and drew a nipple into his mouth, sucking.

With a held breath, she grasped the edge of his pants, her finger dipping behind the fabric and reaching down as she ached for more of him but was a bit too nervous about committing a whole handful.

He pushed his hips up, craving more of her attention. A soft moan shaped his lips as her hand reached in after such encouragement. The space between his clothing and the heated skin of his hard member barely gave her enough room to move.

He rocked into her hand before his lips captured hers with urgency, his own hands coming to the clasp of her trousers, having a much easier time getting through them than she had with his. She lifted her hips as he pushed her pants down her legs. The cold air of the room collided with her feverish skin, raising goose bumps along the way. He pulled away from her to his knees.

A complaint formed on her lips, but before the words entirely left her, the hungry look in his expression intensified as his eyes raked down upon her newly exposed skin. His hands came to his pants, and she focused on the way he unbuttoned and pushed them down along with his underpants.

His whole length sprang out, and *oh, wow.*

"Big boy," she breathed out, and her cheeks heated. Had she said that *out loud?*

Mortification hit her hard, and her stomach turned with embarrassment. Why did her brain-to-mouth filter fail her so? She covered her face, and Arkimedes's hand pulled it aside. He seemed to find it funny or possibly endearing, if the sappy smile that stretched across his lips was anything to go by.

He finished taking off his shirt and was gloriously naked on top of her. She ached all over, wanting to touch and taste all of him. His lips traveled the side of her ribs and down her body.

Nava squirmed, and a laugh escaped her lips. He grinned against her skin, sending a wave of gooseflesh along the expanse of her body. His expression lit up with amusement as he proceeded south.

"That tickles," she huffed, and he rewarded her with the most beautiful smile she had ever beheld.

"It will be worth it." His voice was deep.

Her insides fluttered as he proceeded with his ministrations. She grew more nervous, and as his lips reached the top of her underwear, she swallowed the thick knot that had formed in her throat. What followed next shocked her system. His lips crashed over her sensitive center, over the thin cotton fabric of her clothing. A moan escaped as pleasure exploded through her.

Her hips bucked under him, and soon his hand landed on top of her navel, pinning her to the mattress. As he continued down her thighs with open-mouthed kisses and a trail of his tongue, his stubble burned the sensitive skin of her thighs, and they would be red in the morning.

It was as if he wanted to taste every inch of her skin, and the feeling was new and scary.

She had been intimate with one person in her life before this, a stupid mistake when trying to prove to herself that she didn't need to wait for her soulmate to have fun, to enjoy the company of a man. She had liked Hale. At least she'd been more attracted to him than any other male in her life.

But the experience had been *so* lackluster, and she hadn't been able to see his face ever since. This, with Arkimedes, was different. Her heart nearly bursting out of her chest was enough of a sign to tell her. They hadn't even gotten to the best part yet.

Her gaze was unfocused somewhere on the top of his head. He pulled down her underwear, and she grasped the mattress, trying not to squirm and fighting the feeling of wanting to cover herself.

The only light in the room filtered in from the closed curtains and the supernatural light from his eyes. When his attention came to her sex, his expression grew more feral.

A stroke of his tongue made her tremble, and she

brought her arm up to her lips to quiet the sounds that started to escape her. Pleasure extended through her body. The softness of his tongue moved up and down and over her clit. His lips closed over the sensitive nub and sucked softly, making her toes curl. She blinked at the sensation as she held her breath and tried not to moan as loudly as she wanted.

It built through her body. Something was going to explode inside her. Not sure of what to expect but wanting to ask him to stop *or* keep going—she didn't know what her mind wanted. She grabbed the strands of his hair and pulled. It was like trying to move an unmovable force. His merciless tongue was going up and down and around.

"Ark—" She gasped.

She went rigid for one second before ecstasy exploded behind her closed lids. She gasped and moaned loudly, and with the last strokes of his tongue, he carried her down from the previous waves of her orgasm.

This was what Simone had been talking about all along.

Nava grabbed his shoulders eagerly, and he came up to her. His lips crashed down on hers as she brought her hips up to rub against him. His lips tasted like her and desire. His body fit hers perfectly, like a puzzle made by the gods for her.

Arkimedes's cock was trapped in between her navel and his abdomen, throbbing as her lips came down his jaw and her tongue licked his throat. His skin was soft, a contrast to the prickly sensation of his beard against her well-kissed lips.

He moved then, and his length fell into the place she craved him most. The kiss deepened, and a moan escaped her lips as she tried to get him to move. He stilled.

"What?" Her voice didn't sound like her own.

"I— Have you been with anyone?"

Her skin grew warm as an intense flush took over her face. Her complete mortification over his question dampened some of the burning desire that had been raging through her veins. "Er . . ."

"You can tell me. I'm not going to judge you if you have." His finger traveled down her face. "But I need to know because—"

"I was with someone else!" she blurted.

He leaned away, his brows coming down into a deep frown. Well, she guessed he *did* mind, after all. It wasn't like she wanted to learn if he had been with anyone before her, but judging by his clear experience before going down on her, she would take a wild guess that he *had*.

Nava's stomach churned, and a possessive part of her she hadn't even put thought to burst to life, and her fingers dug into his skin. *This* had to be a part of the soulmate thing because Nava had never been one for being jealous or anything of the sort.

But he made her break that gentle side of who she was, and her nature took over.

She pushed up with her elbows and captured his lips, trying to make a point that he was now *hers*, and by the way he answered said kiss, he was making the same claim.

It wasn't like the kisses before; this one was teeth and tongue and everything raw in nature. He pressed into her slowly before his face buried deep within her neck.

He pushed, his girth filling her, and she was captured between that fine line where intense pleasure met a bit of pain. She had been with one person, and he had not been this well-endowed.

"Please." She needed more.

"What?" he breathed against her ear.

"I need more, Arkimedes. I need you."

His eyes found hers. "To do what? What do you need?"

The tingling sensation of embarrassment rushed through her mind.

"Don't go shy on me, Nava." His voice was like honey and sex.

Who knew Arkimedes would be one to like dirty talk? "I want you to fuck me."

"That's my girl," he purred.

Before she could even quip something funny about that, he pulled out, leaving just the tip in before he slammed inside her. She enjoyed the feeling before his teeth nipped at her skin, making her moan with need.

His tongue soothed the area he'd bitten before, and he fully sank into her. Their gazes met, and something else lingered in between them, the intensity of hearts beating together in the same rhythm.

A connection, her mind supplied behind the daze of lust.

Arkimedes's rhythm picked up as he moved in and out of her, their flesh coming together with a mixture of wet slaps and heavy breathing. He groaned, setting a torturous pace that drove her senseless. Her lips were unable to keep her pleasure in any longer, and her moans filled the room.

"This is unlike anything I have—" He roared before she lifted her body in a way that brought him in even deeper. His hand traveled down her leg and pulled it up over his hip, and he pounded into her, in and out, over and over again. "You feel so good."

Pleasure fully took over and expanded through her body as it grew hot like coal.

His rhythm didn't stop, and his groans filled the air. Nava's body was coiled with tension as he hit the spot within her again and again, bringing her higher.

"Let go," he whispered.

Her breaths stuttered, and she tensed beneath him

once again, feeling the waves of pleasure through her body. This orgasm hit her out of nowhere. He pushed past it, extending it as his movements became more erratic. His face morphed into one of pure rapture as he climaxed within her inner walls.

They tangled together in a pile of limbs and heaving bodies. Arkimedes pulled out, bringing her into an embrace. With the heat of the moment, the room's frigid temperature hadn't registered; she shivered. He got the cover over both of them, and she smiled against his skin.

He looked down, raising a brow in question. "What?"

"I think it's funny. In the thrust of passion, *you* are the chatty one," she said, and her grin grew more prominent.

He chuckled, shaking his head. "Thrust of passion? Who says that?" he teased her back.

"I do." She snuggled closer to him, enjoying the warm masculine scent of his skin, feeling fulfilled and happy. Her fingers patted the taut skin over the muscles of his chest. His face morphed into an unfocused smile. "I'm not broken, after all," she murmured.

Arkimedes's hand stopped caressing her back as he looked at her with curious intent. "Broken?"

"I— Um, I thought maybe I couldn't, you know . . . come." Her cheeks warmed.

He lifted a brow. "Why would you think that?"

"Well, I was unable to do so the one time I was with Hale—" She paused, a bit unsure.

Arkimedes took a sharp breath, and his brows furrowed. "He didn't make sure you came?"

She shrugged, and his hand brought her closer to him, his lips crashing on top of her head, but then he shook his head.

"Selfish bastard—you'd better hope I never cross paths with him."

Nava's lips pulled up. She had never considered it, but once upon a time, when she had talked about it with Simone, her friend had seemed to believe Hale lacked in that sense as well. Nava had had such a difficult time connecting with anyone romantically before. She figured that had been part of the problem.

"You are *not* broken. To me, you are perfect," he said.

"You are not so shabby yourself." Her lips came to his cheek before she let out a sigh. Now that they had gotten this out of the way, exhaustion caught up to her. Nava closed her eyes slowly, enjoying this warmth. "When we were . . . When you were inside me, did you feel a connection?" she asked tentatively.

"Yes." His hand resumed the soft calming circles on her back. "The bond might have grown stronger tonight—I guess we will find out together."

She nodded and yawned. Nava didn't want to spoil this with concerns about secrets and lies, about how her heart ached from what had happened before. There would be other times to speak, and she wanted to enjoy this intimacy, even if for tonight.

Tomorrow war awaited them.

CHAPTER THIRTY-FOUR

a distant buzzing pulled Nava out of her dreamless slumber. An insect flew across her face, making her grumble. She swatted around. The warm body lying next to her beckoned her to keep still and go back to sleep, but the nagging insect wouldn't go away.

Nava snuggled back, enjoying how the muscles of his arm flexed, receiving her, as his nose buried behind her neck. Lips traveled across her skin toward her shoulder, and the tingling sensation spread.

"Mmm." The sigh escaped her lips, encouraging him to keep going.

She pushed against him, and the hard shape of his cock pressed into her lower back. Her stomach swirled, and her inner thighs moistened as she let her mind wander to how much she would enjoy that hard part of his somewhere else.

The body of a bug landed on her forehead, cold and hard contrasting against her heated skin.

She opened her eyes, the hair of her arms rising as the

bee crept across her skin. Her whole body filled with tension, and something else came into her mind.

Arkimedes realized the change in her and lifted his torso with one of his arms, his brows dipping as he took in the bee.

There was not a sound inside the house except for the howling of the wind. Her stomach sank as another bee landed on top of the bed's covers.

She turned to Arkimedes, and his skin was pale. A finger came to his lips, signaling her to be silent, and he moved out of bed with the grace of a feline, barely making a sound. He picked up his pants and shoved his legs through the holes, and Nava followed suit. By the time she was dressed and ready, bees filled the home.

Thunder rolled through, making her stomach drop. Devon Black was close and unleashing another storm.

"He knows you escaped," she whispered.

Arkimedes nodded. His arms extended, and he patted the roof over them. "I'm not sure how close they are. I would fly us down, but there isn't enough space for my wings."

Nava knew her nerves would enhance her clumsiness, but she followed him down the narrow steps of the loft, trying to keep her arms from shaking as adrenaline coursed through her body.

The rain fell hard as Nava tied the belt holding her two daggers across her hips. Arkimedes was by the door, she assumed checking on the wards he had set the night before. His face tilted to her, and she understood without words that they had to get out of the house or it would soon become their prison.

Arkimedes waited by the front door, resting a hand on the handle for a second while he took a sharp breath in preparation. He cracked it open, studying the street from his vantage point.

Ebony tendrils of magic lifted from his skin. The blue light of the early morning highlighted the side of his face. It was colder today than it had been the past few weeks, with the wind howling outside, moving the remnants of ash and dust that had covered the stone roads the night before.

The heavy raindrops were unforgiving as thunder roared high within the sky. The air smelled like wet ash, smoke, and charred meat that made her insides churn, a smell she would never forget.

His eyes cut to her, and they were as ready as they could get in their current circumstances. Bees circled her body. The heavy drumming of her heartbeat was high in her throat, muffling any sound around her.

Even if they were nearby, the army, however big, still didn't know they were in this particular house.

It was now or never.

Arkimedes opened the door and exited first, the waves of his magic covering the whole doorframe. The dreary light from outside peeked through. Nava rushed behind him, her dagger out as she studied her surroundings. Everything was dark, wet, and cold.

She shivered when the icy caress of water hit her exposed skin. A blinding light came rushing to them. Bees flew everywhere in front of them. Arkimedes's magic wove in between their bodies, and the attack bounced off.

Nava hissed. Her heart pounded as the charred bodies of her insects fell to the ground, a sob dying inside her throat.

No.

Arkimedes's wings were out in the blink of an eye, and before the gasp had escaped her lips, his arms banded around her waist, and his wings flapped, lifting them in the air.

Her arms wrapped around his neck. Nava's stomach dropped with the motion. Arrows whizzed by, and spells followed them with different shades and brightness.

Arkimedes barely dodged them, his arms straining around her tightly. Nava buried her face in the crook of his neck. She was heavy, and flying already strained his injured body.

The cold wind burned her exposed skin, and Nava focused on the energy around her, calling for something to shield them. When she opened her eyes, a swarm of bees made of light flew around them.

"Hold on." He flew them quickly over gray skies and out of the heavy rain cloud. The momentary brightness was soon extinguished when he dove under the thick canopy of the forest.

Nava's stomach churned, and she nervously looked at the approaching shapes of trees and branches. She held on tighter and tensed all of her muscles, awaiting a crash.

They were going to *die*.

"No, we are not."

Arkimedes's arms jolted, taking the brunt of the fall. His legs buckled under the heavy weight of their bodies. She was cocooned inside long soft feathers and thick muscle. The wings fell to the earth, and Arkimedes's breathing settled. She pushed up over her arms, examining his body and face.

He was scraped all over, blood peeking through his shirt from his old stab wound.

Nava's shaky hands came to him. "Why did you do that?"

"I'm not used to flying with someone else."

She rushed to her feet, her gaze snapping to each side,

examining the area as bees flew around them. The feeling of impending doom had settled somewhat, but they still needed to hurry.

He took a sharp breath while getting to his feet. His wings disappeared behind his back. Something fast and heavy landed right next to Nava. She winced, and Arkimedes's magic flared to life around them. She focused on the long, looming shape of Ari as his head tilted to the side.

"Tell him not to do that again!" Arkimedes's brows furrowed as he stared at the creature.

"He can hear you."

"*That was close,*" Ari said. His tone of voice was reproachful. He gazed at Arkimedes and then back at Nava. Something seemed to click behind his expression. "*We are finally mated to the Dark One.*" His voice was soft, and her face flushed in embarrassment.

"Oh, no, we are not talking about that." She shook her head, walking past the creature and toward Arkimedes, whose brows raised in question.

"What?"

"You don't want to know." She shook her head. She would have a conversation with Ari about the use of terms because *she* alone was mated to Arkimedes.

Arkimedes looked like he wanted to argue. However, he chose to let it go for the time being. "We need to get to the camp. One thing I did notice was Devon didn't have as many soldiers with him this morning. I'm guessing yesterday's attack weakened him greatly."

NAVA AND ARKIMEDES TREKKED FOR HALF a day over rough terrain, on muddy paths that had not been walked on by humans in a long, *long* time. The earth was soggy, and the scent of moss and wet dirt surrounded them.

They had been quiet, keeping alert for any possible noise that would tell them they were in danger from either Devon, the Neems, or anything else lurking in the forest. Real bees and ones made of light flew sparsely and protectively around the three of them; their message wasn't one of pure panic like it had been that morning in the cabin, but one of constant alert.

"Does it take a lot of magic to put your wings away?" Nava asked in between breaths. She was determined not to complain, especially since Arkimedes was injured and still managed to walk faster than her.

"Yes." His face turned to her as he dipped under a large tree. "Blending in is not easy for me."

Ari made a noise that was hard to decipher, just as interested in the conversation.

"Well, I like them." She gasped for air. "You can leave them out always."

"They do get in the way."

"You are large everywhere," she said and stumbled on her feet. "Not like that! I mean as in tall and strong. But I guess . . ."

Arkimedes cleared his throat, and her words stopped. "It was a close call earlier today. We need to keep alert now."

She narrowed her gaze on him. ' Is that code for shut up and be quiet?"

He flashed her a look that shone with amusement. "Yes."

"Fine."

It wasn't like she couldn't keep her mind busy with all that had happened during the early morning. Not the attack, but them mating. The bond was strong and present, like an invisible string that tied them together. If Nava let her mind grow quiet, she could feel the murmur of his emotions.

Pain was present in his tired body, his wound aching deep in his rib cage. Her brows creased in concern, but there was no point in bringing it up. After all, he needed rest and a healing potion. And they wouldn't get any of those until they got to Roman's camp.

She remembered Arkimedes's words from earlier and held onto the silver lining that maybe Devon was debilitated and they might have a chance to get out of this alive and with their freedom intact.

CHAPTER THIRTY-FIVE

*I*t was past midday by the time Nava and Arkimedes made it to the west side of the village. The wards meant to detract the enemy held them back as an invisible shield for hours before they were able to break through.

The vision of the town in front of them was chaotic. The trees that had been full of life were now columns of blackened wood. The town smelled like burnt pine and cedar and other scents that made her pause.

In the background, behind trees and buildings, the billowy smoke lifted through the air from homes still burning with blue flames.

People rushed in between buildings. Everyone was dirty, bloody, or both. The people of the town stared at them but dismissed them as they approached the center of town. At first, Nava didn't recognize the place. Tents were lifted around the area where she had danced with a blond man and listened to two girls gush over Arkimedes's hotness.

It seemed like such a long time ago. So much had

passed since. The willow trees still stood tall around the small plaza. Tents were housing people lying on cots and crying in pain. Nava's hand flew to her lips as they approached the wounded, coming across bodies, searching for a familiar face.

A mixture of anger and complete despair ran through her as nausea racked her body. Unlike anything she had ever experienced, the smell was overpowering—a combination of burnt flesh, blood, body odor, and magic.

There was a table with food around. No longer could she hear children in the street. Her heart churned as she took in the despair around her. She reached for Arkimedes's hand and held it as he led her forward.

"Do you know where we can find Roman?" he asked a woman walking in front of them. She was carrying clean bandages, wearing pants and a blood-stained green tunic.

Her lips went slack as she studied Arkimedes's face, then her gaze flashed to Nava's, then fell on the tall body of Aristaeus behind her. The Beekeeper's face was devoid of any natural expression, and his pitch-black eyes stared back at the woman expectantly. Bees raced around his beehive.

Her face turned pale, and Nava expected her to run. However, her shaky hand pointed them to a spot deep within the tents. Arkimedes walked past her without another word.

"Thank you," Nava said.

They marched on until they found the Commander's familiar shape. He leaned against one of the posts that held up the main tent. His face was scraped and darkened with soot and dirt. Worry etched his features as his attention went to a bed where a body lay.

Nava followed his gaze, and a scream escaped her as she dropped Arkimedes's hand and ran to the cot where the unconscious body of her friend lay. "Gavin!" she exclaimed.

His face was pale, and his head was wrapped with a tight gauze tinted in angry red. One of his eyes was visible and closed. His breathing was slow but steady.

Nava almost missed Violet kneeling by the cot with her hand grasping his. Violet's eyes narrowed when they landed on both Arkimedes and her.

"Oh, now you come," she grunted and pushed to her feet. Nava huffed as Violet shoved her shoulder back with one of her hands, making her lose balance and nearly fall.

Arkimedes was by her in the blink of an eye, holding her by her elbows, giving Violet a stern warning. "Watch it," he growled, pinning the other woman down.

Violet was seething in anger. A spike in her own emotions got the best of her, but she took a deep breath and tried to get herself to calm down. Violet was in an emotional state Nava couldn't even begin to grasp.

"How bad is his injury?" Nava asked, turning to Roman, who looked at both of them. His face, however, unlike Violet's, was relieved.

"We don't know. Gavin was our senior healer. Marianne, our second healer, has had her hands full, and her experience in combat healing is less." Roman studied the tent toward where the red-haired woman they had seen before was. She was wrapping gauze around a man's chest.

"What happened?" Arkimedes asked.

"What do you care? You left us here to handle your poison on our own." Violet's eyes raked up his body. Fire burned behind her pupils. Her aura was coming up in gray wisps. She wanted to release steam, but picking on Arkimedes was not the best idea.

"Violet, stop it," Nava snapped, coming a step closer to the woman who had helped her a day ago. "Stop trying to make Arkimedes into a villain when he had nothing to do with this attack, much less with what happened to Gavin."

"You are right. Maybe it's you I should be blaming," Violet said.

Nava breathed, and her weary gaze stayed with the other woman.

Roman stepped in, and his large hand landed on the woman's shoulder, squeezing it. "Calm your fire. Nava is right. We could use all the help we can get. Devon's army has already done enough damage, and the wards won't hold much longer. We don't know how much manpower he has."

It was clear he had not slept through the night, and a pang of guilt crept into Nava's head. She had slept and more. Nava should have been here. Even with their exhaustion the night before, they should have tried to make it.

The knot forming in her throat became larger, and her vision glazed with unshed tears.

"I flew over his campsite last night. His army has dwindled. One hundred, one fifty max," Arkimedes said.

Nava silently pleaded, stepping closer. Violet knelt down, giving her a reproachful nod.

Nava had healed both Ari and Arkimedes. Maybe due to a healing gift she was not trained to use. However reliable, it was worth a shot. Her eyes landed on the young healer who was tending to another injured man. Nava walked there, drawing everyone's attention as Ari, her Beekeeper, trailed after her. "Excuse me, Marianne?"

The young woman's face snapped to her. Recognition painted her tired features, but a fire lit behind her expression. "Who told you my name?" She squinted suspiciously.

"Roman. I was hoping I could bother you for a couple of healing potions?"

Marianne stared at Ari before letting out a resigned breath. "I don't have much left. What do you need it for?"

Nava's jaw clenched, and her eyes flew to the cot where Gavin lay.

"If it's for Gavin, I already applied a dose of it this morning, which I told Violet *three* times. Not that she ever listens to me."

Nava nodded. "It is for him, and also for my mat— man, I mean, boyfriend." The word was too insignificant, as Arkimedes was so much more than that. They would have to talk about titles at some point. "I'm a potion maker and could help you make larger quantities of it as soon as we are out of danger. I need a little bit of it . . . to try something."

Marianne started shaking her head when Ari's lips opened in a snarl that would have scared the bravest out of their pants. The redheaded woman jumped back, her features turning pale once again.

"Please." Nava forced a smile to her lips.

The woman gaped at Nava but searched the apron's pockets underneath her green coat and handed over two vials with a purple liquid. "It's Gavin's. It seems appropriate that if I'm going to be *bullied* to give a couple away to you, it would be his."

"I assure you my boyfriend does need one. He was stabbed a day ago." Nava didn't feel an ounce of guilt. She turned around and walked toward Gavin, knowing Ari was behind her. Whatever she had done before, she hoped she could replicate it.

Nava pulled the lid of the vial with her free hand and brought the potion to her nose. She could make out most of the ingredients by the freshness of the brew. It was probably three weeks old, not new enough to be at its full potency, but not fully expired, either.

When this was done, she would have a talk with Gavin about keeping his potion stash fresh.

The burn of Marianne's gaze followed her as she knelt in front of the cot, next to Violet, who gave Nava her best mean stare.

"What do you think you are doing?" she asked with menace.

Nava steeled her temper. "I'm going to apply a healing potion on his head. Is there anywhere else he is injured?"

Both Roman and Arkimedes had approached the bed, following the interaction.

Violet's face softened. She cleared her throat, and her hand came up to his shoulder. "One of the explosions broke part of a building from the trees. Gavin pushed me aside—it fell on top of him. We don't know how bad his inner bleeding is," she admitted, her face colored with guilt.

"It's not your fault," Nava said, but Violet's hand came up, pausing her.

"I don't need your sweet words."

"He would also be saying to you to stop being so unpleasant," Nava said without missing a beat.

Violet's lips twitched. "Yes, I guess he would." She let her body sink onto her knees.

Nava held the potion in her hand and perused her friend's body, swallowing as she took in his bruised skin.

Ari stood beside Arkimedes—his inky eyes bored into her, and she had to try. Nava had to trust in herself that she was good enough to help him. She had done it before, not once but two times.

She took a sharp breath, her body vibrating with pent-up energy. The scent of spice surrounded her, her skin glowing yellow and white.

She brought the liquid to Gavin's slacked lips. Her free

hand came to his neck, lifting it as she pushed the vial closer and dumped the whole potion inside his mouth. His Adam's apple bobbed. Nava brought him down gently to the soft wool blanket beneath him. They waited for a charged moment in silence, but nothing happened.

The disappointment grew within her like a festering wound. Her lips pursed together as she studied the pale complexion of her friend.

One warm hand landed on her shoulder and squeezed. She lifted her face and found Arkimedes staring down at her. The side of his mouth pulled up as he nodded in encouragement, understanding shining behind his sable lashes.

She pushed to her feet and fell into his arms, letting the soft caress of his embrace soothe her. Her cheeks were wet with tears.

"I know what you did," he said against her ear. "Give it time. Have faith in yourself and him "

She blinked. His hand brushed the side of her face, and she nodded, bringing her hand up to wipe the tears that streaked down.

"We need to prepare for the wards to collapse. Any able body available to protect the village needs to be rested and ready." Arkimedes's voice was stern as he took a look at Roman. "Including you."

Nava expected Roman to tell Arkimedes where to shove his opinions.

"Yes, I need to rest—and so does everyone else," the man said tiredly. "Devon took a lot of our strongest people as prisoners yesterday. We might have a chance now with you two here." His words made her head snap to him.

Something warm shook her stomach. The Commander's attention came to Nava, and something that wasn't there the day she'd met him bloomed. Respect and *hope*.

The hope of something being better because of her magic startled her. She was not a simple woman making ends meet to keep her brother alive while empty and unfulfilled. This rang truer to her character, someone who in the past month had grown to be much more than Nava Forrest, the potion maker of Willowbrook.

Her whole life, she had been afraid of this, of being around magic, sorcerers, and creatures. She had been afraid of falling for her soulmate, something legend said was sacred and special. She had been afraid of it all, and now she had given in to every single one of her previous biases.

Her gaze cut across people around her, all the things she had once feared that were now her people. She would fight for them, for their freedom and hers and Cameron's.

She wouldn't run anymore.

"You guys should get some rest. There is food outside." Roman's voice broke the silence. "You can take the house with the blue door. It's hard to miss it from here. Please make sure you take the Beekeeper with you."

He scares the shit out of everyone. Roman didn't need to say the words. He eyed Ari, and the Beekeeper's mouth opened. Sharp teeth made of wood made an appearance, a gaping black mouth dripping with honey.

It was hard to tell if that was a smile or something a lot more menacing. Nava opened her lips to complain, to say she was not hungry or tired, but Arkimedes grabbed her hand and pulled her away.

They walked to get food in quiet companionship and then retired to the offered home, where she proceeded to apply the second vial of potion she took from Marianne on Arkimedes's wound. And then they laid down to rest.

CHAPTER THIRTY-SIX

$\mathcal{N}$ava had barely closed her eyes for what she told herself would be a quick nap when pops and cracks jolted her awake. She was alone in the soft bed of their home for the day. Her eyes traveled around the room, and she swung out of bed, touching the floor's worn grayish wood.

The room was sparse and impersonal. White painted walls, no art, the bedding a mix and match set of sheets and blankets. She didn't linger and instead padded outside of the room barefoot.

"Ark?" She pulled up her pants from the belt loops as they lowered down her hips with each step she took. The clean clothes Roman had provided were made for a much larger person. Earlier in the day, Nava had thrown her daggers on top of the table before she had gone to sleep.

She studied the room with neutral worn furnishings made of leather and wood. Nava's hand came to rest on top of her soulmate mark. The pit in her stomach settled at the emptiness around her. The soft humming of the magic that ran inside her body calmed her nerves. She wondered if somehow she was feeling Arkimedes beneath the layers of her magic.

Arkimedes was not only away from the cabin, but farther than she would like, judging by the pit in her stomach. He was gone.

Screams started outside as she dropped her hand in a rush and finished tightening the belt around her hips. She hustled around, picking a pair of socks that were on the clean pile of clothes Roman had dropped earlier. They were made of scratchy wool but were warm for the late-fall day ahead. She put her boots on as she jumped across the room, scanning for the rest of her things. Her chest vibrated with energy and nerves.

Nava picked up her tunic on her way out of the door. She stared at the sky, her lips slacking. Beyond the trees' foliage, a red fiery crack opened in the invisible shield. It burned with flames as arrows plowed toward it, though most of them bounced off.

Her attention followed the frenzy of the crowd. Most people were dressed in battle gear and ran through the cobbled streets, carrying weapons, their faces twisted in determination. Their auras formed a glow around their bodies in various shades of gray. She tried to find someone familiar, the face of her soulmate, to no avail.

"Where did he go?" she mumbled.

Something landed right next to her. This time she didn't jump. Ari's gaze fixed on the fading wards over them, bees flying impassively around his head. His face pointed to the direction where most of these people were heading. Likely where Devon's army was about to plow through once the wards fell.

Arkimedes had left her behind *again* with some noble cause of protecting her. Nonetheless, her stomach burned with anger. He would hear about it.

Ari grunted and nodded, and they both made their way toward the commotion, following the river of soldiers.

Another pop echoed around, louder this time. With horror, she followed the cracks in the shield, and the pieces fell. She brought her arms up and around her head, expecting large amounts of debris to fall on them, but nothing came, just the heavy scent of burning spices.

"Arrows!" someone yelled as dots flew in from the sky toward the river of people. Most buried in trees and foliage that provided natural shelter from the attack. Few made it through and bounced off people's magic shields.

Nava gaped, her heart beating as adrenaline rushed through her body, and she waved between the multitudes. Ari jumped to a tree, his jerky moves more fluid as he made his way from branch to branch, a swarm of bees trailing him, calling the bystanders' attention.

Arrows rained in again, and Nava took immediate cover behind a tree when the shout came. This time, their shields were less strong, as some had exhausted their energy. Screams bellowed around her. She ran around and behind trees, following the pitter-patter on her soulmate mark.

It was coming alive and acknowledging his presence. He was close.

Ash drifted in the air as the never-ending blue flames still burned buildings in the distance. The path was littered with debris from the day before and some from today. Mushed leaves and mud stuck to people's feet. The buildings made of stucco were cracked and broken.

As an inexperienced fighter, she kept behind buildings, her skin crawling with the appearance of enemy soldiers wearing the same tunics as the day before.

Magic wafted through the air, and the tingling of her own came to life inside her blood as she pulled both daggers out of the sheaths. Bees made of light swirled around her.

The scream of a woman nearby forced her out of her hiding hole. A soldier was upon her, not killing her. She realized ropes swirled around the woman's body like snakes, wielded by an enchantment.

Nava didn't hesitate and sliced the soldier across his back. His high scream burned in her memory, and he turned to her. Nava stumbled back in shock when the face of a child came into view.

Not a child, a teenager, not much older than she'd been when she met Arkimedes.

She gasped, and hot air burned her throat as the man —no, the boy—fell to the ground, a scream on his lips. The ropes that had been wrapping around the woman fell. She recognized the face of the blonde who had been gushing about Arkimedes that one night. Their eyes met and then she was off.

She kept going, knowing she was closer to Arkimedes by the increased fluttering in her stomach. The battle raged, people of both sides fighting for life and freedom or power and dominance.

Magic and weapons were swinging around the narrow roads of a fallen town. Nava's anxiety debilitated her. Her legs froze as she relived the memories of the day before, of killing and fighting for her life.

She couldn't move, barely able to breathe as her blunt nails dug into the hilt of her weapon, and everything grew slow and fast at the same time. The prickle of fear crawled across her scalp and backbone.

She found Arkimedes in the distance. His majestic magic billowed as he moved with lethal grace. Dark mist plumed around him and followed his moves as the arms of his power pulled people high up in the air. His wings flapped with power and grace, allowing him a higher vantage point.

Arrows bounced off the surge of his magic, and the shadows of soldiers around him became alive, attacking their masters.

Arkimedes's eyes shone with green light like they had the night before when he made love to her. However, the anger in them was nothing like the heated expression she had seen before.

She froze when his eyes fell upon her; even in the distance, his growing panic pushed through their bond. He threw a soldier across the street and into a large tree. The man's body cracked, bent into angles a body shouldn't, and fell to the ground with a loud bang.

She couldn't move. Nava had never had an anxious breakdown like this. It blindsided her.

Snap out of it, she told herself, and her hand shook the metal of her dagger. She stared at a couple of soldiers who approached her in a run, their faces twisted.

Ari landed on one. His long twisted arm reached to the other with sharp fingers, clawing at his chest where a red stain bloomed on his gray tunic. The man screamed and stepped back, taking in the appearance of the Beekeeper in front of him.

A wave of calm reached her as Ari faced her, his face contorted in worry.

"*You were under a spell,*" he said.

She blinked the daze of her panic away. "By whom?"

Ari shook his head. The upcoming attack shortened their conversation. Two, *no*, three soldiers rushed to them. Their screams were lost among all others. Nava's magic flared as she met their attack, a long sword against her blades, while Ari battled the other two. Their magic fed one another, and bees attacked their enemies.

She separated from the Beekeeper and chased down a soldier. The roads that once had been green and alive with moss were covered in red and gray.

The town was chaos. She could tell Devon's army was failing as they claimed back part of the town they had lost the day before. Nava ran down the streets. The trees shook with the beat of her steps. Branches swung like arms, hitting thatched roofs that sent large pieces of a building flying toward the fleeing soldier. His body was buried under rubble with a precision she wouldn't have had under normal circumstances.

Nava stopped heaving as she studied her surroundings and followed the shape of Arkimedes. He landed a block away from her. Fire burned from the buildings, making ash rain over them. Her view was hazy, his magic contrasting against the white billowy shape of smoke.

Arkimedes's body was taut as he took a few steps toward her. The shadows of soldiers retreated behind the smoke while being pursued by the village warriors. They were *winning*. She scanned the bodies around her.

Black stains of soot marked Arkimedes's face. His eyes raked down her body, checking for injuries. She smiled at him, but her stomach sank when her soulmate's expression shifted to one of pure unadulterated fear.

A chill ran down her spine when a body pressed against hers, so fast she barely had a chance to gasp for air. Nava was as frozen as she had been moments ago when Ari helped her. Someone had cast a spell upon her once again. A hand wrapped around her neck and another one around her arm. The air became heavy as the tightening grip burned her skin.

"Well, well, well. Look who we have here." His voice was silk and poison. His warm breath hit her. Goose bumps rose in its wake, prickling her skin as her stomach rolled.

She made no moves. The grip on her arms tightened. She gasped as pain ran through her arm and neck. It wasn't regular strength but the magic that chilled her bones.

Arkimedes had made it to them fast. "Devon, let her go." His magic flared around him.

Devon's grip tightened again, and the smell of magic wafted around them. "And why would I do that?" Menace dripped off each word. "Keeping her will ensure you don't kill me, *brother*."

"If you don't let her go, I *will* kill you," Arkimedes promised, but he didn't move a muscle. His arms opened in a sign of yielding. His throat bobbed.

"Tsk, tsk. You aren't in a place to make threats," Devon said in a mock tone.

Nava tried to move, to writhe in his grasp, but couldn't. She cried when a bone-melting wave of pain coursed through her body once again. He had paralyzed her, but not her ability to scream or cry. A way to torment Arkimedes. Tears streamed down her face, blurring her vision.

"Imagine my surprise when I found you had escaped yesterday, even after I commanded them to make sure you couldn't so much as *think* about leaving. I guess I underestimated this kitten." Devon's lips touched her neck.

A cry escaped her, and Arkimedes came toward them a step closer.

"Don't!" Arkimedes warned.

"I knew the day we found her something had changed with you. I always guessed your friendship with Celeste was the reason why you left." Devon's voice became sharper. "The golden boy of our Society had found his soulmate in the fugitive daughter of Celeste Forrest. And to think they all mourn your death. I knew better. Something was off in the way Forrest vanished. But also you, and this cat."

Nava screamed as the pain that coursed through her intensified. She tried to bend over, to curl up and wallow in her misery, but he gripped her in his magical clutch.

"Devon, you don't have to hurt her, please—"

"Where is the fun in that?" he snarled. "I came here looking for deserters, following a blind lead of maybe finding my brother. To find what might have happened to my best friend. And here you are, happily alive, waiting for some pussy to show up."

Arkimedes's face sobered. "If you were searching for me, what makes you believe I would be okay with this crazy behavior? Hiring bounty hunters—working with the crown like we're theirs to command? This is madness, Devon."

"I had to bring as many deserters as possible. You know they can't just leave—we hang in a fine balance before extinction," Devon snapped. "We swore to our gods to maintain it."

"How much did the crown pay you to bring them back?" Arkimedes challenged.

Devon cursed behind her, and a sob escaped her lips. She tried to keep her eyes open, but the pain was too much. Bees swirled around them. She doubted Devon could even see them, as he focused solely on Arkimedes. He knew nothing about her and her connection to nature or bees.

He wasn't aware she was a Beekeeper.

"We don't work for the crown. We swore to protect, to keep balance," Arkimedes said again.

Devon's laughter shook her. "So naïve, brother," he said, amused and also sad. "I'm tired of living under your shadow. I'm going to prove to them how weak you are, how much of a two-faced liar. Even with all your powers, your wings, and your boring bravado, you have been hiding for all these years. While I was there in the kingdom, trying to save magic from disappearing."

Nava grew tired of his voice, of his hands touching her. It was Arkimedes's shifting expression that sobered her mood.

"What is it you want? You lost. Why are you doing this?" She forced her words out and tried to distract him.

"I will take you back home. He will follow, I'm sure. The Society can see what they want to do with the two of you then." If the context had been different, she would have assumed by his calm pleasant voice that he wasn't torturing her.

"I'm not going with you anywhere." Anger burned in Nava's body, and the buzzing around them became louder. She focused on the pain, and magic wrapped down her arms like ghostly fingers on the fabric of her tunic.

She had to unwrap them or, better yet, burn them away.

Once, her mother had told her magic was part of her essence, that she controlled her energy and, with enough practice, could bend it to become what she needed.

Nava was earth and fire, and the pain was no longer coming from him but the growing pit of anger in her body. Anger with Devon. With the crown and Crows. With her mother and her secrets.

The memory of the young sorcerer soldier she had cut not long ago flashed through her mind, as if her subconscious brain was giving her a fraction of a reason why her mother had done what she had.

Nava always hid behind a mask of pleasant smiles and fumbling words, but she was angry. With herself. For turning a blind eye to her nature and allowing fear to dominate her.

Her disgust toward the man behind her burned hotter than her pain. Her body was warming up to scalding-hot. The earth shook beneath her feet. Devon gasped in pain, yelling as he backed away, and Nava stumbled forward out of his hands, onto the cobbled street. Her hands broke her fall, and it shocked her to see the blue fire burning over her skin like a halo.

She turned to Devon. His face was red and burnt, his inky gaze wide with surprise.

"You are a slow learner, Devon. You have underestimated me again." Her voice came out rushed, and she bolted toward Arkimedes, whose own magic swirled around him.

The bees descended on Devon, a cloud made of swirling brown and light. The screams that followed were terrifying. Their bodies landed on him, but where he burned them away, more appeared. Thousands of bees came upon him.

Arkimedes welcomed Nava into his arms. She buried into his large chest, and they both stared in horror as Devon fell to his knees, screaming, trying to save his life with magic.

Arkimedes flinched and stepped toward Devon. "We can't let them . . ." His face paled, and his gaze moved around his old friend's body, brows lifting as panic settled.

She tried to find Ari, but she couldn't see him in the smoke of the burning town.

"Nava, stop them."

Her stomach shook as understanding hit her hard. This wasn't Ari's doing. It was her anger fueling the bees to protect her and Arkimedes from the crown and the Crows.

Her face snapped back to Devon's body as he barely

held himself against the ground. "*Stop*." The word was loud even to her ears.

The bees all lifted from the warlock at the same time, hovering close to his body. His shaky arms held him upright before he collapsed to the ground.

Arkimedes rushed to the man, and Nava followed behind. Devon's skin was red and swollen, covered in black stingers, and she couldn't bring herself to care enough about what had happened to him. No, this man had killed *many* innocents and had tortured others, including herself, Gavin, Violet, *and* Arkimedes. He had terrorized her, forced her to leave her brother behind.

She crossed her arms over her chest and stilled when Arkimedes's hand came to Devon's pulse and he breathed in relief.

"He is alive." He met her gaze with an expression that was hard to read.

"I don't understand *why* we care." Her voice was clipped.

Arkimedes lifted to his feet and cut the distance in between them. His hand landed on her shoulder pleadingly. "He is my brother, Nava," he whispered, lowering his gaze.

"He is a monster."

"I'm not saying he doesn't deserve a punishment for this." His sigh made her tense posture relax a fraction. "He doesn't deserve much mercy, but it shouldn't be our decision alone to make. He hurt the people of this town. They should be the ones deciding his punishment."

She shook her head, and her eyes landed on where his wound was. "He tortured you, commanded Mort to hurt you."

"Killing for self-defense, it's different from killing out of anger. I'm damaged because of what I have done in my past. I don't want you to go through that."

Nava knew he was right. She had not been in danger when the bees had kept going. Devon was fully incapacitated, a pile of swollen flesh barely hanging on after such an attack. Still, she'd almost kept going. A bit too far, probably to the point of no return.

"He is a crappy-ass brother."

"He's not a great one," he agreed.

"Also, I haven't forgotten the fact that you left me asleep today and came to this battle on your own."

He shrugged. "I would do it again."

Her lips slacked. "What?"

"I promised I wouldn't lie to you again. I'm never going to stop feeling protective. If I can keep you away from danger, I will."

"Well," she huffed, and she could tell him who was not getting laid tonight, but she took a sharp breath and turned her head to face Devon once more. "So what do you suppose we do with him?"

"Roman can decide," Arkimedes said.

Nava assessed the body of her enemy. It was over—at least for now.

The echoing steps in the distance called their attention from the body on the floor. The silhouetted shape of a tall man approached at a slow pace, his sword drawn out as he investigated the area with careful measures.

She recognized him even among the gray mist and smoke around them. Roman's feet moved with caution, his head snapping from empty homes around them, coming to fallen bodies that peppered the ground. His face contoured in a mixture of anguish and anger.

The blue-and-black shades of Devon's outfit let him know who that was. Roman brought down his sword and put it back in its sheath with a quick movement. His steps were faster to reach them. His black hair stuck to the sides of his sweaty face, his skin marked with blood and soot. "Is that . . . ?"

Arkimedes nodded, stepping away from his brother's body. He didn't say a word, but she could tell by the tense line of his shoulders that he was teetering on the edge of something dark.

"Is he dead?" Roman asked, the large tip of his boot pushing on Devon's leg.

"No," Nava ventured to say before taking a deeper breath. "We figured it would be fair for you and your people who suffered the most from his attack to determine the level of his punishment."

Roman's warm brown gaze snapped to Nava, his thick lips pursing before he nodded. "We are not savages," he mused with understanding. "Here, we adhere to and follow the rules of our village. We will lock him up to wait for trial. I understand you two were close once upon a time. I remember."

No wonder Roman had been so hostile when learning about Devon's impending attack.

"He deserves his punishment. He attacked a village of innocents and was not following our—the Society's law I grew up believing and the reasons why we upheld certain things." Arkimedes shook his head, pursing his lips. "With the dwindling number of magical humans being born, we were supposed to be doing this for the benefit of people. It was never about the crown and doing their bidding."

He took a deep breath and rested his hand on her lower back as if needing contact to steady his nerves. Her own body trembled as the adrenaline dwindled from her system.

Her heart filled with hope, and it relieved some of her

momentary anger. They had to work hard on their communication. She had a broken man, someone who had suffered disappointment and pain. The kind of abandonment she'd never had to deal with, other than when her father had decided to let himself die.

"We are not executioners," Nava said with a nod, and she focused on the body she'd almost, albeit unknowingly, killed. Her stomach churned with the realization.

"Good," Roman said, and more people approached. The three of them relaxed as they took in the approaching shapes of the villagers.

"Would you stay here with us?" Roman asked.

"If it's not much trouble, we would appreciate somewhere to rest before we have to go back." Arkimedes's eyes came to her, a question painted on his features.

She nodded.

"We didn't start on the best terms, but you're welcome back here anytime." Roman extended his hand to Nava, who shook it, and to Arkimedes, and the previous tension that had flowed around them melted as soon as Arkimedes's hand grasped Roman's.

"Thank you."

The older man nodded and bent down, lifting Devon's limp body with ease and dropping it over his broad shoulder.

Nava eyed their retreating shapes, focused on Devon's previously pale features, which were now covered in angry welts.

"We should go help with the injured. Hopefully, we will get some rest tonight," Arkimedes said, and she nodded, letting her mind go blank as she got to work.

CHAPTER THIRTY-SEVEN

*I*t had been a tiring three weeks since Devon Black's army had attacked the northern town in the forest. The days grew shorter and colder, and the sky was no longer gray with smoke and magic-induced storms. The sun shone, but everyone was aware bright winter days were the coldest.

They had moved patients back to their respective homes with the dropping temperatures. The few army sorcerers who had not escaped that day had been taken as prisoners and were held in the town's jail.

Nava had been surprised this existed in a lost village in the middle of a forest, but the longer she stayed, the more she realized the place wasn't as small as she had once imagined.

She found herself among the healing team, including Marianne, who disliked her but tolerated her based on her potion-making skills. Nava had been hard at work, brewing healing potions and pain management medicines every hour of the day she wasn't sleeping.

She had not performed any other healing spells, like the one she had done with Arkimedes, Ari, and Gavin.

Her steps were loud in the quiet morning, her boots clicking over stone roads that serpented the village. The sun shone through the tall trees. The homes protruding out of the giant trees no longer appeared jarring to her; she knew this area well.

She turned left and headed to a home she had been in and out of each day for the past week. The façade was thin and tall, the walls made of clay and sticks painted a warm cream that made the red door contrast against it. Pine needles were scattered all over the entrance steps.

She knocked on the wooden door a couple of times before she buried her hands inside her pockets, trying to shelter her skin from the biting weather. Nava heard quick steps before the door cracked open, and Violet's face appeared in front of her with a scowl that morphed into a somewhat pleasant expression.

"Oh, you are here," she said, opening the door wide to allow her in.

Nava cleaned her boots furiously on the doormat, not wanting to be scolded by Violet like she had the first day she'd shown up. She studied the warm home with a comfortable red couch in the center and a wood table that held multiple volumes of books, like the bookcase behind it.

The kitchen was quaint. There was a woodstove in the corner surrounded by sage-green cabinets, and copper pots and pans hung from the wall.

Nava's icy fingers came to the back of her neck, cooling her heated skin from her brisk walk here. Violet kept her home warmer than she was used to, and she was too afraid to take off her coat and drape it anywhere, as the woman was particular about how neat she kept her home.

"Is he in the bedroom?" Nava asked, shrugging off her coat after some deliberation.

Violet pointed to the coatrack by the front door. "Yes, where you last left him, kitten."

Nava grumbled, deciding not to say anything about the forsaken nickname this time.

She picked the potions out of her coat pockets and followed Violet past the narrow hallway of her home to the master bedroom, where Gavin awaited. "Good morning, sunshine," Nava said cheerfully when she found Gavin's bright face tilted at her from the bed.

It was a decent size and was covered in multiple blankets of different bright colors. The room was neat and homey. Nava came close and put the three vials of potions on top of the side table, her fingers coming to the bandage that covered half of his forehead.

"Nava," he greeted, his voice a bit more like himself and less groggy and tired. His face was less pale, though the gashes were still present and likely to leave a scar. "You have taken well to being a healer."

"What can I say? I can't let Marianne have all the fun." She was happy the wound on his head was healed. She applied the potion on top and wrapped the gauze around him again.

"She can be difficult sometimes," he agreed with a nod. "I seem to find myself surrounded by strongheaded women."

Nava's grin grew as a huff came from where Violet stood. "Please, the girl is barely a woman."

"Who, Marianne or me?" Nava handed Gavin one of the vials.

He scrunched his nose, and his coffee-colored eyes

came to her, his expression imploring. Healers were the worst patients.

"Marianne," Violet answered with a growing smile. "You were a virgin, not a girl."

Nava turned to Violet, lifting a brow. "I was not a virgin. I told you."

"Oh, you were, in a way. Glad that's not the case anymore." Violet laughed louder.

"We can stop talking about it now."

"Please. As much as I like Arkimedes and you, I'd rather not imagine you two going at it like hungry beasts." Gavin's face scrunched.

"I wouldn't mind hearing more about it, soulmate sex —it's gotta be special."

Nava gaped before shaking her head and getting up from the bed. "This is weird, and I'm going to go home."

"Soulmates are so rare, and when they find each other, they keep it to themselves. The connections that undoubtedly happen in between you are a mystery." Violet's gaze shone with curiosity, and she followed Nava.

Nava grabbed her coat and shrugged it on. "Make sure he takes the second vial this afternoon. Marianne told me to tell you she will be coming here tomorrow morning."

Violet paused a few meters away from Nava, searching her face. "And where will you be, kitten?"

"Arkimedes and I are traveling back to Willowbrook tomorrow morning. My brother is waiting for me," she said, and they both stared at each other in silence.

"Will you be back?"

"I'm sure we will be, someday." Nava nodded. "Never thought you would be so sad to see me go."

The woman in front of her scoffed and crossed her arms over her chest, shaking her head. "Don't get it wrong.

I'm curious because I want to learn more about the . . . soulmate bond."

Nava laughed. "If you say so." She opened the door, and a wall of freezing air hit her body, a clear contrast to the warmth inside. "I'm really terrible saying goodbye, so please tell Gavin I will see him soon."

Violet didn't say another word. Clearly, goodbyes weren't her forte either, and with this bittersweet moment, Nava walked back to the home that had been theirs for the past weeks, a place where they had been able to spend time together and not worry about the impending capture.

No more running. No more hiding.

For the first time, she had been able to breathe and enjoy him and their connection. It wasn't always pleasant, and there was that wedge he drew with secrets.

With the danger of war removed, it was easier to open up and live. Arkimedes worked hard to help Roman capture the soldiers who had tried to escape, a chase that had lasted at least a week. It was fitting that they had been the ones being hunted down.

The rebuilding had started a week after the battle. The broken bits of the town's east side were piles of rubble, ash, and buried bones. The blue fire that hadn't ceased to burn for days had taken down buildings and century-old trees. Gray ashy rain had fallen upon the town for days, and the smell of burning cedar and pine lingered almost a month later.

She had not wanted to know how they'd disposed of the battle's dead bodies, but some rituals had to happen for the spirits to rest in peace and not haunt the grounds where this village stood, to not become part of the haunted souls that still plagued her nightmares.

Leaving this place gave her a mixture of feelings she

had a hard time reconciling within herself. A yin and yang battle over what she wanted.

She had always struggled to find her place, to connect with people. Here, it had been easier to let go and embrace all facets of what made her.

And to think her little thirteen-year-old brother had been right all along.

She spent the whole day making potions for Marianne and the rest of the healing team to use when she was gone. Her heart was full of excitement to see Cameron, Laurie, and Simone again when the sun was setting over the trees and the door opened to Arkimedes, who was coming home.

CHAPTER THIRTY-EIGHT

*N*ava opened her eyes with a flutter and focused on the sharp features of Arkimedes in front of her. The morning sun burned warm against the skin of his cheeks, outlining his sharp jaw and chin.

He eyed her intently, and he beamed at her. Her stomach flipped as her heart stumbled in its beats.

"Morning." Her voice was tinted with layers of sleep as she cuddled closer to him, enjoying the heat of his body.

"Good morning."

She sighed against him, goosebumps rising along her skin. The sheets smelled like him and like home, even though she had been here for such a short time.

He pulled away, and his expression turned amused. "We should get some breakfast."

Nava groaned a complaint because she wanted a different kind of breakfast. It surprised her, the sex fiend she had become. She'd had to up the doses for contraceptives three weeks ago to make sure a surprise didn't pop up when she least expected it.

The potion was an easy one to make, and it had been

one of her best-selling brews back in town. Here in magic land, the recipe was different, and it carried ninety-nine percent success in pregnancy prevention, according to the local gossip.

"I'd rather eat something else entirely." Both of their faces turned bright red. "I didn't mean to say that out loud!"

A rolling laugh escaped him. "I imagined that was the case." He stole a kiss. "We should talk, though—about what happens next."

Nava's stomach fluttered, and she cuddled her pillow. His hand traveled from her shoulder to her back, the caress of his fingers igniting her nerve endings. "What do you mean?"

"I mean past today, about Cameron. Are we going to go back to the town and stay there?" He was nervous, and it was endearing.

They had been taking things slow, or as much as they could for being two bonded soulmates who could feel each other's moods and had to be close to survive.

She was concerned about him being in that non-magical town, what it would do to his half-fae side. She was also uneasy if Cameron would love him, or vice versa, though even, in her biased position, her brother was pretty hard to dislike.

"I—I guess I thought we would take it one step at a time?" she conceded, meeting his gaze and finding it nonjudgmental.

"I don't want to force you to be here because of me."

"What do you mean?" She searched his face for better understanding. He didn't mean them apart, right? Her previous insecurity reared its ugly head. She reached into the depths of their connection and learned he wanted the opposite.

"I would stay in that town if it's what you want."

She released a deep sigh, her mind going around everything that had happened in the past months, all the horrors she had seen in the forest, all the wonders she had encountered. Her life had changed irrevocably.

No longer did she feel magic was her crutch. She brought her hand to his face and smiled. She also couldn't be away from Ari—he was a part of her, and it was her duty to be there for him.

"This journey didn't only bring me to you, but it made me accept this part of me that was always missing," she whispered, and the flutter in her chest became more pronounced. Was it her heart or his? "While in Willowbrook, I always felt *numb*, like a hole I always assumed was my missing soulmate, but it was much more than that. I was missing a part of what makes me, me. That made a lot more sense in my head."

"It makes sense."

"What I mean is . . . I want to go and get Cam and Laurie and bring them with us, maybe back to your cabin?" She scanned the room of their provisional home in the Northern Village, and a crinkle formed in between her eyebrows.

"What?"

"Actually, your home might be too small for the four of us. I don't really want to share a room with Cameron, much less Laurie."

Arkimedes blinked before snickering, letting his head fall onto the pillow. "No, that wouldn't be good, especially with how you have been lately.' He paused, waiting.

Her lips parted in offense. "Arkimedes Valeron, how dare you? You won't be getting in my pants again, since apparently, I'm this sex monster perverting your sensible elven ways."

He breathed a laugh that grew and made her stomach flutter, and she found herself laughing as well.

"I'm serious," she insisted, but with her clear sexual awakening, she wasn't sure she was fooling anyone in this room.

His eyes fixed somewhere on the ceiling. The thick wood beams were sturdy and rustic like everything here. Somehow, when they'd arrived at this house, it felt like it didn't have any personality. Bland, even. But now it gave her space to focus on all she had around her. "I built that cabin filled with so much anger and loneliness. I had left my whole life behind, the family I knew, to follow the unknown and also something that at the time I disagreed with wholeheartedly," he explained.

"You mean being a deserter? Or having me as your soulmate?" she offered with a raised brow.

"No, not you. I didn't want to be a deserter. At the time, I believed blindly in what they preached in the Society. I still do believe in some things. It's not black and white for me—there is a problem with magic fading in our world."

"Maybe it's what the gods want." She shrugged. "There is the gift of magic being given. Look at me. Born from a non-magical father and a magical mother. They came together as they should have, and I was born *with* magic. Forcing a hand breaks people apart. It doesn't make for a healthy nation."

"No, it doesn't. I don't agree with them forcing people together or apart. And the cabin, it reminds me of that past belief. I think maybe it would be good if we make our home somewhere else," he suggested and awaited a reaction.

"Where do you suppose?"

"Roman did offer for us to come back. He said his village would always welcome us in." His voice was unsure.

Nava lifted a brow. "A month has changed a lot of your dislike for Roman and how badly they treated you."

"Roman and I have a rocky history. I don't blame him for not liking me," he said. "And it doesn't help that the Crows tried to force Mars into marrying some high-society sorceress."

"No way." Her lips slacked.

He nodded. "Yes. She fancied him and worked her influence with the crown."

"Ark, you are a gossip master." Nava gasped.

His cheeks turned a deep shade of crimson. "Mars talks a lot," he defended. "I have never met anyone who gives so much information in a minute."

She chuckled. Never in her life would she have guessed she would be sharing gossip with the stoic, hunky man of hers.

"*Either way.* Here, Cameron will grow close to kids his age and learn magic the way he is supposed to."

"What I'm hearing is you don't want him to always be around us. Which means I'm not the only one around here burning for . . . intimacy."

Arkimedes pinned her to the mattress. His movements were so quick, it made the air leave her lungs. His lips met her jaw in a wet kiss. "We are recently mated, bee. I definitely don't want your baby brother around us all the time."

Her cheeks warmed. "Well, technically, we found each other ten years ago, when I was working on the garden and you so rudely interrupted me."

Arkimedes's eyes danced with mirth. "Is that so?"

"Yep, get it right."

"Hard to forget. My mate was a gangly, pimply teenager."

Nava hit the side of his shoulder, her lips parting. "I didn't even have pimples."

"Are you sure?"

She pursed her lips. "I might have had a couple because it was summertime, and it was hot." She fumbled over her words. She had looked an absolute mess that day. "Who's to tell? Maybe you weren't this perfect, handsome, strong man. Maybe you were also a skinny, pimply twenty-year-old."

Arkimedes raised a brow, and her annoyance grew, because who was she kidding? There was *no way* Arkimedes had been that. Her memory supplied the image of his strong, tall body filling his Society of Crows outfit.

She somehow knew his face had been as striking as it was now. Maybe with rounder cheeks.

"Your ego has no end. Not all of us have perfectly perfect elven genetics and are gorgeous always."

"You were cute then, but now you are gorgeous," he said, and his expression softened.

A warm wave ran through her body, making her light and happy. "Thank you."

"It's the truth."

"The Northern Village, then? It would be nice to see Gavin more often," she whispered, lost in her own thoughts.

Arkimedes's growl made her giggle as his fingers tapped the side of her ribs where she was the most ticklish, something he'd found soon after the war was over.

Laughter exploded from her lips, and she squirmed to get out of his hold. He held her against the mattress, his fingers relentless as she gasped for air, trying to escape.

She bucked under him as he held her close, leaving her

breathless. She moved against him again, the hard planes of his chest pressed over hers.

She stopped when his growing desire became more apparent. His naked body was against hers with a thin sheet separating them. The movements of both their bodies had brought them closer. His hands stilled as their gazes met, his pupils hiding most of the turbulent green shades in his irises.

"We are going to need some boundaries about you bringing other men up when we are in bed together." His voice was husky.

His words shook her all the way to her core. "So sensitive," she breathed and pushed her hips to him, rubbing herself where she needed him.

He zeroed in on her mouth as her heart stumbled. His touch traveled to her hips and dipped past her navel in a soft caress that made her tremble with building desire. His hand pulled aside the sheets that had tangled around her in a slow, calculated move.

A breath shook her as his fingers dipped into her, and pleasure exploded through her body when his touch met her throbbing center. She held his shoulders, her nails digging into his golden skin where his wings were tattooed. She held the moan, bringing her lips instead to his chest.

"Let me hear you," he commanded.

She panted as he added a digit. In and out of her in a torturous pace that built her up and tied her into an endless knot. Her breathing was loud. The soft roaring of the fire in the fireplace provided warmth to their bodies in the chilly morning.

His lips traveled the base of her throat, his tongue marking her skin.

"I need you," she urged him on, gasping when his touch abandoned her.

The tip of his length pressed against her entrance. The hard length of him pushed in, stretching her in a way that was too much and not enough.

His lips captured hers in an open-mouthed kiss that moved fast and asked for all of her. His arms landed on each side of her head, muscles contracting as he held himself up and rocked into her, pushing her closer to where she needed to be.

The coil in her core grew tighter with each thrust of his hips, and both of their moans filled the room.

"Let go, Nava."

"I love you," she gasped as ecstasy exploded inside and around her.

His movements faltered, and she found his fierce gaze on her. Her heart was drumming from the last waves of her orgasm, but in the haze of her pleasure, she had said the words out loud. Before she could say anything else, his lips crashed onto hers, and he resumed his punishing pace.

"I love *you*, too," he said against her lips, and she held on to him tighter as his own movements became erratic, and soon he was also pushed past the edge and collapsed onto her.

CHAPTER THIRTY-NINE

*N*ava's things lay scattered on top of the table. The half-used cardamom soap Cameron had gifted her. Her tent was folded into a pile. Her vials of potions had been refilled, with a new, fresher batch containing improved brews with magic inside.

She moved her gaze over her things until it fell onto the leather-bound journal her mother had left her. Nava swallowed and reached for the item, unwrapping the rough leather bind. The parchment map tumbled to the wood table. She focused on the familiar scribbles of her mother's writing.

Nava took a deep breath and opened the page, passing notes of travels around the forest. Plants she'd picked for her father to use in potions.

She paged through to the end where the pages became sparser with content and paused.

Nava,

If you are reading this, I fear I never got around finding the strength to speak with you. I know you will be angry and confused.

I'm ashamed of what I did to protect you, and this has been a secret eating at me for the past few years.

In this journal, you will find a map that will take you to Arkimedes, your soulmate. Please don't go to him until you are ready, because the soulmate bond is wonderful but all-consuming.

We don't talk about him. In truth, it's hard to see you so young and already destined to something dangerous.

Arkimedes is too powerful, and with it comes the dangers of what might corrupt his soul. We have never known of his kin, but few can inherit such power and not have to answer for it.

He is mostly good, and I always thought he would pull away from his own darkness. Eventually. I cursed him to prevent him from coming to get you too soon. He is not ready. Neither are you, but I wasn't ready to let you go.

The curse I used was black magic. To use such hexes, you have to give a part of your soul away. His magic is so different. The curse has backfired on me. With the passing of days, I've become weaker. It's the price I pay for acting out of selfishness, for defying the gods.

I told him he had to do a selfless act for you. The real way of breaking the curse is for you to accept him fully as yours. I hope this will give you the choice you deserve.

I love you.

Nava gasped. Tears streamed down her cheeks as the journal shook in her grasp. Answers. She'd had all of them here with her the whole time.

Laurie had told her she had been holding back until Nava asked. They had always wanted to give her a choice. She could have broken Arkimedes's curse before. She would have known who he was had she read on.

Had she not been so angry, so stubborn.

Nava closed the journal with shaking hands. Her mother had died for cursing Nava's soulmate. For trying in vain to slow down time.

TRAVELING TO HER OLD town was bittersweet, the short days and long nights making it harder to journey along the forest's winding trails. The trip back had been quicker than their whole journey to the Northern Village, backtracking to areas she remembered well, some with longing, some with dread.

It had been three months since Nava left the town. She and Arkimedes approached the edge of the forest, where the trees became more sparse and less imposing, where tall grass of golden tones stood dancing in the wind. She could see the houses nearby, starting with ranches with terracotta tiles on their roofs and the warm stucco walls.

She took one step after another, her stomach churning with the anticipation of seeing Cameron once again, and as she walked, something shifted inside her.

A hollowness that grew somehow.

Arkimedes paused, studying his surroundings, and he was no longer walking by her side. She turned around and adjusted the weight of her backpack, the one thing she had refused to leave behind, much to Arkimedes's amusement.

It was no longer heavy, as her own endurance had grown exponentially from the start of her journey, and she had been working on practicing her magic by making it light as a feather and not exhausting her energy. The straps had marked her skin with angry red marks that told her they hadn't taken a rest in a few hours.

Arkimedes hesitated, his hands buried inside his pockets.

"Is there something wrong?" She took a few steps back to him as he frowned at the nothingness. Nava's lips parted, and she understood the predicament ahead.

It was the invisible shield that held magic outside of town. Her gaze traveled up the trees in the distance; maybe she had imagined it. Ari lurked in the background, unable to follow them past this point. A tortured gaze from afar morphed his features.

It had been something she had discussed with her Beekeeper. She couldn't stay in town without visiting the forest at least a couple of times a week. It was unclear how her being in the forest would set things in motion, but whatever magic she had in her helped maintain a balance.

The buzzing of her magic had gone dormant once again. The hollowness inside her made her breathless. Her hand came to her chest. This had been the way she'd felt all these years, as if missing something.

The village's spell had taken this away from her. She couldn't stay here long.

"I feel a pushback." He hesitated before his hand rested against the invisible shield. It resisted allowing him in, and they both held their breaths before it popped and allowed his arm in. His throat bobbed, right before he forced his body through.

They stayed frozen in silence, and she stared at his tall, strong figure. It was the same breathtaking sight of a handsome man, but her lips parted when she stared into his eyes. Gone was the magical storm raging inside his irises. Staring back at her were pale green irises, and he appeared more human than before.

She walked to him, grabbing his face as she examined every single inch of him. "Your eyes—they changed," she blurted.

His hands came to his face, patting over his black

eyelashes. "They feel the same," he started, squinting around him. "Maybe the colors are a bit duller."

"Really?" she gasped.

"No, not really." He smirked, and a soft laugh escaped his lips as she whacked his shoulder.

"You wicked man. Do you feel all right, though?"

He nodded, and his hand came to her shoulder, squeezing it softly. "I'm fine."

They started down the hills that led them to Willowbrook. Cattle roamed around fenced fields, the landmarks peppered with trees of changing sizes, naked except for the occasional evergreen.

When she crossed this path months prior, she had been running for her life, not taking a second to breathe in the clear air on the edge of town or appreciate its beauty. The sun was midway through the sky, not quite as hot as in the summertime, bringing a pleasant warmth to their bodies as they hiked the winding dirt roads.

They walked in silence. The day of nonstop trekking caught up to them as they approached. Her heart was already beating as the vision of the packed cliffside town and its cobblestone roads came into view. The homes closed in on them.

She hadn't written or heard about her family for months. She suspected they would be in Simone's house since Devon's ship was still likely docked in town, waiting for him to come back, something that wouldn't happen.

Large arches of caramel-colored stones marked the town's entrance, with buildings of similar tones surrounding them. Wooden flower boxes were outside each window, painted in greens and reds. All vegetation had died and wilted from the cold weather.

The pleasant scent of burning wood and the crisp feeling of winter welcomed them in as people wearing various attires walked past them, barely sparing them a glance.

Arkimedes's gaze hovered over shop windows and studied a town lacking magic. His hand was firmly placed over the small of her back as she paused to allow a cart carrying large metal cans of fresh milk from the local farm to pass by them.

"We aren't far away from Simone's," Nava said, tilting her head to Arkimedes, who nodded, his face morphing with a curiosity she found endearing.

She smiled as they pushed past shops and mundane life by making their way down alleyways she knew well to the home of her best friend.

She half expected the vision of her house to be nothing but rubble. She had even entertained the idea that it had been burned to ashes in a fit of anger by Devon's goons after her escape, having found Simone was hiding the fugitives.

Her stomach churned as her attention fell upon the familiar shape of it, her friend's modest home. Narrow and close to her neighbors, it was made of strong stucco walls and white paint. Smoke was puffing out of the chimney as she pushed open the gate of the small front yard. Simone, unlike Nava, had never had an excellent green thumb, so Nava usually made her way here in spring to work in her garden.

It was all dead and brown.

Her hands were shaking when she reached for the door handle and stopped a few centimeters away from grabbing it. Nava's stomach awoke in a flutter, and her hands moistened with sweat. A warm touch grounded her as Arkimedes came close to her, giving her strength without the need for words.

"I bet you want to see him," he encouraged. A handsome smile illuminated his features.

She took a deep breath, steadying herself before she knocked on the door a couple of times. Where before there had been soft noises coming from inside, silence descended.

He nodded, his chin pointing to the door.

"Simone, Cam?" Her voice quivered even to her own ears.

Steps came rushing to the door. Clumsy long strides pounded over creaking wooden floors. It had been a few months since she'd held the freckled boy who stood in front of her with a gaping mouth as he took her in.

"Nava?" His voice was the one of a kid. If she closed her eyes, she could almost forget he was so tall.

"Of course, caterpillar," she said with a smile as tears blurred her vision.

Her brother jumped into her arms with a bone-crushing hug. "I thought I would never see you again. I— Simone said you would be back, that you were strong, and of course, I *know* you are strong. I never doubted that for a second. The house was such a mess. Like they had taken you. We were so afraid." The words tumbled out of his thick lips, but she enjoyed the smell of his skin and the feeling that she was home.

"The quickness of talking is something you *can* inherit." Arkimedes's voice broke the moment as both siblings pulled out of their embrace and turned to him. He had a smile on his lips, but he twisted his fingers as he stilled under Cameron's gaze.

"Cam, this is Arkimedes, and he is— Well, he is my soulmate." There was no use beating around the bush. Her brother's lips parted in shock as his bushy red eyebrows lifted to the edge of his forehead.

"Nice meeting you, Cameron."

"Whoa, wooow, wait—*wait*, you found your soulmate? The Crow?" Cameron shook his head as if trying to get his thoughts in order before pushing himself from the door and walking inside.

Nava followed behind. She knew Simone's house well, and while she studied the clean, neat place, she was unable to find a sign of her friend. The woman was likely in her bakery and wouldn't be back here until later that day.

"Yes," Nava answered her brother's questions and turned around to make sure Arkimedes was following. He had, but he stayed by the door with both hands in his pockets as his gaze followed the boy walking around the room in a wind of energy and emotions. Clumsy steps of someone who had grown too fast in the past few months.

"But . . . they are our enemies, no? Wasn't it a Crow who came and forced you to leave?" Cameron's gaze landed warily over Arkimedes, who looked at Nava for help.

"Cam, you might want to sit. It would be good for us to explain."

Cameron stopped and nodded, walking to the large sofa in the living room and letting his body fall unceremoniously onto one of them. "Are you having dreams? The ones of him, the ones that can take you away?" His voice was small. His attention focused on both her and Arkimedes as they settled as well.

"I stopped having them when I met Arkimedes. I know you are going to ask, but no, I wasn't aware he was my soulmate when I met him," Nava said, and she told him all that had happened, skipping a few bits of information he didn't need. She didn't want to scare him, after all.

"Where is Laurie—and Simone?" Nava got to her feet and made her way to the kitchen. She was starving and wanted to get something in her before making a trip to her house to see what state the bounty hunters had left it in.

"Laurie went to the market, and Simone is working."

Nava nodded, her palms damp from anticipating the two women reacting to her being back, with her soulmate in tow.

"So, you are a Crow? And we are fine with that?" Cameron's attention snapped to both adults in the room with a held breath as Nava nodded.

"We are okay with *Arkimedes*," she agreed.

"I don't want to lose you like we did Dad. I was afraid you would never want or consider us going back to Iron City to find him. So I wanna say . . . I'm happy that for whatever reason, he was here, instead." Cameron's brow raised. "*Why* were you on the island? You aren't some stalker, are you?"

"Cam!"

"No, it's fine. It's a fair question. I wasn't stalking your sister. I wasn't able to even get into this town. I had to be on the island to be near her and not be taken like your father by the dreams. Soulmates need to be close."

"The dreams . . . happen because the soulmate is away? Well, that makes sense."

"Yes."

"But Mom, didn't she know it would happen? Why would she take Nava away from you and risk it?"

Her stomach dropped as she cleared her throat. "She did, and she expected he would follow."

"Which I did."

"It doesn't seem fair. Nava suffered through dreams for years," Cameron said.

"Mom left me a note," she admitted, lowering her gaze but feeling both of their eyes boring into her. "She explained it all, who Arkimedes was—" She met the man's confused gaze. "I found it in her journal when I was packing."

His lips parted.

"So you are accepting the bond? You didn't want it, right?" Cameron asked, unaware of the intensity hanging in between them.

A silence extended, and Arkimedes's brow lifted as a smirk appeared on his face.

"I wish I hadn't been so eager to voice such things to everyone," she mumbled. "It doesn't feel forced. It feels natural and real. I didn't understand the magic of it because I hadn't been able to experience it. We got to spend time with each other before we both chose one another."

"So—you love him?"

Nava's skin warmed as she held her breath.

Cameron turned to Arkimedes. "Welcome to the family."

"Thank you."

Nava was truly and unabashedly happy. They were not to stay here. The loss of her magic, being away from Ari, and her concern about whatever this was doing to Arkimedes's fae side were too much for her to grasp.

Sure, it would take them time to figure out what to do, to sell all their belongings and move across an island, but she was ready for this new life to begin.

She caught the brown body of a bee flying around the house. It landed on the arm of the sofa she had settled on. She turned her hand and opened her palm, and the bee crawled to it. Its soft humming energy coursed through her body.

Her eyes lifted to meet Arkimedes, and her mark soared.

It was *magic*.

CHAPTER 1

CHAPTER 1

Nava

*N*ava had been waiting for a while for Arkimedes to join her in the bath. She stared at her pruny fingers while moving her arms over the milky water. What was taking him so long? Surely getting wine from their kitchen wouldn't have meant leaving her alone for the evening. Not when he'd been kissing her senseless recently.

"Ark?" she called, frowning at the water around her that now cooled her heated skin.

Her heart skipped a beat at the silence. She lifted out of the water, and there was a heaviness in her stomach that hadn't been there before, something that made her pause.

She got out of the tub, reached for her nightgown, and draped it over her body, not caring that it would get wet.

Thunder rolled, and the pitter-patter of the rain fell harder against the glass window. She walked to the door, unsure why she tried to keep her steps weightless, but the uneasiness grew more assertive.

The prick of panic settled in the back of her mind like a whisper. Nava's steps slowed down as she tried to understand what was happening. She stilled her hand, then extended it to the doorknob. The only sound other than the rain was her loud heartbeat.

Out of nowhere, a stab of pain rattled through her. Her soulmate mark was aching like someone had branded her with burning iron. A loud bang roared from downstairs, followed by the cracking of wood.

She couldn't move and her vision blurred with tears as the scent of cayenne wafted around the room. Magic always carried a spicy note.

Devon, the member of The Society of Crows who'd attacked the village a year ago, had frozen her under a spell similar to this one in the middle of a battlefield.

Her body glowed as her magic awakened. Bees made of light formed over her skin, giving her the power to snap out of whatever had her frozen. She and Arkimedes were under attack. Her fingers twitched, and Nava focused her attention on them and closed her hand into a fist, grasping at the door and stabilizing her body weight on the frame.

Arkimedes had taught her earlier in the year how to battle a paralyzing spell by focusing on each part of her body and funneling her magic to it. Her muscles spasmed before she regained control.

She rushed down the stairs, her power around her like a shield. Candlelight illuminated the first floor. The sound of soft crackling came from the fireplace. The door that led to their garden swung with the loud wind from the storm outside.

Nava studied the space. The green glass of the bottle

of wine on top of the wooden table mocked her. Her stomach churned.

Arkimedes. She tugged on their mating bond like a string, but panic tasted bitter in the back of her throat at the lack of response.

She ran past the threshold of the door and out into the rain. Her bare feet pounded the ground as she followed the pull towards him. Arkimedes held his head in his hands. Kneeling while hunched over, a gasp of pain escaped his full lips. Her heart wrenched as she felt his pain vibrate through her body.

Their bond was aching, unable to contain this anguish any longer.

The darkness of the night veiled them, but she knew this area well and could roam it almost blindly. The scent of wet grass and summer rain enveloped her in a humid embrace, the tall trees of the Grey Forest their constant companions.

Nava was closer to him. His white knuckles tightened around his brown hair, pulling harder. "Ark—" She reached to him.

Arkimedes' head snapped up, and his wild green gaze came upon her. "Stay back, bee." He forced the words through tight lips. His handsome face was usually bright and healthy, but it had lost all its color.

Shadows of mist and smoke billowed around Arkimedes. It had to be the aura of his power. But these were wrong, like an evil presence of torture—ghosts made of dark magic and ancient, raw power.

Her heart lurched as an icy caress went down her spine, and she stopped panting for breath. Her body broke out in a thin layer of sweat. The aura around him resembled Arkimedes' power when he was in a fight.

The smell of magic and a mix smoke, enveloped her.

The weight of the shadows' stony gazes made the hairs on her arms stand. Nava watched with horror as Arkimedes' face contorted, his lips opening with a silent cry. She took a step closer, but he shook his head in a plea.

"*No!*" He shouted in her mind. "*Stay. Back. Nava.*"

The bodies became sharper, almost taking the appearance of a human. Tall, with slim waists and broad shoulders, something wicked blooming behind their bodies. Wings. She couldn't tell their shapes in the darkness of their yard, but the clear silhouette of feathers became apparent, so similar to Arkimedes'.

She counted seven, maybe eight winged creatures who flickered in and out of focus. Her chest burned, and she tried to swallow the thickness that had formed in her throat and made it hard for her to breathe.

The tendrils of a dark spell approached her. They grew like a weed over the ground, fingers extending at a rapid pace. Nava took a few steps back as a distance buzzing tickled the edge of her mind.

She was quick on her feet, backing away, focusing upon her soulmate. The ache emanating through their bond distracted her.

The bees surrounded her, but for the first time since Nava had learned she was a Beekeeper, they did not offer relief.

Nava was losing sight of Arkimedes behind the shapes of her insects.

No, *no*. She pushed her hand through the shield that enveloped her. Bees covered every inch of her body, constricting her movements. Her power blinded her, even as it tried to protect her from harm. But she didn't want this—she wanted to see Arkimedes, to help him.

Nava waved her arms around, the scorching sensation in her soulmate mark intensifying. The bees lifted her body in the air. The buzzing grew louder as a cry of desperation left her lips. Was Ari controlling the bees? Was the second Beekeeper nearby? "Arkimedes!"

The bees uncovered her face and the humid air of the summer night hit skin. From the ground below, his face lifted, staring at her with pained eyes.

And then he was gone, disappearing in a billow of mist.

"No!" she gasped, and her heat spread through her veins and her skin. The bees flew away from her body, and she dropped a few meters down. She landed poorly, but even as she stumbled on her feet, a deep hollow pain in her chest grew like a festering wound, making it hard to breathe.

Nava made it to where Arkimedes had been but a few moments ago. The weight of his body depressed the grass. She dropped to her knees and ran her fingers over the blades of grass. They were warmer than the cool ground. He had been here, and they had taken him away from her.

She heard something land behind her, but she didn't need to turn around to see it was the creature who was bound to her and Arkimedes. Aristaeus' presence had become second nature to her. Her friend, companion, and the first Beekeeper.

"He is gone," he said.

She lifted her head, and the raindrops were warm in contrast to her icy skin. Her chest seized as tears ran down her face. "Where?"

"The Dark Ones' kingdom, I presume." But she couldn't form a cohesive idea as she gasped for air like she was drowning. Aristaeus tilted his head, wood groaning at the movement. *"Sleep, dearest one."*

The hard sticks that were his fingers wrapped around her shoulder, the touch numbing. Her vision became spotted and the stale taste in her mouth was replaced by the sweetness of honey, and then there was darkness.

* * *

Nava squinted in the warm morning light. The storm had passed, giving way to a sunny morning.

The shape of trees and twisty branches hung above her. Her body ached from sleeping on top of a bed of leaves. Nava sat up and took over her appearance. Her white cotton nightgown was stained with greens and browns. Mud crusted her bare legs and feet.

It wasn't her appearance that gave her pause or the fact that she'd slept outside, but the sinking inside her chest. The slow ache that reminded her of all that had happened the night before.

Nava brought her shaky hand over her soulmate mark. Her chest caved in, and the wrecked sound that escaped her lips was empty. Not a dream, the shadows had taken Arkimedes.

She stared at a lost point between the trees while her body shook with the intensity of her sobs. The sparse grass made the puddles more visible.

Her body was numb and heavy like lead. She had not an ounce of energy to move, her thoughts muddled. From her vantage point, the movement between the trees called to her.

Ari's wooden frame appeared in front of her, thick trunks and branches covered in lichen and moss. He took her in with a gentle, ebony gaze. It was hard to read his expressions, since he was a creature made of wood. But the underlying pain through their strange bond was present.

He'd used his magic to put her to sleep the night before. Had settled her in this pile of garden brush that Cameron had refused to throw away before he'd left for his travels with Gavin and Violet.

Her younger brother had taken an immediate liking to both sorcerers as soon as they'd moved to the village earlier in the spring. It had surprised Nava that Violet liked children. For someone who'd been so standoffish the entire time they'd traveled together, she had warmed up to her younger sibling rather fast.

"You put me to sleep." Her voice sounded broken to her ears, wobbling at the end.

"You were about to faint, and my magic has numbing qualities that would allow you to rest."

Nava rushed to sit down, and the hard edges of wooden sticks buried into her back and sides. "We should've followed the Dark Ones. Find Arkimedes and help him. I didn't need to sleep, Ari."

The Beekeeper tilted his head, slowly blinking. *"And how were we supposed to? Did you master your transporting skills overnight?"*

Her Beekeeper had been spending too much time with her little brother. His sarcasm levels had shot to the sky during the last few months.

Nava took a deep, calming breath. "I don't need the attitude right now," she huffed. "You know I haven't mastered it yet." It was imperative she learn to harness her Beekeeper's magic and transport, the way Ari could move around the forests. Magic connected them to nature, and thus they could become part of it. She rubbed her chest, going over the memories of the night before. Something came up. "Yesterday, you said you presumed he was in the Dark Ones' kingdom?"

The Dark Ones—the name people liked to call Arkimedes, the reason the entire town had was so afraid of him months ago when she and Ark had been in the village for the first time, battling Devon's army.

Arkimedes had once told her that everyone else but her

saw him always surrounded by his power. Something wicked and dark. She hadn't understood what that would look like. Why would people be so afraid? Today, she knew better.

Ari nodded, and the tremor of dread that built in her stomach grew. The shapes from the night before were part of whatever he was from. When he'd shared about his past, he'd mentioned where he'd tracked his origins before he had stopped searching further.

She got up from the ground and dusted her nightgown. "He found his kin in the Copper Kingdom. I have to go there—what does that mean for us?"

The Beekeeper nodded. *"Magic bound the three of us long ago. I shall go with you and stay in the forest's near the city. We should be able to maintain the balance in nature from there."*

Balance in nature, words Ari liked to throw at her, even though she had a hard time grasping whatever he meant. It had been almost a year since she'd discovered she had a larger fate than being a potion maker in Willowbrook.

Not long ago, she'd thought she would always stay in that non-magical town. But once they'd returned after the Crown's attack, she couldn't take it for longer than a couple of months. They'd stayed there long enough to pack a few things and make their way back to this village. She wanted to raise Cameron in a life that embraced their newly accepted nature, and she also needed to be closer to Ari.

Nava wished she hadn't been coddled over her whole life, so maybe leaving this island towards the unknown wasn't adding to the dread already piled over her. There was no other way, however. She had to get to Arkimedes as fast as possible; their soulmate bond demanded them to be close.

How long would it take her body to deteriorate now

that he was continents away? How long did they truly have?

Weeks, months? She didn't even want to consider being away from him for longer than a few days. Nava wished she could ask someone about how her bond might affect her by being away from her soulmate, even though they were both still alive--at least she hoped that was still that case. Her heart constricted at the way her thoughts twisted, and after a forced intake of breath, she took her mind away from that line of thinking.

There was one person who knew more about soulmates than she did—Violet. However, the sorceress was away for a month to do research in the enormous libraries of the Pearl Islands.

Cameron had begged Nava to let him come with Violet and Gavin, fascinated to learn more, and the largest magical library in the world had made her little brother tremble with excitement. She could use his hug to bring back her strength.

"We don't have long," Ari said, and Nava met his eyes, her stomach dropping. *"Your bond is fully formed now. We will deteriorate fast."*

"You are full of good news, Aristaeus."

The bark that made his brows dipped. *"The Zorren will come for us in our weakened state and make sure they finish what they started months ago when we first met."*

Great. The pit of dread in her stomach grew. She'd found Ari nearly dead almost a year ago. The Zorren had attacked him, who she'd learned were creatures of a shadow dimension that sought destruction in the world. The only information Aristaeus had given her was that they fed from life.

They were the mortal enemies of the Beekeepers. *Her* mortal enemies, even though she'd never seen one before.

"So what then? We transfer there? How long would it take me to master this?"

"*We have been working for a couple of months. You tell me.*"

She tightened her lips. "Cut the sass."

As if to prove his point or to annoy her further, Ari disintegrated in front of her. His looming body faded to shapes of bees, dust, and pollen. He flew away from her and headed to the forest, leaving her standing on her land.

Whatever peace of mind Ari had given her was gone. Throwing her back into despair, she walked to her home, ready to get on with her tasks at hand. First, get dressed. Second, get her weapons. And third, find Roman.

The Commander knew about the Copper Kingdom. She remembered that detail being mentioned before and was hopeful he would aid her. Nava couldn't march there and bring Ari along with no actual knowledge of what to expect.

Had she honed her power and transfer, maybe they would already be there. She took a breath to lighten her heavy heart, to not be annoyed at herself and her failings. She'd been doing magic for less than a year. Arkimedes always told her she was her own worst critic.

Nava lifted her hand, chasing the cool brass handle of the back door. The aroma of leather, lavender, and cedar hit her in a wall that reminded her of home, but also of the clear hole staring at her with a sense of growing doom. She'd be of no use to Arkimedes if she crumpled now.

Like the dinning chair that lay on the floor, turned on its side, the leg twisted and broken. The sound of it falling had been the only alert she'd gotten that something had been wrong the night before.

Nava walked to it, grasping the cotton fabric of her nightgown as she went over the splintered wood. She kneeled down and studied it longer than time itself. A few drops of dried blood stained the floor, and a breath caught in her throat as anger exploded inside her stomach, spreading like wildfire through her veins.

Nava wasn't the scared woman who'd run from her town a year ago. She was powerful and determined, all in one.

She would find him, whatever it took. And they would pay.

SIGN UP FOR MY NEWSLETTER!

For updates on future books, and to get extra scenes, character art and more, including this fun short story!

Go to

SIGN UP FOR MY NEWSLETTER!

WWW.ABBEYFOX.COM
To learn about the Kingdoms, see mood-boards and
other fun stuff!

ABOUT THE AUTHOR

"Abbey Fox has always loved storytelling. Ever since she was little, she created characters for fun and got immersed in their life stories, worlds, and magic systems. This naturally progressed onto writing. Her first story being a cringe worthy teenage high school Romance, which she wrote at the age of thirteen in a notebook that was half falling apart by the time she wrote the end.

As time has gone by, she has dived into writing other genres, from YA Fantasy to Mystery Romance, Romantic Soap opera Sci-fi. Now she focuses on her love for Adult Fiction in the Fantasy Romance/ Paranormal Romance genres.

Her debut novel is coming out later this year. It is part of an enthralling series set in a magical world where soulmates are real and power corrupts the kingdoms.

When Abbey is not writing, she enjoys spending time with her husband and her four-year-old son. She also enjoys tending to her indoor tropical jungle and painting fun characters with watercolors. "

facebook.com/abbeyfoxauthor

instagram.com/abbeyfoxauthor

www.ingramcontent.com/pod-product-compliance
Lightning Source LLC
Chambersburg PA
CBHW051529100726
47898CB00005B/1622